GRACE E. ROBINSON

I0612965

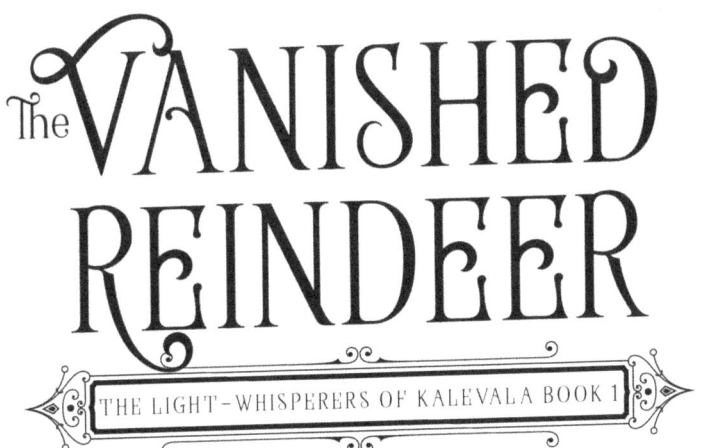

The VANISHED REINDEER

THE LIGHT-WHISPERERS OF KALEVALA BOOK 1

The Light-Whisperers of Kalevala
Book 1
The Vanished Reindeer
By Grace E. Robinson

Table of Contents

Maps

Map of Finland... 4

Map of Pohjola... 5

Chapters

Chapter 1: Inari... 6

Chapter 2: Pohjola 41

Chapter 3: The Mountains of the Moon.............. 85

Chapter 4: Sápmi..157

Chapter 5: The Western Fells.............................188

Chapter 6: The Dancing Ground 258

Chapter 7: Ice-Dark..325

Chapter 8: The Edge of the Darkness 383

Chapter 9: Suomi..463

APPENDICES

1: The Kalevala..519

2: Finnish Language and Pronunciation Guide 519

3: Sami Culture, and Language and
Pronunciation Guide...520

4: Music...521

Author's Note..524

About the author:..525

MAP OF FINLAND

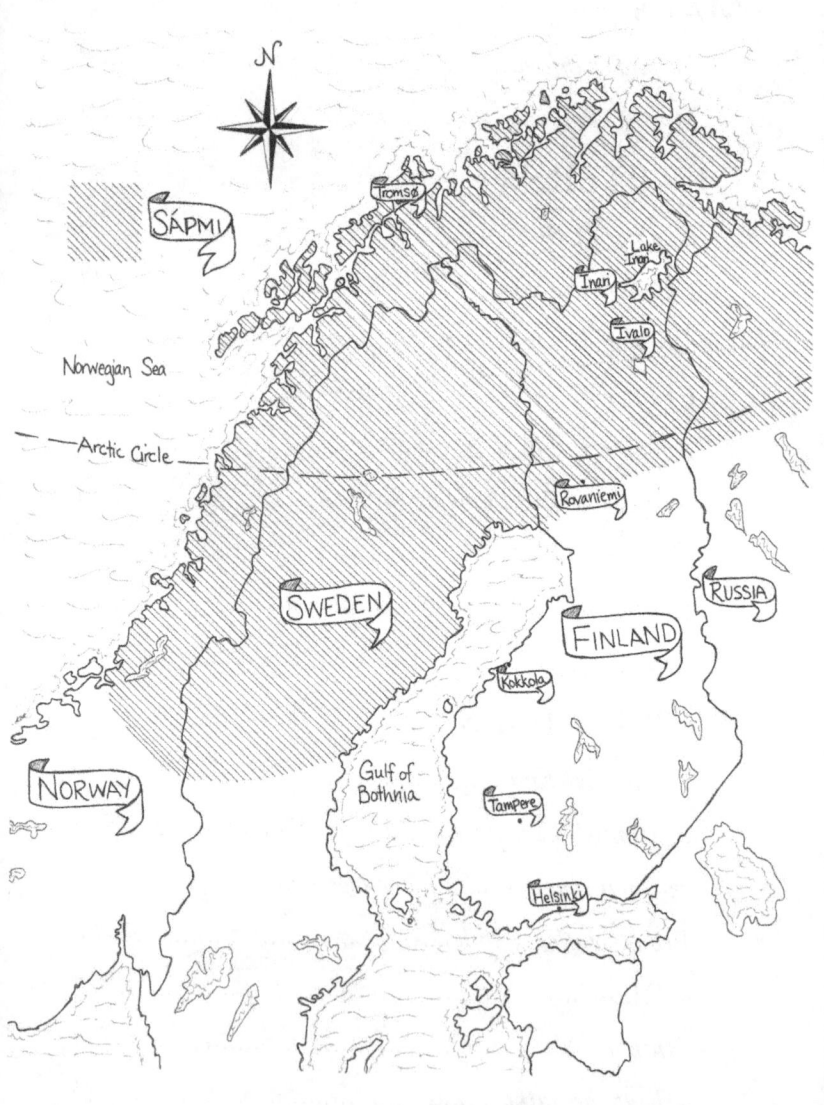

MAP OF POHJOLA

CHAPTER 1: INARI

I t was barely dawn when Detective Lyylia Niiranen hauled her suitcase out of the trunk of the taxicab. She pulled out the handle of the suitcase, tightened her scarf around her neck, and entered the train depot.

Inside she was free from the frigid wind blowing in off the bay, but she kept her purple and blue scarf wrapped around her neck. She picked up the ticket that her boss, police chief Mikael Sjöberg, had purchased the day before, then took a seat to wait for her partner to show up.

She looked around the quiet station. A good number of people in Kokkola traveled early in the morning, silently sipping their coffee or looking at their phones. Kokkola was a nice enough little historic spot on the map, a town that always smelled of frozen salt water and chemicals from the industrial plants. Lyylia missed the bustle of Helsinki. True, big cities came with bigger problems, but back in Helsinki she felt she'd been making a difference. And Helsinki was her home. Her mother and sister Teija still lived there, her father was buried there. Her job transfer to Kokkola seemed longer ago than just a year.

Her partner, Detective Jassu Toivonen, came striding into

the train station, whistling much too loudly for the early hour.

"Lyylia!" he bellowed. "Morning! Ready for our adventure in Lapland?"

"As ready as I'll ever be," she replied. "Get your ticket at the window. You have to show ID, so they wouldn't let me pick up your ticket."

"Okay." Jassu went to the window. Lyylia stood and snugged up her scarf, preparing for the arctic air in the loading zone. There weren't many passengers waiting to board this particular train. No surprise there—who would want to be going to Lapland just as winter was setting in? It was still autumn in Helsinki, Lyylia thought wistfully. Here in Kokkola, much farther north, the colors on the trees were already fading as the cold air of winter moved in. Worse, they were going to the Lapland capital of Rovaniemi and then Inari, up past the Arctic Circle.

"Okay, let's review the files that the chief gave us yesterday," Jassu said after they were settled on the train. He rummaged in his backpack at his feet and pulled out several folders.

They spread the files out on their laps as the lights of the train station and the city of Kokkola snapped past the windows. The case: a herd of reindeer, exact number of animals unknown, missing in Lapland, near the village of Inari. Suspects: no one and nothing. After investigating the disappearance for several days now, the Sami police from both Inari and Rovaniemi had no more leads than they'd started with. Their request for outside assistance had found its way to Chief Sjöberg's desk in Kokkola.

"The first people we should talk to are the reindeer herders," Lyylia said. "Ávgos and Sirkka Heikkilä and Maden Lahti are listed as the owners of the reindeer. If these records are accurate, it looks like Ávgos is the only one who's given a statement."

Jassu held up a sheet of paper. "This lists some coordinates from a GPS. Isn't there a map in this file somewhere?"

Lyylia shuffled through her papers until she found a map of the Inari region. They both looked at it.

"Okay, so according to this report," Jassu said, "Ávgos tracks his reindeer with GPS collars. But two of the signals stopped transmitting, which is why they can't find the rest of the herd."

"Looks like there are only four signals total," said Lyylia, peering at the paper. "So, only four collars for hundreds of animals." That didn't seem very effective, but then again, she knew nothing about how much these GPS collars might cost. And reindeer were *herd* animals, after all, so presumably they all stuck together. Except for this incident, of course. "Two signals stopped transmitting near the lake."

"Or in the lake," said Jassu, pointing at the map. "I think. It's hard to read this thing. Let's ask for a more detailed map when we get to the precinct in Rovaniemi."

They set the map aside.

"We should also talk to these scientists," Lyylia said, picking up another sheet of paper.

A small team of aurora scientists was listed as the only group of visitors who had arrived before the disappearance of the reindeer and remainedin the village. Apparently they hadn't been questioned at all yet. That needed to be remedied as quickly as possible, Lyylia decided. Not that visitors were automatically suspect—but they always had unknown motives, as well as a different way of observing things from those who were locals.

"I agree," said Jassu. "And there might be more up-to-date reports when we get to Inari—all of these reports are from three days ago, when the Rovaniemi police put in the request for help."

"I hope they've found out something more." Lyylia looked at another report. "Because all we've got besides Ávgos Heikkilä's statement is a report by an anonymous resident who claimed to have seen 'evil spirits' in the lake."

"Great. Superstitious nutjobs always make any assignment more fun."

Lyylia sighed as they returned the papers to the folders. Hopefully the Sami police were not quite as ineffective as these reports made them sound. Even in the vast wilderness of the northern part of the country, one hundred-plus reindeer couldn't stay lost forever. Could they?

Traveling as they were deep into the world of the Sami, Lyylia found herself slightly embarrassed about how little she knew of her country's indigenous people, or their primary livelihood, reindeer. She pulled out the Sami-Finnish-English dictionary she'd bought last night and thumbed through it. It had been written specifically for tourists, so there were all sorts of words and phrases that she'd never use, like *'does the skiing trail start here?'* and *'when do the reindeer races begin?'*

'Where is my room?' That might be a useful question. *"Gos mu latnja lea?"* she stumbled over the words.

"Huh?" said Jassu.

"I bought a Sami guidebook," she explained. "I'm trying to find some useful words and phrases. *Hotealla* is hotel, that's pretty easy. *Jávri* is lake—that could be useful, too."

"Good," said Jassu. "Well, wake me up when you find out how to say 'My God, I can't believe we're being sent to Lapland.'" He settled in for a nap.

Unfortunately, that phrase wasn't in the book. After a while, Lyylia put the book aside. The sun had risen, and she unwrapped her scarf and smoothed her blond hair. She kept her hair to just below her shoulders, because long hair was a hassle and not important in police work. However, to wear her curly hair short would be to endure more frizz than a metal band from the 1980s.

She wanted to talk to Teija. When her sister had called last night, Lyylia had briefly told her about her new assignment, but they hadn't talked for very long. Even though their careers had taken them down different paths—Teija worked for a software development company in Helsinki—they were still as close as they'd always been. But now that Lyylia lived in Kokkola, it had been months since she'd seen her sister.

Teija was probably at work by now, so Lyylia sent a text message.

Hey! Sorry I had to cut your call short last night. Frantic last-minute packing for this assignment.

So you're on your way to Lapland now? Teija replied.

Yeah. Rural Sami villages and reindeer country, here we come.

I know you're a big-city cop, but you'll do fine. She could almost see Teija's bright, encouraging smile through the text message. *You're a great detective! :)*

LOL, thanks.

Bring me back a Sami souvenir!

I'll see what I can do! Lyylia smiled as she closed the text message thread. She wished she'd brought a coffee with her, instead of rushing to finish a cup early before she left her apartment. Thankfully there were several stops before they reached their destination. She'd get some coffee then.

She leaned her head back against the headrest and opened the music player app on her phone. Putting in her earbuds, she selected her Apocalyptica playlist and settled in to the soothing cello notes as she watched the landscape of rural

Finland sliding past her window.

In Rovaniemi they met with Bierža Syrjälä, the Sami officer in charge of the case. Even though there was no new information, Lyylia was impressed with his thoroughness and attention to detail. He gave them a map of the village of Inari and the nearby lake, complete with key locations circled and notated. And he spoke Finnish perfectly.

The rail ended in Rovaniemi, so Lyylia, Jassu and Bierža boarded a bus. The seats were less comfortable than the train had been, but the bus was heated, at least. A family with two children sat near the front. The little boy wore a hat trimmed with bright red, blue, and green ribbons: the colors of the Sami. Both children were quiet, so Lyylia couldn't hear what language the family might be speaking. The family got off the bus in the Sami village of Saariselkä, still several hours and several stops from Inari.

They finally arrived in Inari village, long past sunset. The bus depot was right next to their hotel.

"Okay," Jassu said, as Bierža checked them all into their rooms. "First thing tomorrow, we'll talk to the reindeer's owner, Ávgos Heikkilä, and his family. Then we talk to this team of scientists, since they're the visitors who have been here the longest. It's a Norwegian group, I think…is that what the paperwork said?"

"Yes, but I don't think all of the scientists are Norwegian, though," put in Bierža. "One of them is American, and I think there's a Russian with them, too."

"We may need to find a translator, in that case," Lyylia said.

"If they speak English, you can talk to them, Lyylia," said Jassu. "You know more English than I do."

"I can arrange for a translator, if necessary," Bierža said.

"Thank you," Jassu said. "All right, so we'll meet here in the lobby tomorrow morning, seven-thirty."

Upstairs in her room, Lyylia was pleased with the modern and cozy atmosphere—wi-fi, satellite television, and a large sauna at the end of the hall. Looking out the window, into a night sky much darker than the light-washed sky of a city, she saw a flicker of green. The northern lights, she realized. She saw them every winter, of course, in Kokkola and Helsinki, but not usually this early in the season. And here the color was more vivid in the rural darkness.

She checked her email, then saw she'd missed a text message from Teija.

I talked to Mom today. She sends her love and says to stay warm. As if you went up there all unprepared. I'm just delivering her message! :-P

Just got to Inari, Lyylia replied. *Nice little town—not as primitive as I was expecting. You can tell Mom I'm staying warm!*

Haha, okay. Teija's reply came back almost immediately. *Go get 'em, sis.*

Lyylia smiled. *Thanks. I'm going to bed now. I miss you. Love you! Love you too, Lyylia!*

The pounding on his hotel room door dragged Shaun Abernathy from his somewhat fitful sleep. Groggily he looked at the clock, wondering who would have the nerve to bang on his door this early.

It was nearly two in the afternoon.

Shaun scrambled out of bed as the knock came again. Apparently his roommate and fellow scientist, Paul Banks, had already gotten up and left. He wondered if the other two men on their science team were also up. But since their team did most of their work during the night, he didn't feel guilty about sleeping half the day.

Shaun switched on the light and opened the door. Elias stood there—the Sami man who was the guide and translator for their team as they set up their aurora observation equipment around Lake Inari. With him was the most beautiful woman Shaun had ever seen, and suddenly he wished he'd taken a few extra moments to straighten his hair and put on something nicer than his bed-rumpled t-shirt.

"Terve." The woman greeted him in a business-like tone, giving him a brief, painfully polite smile. *"Nimeni on Rikostarkastaja Lyylia Niiranen. Kokkolan poliisi."* She held up an official-looking badge.

"Um, *terve.*" Shaun returned the greeting, and glanced at Elias. "I'm sorry, I don't speak much Finnish."

"My name is Detective Lyylia Niiranen." The woman began again, in clear but heavily accented English. "Kokkola police." She flashed the badge again.

"Police? Did I do something wrong?" He looked at Elias again. The Sami man's face was perfectly placid.

"May I ask you some few questions?" said the detective. "You are not suspect, but a witness perhaps."

"Um, okay…" said Shaun, a little nervous about where this might be going. The science foundation they worked for had given all the team members information about local and federal laws before they'd arrived. And Pål, the team leader, had hired Elias Viiri once they arrived, to make sure they didn't accidentally screw something up. "Could I get dressed first?

Give me two minutes."

The detective nodded curtly. Shaun shut the door and hurriedly threw on some clean clothes, slapped some gel in his unruly brown hair, and brushed his teeth. His stubbly beard was a bit longer and scragglier than normal, since he hadn't shaved in a few days, but he didn't want to take the time to tidy it right now.

Then he quickly neatened up a bit, smoothing the blankets over his rumpled bed and tossing his scattered clothes and toiletries back into his suitcase. His roommate, Paul, was British, and fastidiously clean and organized. His bed was made, his clothes all hung in the closet. Even his physics journals were in a neat stack on the bedside table.

In just under two minutes, Shaun opened the door again. Elias and the detective were standing there patiently, and now that he was more presentable, he took a longer look at the woman. She wore jeans and a black coat, rather than a uniform, probably because she was a detective. Her blond hair was pulled back in a clip, leaving several stray curls loose around her face and looping around the gold stud earrings in her ears. She still wasn't smiling, but she was beautiful. Too bad she was a police officer.

"Would you like to come in?" Shaun said politely, stepping back from the door.

"Thank you." She strode in, followed by Elias. Shaun noticed that she didn't have a notepad or recorder or anything with her. Apparently she intended to memorize everything?

"I am sorry to bother you, Mr. Ahpbernahtoo," she said, mangling his last name.

"Call me Shaun," he said, not bothering to correct her pronunciation. Most Finns had trouble with his name.

"Mr. Ahpbernahtoo, I am here to investigate the

disappearing of a reindeer herd. The animals vanished five days ago. I'm looking for witnesses or clues. Mr. Viiri says you are American, here for studying the northern lights."

"Yes, ma'am." Shaun tried not to be distracted by the enticing way she rolled her r's. He wondered if she'd already questioned Pål, Paul, and Sergei, and if they'd been just as distracted. Why couldn't the police have sent an ugly, middle-aged guy?

"When did you arrive at Inari?" she asked.

"Six days ago—no, I guess it was seven days."

"Have you come to Inari before now?"

"The municipality of Inari, yes—Inari village, here, no, never before." He probably should be as specific and accurate as possible. He didn't feel like getting on the bad side of the local law enforcement. "Last year we came to another Sami village," he elaborated. "I'm afraid I can't remember the name. Somewhere to the west, near Norway."

"You came in autumn, to study aurora then, also?"

"Yes, ma'am, Detective—I'm sorry, I've forgotten your name."

"Detective Niiranen," she supplied. "Where do you study?"

"Where? Well, outdoors, obviously…" He trailed off with a chuckle, which he cut short as he saw Elias giving him a serious look. Detective Niiranen didn't crack a smile.

"Outdoors, specifically by Lake Inari," he resumed. "We have our equipment set up in several spots near the edge of the lake, as well as on one of the islands in the lake. All to the south of Inari village, and away from the main hiking trails, as well. We got all the necessary authorization from the Inari officials before arriving."

"You study outdoors at night, to see the northern lights?" she asked.

"That's right."

"You said you are at Lake Inari, or nearby to it, as you study your equipment?"

He nodded. "The four of us on the team take turns at the scanners that we have spread out at different sites. They cover a good twelve kilometers or so. Most of them are fairly near the lake. They're set up in different spots, based on elevation, tree cover, mean air pressure and temperature, and so on. For magnetic observation, some of those factors matter, but for the visual spectrum, a clear shot of the sky is necessary."

The detective nodded as if she'd fully understood all of that. "During the night, when you are outside studying the lights, do you ever see reindeer?"

"Quite a few," Shaun said, then second-guessed himself on that vague amount. Accustomed to the suburbs of Philadelphia, seeing even one reindeer constituted a lot for him. "A couple of times when we've been out at our observation sites, we've seen reindeer in the distance—a large number of them, like a herd, I guess."

Detective Niiranen nodded again. "Lake Inari. Is your science equipment at the shore of the lake?"

"For the most part. Not on the actual banks of the lake, but close by."

"Can you take us to there now? To the exact places where you have your science equipment?"

"Sure," he said. "Just let me grab my coat and boots." As he went to the closet, he wondered what the other guys on the team would think of this. As a general rule, they all closely guarded all of their equipment and didn't freely share any information with anyone. But that secrecy normally applied to busy-body locals or other scientists. Not law enforcement.

"It's about a two-kilometer hike," Shaun explained as the

three of them went downstairs and left the hotel. "We've placed our scanners in places away from paths and trails. We don't want people stumbling across it and accidentally injuring themselves or damaging the equipment. It's expensive, delicate stuff. I've actually designed and built a couple of the pieces myself."

Shaun led them through the paved streets of Inari, heading for the south end of town and the lake and wilderness beyond.

He glanced at Elias; the Sami man had been silent this entire time. Shaun wished he could talk to him privately.

He got his wish almost immediately as the detective's phone rang. As she answered it and began talking away in Finnish, she dropped several steps behind Shaun.

"So what is all this about?" Shaun asked as Elias stepped up beside him, keeping his voice low even though the detective was several steps behind. "Why am I being questioned? Is she really a police officer?"

"Yes, she is," Elias said. "Her partner is talking with Pål and Sergei, and she already spoke with myself and Paul this morning. As she said, you are not a suspect—they are simply trying to find clues."

"Clues to what? Missing reindeer?"

"Yes. Apparently part of Ávgos Heikkilä's herd went missing last week, presumed stolen. The police are simply talking with everyone who was in the area at the time the animals disappeared. They were last seen to the southwest of the lake, not far from some of your observation sites."

"Who would steal a whole herd of reindeer?"

"Certainly not a Sami," said Elias, with a tone of mild indignation.

"So they think one of us did it, because we're not Sami?"

"I don't know what the detectives are thinking, but they say that none of your team is a suspect. I simply meant that no Sami who respects himself or his culture would dare to steal another Sami's reindeer."

So, as outsiders, the science team was automatically suspicious. Shaun wasn't worried, though, or offended. He certainly hadn't stolen any reindeer, and he knew his teammates hadn't, either. He wondered why the police were bothering with missing reindeer at all, though. With the hundreds of miles of unpopulated wilderness in this part of the country, how would anyone know if a bunch of animals were "missing" at all?

The paved streets had become a dirt road as they'd left the outskirts of the village, and now the road was more of a path. Shaun knew the route by heart, after a week of hiking along this trail in the dark to check the aurora scanners. However, the surroundings looked different in daylight.

At this point the path was still wide enough for three people to walk side-by-side, and Shaun found himself walking beside the detective. She'd finished her phone call and put on a pair of sunglasses which hid her blue eyes, but he still couldn't help glancing at her as they walked.

"Elias," she said. "My documents says there are many reindeer herds in this area, near to this part of the lake. How many herds might be in this area last week and this week?"

"Two or three, maybe six or more," he said. "We've just finished the separation of the herds, so it would depend on where the herders are taking their animals for the winter grazing, how many young are with them, and other factors. Many herds travel by this part of the lake, as it's good grazing and watering for the reindeer at this time of year. The water is deep there, even at the shore, and so it does not freeze as quickly at night. I don't own reindeer, so I do not know all the paths that are taken by the herds and their drivers."

Detective Niiranen seemed to be finished with her questions, and so the trio walked in silence as Shaun tried to figure out something to say to her to get her talking again.

"So, Detective," he began. "What made you decide to become a police officer?"

"I like to fix problems and discover things," she answered, turning her head to glance at him through her sunglasses. "What made you decide to become scientist?"

"I like to fix problems and discover things, too," he said with a smile.

"Are you fixing a problem here, or just discovering?" Her tone, while still businesslike, held more of an edge of pure curiosity than rapid-fire police questioning.

"Well, we know what the aurora is—charged particles from the sun reacting with the magnetism of the earth's poles, to put it simplistically. But there's so much more to it. Our team is here to observe, record, and analyze the auditory properties of the aurora. The sounds that the electromagnetic energy of the aurora generates, which is usually inaudible to the human ear. Many people in the scientific community still don't believe that the aurora makes sounds at all."

"I have heard the northern lights," said Elias. "Many Sami have."

"I know, exactly," Shaun said, nodding with excitement. "And so have the Inuit, and the Eskimos, and so many native people who aren't all mired down in the tradition of their 'university science.'" He wasn't sure if Detective Niiranen was following all of this, but she kept turning her head to look at him as he talked, so he kept going.

"So I'm out here with this team measuring the sounds the aurora makes. I'm also experimenting with trying to harness the electromagnetic energy of the aurora." He tried to keep his voice calm in his excitement. "The lights at our poles, that are there all the time even in the summer when you can't see them, could potentially power personal electronics and home appliances, or even more, if we could figure out how to harness the energy."

"Very interesting," said Detective Niiranen. She sounded sincere.

The path began to narrow, forcing them to walk single file. Shaun had to lead the way, but he mused that it would be a nicer view if the detective could be walking in front of him.

"This first observation site where we're going," Shaun explained, "is a key spot, where I put one of the devices that I invented and built myself. It's primarily for measuring and recording the aurora's auditory properties, but the unique thing about this piece of equipment is that it's powered solely by the aurora. In fact, it's receiving power right now, even though it's daytime and there isn't a visible aurora display at the moment. I'll show it to you."

Soon he had to lead them off the path, and down a less well-defined trail through the woods and thick foliage. Dustings of snow and frost lay in the perpetually shady areas. The land began to slope up a hill. "We're almost there," he said, looking back over his shoulder. "Everybody okay back there?"

"We are fine," said Elias, and the detective added, *"Kyllä."* Shaun remembered that meant "yes." He was trying to re-learn what little Finnish he had picked up on his first trip here. He'd started learning some Russian—enough to have a small-talk conversation with his teammate Sergei. Pål spoke English very well, as well as his native Norwegian, some Finnish, Swedish, Russian, and probably several other languages. And Paul, being British, refused to learn any other languages besides English.

Finally they climbed up the hill to the observation site. It was a short trek, but a tough one with the rocky ground and brambles trying to overtake the narrow path. Shaun was always winded when he got to this spot. Detective Niiranen was also breathing hard when they reached the summit, but Elias seemed fine.

"Well, here we are," Shaun said, and gestured toward the small plastic tub that sat under a scrubby little tree. "Every night I come out here and place this out in the open, like so…" He knelt down and opened the lid and removed a sturdy waterproof protective case with a laptop inside. "See, it's basically a modified laptop attached to the guts of an electromagnetic scanner and several types of microphones and E.L.F receivers." He set the laptop on a flat rock where it had an unobstructed view of the sky and began connecting wires and cords. "And, of course, the battery, powered by the aurora itself."

He had two batteries—one to power the computer, the other to sit out and charge. Larger than the average laptop battery, the black rectangular power source hooked up externally to the computer. The charging battery sat on a rock, attached to a small solar panel that he'd configured to receive power from magnetism, not sunlight.

"It's smaller than I expected," Detective Niiranen said.

"Most of our scanners are small, actually—just different sorts of radio receivers hooked up to computers. But this particular one, with the aurora-powered battery, is just a prototype, after all. And I designed it to be portable." He tapped the waterproof case around the laptop, and then gestured toward a backpack in the plastic storage tub.

"Interesting," said the detective. "So from here, do you see reindeer?" She turned away and looked out over the lake. This little pinnacle of rock afforded a beautiful view of the expanse of Lake Inari, Shaun realized. He hadn't been out here during the day very much. And as many scenic places as he'd been in recent years, he was always more concerned with the view of the sky and never paid much attention to the landscape.

"Yes—well, like I said, it was just a couple of times that we saw reindeer, in the distance. And it was dark. But I guess we saw a herd over that way." He came up next to Detective Niiranen and pointed to the southeast, along the shoreline. The lake stretched to the horizon, smooth greenish-gray water dotted with tiny islands; thin white films of ice were visible in some of the shallows.

"When did you see reindeer? Which night?"

Shaun looked at her. She had pulled off her sunglasses and squinted in the bright sun, but was gazing steadfastly out over the lake. The light breeze tugged at her hair, pulling more curly white-blond wisps free from the clip.

"When did you see the reindeer?" She repeated her question, startling him.

"Oh, right. Well, let's see…" He struggled to remember. "Yeah, I think I saw some reindeer when I was out here first setting up. That would have been almost a week ago."

The detective turned to look at Elias. "Do reindeer ever go into the water?"

"Yes," he said. "If the herds are being moved across a river or an inlet of the lake, they will swim across. Reindeer are strong swimmers."

"Would they swim here?"

Elias shook his head. "Perhaps. I'm not sure. As I told

you, I am not a reindeer herder, so I don't know the paths that herds might take. This area of the lake is a common spot to find herds from time to time, especially at this time of the year, but if there is no need to swim the herd, they probably would not go into the water."

"You know, I think I did hear some splashing the other night," said Shaun, a vague memory coming back to him. "It might have been the same night we saw the reindeer, I'm not sure. We heard a lot of splashing in the water, coming from sort of that direction, I think." He waved towards the same area where he was pretty sure he'd seen some animals moving in the distance under the starlight. "I wasn't really paying any attention to it. I never thought about reindeer being able to swim or not, but I guess they might have been."

"You say 'we,'" said Detective Niiranen. "You were not alone?"

"Paul was with me." He looked back at the computer. "I first set up this station six days ago. I know I didn't hear the splashing that first night, so it was probably five nights ago, or maybe four, that we heard it."

The detective's phone rang again. She stepped several paces away from him and Elias to answer it. Shaun wished he could hear her more clearly—not that he knew enough Finnish to try eavesdropping. Her slightly stumbling English and thick accent were very cute, but he wanted to hear her speaking her native tongue.

His musings were halted as she hung up the phone and came back over. "I need to return to Inari village. Thank you, Mr. Ahpbernahtoo, for showing me this and telling me all."

"You're very welcome, Detective." He put the laptop and other equipment back into the storage box, shoved the box back under the brush, and led the way back down the hill.

After a time, when the path widened out again, Shaun made sure to walk beside her, and tried several more times to strike up a conversation. She obligingly answered his questions, and asked him several in return, but clearly small-talk that did not pertain to her case of missing reindeer did not interest her.

As they came back to the streets of Inari village proper, she thanked him again, and then set off briskly down another street, leaving him and Elias on the road that led to his hotel. Shaun sighed and stared after her until she turned a corner and disappeared.

"She is a police detective, Shaun," Elias said quietly.

"I know that, Elias. But a guy can dream, can't he?"

Elias gave a small smile and said nothing.

Shaun's phone rang. He pulled it out and saw that it was Pål calling. Probably the other guys had figured out that he'd taken one of the detectives out to an observation site and revealed details about some of their equipment. Even though that didn't pertain directly to her case, it was still a violation of sorts of the agreement they all had. Shaun didn't really want to answer the phone.

Either way, though, the other three guys would give him a lecture sooner or later. He took a deep breath and answered the call, bracing himself for a good chewing-out by one of his senior partners.

The next morning Lyylia met Jassu in the lobby of Hotel Inari. "Where's Bierža?" she asked, glancing around. The lobby was empty except for the desk clerk, filling a pot of coffee.

"He's on his way," Jassu said. "He went to get a boat."

Late the previous night Bierža had gotten a call from a local Inari resident who had found a dead reindeer washed up on one of the islands in the lake. A possible clue.

Bierža came into the lobby, bundled up in gloves, hat, and parka. "I've got a boat ready," he said. "Ávgos Heikkilä is waiting for us there."

Lyylia tugged on her gloves as they followed Bierža outside. It was still dark, and Bierža pulled out a flashlight. A walk of several minutes took them to the shore of Lake Inari. Ávgos Heikkilä was already there waiting for them. A short man with close-cropped brown hair, he wore a serious expression on his face. But he greeted them with a friendly tone.

At least Ávgos had finally confirmed for them yesterday the exact number of animals missing from his herd: one hundred thirty, out of a herd of three hundred seventy-two. The paperwork had said "five hundred or less." Bierža had explained that it was culturally unacceptable to talk about the specific number of reindeer that one owned—it was like telling a stranger how much money you made and how much your bills were. Lyylia understood the concept, but it was still frustrating when everyone they had questioned yesterday gave vague amounts that ranged from "some" to "a lot."

Everyone climbed into the small open boat. Ávgos sat in the back with Bierža as he drove, and Lyylia and Jassu sat up front. The boat cut through a thin film of ice on the surface of the water, and Lyylia tightened her scarf against the wind.

"This is the same area where the American scientist said he saw reindeer," Lyylia said to Jassu, pointing at the shoreline as they went past. "That hilltop is where he took me."

"I'm glad you got that much information out of him," said Jassu. "The Norwegian and the Russian on that science team were pretty uncooperative."

"Well, the British scientist didn't tell me much," said Lyylia, lifting a hand to shield her watering eyes from the cold wind. "But the American was surprisingly forthcoming. It must be true that Americans like to talk a lot."

Jassu laughed. "I once dated an American girl when I was at university. She was a talker, all right. Among other things."

"I'm sure," Lyylia said, rolling her eyes. "You know, I was so concerned on the way up here about being able to communicate with the Sami; I wasn't expecting I'd have to speak English."

Jassu laughed again. "Well, you volunteered to talk to the English-speakers."

"That's because you can't speak anything but Finnish and Swedish," she countered. "And neither of those too well, either."

Jassu chuckled.

Bierža guided the boat through a network of tiny islands. Lake Inari covered over a thousand square kilometers, Lyylia remembered from the paperwork, and it boasted over three thousand islands. Searching the entire lake and all of the islands would be a daunting task, if it came to that.

Bierža slowed the boat and pulled up at one of the islands. This island, like so many of them, was no bigger than a large house. Even in the morning darkness, Lyylia could see the dead reindeer lying tangled in the bushes a few meters away.

Lyylia and Jassu pulled out their flashlights as they climbed out of the boat. Yesterday when they'd met Ávgos, Lyylia had been surprised to learn that reindeer were so small. Visiting her grandparents in Kuusamo when she and Teija were young, she'd seen moose, which were alarmingly huge—but in contrast, reindeer were barely the size of a small pony or even a large dog.

This animal still had its antlers—both males and females shed their antlers every winter, Ávgos had told them. It lay right at the edge of the water, partially tangled in the small bushes growing on the island. Brambles and thorns were snagged in its gray fur. If it had been a human lying in that place and in that position, Lyylia would judge that it had washed up on the shore already dead, rather than climbing out of the water and then dying on land.

Ávgos squatted down beside the animal, and Lyylia and the other two shone down their flashlights. "My earmark," he said, lightly touching the reindeer's left ear. "These marks cut into the ear mean it belongs to my herd."

Jassu hunkered down beside him. "I'm not a forensics expert—especially with animals—but I'm not seeing any signs of injury."

Ávgos poked at the stiff animal. "No wounds," he agreed. "No broken bones, either, I don't think. This was a healthy male, two years old. It looks like it's been dead for several days. The cold would've kept it from decomposing."

"Did it drown?" Lyylia asked.

"That would be my guess," said Ávgos.

"I thought that reindeer can swim," said Jassu.

"Yes," Ávgos answered. "But even people who can swim can drown. He could have panicked if he became separated from the herd or lost sight of land."

Lyylia looked around at the dozens of little islands and skerries that rose up like shadows from the dark water. "If that was the case, he may not have drowned in this area. How far out into the lake would a reindeer have to be to lose sight of land?"

Ávgos stood up and looked out over the lake. "Several kilometers."

"So this is not one of the animals that you put your GPS tracker collars on?" Jassu asked.

"No," said Ávgos. "My father had GPS collars for only four reindeer—ones that are usually leaders of smaller groups within the larger herd. I've been wanting to collar more of them, but what with managing everything else since my father died last year, I just hadn't gotten around to it yet." He sighed.

"Are the collars waterproof?" Lyylia asked.

"They're supposed to be, but the ones I have are an older model, so the waterproof aspect may not be reliable anymore. If the herd swam through the lake long enough, that might be enough to short them out. That was my first theory when I first noticed the animals were missing and two of the collars weren't showing up on my tracking app."

Lyylia nodded as she looked out into the darkness of the vast lake.

"A lot of things can interfere with the collars' signals," Ávgos added. "Like intense aurora, or the batteries getting low. I charged the collars in the spring. The batteries are supposed to last at least six to eight months, but like I said, these are an older model."

They spent the rest of the day out on the lake. Once the sun finally rose, it made the search easier, though the overcast daylight brought no warmth to the air. Lyylia kept her scarf wrapped securely around her neck to block the wind as Bierža drove the boat from island to island. Snow flurries filtered down, off and on. They found no evidence of other reindeer, foul play, or anything else.

That evening, Lyylia and Jassu sat in the hotel restaurant going over their notes. Lyylia was grateful for hot food and to be inside out of the wind. She had always admired her father for not only what he did—running a search-and-rescue boat on the bay of Helsinki—but simply for being out in the elements all the time. She missed him, as she had every day since he'd died.

Jassu pushed his empty plate aside and tapped a finger on the map of Lake Inari spread out on the table between them. "So all we managed to look at today was this tiny corner of the lake. If you really think that all of the missing reindeer are in the lake, we're going to need some serious backup to help us search. I don't know if we'd be able to get any dredging equipment up here before the lake freezes. And if the animals are alive, and hanging out on some of the islands farther out…" He shook his head. "We're still going to need back-up."

"I think the lake is where we should begin," said Lyylia. "That's where the two GPS collars stopped transmitting, and now with the dead reindeer we saw today..."

"I agree," said Jassu. "I just don't know how feasible this is going to be."

"Well, feasible or not, we can't just call it a cold case and go home." Lyylia took a sip of her coffee. "And we have a suspect: Ávgos' cousin."

"Right. Mađen Lahti." Jassu looked at one of the papers. "He was here in Inari at the time that the animals disappeared, but two days later he left on 'business' and still isn't back. Ávgos and his wife, Sirkka, avoided our questions about him yesterday, and Ávgos was just as vague today in the boat. He knows where Mađen went—and why—but he's protecting him for some reason."

"I think Mađen went to Rovaniemi," Lyylia said.

Jassu looked at her.

"When we were talking to the family yesterday, Ávgos' sister, Elbmá Somby, mentioned that Mađen had lived in Rovaniemi for a time, but he'd come back home to live with the family. So if he went somewhere on 'business'—that had nothing to do with the family business of reindeer husbandry—Rovaniemi is the first logical place."

Jassu wrote in his notes. "Well, it's something to go on. Okay, so we'll definitely need more manpower if we're going to track down Mađen Lahti *and* search the lake."

"Let's send Bierža to Rovaniemi to find Mađen," said Lyylia. "That's his city, so he'd have the knowledge to track down Mađen quickly if he's there. And he might be able to get some manpower and equipment sent up here."

Jassu nodded. "Good idea. I'll call Chief Sjöberg and request backup from Kokkola, too, since this is our case. Maybe between those two jurisdictions we'll actually get something before the lake freezes over."

"Let's hope so." Lyylia put down her coffee mug and made some notes. "Okay, you call the chief, and I'll call Bierža."

"It's a deal." Jassu began gathering up his papers.

Lyylia stood up and collected her papers and the map. "I'll have to go outside to make the call. For some reason I have hardly any signal inside this hotel. I can text, but all my calls drop. How is it that you have service and I don't?"

Jassu shrugged. "I guess I just have a better phone. You're still using that archaic decade-old device."

Lyylia made a face at him. "My phone is not that old, thank you, so just shut up about your cutting-edge technology."

Jassu shrugged again, more dramatically this time. "I don't have to say another thing. The proof is right there—I have signal, you don't." He gave a superior-looking smile.

Lyylia just shook her head. "Good luck with the chief."

"Thanks." He grinned. "See you in the morning, Lyylia."

Lyylia went up to her room to deposit the papers, use the restroom, and put on her coat and scarf. She thought of her sister, and felt farther away from her family than ever, here in this little village at the top of the world. Glancing at the time on her phone, she decided it wasn't too late to give Teija a call once she finished with Bierža.

Grabbing her flashlight, since Inari village had very few streetlights, she went outside to make her phone calls.

"So we spent the rest of the day out on the lake, but we didn't find anything else." Ávgos looked at his wife, Sirkka, as she rinsed the last plate in the sink. He took it from her and dried it.

Sirkka sighed as she wrung out the wash rag and hung it on the oven-door handle. "What are we going to do, Ávgos? What if all of the missing animals are dead? If we never get any of them back, how will we make enough money with only half a herd? And the baby will be here in January…"

Ávgos put the plate away in the cupboard. "We'll figure it out, Sirkka. We'll manage. I promise. These are big-city police detectives—they have different methods from the police up here. They'll find something." He laid his hand gently on her pregnant belly.

Sirkka smiled. She was a strong woman, he knew—stronger than she really should have to be. Wanting to advance beyond the average Sami lifestyle, both he and Sirkka had gone to university in Turku and had started making a comfortable living in southern Finland. But then, when Ávgos' father died last year, they'd given all that up and come back to the north to manage the family herd. And now this new life that they hadn't even really wanted had been pulled out from under them.

"I'm going to go out and check on the herd once more," Ávgos said.

Sirkka nodded, and they both left the kitchen and went into the living room. Their three-year-old daughter, Piijá, was playing on the floor; Ávgos' mother, Máddji, sat on the worn brown sofa, watching her.

"Come on, Piijá, time for bed," said Sirkka. "Say goodnight to your father. He's going out to check on the reindeer."

Ávgos picked up his little girl and gave her a kiss on the cheek. "Goodnight, sweetheart."

"Goodnight, Daddy," she said.

He kissed Sirkka. "'Night, honey. You'll probably still be up when I get back—I won't stay out long." He handed Piijá to Sirkka, then looked at his mother sitting silently on the sofa. "Goodnight, Mother."

Máddji looked up at him but didn't say anything. She was always so quiet now. Sometimes she'd go for days without saying anything at all. She'd been that way ever since his father died.

Making sure that he had his phone, flashlight, and keys, Ávgos went out through the kitchen door, where his boots and coat were waiting in the tiny mudroom off the back porch.

For the past week, they'd been keeping the remainder of the reindeer herd corralled in the small paddocks near the house that were normally reserved for earmarking and slaughtering. The separation of the herds had been finished over a week ago, so his animals had been corralled in the larger paddocks several kilometers away when the theft had occurred. So far, no one and nothing had disturbed the remaining animals in their small paddock.

The reindeer lowed and whickered at Ávgos as he shut the corral gate behind him and moved amongst them. They all seemed fine, and none were missing. He tossed a few more bales of straw into the paddock and broke the ice in the water troughs.

He started back towards home, but then decided to take a slight detour, turning southeast to head along the road that led toward Lake Inari. He wanted to get back home to Sirkka, but it was such a beautiful night that he wasn't quite ready to go back inside. While he missed the city of Turku, the wide sky and open tundra of Samiland touched him in a deep place inside his soul. He hadn't wanted a career as a reindeer herder, but he'd never stopped being a Sami.

The thin clouds from the day had cleared and thousands of stars all showed up with crystal clarity, undiminished by the brightness of the moon. A faint wisp of color, like a green and purple cloud, floated across the sky. Briefly looking up at the northern lights, he pulled out his phone and called his cousin again.

"Any news?" Maðen's voice answered the phone, terse and with no greeting.

Ávgos told him about the dead reindeer and the day spent searching out on the lake.

"So these cops think that all of the reindeer drowned?" Maðen said. "They're big-city cops from the south—what could they possibly know about reindeer?"

"They don't know anything about reindeer, but they know how to find clues and hunt down criminals. And this is more than we've had to go on since the herd vanished." Ávgos paused, and when his cousin didn't say anything right away, he continued. "Mađen, you should really come back home. We need you. And I had to lie to the detectives—I told them I didn't know where you were."

The silence continued on the other end of the line. "Just give me a couple of more days, cousin," Mađen finally said. "I think I can meet with one of my contacts tomorrow."

Ávgos sighed. "Mađen, I appreciate that you're trying to help this way, but it's dangerous. And I don't think—"

"I know what I'm doing, Ávgos," Mađen cut him off with a growl. "I can handle it. Just keep the cops off my back for another day or two."

"I'll do my best," Ávgos said with another sigh. "But if one of the cops finds you in the wrong place at the wrong time…"

"I know, I know. I'll be careful. And I'll be back soon. I promise."

"Please come back as quickly as you can, Mađen. This is your home—you know you'll always be welcome here."

There was silence again on the other end, and then Mađen finally spoke. "Thanks, Ávgos. I'll finish what I came here to do, and then I'll be back home. I promise I won't let the family down again."

Ávgos managed a small smile at his cousin's words. "Okay. We'll see you soon, then."

He ended the call and put his phone back in his coat pocket. Mađen had made some poor choices and some dangerous friends in the past, but when Ávgos' father had died last year, the tragedy had pulled together the scattered bits of the family. Or at least, that's what Ávgos had believed at the time. No, he still believed it. His cousin had changed his ways; but if only he could just manage to completely forget his old mistakes and stay at home in Inari...

Wishing for everything to go back to the way it was before

was pointless, of course, but Ávgos wished it anyway. They'd been a happy family with a large herd of reindeer, all working hard together to make a new life.

Ávgos continued his walk, finally switching on his flashlight despite the blush of aurora and the brightness of the half-moon. Hopefully these big-city police officers could find his reindeer, find the culprits, and he and his family could get back to being a family again.

Ávgos had lost track of how long he'd been wandering along the path when a voice startled him.

"Hello?" called a voice from behind him suddenly. "Ávgos Heikkilä?"

He stopped and turned around, waving the flashlight up to see who was there. It was one of the police detectives, the woman. She held her flashlight angled at his feet so he wouldn't be blinded.

"Detective Niiranen," he called back, also lowering his flashlight. "What brings you out here so late?"

"No cell phone signal inside the hotel," she said, catching up to him.

Ávgos gave a small chuckle. "Cell service is spotty up here. I was out checking on the herd earlier, but I wanted to take a walk before going back inside."

"All of the animals still accounted for?" she asked.

Ávgos nodded. "They're safe and sound."

"May I walk with you?" she asked.

"Certainly." Ávgos felt reluctant to say no to a police officer, but he hoped she wouldn't ask him more questions about Maðen.

"I do my best thinking when I'm moving," the detective said conversationally as they walked along the winding path towards the shore of the lake.

"You won't want to do this for too many more nights," said Ávgos. "I'm surprised we haven't gotten much snow yet. Samiland is beautiful in the winter—but I certainly hope you won't have to be here that long."

"I hope not, either," she said. "I'm sure it is beautiful, though."

Ávgos had always loved Samiland in the winter—or in any season, really. But he couldn't help thinking of his recent winters in a city: soft pools of light from streetlamps on the snowy sidewalks, ski tracks winding through the city parks, icebreakers chugging through the harbor clearing the ice for the ferries and cargo ships.

"What was that?" Lyylia said suddenly, stopping.

Ávgos looked where she pointed with her flashlight, and saw a light flickering amongst the trees at the top of a hill. It looked like another flashlight, waving erratically through the trees.

"Perhaps the foreign scientists," Ávgos said. "I've encountered several of their computers and things in this area—I think they're here studying the northern lights."

"Yes, that's right," said Lyylia, looking around at the landscape.

"I had never thought about studying the aurora before," said Ávgos. "I suppose as a Sami I just accepted the lights as part of everyday life. Tourists come in the winter to see the lights, but I never imagined that someone would purposefully travel from another country to make a career of studying them."

"It's fascinating, I agree," said Lyylia. "I'd never thought about it before, either."

The flashlight on top of the hill continued to sporadically wave about. Then they heard a shout, coming from the hilltop, and the movements of the flashlight became frantic and rapid.

Another shout, this time sounding like a yell of panic.

Lyylia took off running up the hill, and Ávgos followed. The frantic yelling got louder, and was joined by the distinctive sounds of hitting and scuffling and crackling underbrush, as if someone was trying to wrestle off an attacker. Tossing her flashlight to her left hand, Lyylia reached into her coat and pulled out her gun. Ávgos hoped it wasn't a bear. He—foolishly—hadn't brought his gun or bear spray with him.

They were almost at the top of the hill and Ávgos was beginning to feel winded. The sounds of a fight were louder and more distinct. Snarling sounds and more yelling came from the trees.

"Police!" Lyylia shouted. "Stop where you are!"

When there was no response, she looked over at him. "Ávgos! Say that in Sami!"

Ávgos repeated Lyylia's police threat in Sami. The snarling sounds continued, and the frantic flashlight had stopped waving.

"Stay here," she hissed at him, and then scrambled over the last rock and into the clearing at the top of the hill.

Happy to obey, Ávgos hunkered down with his back to a tree, pointing his flashlight down at the ground.

"Detective!" came a shout in English. "Help!"

Ávgos saw Lyylia's flashlight waving around. "What's happening?" he heard her demand, also in English. "Who attacked you?"

"I don't know. It was like a swarm of little people. They just jumped out of the trees." Ávgos assumed it was one of the scientists speaking, since they were all foreigners and spoke English. "I fought them off and grabbed my scanner, but I know they're still here somewhere."

"Little people in trees?" Lyylia's voice asked.

"Look, I'm not crazy—several somethings just jumped

me. At first I thought they were bears, but they were little, like kids or something. I wrestled them off, but one of them bit my arm. I know they're still here—I heard them snarling just a second ago."

Ávgos rebuked himself again for venturing outside at night without any protection. He picked up a large sturdy stick lying in the underbrush, and came up over the top of the hill.

"You are injured?" Lyylia said, shining her flashlight through the forest, glancing briefly at Ávgos as he came into the little clearing.

"I'm not hurt. I'm wearing, like, four layers," said the scientist. He had a large backpack on his back, and a rock in his hand. His flashlight lay on the ground, pointing back into the trees.

"What you're describing doesn't sound like bears," Ávgos said in English. "Or any other kind of wild animal."

"I know what I saw. I mean, what little I saw," the man said. "Did you hear them, though? Snarling, like cats or something. You guys didn't see or hear anything?"

"I heard sounds," Lyylia said. "Ávgos—" Her words were cut short by a shout from the scientist at the same instant that something blurred past and slammed into her back, knocking her flat into the underbrush.

Ávgos instinctively ducked, and swung out with his stick. Lyylia rolled over on the ground, keeping a grip on her gun and her flashlight, and kicked the creature backwards into a tree trunk.

Swinging his flashlight and his stick around, Ávgos tried to get a look at it. He saw a glimpse of something that was about a meter high and covered in white fur, but then it was gone, scurrying back up into the treetops.

Then with a flurry of snarling and hissing, creatures

dropped out of the trees all around them. Ávgos swung his stick and hit one of them, but then suddenly his legs were yanked out from under him. He heard the other two shouting, and the detective's gun went off.

He scrambled around in the brush, searching for his flashlight. Lyylia landed right beside him, one of the furry creatures on top of her. Her head hit the rocky ground with an audible crack, and she didn't try to get up.

His hand found his flashlight, and he slammed it into the creature. With a hiss it tumbled away into the brush. Ávgos switched the flashlight back on and looked at the detective. Her eyes were closed, but he didn't see any blood.

Whatever these things were, they most certainly weren't bears. Ávgos stayed on the ground next to Lyylia and swung his flashlight around towards the scruffling sounds close by.

The American was still trying to fight off the creatures. Two clung to his arms and back like monkeys, then two more dropped out of the trees again.

Ávgos saw Lyylia's handgun lying in the leaves, and he crawled forward on his elbows and grabbed it. But before he could try to get up or even find anything to take aim at, claw-like grips closed around his ankles and he felt himself being dragged.

Ávgos bumped and slid down the hillside. More of the creatures were dragging Lyylia and the scientist, as well. Both his legs were secure in the grips of the little white-furred creatures as they scampered down the hill. He tried to kick, but had no leverage. He still had a grip on the detective's gun, and so with brambles and underbrush slapping him in the face, he aimed for the nearest creature he could see well, and fired.

He missed, and the little monsters responded with snarls of protest and dragged him faster. His back and head were aching now from the rough, tumbling trip down the hill. He glanced around in the moonlight.

Lyylia was apparently unconscious—hopefully not worse. Her body was limp as the creatures dragged her across the ground. The scientist was still trying to struggle, but he was being fully carried, with creatures holding his arms and legs.

They reached the bottom of the hill, and the creatures kept on going. Straight towards Lake Inari.

Taking a deep breath to quell his rising panic, Ávgos tried to take aim again with the gun, but he couldn't focus on the creatures well enough. They were almost at the shore of the lake. He stuffed the gun into his coat pocket, hoping it wouldn't go off accidentally with all the jouncing around. Being a police weapon, it probably didn't have a safety. Then he fumbled in his other pocket for his phone. He automatically dialed his home number rather than an emergency number, but before the phone connected the call, he was jerked against a rock. Pain lanced through his shoulder and the phone fell out of his hand.

Tumbling over the rock that he'd been slammed against, he hit the water face first. Heart pounding, he thrashed wildly. The water churned, and little clawed hands grabbed at him and pulled him down. As the dimness of the night disappeared above him, all he could think of was Sirkka.

CHAPTER 2: POHJOLA

S haun just knew he had to be dead at this point, but his body hurt far too much for that. He remembered the little hissing monsters jumping out of the trees at him. Then the detective showed up, and there was another fight...then water. The creatures had dragged them down the hill to the lake—he'd been conscious enough to remember that, but he hadn't been able to fight back. His memories grew foggier after they'd hit the water—so cold he could hardly breathe, then he couldn't breathe at all, and so he figured he must be dead by now.

But now he was suddenly feeling very awake, and realized he was warm and dry and lying next to a fire, wrapped up in a fur blanket. Blinking and squinting in the bright flickering light, he slowly turned his head and tried to look around. Over the crackling of the fire, Shaun could hear voices murmuring nearby in conversation. Shifting around in his fur blanket, he realized that he was lying in snow. Footsteps scuffled, and a small man crouched down beside him.

He was short, with a round youthful face and shaggy light-brown hair. He was dressed in a primitive-looking costume: fur coat with a big hood, leather pants, fur boots, and a rough leather belt strapped around his midsection.

"Who are you?" Shaun struggled to sit up and back away at the same time, and neither one worked. He was well cocooned in the furs, and every muscle in his body hurt and refused to work properly.

"I won't hurt you," the man said with a broad smile. "My name is Boots."

Shaun blinked at him. "Boots, huh? Okay." Odd name. "Um, my name is Shaun. What...uh, what happened?"

"You were attacked by hiisi. We rescued you," said Boots. He leaned back on his heels, and turned to poke at the fire with a stick.

"What's a, um, *hee-see*?"

"Those are hiisi." Boots pointed with his fire poker.

Shaun managed to prop himself up on one elbow in his fur wrapping and looked where Boots was pointing. Just a few yards away in the snow lay a pile of bodies: bodies that looked like white mutant chimpanzees. The creatures looked like they were maybe three or four feet tall, and were covered in nappy white fur. The faces that he could see were gray and squinting and grotesque, with sharp teeth and wide flat noses.

Shaun shuddered at the sight. "Those are the things that attacked us? What the hell are they?"

"Hiisi."

He looked back at Boots. "Yeah, I got that part." Shoving himself up to a fully sitting position, he was able to get a good look at his surroundings. Just a few feet away from the pile of dead bodies stood another man: a short, youthful-looking man like Boots, also dressed in an outfit of furs. He held a long spear and stood motionless, like a sentinel. A husky-type dog sat next to him.

Just past the fire, Shaun could see the shore of a lake,

where a small wooden boat was tethered and bobbed gently in the water. The fire had been built in the shelter of a small rocky hill at the edge of a forest. Shaun assumed they were somewhere along the shore of Lake Inari, but then he realized that there was snow everywhere—a good three or four inches deep, at least. The sky had been clear, last he remembered, with only a dusting on the ground from a few days earlier—so how long had he been knocked out?

And then he finally noticed the light. The landscape was lit with a silver hue, like moonlight, but much clearer and brighter than even the brightest full moon. He looked up at the sky, and his heart skipped a beat. There was the moon, large and about half-full. And the stars—but they were all so large. He recognized the northern wintertime constellations, but they were too big, too bright, as if he were looking at a planetarium show with everything enlarged beyond its actual size. And directly overhead was one giant bluish-white star, too small to be the sun but much too large and close to be any other star, illuminating everything with its silvery-blue light.

Panic set in. He could handle strange primitive people and even the miniature yeti creatures, but the sky…this was not a sky that should exist, that *could* exist. Struggling with his fur blankets, he tried to stand up.

"What…where am I? What's wrong with the sky?"

Boots put his hands on Shaun's blanket and gently pushed him back down. "There's nothing wrong with the sky—this is the way the sky always looks. The sky in your land must look different, then?"

"What? What are you talking about?" Shaun stared at the man's round, gentle face and tried to get his heart to stop thudding frantically in his chest. "Where am I?"

"Pohjola." Boots smiled and spread his arms wide. "Our

beautiful land of forests and rivers, meadows and lakes, mountains and fells. Everything lit by Pohjantähti is our land. On behalf of Kuu our Queen and all my fellow Menninkäinen, I welcome you to Pohjola!"

Shaun swallowed hard. "Pohjola. So…so is this another planet or something?"

"I'm not sure what 'planet' means," said Boots. "We have legends that tell of a gateway to another world, a place called Kalevala. Just recently we discovered that this gateway is indeed real—and it's in this lake. So we can only assume that you've come from Kalevala, since we caught the hiisi dragging you through the lake. We've never seen people like you before."

"I'm from America," said Shaun. "And the last thing I knew, I was in Finland. I don't know what this Kalevala is, or any kind of gateway in a lake." He shook his head. "Is this for real?" He rubbed at his head. He remembered the white-furred hiisi dropping out of the trees… "Wait, where's the detective and that other guy? There were two people with me."

"They are fine," Boots said, pointing. "The man named Ávgos woke briefly just before you did, but he's resting again."

Shuan finally spotted two human-sized bundles of fur in the snow near the fire. Then he noticed a tangle of curly white-blond hair at the end of one of the bundles. "Detective Niiranen!" He struggled up to a standing position.

Keeping the furs wrapped tightly around him, he shuffled through the snow toward her. As he did so, he suddenly realized he was barefoot, and completely naked under the furs. "Hey, where are my clothes? What the hell did you do with my clothes?"

"Your clothing was wet. You were in the lake," Boots said matter-of-factly. "All three of you were nearly dead from the cold when we pulled you out of the water." He pointed to several branches propped up on the other side of the fire, from which dangled coats, pants, and other familiar articles of clothing.

Securing his blanket again, Shaun made it over to where the detective lay.

"Detective Niiranen," he said, crouching down beside her. "God, I wish I could remember your first name." She looked asleep, her head turned to the side, her lips slightly parted. Then he saw a reddish-black mat in her blond hair near the back of her head. "She's been hurt! Boots, did those hiisi things do this? She's been bleeding!"

"Yes, it looks like her head was struck, but the cold water stopped the bleeding," said Boots, coming up behind him. "Tip and Eider have gone hunting to gather more food, and they are also looking for some healing moss that will help her."

"She could have a concussion—or worse," Shaun said. He slid his hand under her head. Boots was right—she was no longer bleeding, but he could feel a distinct knot on the back of her head, under the mat of dried blood. What if her skull had been fractured?

Suddenly she stirred. Maybe poking at her injury had woken her up. That was good—at least it meant she hadn't slipped into a coma or something. She groaned softly and moved her head. Shaun moved his hand to cradle the back of her neck.

She opened her eyes and squinted up at him.

"Detective Niiranen," he said softly. "It's me, Shaun Abernathy. The aurora scientist. The American."

She mumbled something in Finnish and closed her eyes again.

"Can you understand what I'm saying? Please, just say something—I need to know that you're all right."

She spoke more loudly this time, and started to roll over.

This apparently was painful, though, because she gave a sharp gasp, and opened her eyes again.

"You're injured," Shaun said. "Please, can you understand me at all? Just tell me what hurts."

She mumbled, sounding somewhat snappish this time, and made a move to sit up. Shaun kept his hand behind her head, and supported her back with his other hand to help her up.

"You were hit on the head," Boots said, squatting down at her other side and also helping her to sit up. "So yes, that would be the reason why you say everything hurts. I'll soon have some healing moss and a hot drink for you, though—that should help."

She stared at him. "*Kuka sinä olet?*"

"My name is Boots. My friends and I pulled you out of the lake. You were attacked and brought here by hiisi. Your friend Shaun can tell you all about it."

"Wait a second…" Shaun said. "Boots, you can understand what she's saying?"

"Of course," he said. "Just the way I can understand you. Neither one of you is speaking the Menninkäinen tongue."

"I guess not, but…okay, so how can I understand you?"

"We Menninkäinen can understand and make ourselves understood to any creature intelligent enough to have a language. We speak to our dogs and our horses, and sometimes to birds. And we can understand the hiisi's language, too, which is how we knew you must have come from Kalevala."

"Nice talent to have. Well, I have no idea what she's saying. Can you ask her if she remembers how to speak English?"

"I speaks English fine," the detective said, turning to look at Shaun. "My head…is pain. Where…?" She seemed to run out of words.

"Long story. And I'm not sure I'm ready to believe any

of it. How do you feel?"

"Very terrible." She worked a hand free from the furs to touch her head, and winced.

"I don't suppose you have any painkillers here?" Shaun asked Boots.

"The healing moss, like I told you," Boots said patiently. "Tip and Eider will be back soon. Unless you'd rather I went off in search of some moss and left the three of you here with only Claw to protect you." He nodded in the direction of the spear-holding man who was still stoically standing by the heap of dead hiisi. "Claw is quite capable, but if more hiisi were to show up, I'm sure you'd rather have more than one of us to help you. None of you is in any condition to be fighting hiisi right now."

"Okay, fine, we can wait," said Shaun. Boots had a point. Assuming all of this was really happening. "I'm just concerned about her, is all."

Detective Niiranen lifted her head and looked at Shaun, and then looked over at Boots, staring hard at him as if really seeing him for the first time.

"You speak Finnish or English?" she asked.

Boots gave a shrug and smiled. "Neither one. I can understand both of you, and apparently the Menninkäinen gift of understanding enables you to understand me, as well."

The detective looked back at Shaun. "*Mitä?*"

He shook his head. "Don't look at me. I'm completely lost at this point. Maybe I hit my head, too."

Boots moved a few steps away to put more wood on the fire. The detective gave an unhappy-sounding grunt, and moved to lie back down. Then she paused, and looked up at Shaun. "Where are my clothes?"

"Over there, drying," Shaun said, nodding at the campfire.

He tried not to think about the fact that she was naked under the fur blanket. He gently helped guide her back down to a comfortable lying position, keeping one hand resting on her shoulder.

"I remember we were attacked," she said quietly, looking up at him. "Little creatures in the trees…like people, but of fur." Her blue eyes focused on his face, and through the thick furs Shaun felt her body tense beneath his hand. "Ávgos. Where is he?"

"Asleep right over there," Shaun said. "Boots said he's okay."

"And we are believe everything he says? We don't know this place." She looked up at the sky. "Where are we? Is that the moon or sun?"

"Neither one, I don't think," said Shaun, glancing up at the disconcerting blue-white illumination. "Detective, I hate to tell you this…but either we're sharing the same nightmare, or we're somehow not on Earth anymore. We're definitely not in Finland. Or Kansas."

"Kansas?"

"Never mind. Boots said we came through a gateway in the lake, whatever that means. I do remember water. According to him, the things that attacked us are called hiisi. There's a pile of dead bodies over there."

She twisted her head and tried to sit up to look, but then winced in pain again and settled back down.

"He says this place is called Pohjola, and he seems to think we're from a place called Kalevla or something."

"Kalevala?" she said.

"Yeah, that was it." He looked down at her. "You've heard of it?"

"Kalevala, Pohjola, Menninkäinen…I am dreaming, or crazy with hitting my head."

Boots turned from the fire to face them. "So you are from Kalevala? The legends are true!"

"Kalevala is a legend!" the detective said with sudden energy, and hoisted herself to a half-sitting position, supporting herself on one elbow. "What are you?"

"My name is Boots. I'm a Menninkäinen. What are you?"

"*Suomalainen,*" she said.

"We're humans," Shaun supplied. Boots looked human enough, even though he was a bit shorter than the average adult man.

"I don't know what *Finnish* or *humans* means," said Boots. "But we have a legend of another world called Kalevala. Apparently the hiisi found the gateway, curse them all. It's beneath the water of the lake."

"So, Detective, would you like to fill me in on why you've heard of this Kalevala?" Shaun asked.

"It is our story, the legend and myths of Finland," she said, still staring at Boots as she talked. "The country peoples, Karelians and Ingrians and others, told stories and legends long ago when we still were ruled over from Sweden and Russia, stories about our Finnish culture."

"Okay," Shaun prompted when she paused. "Go on."

"*Kalevala* is the name of stories and poems and old songs. Legends of Väinämöinen and others, and Sampo, and north land of evil, Pohjola. Myth, stories." She glared at Boots. "Kalevala is not a real place!"

"Kalevala is a legend in your world, too?" said Boots, sounding astonished. "And you have a legend of Pohjola? But Ice-Dark is the northern land of evil, not our land."

"What's Ice-Dark?" asked Shaun.

"The land on the other side of the lake. It's a place of evil. That is where the hiisi live."

Shaun looked at Boots, and then back at the detective.

Boots stood up and brushed snow from his leather pants. "Well, once you three are strong enough to travel, we'll be taking you to the Queen—she'll know how to stop the hiisi and to help you return home. You're not the first creatures that have come through this gateway."

"We're not?" Shaun said. "Who else came through? Were they from our world?"

Boots shrugged lightly. "I don't know where they came from. But they were just more creatures of myth, so don't worry about it. Detective probably wouldn't believe me, anyway."

"Detective is my title," she said. "My name is Lyylia."

"*Loo-lia,*" Shaun repeated. Now he didn't have to be so formal with her.

"Well, get some rest, Lyylia," Boots said in a gentle tone. "There will be food and healing moss for you soon. And even if you believe nothing else that I've told you, please believe me when I tell you that I and my Menninkäinen brothers will keep you safe." He smiled warmly, and then went back around to the other side of the fire.

"He's right, Lyylia, you should get some rest," said Shaun.

She lay back down, but looked up at him with a frown on her face. "I don't trust him."

"Well, we don't have a lot of options right now," Shaun murmured back. "They saved us from those hiisi things that attacked us by Lake Inari. And you're in no condition to be doing anything right now."

Lyylia muttered in Finnish under her breath, but she settled down and closed her eyes. She must have been exhausted, because within moments, her breathing was slow and regular. Shaun remained sitting beside her, feeling a strange jumble of confusion, panic, and awe as he stared up at the strange and vivid sky.

Lyylia was finally dressed—her clothes were warm and dry, but smelled strongly of woodsmoke from where they'd been drying by the fire. She dug into the pockets of her jeans and her coat one more time to take inventory of everything: hat, gloves, police badge, wallet, hotel room key, dead cell phone. But her gun was missing.

The short, round-faced man came around the edge of the fire, a bundle of sticks in his arms. "Oh, you're up and dressed now, I see," he said, tossing the sticks onto the fire. "Feeling better?"

"My head hurts and I'm a little dizzy," she said, sitting down on a log next to the fire. Her head throbbed and every muscle in her body ached. All of this had to be a dream, except that she was in too much pain for that. "Is there more of that porridge?"

"The rabbit stew? Yes, of course. And it has some healing moss in it, so it will help with your injury." He bent over the pot by the fire and spooned some into a wooden bowl.

"Thank you." She wanted to be cautious about eating strange food in a strange place, but survival options seemed limited at the moment. "I'm sorry, I've forgotten your name."

"Boots," he said with a cheerful smile.

"Thank you, Boots."

She looked around at the snowy landscape as she sipped on the porridge. Everything was tinged sharply with a silvery-blue light from the enormous blue star directly overhead. All the stars seemed bigger and brighter than they should be, almost as if the entire sky was like a blanket that had been pulled closer to the earth. "Where am I?"

"Pohjola," Boots said. "At the edge of the northern woods next to Dark Water Lake. Now that you're more clear-headed, maybe you can tell me the name of your world. You and Shaun seemed to be having a disagreement earlier about where you were from."

"I'm from Finland," she said. "But he's from America. Different countries."

"Ah," said the little man. "That still makes no sense to me. Well, whatever you call your world, I will continue to call it Kalevala."

"Kalevala is just old stories," Lyylia insisted.

"Yes, so you said. It's old stories here, too. A strange coincidence, yes?" He gave her a grin as he stood up.

Lyylia stared at Boots. How could people on another planet—if that's where they were—have the story of *The Kalevala*? It was uniquely Finnish—something that even the Swedes and the Russians hadn't taken from them.

She spotted Shaun and Ávgos a short way from the fire, both crouched over, examining something in the snow. She finished the porridge and carefully stood up. All her muscles were stiff, and a spike of pain went down her neck. She snugged up her scarf and slowly started walking.

Shaun and Ávgos both stood up to greet her as she approached. "You're looking well, Detective Niiranen," Ávgos said. "I'm glad to see that your head injury wasn't too serious."

"My head still hurts, and I feel sore all over," she said. "But I'll be fine."

"You look great, Lyylia," said Shaun in English. "I mean, you're looking like you're feeling great, feeling much better."

"Yes," she said, struggling to switch her brain around to English mode. "I still feel I am dreaming or nightmare."

"Same here," Ávgos said in English.

"What is that?" Lyylia asked, pointing at what looked like a dismantled computer, lying in pieces on a black backpack in the snow at their feet.

"My aurora scanner," said Shaun. "The same one that I showed you the other day. I was out making my rounds to all the observation sites when those hiisi things came out of nowhere, before you two showed up. I didn't know what they were or what they wanted, so I packed up my device. I was going to take it back to the hotel to keep it safe, but I never got the chance."

The laptop was open and the circuit board exposed. Several miniature screwdrivers and sets of pliers were scattered around. "Even though I had it in its case, it still got wet," said Shaun. "I knew I should have gotten the watertight case, not just the water-resistant one. I think it's mostly dried out now—I just hope it'll still work. I want to be able to test it, but I'm not sure how much juice is left in the battery."

Lyylia wasn't sure if she'd understood every word of his explanation, but she didn't have the energy to ask him to repeat himself or to ask Ávgos to translate. Between the linguistic exercise and moving around, she felt exhaustion pulling at her again. She hoped she didn't have a concussion or some other internal injury. She'd done a cursory check for physical wounds when she'd gotten dressed. Moss and porridge might be about as advanced as the medicine was here, which was not a comforting thought.

Boots came over to them. "Is your magic box dried out and ready for travel, Shaun?"

"It's not magic, and yes, I guess it's as dried out as it's

going to get. Just let me put it back together and I'll be ready."

"Where are we traveling and why?" Lyylia asked Boots.

"Back to our village," said Boots. "It's a two-day journey south of here. You'll be safe there. Then we need to get word to Queen Kuu about your arrival. We need the Queen's wisdom about where you've come from and what to do."

"Why can't we just go back home?" Lyylia asked, switching back to Finnish again so she could more clearly express her questions. To make the language problem more confusing, she heard Boots in Finnish, but Shaun apparently heard him in English, so she wasn't sure what language to use when speaking to him. "You said you pulled us out of the lake. Right? Am I remembering this correctly?"

"Yes," Ávgos said in Finnish. "Something about a 'gateway' under the lake. One side of the gate is apparently in Lake Inari, the other side is here. Wherever 'here' is…"

"Pohjola," Boots reminded him cheerfully.

"Right." Ávgos nodded, looking perplexed.

"So, can't we just go back through the gateway?" Lyylia insisted. "We need to go back home. We can't stay here."

"I understand how much you'd like to go home," Boots said. "But you'd be better off staying with us. First of all, we don't know where in the lake the gateway is located. Unless one of you might know…"

They shook their heads.

"If you'd really like to swim around in freezing waters, in a lake so large that it takes two days to travel along the shore, in water so deep that no Menninkäinen has seen the bottom, I guess I can't stop you. But it seems unwise to me."

"I suppose so," Ávgos said slowly.

"Also, we don't know how many more hiisi might be in this area. As I mentioned before, on the other shore of this lake is Ice-Dark, the land of the hiisi. And there might even still be hiisi on the other side of the underwater gateway, in your world."

"That's a scary thought," put in Shaun.

"All the more reason to go back to home," Lyylia said, still in Finnish.

"I hope that's not the case, either," said Boots. "But as I said, we don't know how to find the gateway. Eider and I will take you back to our village. Tip and Claw will stay here to monitor the lake. But we need to send them reinforcements as quickly as possible, and to do that, we need to get back to the village. We don't have a moon mirror with us, so we can't send a message to the village. I'll explain everything that I know while we travel."

"We're not going anywhere," Lyylia said. "Thank you for saving us from our attackers and for pulling us out of the water. But we don't know you and we don't know this place."

"We mean you no harm and we're telling you no lies," Boots said, looking up at her. "I swear. And please believe me when I tell you that we will protect you and get you safely to Queen Kuu. I know you want to go back home, but as I said, we have no way of getting you there."

"Those things that attacked us, hiisi you called them?" Lyylia looked over at the heap of white-furred bodies a distance away. "How did they find this gateway under the water?"

Boots looked apologetic. "We don't know that, either. But the Queen must be told of your arrival as soon as possible. We must get to the village so that we can send her a message."

"So you go back to your village and we'll wait for you here."

"It's not safe for you to stay here," Boots insisted. "If the hiisi kidnapped you, more might come to try to take you to Ice-Dark. It would be safer for you—for all of us—if we got you away from the lake as quickly as possible."

"What if we want to stay here?"

Boots cocked his head to one side as he stared up at her. "But why would you want to? I just explained—"

"Are you going to force us to leave this place?" she challenged. "Are we your prisoners?"

"Prisoners?" Boots blinked at her. "I don't know what that means."

Now it was Lyylia's turn to stare at him with surprise. It wasn't a language barrier—he seemed to understand everything else they said. How could someone not know what the word 'prisoner' meant? But she'd been a police officer long enough to know when to trust her gut feeling—and right now, her gut was telling her to trust this strange little person. He seemed to genuinely want to help them and was doing what he thought best.

The rational, cautionary part of her mind resisted the idea of traveling into the unknown with these unknown people, while leaving behind the only possible escape route. Nothing he said made sense—nothing about the entire situation made sense—but her gut told her that he was trustworthy. And, unfortunately, his argument was logical.

Lyylia looked at Ávgos and Shaun.

"I don't want to swim around looking for a 'gateway' that we don't know how to find," Ávgos said. "But we have to do something. We need to get home. Can we take the boat out? Is the gateway visible from the surface?"

Boots shook his head. "No one has ever seen it. We would take you to the gateway if we knew where it was."

"Where in the lake did we surface?" Lyylia asked. "Wouldn't the gateway be there?"

"Perhaps," said Boots with a shrug. He pointed out over

the lake. "You and the hiisi appeared some distance away, just past that large island."

"I know I'm missing half this conversation," Shaun spoke up, "since you guys are speaking Finnish, but I think Boots is right."

They all looked at him.

"The gateway is probably an Einstein-Rosen bridge," he continued. "It's the only explanation that makes any sense."

"A what?" said Ávgos in English.

"A wormhole. A bridge or a 'gateway' across dimensions. Wormholes are completely theoretical, but..." He paused and waved at the lake. "I mean, I guess maybe they're real, after all. But either way, an Einstein-Rosen bridge would be highly unstable. Even if we could find this end of the gateway, the other end may not return us to Lake Inari."

Ávgos frowned. "But that doesn't explain—"

Lyylia held up a hand. She hadn't understood half of the words Shaun had just said, and judging by Boots' face, he hadn't, either. "Is there another way back to Finland?" she asked Boots in English. "Or Earth, Kalevala. Another way to travel besides the gateway?"

Boots looked up at her. "I don't know. But if there is another way, Queen Kuu would know."

Lyylia looked at the two men.

Shaun shrugged.

Ávgos gave a resigned-sounding sigh and shook his head. "I'd rather stay here," he said in English. "But if we can't get home and your Queen can actually help us…"

Lyylia looked back at Boots. "Fine," she said in English. "Take us to see your Queen."

"Good!" Boots clapped his hands. "I'll gather what we'll need." He hurried off.

"I will help you with your computer, Shaun," Ávgos said. "But first—a moment with you, Detective?"

Shaun bent down to begin reassembling his equipment. Lyylia and Ávgos stepped several paces away.

"I want to return this to you," he said, pulling out a handgun. "I don't think these Menninkäinen know what it is or what to do with it, and they returned it to me along with my clothes when I woke up. You dropped it on the hilltop at Lake Inari and I picked it up."

"Thank you, Ávgos," she said, taking the pistol from him. "I'd been wondering what happened to it." She checked the magazine. "Two shots have been fired." She vaguely remembered firing one shot.

"I shot one of them, Detective," said Ávgos. "You got knocked down and dropped it. I picked it up and shot at one of the hiisi. I'm not sure if I hit it or not. I put the gun into my coat pocket right before the hiisi dragged us into the water, and that's the last thing I remember before waking up here."

"Thank you," she said again. "And you can call me Lyylia. 'Detective' doesn't mean much here, I don't think."

He gave a small smile. "Very well, Lyylia."

Ávgos went back over to help Shaun. Lyylia wanted nothing more than to lie back down and go to sleep, but if they were about to head out on a hike, she needed to stay alert. She knelt down in the snow and did a quick field strip of her gun just to make sure everything was working properly, though she knew it was designed to survive getting wet. She loaded a bullet into the chamber, just in case; there was no telling what they might encounter as they traveled into the unknown. She secured the gun in the shoulder holster under her left arm.

Then she made her way towards the heap of dead hiisi carcasses. The spear-bearing man standing guard looked up at her as she approached.

"Those are the creatures that brought us here?" she asked, pointing at the pile.

"Yes," he said. "They are hiisi from Ice-Dark."

She went towards the pile of bodies. "Are they all dead? I wanted to take a good look at the things that attacked us."

"They are dead."

The hiisi were all stiff, and clumps of ice hung in their nappy white fur. They looked smaller than the Menninkäinen, probably about a meter high when standing. Lyylia had vague, blurry memories of the hilltop by Lake Inari and strange furry creatures dropping out of the trees. There were at least eight hiisi in the heap. Red-black blood was matted against their fur in places, probably from spear wounds. So these Menninkäinen knew how to fight and how to kill.

Two of the dead hiisi that Lyylia could see had something around their necks, the only adornment that any of them were wearing. Reaching for the nearest one that had its head and neck exposed, Lyylia pulled the crude necklace off over its head. The necklace was a rope of coarse fibers twisted together, and from the rope hung an uneven lump of grayish-black rock.

Shaun came over, his bulky aurora computer backpack slung over one shoulder.

"Boots and Eider are ready to leave," he said, pulling the other backpack strap over his other shoulder. "What's that?"

"Some hiisi are wearing this," she said, holding out the rope and rough-hewn stone. "But not all of them. Maybe this hiisi was the leader."

Shaun took the necklace and turned the stone over in his hand, and then peered down at the hiisi at the bottom of the pile. "It looks like the same kind of stone." Squatting down, he held out the stone to compare it to the one the other hiisi was still wearing. With a click, the two stones slapped together and stuck.

He pulled them apart, and stood back up. "They're magnets. Like lodestone, or some other kind of magnetic ore. I'm not a geologist."

"Keep it," Lyylia said. "It maybe means something, is a clue about these hiisi or this place."

Shaun nodded in agreement and stuffed the stone necklace into his coat pocket.

Boots and Eider approached with small leather packs on their backs. Eider looked a little younger in the face than Boots. His sandy hair poked out from the edges of his fur hood. He was taller and thinner than Boots, but even so, he was still slightly shorter than Lyylia.

Ávgos carried a pack as well. One of the dogs that Lyylia had noticed keeping watch was now harnessed up to a little travois made of sticks, to haul the bulky fur blankets. Apparently they weren't going to make Lyylia carry anything, for which at the moment she was grateful.

"And now, our journey begins!" Boots said, and set off walking towards the line of trees in the distance.

Lyylia took one last look at the lake behind them— apparently housing, somewhere in its depths, the mysterious gateway back home. She still wasn't sure how this could all be real; but if it was, she hoped she wasn't making a monumentally foolish decision. Then she turned and fell into step with the others.

As the group left the snowy tundra and the lake behind them and entered the thick pine forest, Lyylia tried to think of something to ask the Menninkäinen to learn more about their situation and this place. But her brain felt sluggish, and Shaun started asking questions before she could even formulate a thought.

"How long have we been here?" Shaun asked. "I've been looking at the sky—the stars move, and the moon, but that pseudo-sun hasn't moved at all."

"We heard the hiisi in the water about halfway through the night," said Boots, "and it's now late in the day."

"So that never moves?" Shaun asked, pointing upwards at the large bright blue-white star directly overhead.

"Pohjantähti never moves," Boots said. "Should it?"

"So the light is always like this? How do you tell the difference between night and day?"

"Night is when the birds are asleep and the Dancing Lights come," Boots said, as if it should be the most obvious thing in the world. "When the birds wake up and the Lights go to sleep, then it is day and time for us to be wakeful, as well."

"Dancing Lights?" Ávgos asked.

"Yes, the Lights of many colors that dance and sing in the sky every night," said Boots. "Your world must be a strange place indeed—no Pohjantähti, no Dancing Lights."

"You mean aurora?" said Shaun, looking up at the sky again.

Boots shrugged. "I suppose you might have a different name for it. But when the hunter in the sky has moved two more handspans, it will be night and you will see the Dancing Lights."

"The hunter. Which one is that?"

Eider came beside Shaun. "Those stars," he said. Lyylia tried to follow where he indicated, but the blueish-black sky was so dotted with stars, even if there hadn't been tree branches overhead to obscure the view, that she couldn't pick out any constellations. "See, his broad shoulders, the bow he carries, the knife at his belt. He even has a dog that follows behind him."

"My God," Shaun murmured. "It's Orion. We see that constellation as a hunter, too, called Orion, and that's his dog, Sirius Major. So what do you call that one?"

"That's the Great Wolf," said Eider.

"It's a bear for us, Ursa Major, and there's Ursa Minor right there. We also call it the Big Dipper—you know, like a big ladle."

The two Menninkäinen laughed. "A great spoon!" said Boots. "Yes, I guess I can see the shape, but a great wolf is much more worthy of respect than a great spoon."

Shaun laughed. "Yeah, well, I usually call it Ursa the bear. So what about that one?"

"That one is what we call the Great Bear," Eider said.

"This is fascinating, and totally puzzling," said Shaun. "The constellations are the same, just bigger and brighter. And placed differently—it's like we're looking at a circumpolar sky. That bright one—Pohjantähti, you called it?—is in the position of our north star, Polaris. But the stars would only move in a circle if we were at the north pole exactly, the very top of the world, basically."

Shaun continued to ask the two Menninkäinen questions. Lyylia tried to follow them, but she was quickly lost as she realized how little she knew about the constellations—or anything else involving astronomy and the sky, for that matter. She found that she had to pay attention to where they were walking—there was no trail whatsoever.

The snow was not very deep—just a few centimeters—but even so, it hid all of the rocks and dips in the ground, so she had to watch carefully where she stepped. Lyylia struggled to keep pace. She was rapidly growing tired, her head and back ached, and despite the physical exertion she felt cold. In addition to being very much out of her element with the wilderness hiking, she now felt like extra baggage. She was a police officer—she was supposed to be the one leading and helping others, not the one limping along at the rear.

To get her mind off of how miserable she felt, and to make their journey more productive than just talking about stars, she tried again to rouse her brain in order to get some answers.

"So your Queen will know how to get us back home?" she asked in English, for Shaun's benefit, during a lull.

"Yes," Boots said, glancing back over his shoulder at her. "You see, we have always suspected there was a magical gateway between worlds—our legends tell of it. The stories say that it lies somewhere in the depths of the Dark Water Lake. In the past, shamans have tried searching for it, but no one had ever found it. But apparently the hiisi found it.

"The hiisi are from the land of Ice-Dark—a shaman as powerful as Queen Kuu, only evil and dark, rules that land. And so with his magicks he must have found the gateway. For many moons now there have been sightings of hiisi coming and going in the water.

"That's why Eider and Tip and Claw and myself were there by the lake. No one lives near the Dark Water Lake—it's too close to Ice-Dark. But some Menninkäinen on hunting trips here in the north had had encounters with hiisi, and so Queen Kuu commanded the lake to be kept under observation, to keep the hiisi out of Pohjola. We've been camping by the shore for many days now, and that's how we were able to spot you and hiisi in the water when you surfaced."

"You said before that other things come from the gateway," Lyylia said. "People like us?"

"No, not at all," said Boots. "Well, we can only assume they came through the gateway—we never have actually seen them. But they've been spotted here in the north, which is another reason why Queen Kuu commanded that scouts be sent out into the north near Ice-Dark."

"We've heard that other Menninkäinen have seen these creatures," put in Eider. "And some have even been captured and taken to Queen Kuu's castle to protect them from the hiisi."

"So what are these things?" Shaun asked.

"More legends," said Boots. "The Gentle Beasts, they're called in the tales. Stories tell that these Beasts once were wise lords of the woods in ancient times. These forest lords taught the first Menninkäinen the ways of magic and shamanism."

"What do they look as?" Lyylia asked.

"No one is really sure. Like Eider said, no one in our village has seen one since they've reappeared in Pohjola. The old songs say they are like living trees that walk about and sing to the moon."

"That sure doesn't sound like anything from our planet," said Shaun. "Are you sure this gateway doesn't go somewhere else, too?"

"Well, the legends say it goes to Kalevala. Maybe the Gentle Beasts are from there, since you say your world isn't Kalevala."

"*Kalevala* is the name of a collection of poems," Ávgos said. "It's the Finnish national epic, the mythology of our land."

"Yes, so Lyylia kept insisting," said Boots.

"It is true," she said.

Boots gave a light laugh. "Well, until you three figure out what your world is called, to us it will be Kalevala."

"I'm willing to go with Kalevala for now," Shaun said easily. "Since nobody but me seems to want to claim that we're from Earth."

"I never said we weren't from Earth," Ávgos said, frowning at him. "But we're also from Finland."

"*I'm* not from Finland," said Shaun.

Lyylia rolled her eyes and said nothing.

Eider stepped closer to Boots as they walked. "I'm confused," he said quietly.

Boots shrugged. "Me too. Their race must thrive on confusion."

"Well, that's accurate, I think," Ávgos said. Shaun laughed in agreement.

The blueish-white daylight never changed, but Lyylia noticed that the chattering of birds began to quiet, and an owl hooted in the distance. Glancing upwards through the thick canopy of trees, Lyylia saw a brief flicker of light that was distinctly green. It was followed after a moment by pinkish glow, and then suddenly a full-blown aurora display filled the entire sky.

"Oh my God, it's so beautiful," Shaun said, stumbling a bit as he craned his neck to peer up through the trees.

"The Dancing Lights," said Boots. "So you do not have this in Kalevala?"

"No, we have lights like this," Shaun said. "But this is a spectacular display. I can't wait to look at them when we stop."

"Why are you so anxious to see them if you have them in your world?" asked Eider.

"Because I study them. That's what I do—I'm a scientist. I study the lights. The patterns, the atmospheric and celestial conditions, the solar wind, the sounds that the electromagnetism of the aurora produces, that sort of thing."

Boots and Eider looked blankly at each other.

"They must not have scientists here, Shaun," Ávgos said.

Lyylia was grateful when they finally stopped to make camp. Boots unharnessed the dog and unrolled the fur blankets, and Eider pulled out his bow and disappeared deeper into the woods. Shaun began unpacking his computer. Lyylia had been camping a few times as a child and had enjoyed it—but that was in the warm bright nights of a southern Finland summer, in a tent with pillows and sleeping bags, her sister Teija with her and her parents in a tent right beside theirs. This was totally different. There wasn't even a tent.

Dinner was a freshly-cooked dead something, and Boots passed around a bowl of berries that he and Ávgos had collected while gathering firewood. The plump little yellow berries looked and tasted exactly like Finnish cloudberries, the tart relative of the raspberry.

After eating, Lyylia went a short distance away to relieve herself, which was an unpleasant and chilly task. When she came back, Shaun had his laptop open and the screen was lit. Impressive that it still worked.

"It looks like only one of the VLF receivers is dead—I might be able to bring it back to life with some tinkering," Shaun was saying.

"The battery can't have much of a charge left, though," said Ávgos.

"Not at the moment, no. I modified some solar panels to absorb electromagnetic energy from the aurora. Now that I know that the equipment works, I can set out the batteries and the charging panels every night to gather energy from the aurora."

"That's amazing," Ávgos said with an appreciative nod.

Boots and Eider peered at the computer with interest.

"Fascinating," said Eider. "I would like to know more about this Kalevala magic."

"I'd be happy to tell you about it," Shaun said. "But this battery is almost dead—I need to shut the computer down and recharge it and my back-up battery. It should be charged and ready to go by tomorrow night."

"And now we should sleep," said Boots. "If we rise early and travel quickly, we should reach Shaman Pike's village by tomorrow night."

Everyone got settled in the furs. *This has got to be a bad dream,* Lyylia thought wearily, though by now she knew that whatever this place was, it was all very real. Her training told her to stay awake and alert, but the throbbing in her head and her aching muscles were telling her otherwise. Keeping her boots, hat, and gloves on, she pulled the edge of the blanket over her head, and fell asleep thinking of her sister and home.

Shaun looked up through the canopy of trees at the blue-white miniature sun directly overhead. All around them, the woods were alive with birds chirping and flitting through the branches. A weasel, its fur white for the winter, poked its head out of the snow, and then disappeared again. Fresh tracks of a larger animal, possibly a lynx or a bobcat, wound between trees and bushes. As bizarre as this situation was, he felt comforted by the familiarity of walking through a snowy woodland, surrounded by the sound of snow crunching and the sharp fresh scent of evergreens. If not for the sky, this easily could have been a forest in Finland, Norway, or Alaska.

"How about some music for the journey?" Boots said. He pulled a small wooden flute out of his coat pocket. "This is a tune that my father always played, when we traveled to other villages for trade." He began to pipe an upbeat little melody.

Ávgos smiled. "That's a pretty tune."

"Boots plays so well," Eider remarked. "I wish I knew

how to play an instrument."

Shaun looked back at Lyylia as they walked. She'd been very quiet all morning, but she seemed to be keeping pace with the group more energetically than she had yesterday. Shaun slowed so that he was walking next to her.

"You're looking like you're feeling better today," he said.

She nodded. "Better, yes. I am sore, and very cold."

"I know," Shaun said sympathetically. "None of us was dressed for camping outdoors in the snow."

Suddenly the dog halted in his tracks, and Lyylia nearly stumbled over the travois he was dragging. Shaun instinctively grabbed at Lyylia's arm to steady her. The dog gave a low growl.

The others stopped walking. "What is it, Wolf's Bane?" asked Boots, lowering his flute. The dog whined and growled low in his throat.

"That thicket over there," Eider said quietly. He reached over his shoulder for the bow slung across his pack.

"What is it?" whispered Shaun. "Is it more of those hiisi things?"

"I don't think so. Wolf's Bane doesn't know this smell," Boots whispered back. He began untying the dog's harness to release him from the travois. "Slowly, boy," he murmured to the dog. "You don't want to spook it."

Lyylia reached inside her coat and pulled out her handgun. Eider had an arrow on the bow string. As Lyylia started towards the thicket, Boots put out a hand and grabbed her coat.

"No, you stay back here—we will protect you."

"I have a weapon," she said quietly.

"Lyylia—" began Shaun in a whisper.

Lyylia turned her back on them and kept going towards the thicket, gun at the ready. Eider and the dog approached the thicket, and Boots pulled out a knife.

"Okay, I'm suddenly wishing I had a weapon," Shaun murmured. He glanced around, looking for a stick or a rock, but there seemed to be nothing convenient within reach.

"Me too," Ávgos murmured back.

At a gesture from Boots, Wolf's Bane lunged at the thicket with a bark to scare out whatever was hiding. With a rustle of branches and a shower of snow, a brown and gray creature not much bigger than the dog lurched out into visibility. It was a reindeer.

Lyylia lowered her gun.

Ávgos started towards the animal.

"Ávgos, what are you doing?" Boots sounded aghast.

"It's a reindeer," Lyylia said, sliding her gun back inside her coat.

"They're not dangerous, unless you spook them first," Ávgos said. "This one is clearly accustomed to dogs and people."

Boots and Eider exchanged dumbfounded looks, their weapons still poised at the ready. "You know this creature?" said Boots.

"Of course," said Ávgos. "You've never seen a reindeer before?"

Eider started trembling, and he dropped his bow in the snow. "Boots, it's…it's one of the Gentle Beasts! We've found one! They *have* come back to Pohjola!"

Ávgos stroked the animal's neck and murmured to it, while Boots and Eider stared at him with shock and awe.

"Oh my God…" Ávgos said.

"*Mitä?*" asked Lyylia.

Ávgos began talking excitedly in Finnish, and Lyylia came up beside him and looked down at the reindeer.

"What's going on?" Shaun asked. "Boots, what are

they saying?"

"He says this Gentle Beast belongs to him…?" said Boots, shaking his head in confusion.

"This reindeer has my earmark. It's from my herd," Ávgos said, switching back to English.

Shaun went over to them. The animal blew a cloud of steamy breath from its nostrils as Shaun approached, but otherwise seemed unbothered. The reindeer's small antlers barely reached Shaun's chest. Ávgos cupped his hand behind the reindeer's left ear and showed Shaun the little nicks cut into the edge of the ear.

Lyylia began speaking to the Menninkäinen in Finnish.

"What's she saying?" Shaun said to Ávgos.

"She's asking if more reindeer came through the gateway. Remember they said that creatures of myth had come through?"

Shaun nodded, remembering.

"I don't know," Boots was saying to Lyylia. "There have been rumors of strange creatures. And the Queen commanded that if any Gentle Beasts were found, they should be brought to her for protection." He looked at the reindeer. "But we didn't know whether to believe the rumors of the Gentle Beasts' return or not. And until this moment, I didn't know what one looked like." Boots gave a bow to the reindeer. "Welcome to Pohjola, great lord."

"If one of my reindeer is here, then the rest must be, as well," Ávgos said.

"If the hiisi stole the reindeer, they would take them to their own land," Lyylia said. "Ice-Dark is the name?"

"That's right," said Boots.

"Then unfortunately, the Gentle Beasts are probably lost forever," Boots said. He sighed, and looked at the reindeer. "I am sorry, my lord."

"I can't accept that," Ávgos said, looking at Lyylia. "At least, not until I know for sure what happened."

Lyylia looked back at the Menninkäinen. "That is why we were outside at Lake Inari—the lake at our world. We were looking for Ávgos' missing reindeer."

"We must hurry to bring this Gentle Beast to the Queen," Eider said.

"So let's go to the Queen and not the village," said Lyylia.

"We don't have enough supplies to go that far," Boots said. "And we need a shaman with a moon mirror to get word to the Queen about this."

"And we must send back-up to help Tip and Claw at the lake," Eider added.

"What's a moon mirror?" asked Shaun.

"It's what shamans use to talk to the Queen and to one another over a long distance," Boots explained.

"Really?" Shaun said. That sounded like the closest thing to technology or science they'd encountered so far. "How does it work? I'd like to see it when we get to the village."

"Perhaps Shaman Pike can show it to you," said Boots. "Come, we should get moving so that we can reach our village tonight before everyone is asleep."

Boots harnessed Wolf's Bane up again. Ávgos made a clicking noise to the reindeer, and it followed him as he started walking.

Eider kept staring with an awe-struck expression at Ávgos and the reindeer as they walked. "A Gentle Beast, a lord of the woods!" he murmured in a reverent whisper to Boots. "The first shamans in the ancient times sat at the feet of the king of the woods and learned wisdom and magic from him! And this lord of the woods comes from another world—can you imagine the lore and wisdom that he carries in his heart?"

Shaun hadn't been expecting reindeer to be the great creatures of legend that Boots had mentioned before. He glanced over at Lyylia; her forehead was furrowed under her tangle of curly blond hair.

"So what are you thinking about, Lyylia?" Shaun said quietly.

She shook her head. "I'm thinking of reindeer and Inari Lake and hiisi. So many clues now, and some questions answered—but now so many new questions."

"Well, maybe this Queen of theirs can actually help us, or can answer some questions better than they can," he said.

"I hope," she said, sounding doubtful. "But they worship animals, reindeer—the Queen, if she is real, may not be any smarter than animals."

"You think their Queen isn't real?"

Lyylia slowed in her walking so the Menninkäinen wouldn't overhear. "They worship the moon."

"What?" said Shaun. "How do you know that?"

"That's what they are saying," she insisted. "You don't hear them say 'Queen Moon'?"

He shook his head. "I thought her name was Kuu."

Lyylia made a face. "*Kuu* means moon!" she hissed. "It's Finnish legend again."

"Kuu was the moon god in *The Kalevala*," put in Ávgos. He'd dropped behind the Menninkäinen to join them. "Male, not female, if I recall. And this place—Pohjola—was the northern land of evil, where the witch lived."

Shaun looked at him, and then back at Lyylia. "So are you saying that *this* place is actually the evil land, not the Ice-Dark place? Can we trust these Menninkäinen?"

"I don't trust," Lyylia said.

"I'm not saying this place is evil," said Ávgos. "Or that

their Queen is anything like the witch…what was her name…"

"Louhi," Lyylia supplied.

"Right," Ávgos said. "Anyway, I still don't know what to think, or if we can really trust these people or believe everything they say. But I don't know what other choice we have right now."

After a while they came to a quaint collection of huts and cottages. It looked like a picture out of a historic Lapland book—the little wooden houses shaded by trees, the snowy trail following the lay of the land, dogs and small shaggy horses in rough wooden pens. One pen held a handful of spotted sheep, and a row of chickens perched on a log in another pen, but there were no reindeer to be seen.

Boots called out to a man outside a hut chopping wood. In mere moments, a crowd of Menninkäinen gathered at the edge of the village, and more were coming out of their huts.

"Shaman Pike!" called Boots. "We have come with visitors from Kalevala!"

"So the gateway is real!" An elderly Menninkäinen, wearing a long brown fur robe covered in beaded tassels, came towards them through the crowd, leaning on a walking stick. "Welcome, guests from Kalevala! The Queen will be most pleased to hear of your arrival. And especially you, honored lord." He bowed at the reindeer. "You are welcome to stay at my house for the night."

"Uh, I'd rather he not be separated from me," began Ávgos.

"Oh, you are welcome to stay with us, as well," said Pike. "My daughter will show you to our house." A little woman stepped forward and bowed.

"We should have room for Shaun at my home, Shaman," said Boots. "Eider, is there room at your home for Lyylia?"

"My parents and my sister would be honored to host a

visitor for the night, especially one from another world," said Eider, grinning up at Lyylia.

Shaun exchanged looks with Lyylia and Ávgos. As friendly and kind as the Menninkäinen were, the prospect of being separated didn't seem like a safe idea. Lyylia began talking in Finnish.

"I promise my family will take excellent care of this man and the Gentle Beast," Shaman Pike said cheerfully to Lyylia. "Come, it's late and I'm sure all of you are tired from traveling."

A little boy pushed his way through the crowd and threw his arms around Boots. "This is my boy, Track," said Boots, ruffling the boy's disheveled brown hair. "Track, we're going to host a visitor from another world for the night!" Track just gaped at Shaun.

Shaman Pike headed off through the crowd, waving for Ávgos to follow. Many Menninkäinen surged behind them, forcing Ávgos and the reindeer behind Pike. Eider grabbed Lyylia's hand and led her in a different direction.

Before Shaun could protest, Boots, Track, and the rest of the crowd herded him down the path behind Eider and Lyylia. Glancing back over his shoulder, he saw Ávgos being escorted into the shaman's hut. That little cottage was distinguished from the others around it by a large upright stone planted near the front door. Boots stopped at another hut, and Eider led Lyylia several houses further down the path. Shaun scanned the path between the little houses, memorizing the route.

Boots opened the door of his hut. "Silver, my love! I've returned from the Dark Water Lake, and I bring a guest!"

Shaun stayed just outside the door, craning his neck to watch Lyylia until she disappeared into Eider's hut. Then he turned to look into Boots' house.

Across the room, a small plump woman was standing on

a wooden stool, reaching for something on a high shelf. She turned, nearly tumbling off her perch. She wore a rumpled blue dress and brown apron, and had her honey-blond hair piled up on her head in a disheveled bun. "Boots! Welcome home, my love!" She jumped down off the stool and hurried over to them. "So that's where Track dashed off to."

"Giant strangers, mother!" said Track, hopping up and down on his toes.

Boots gave Silver a quick kiss. "I'm going to unharness Wolf's Bane."

Silver turned to look up at Shaun. "Welcome, come in out of the cold! What a story Boots will have to tell! So you're from another world, are you? I always wondered if Kalevala was real! There's some stew still warming on the fire—I'll fix you a bowl. Toilet shed is out by the horse paddock. There's a bath house up the road a bit, but I'm sure you'd rather eat first. Here, sit and I'll get you that stew. Do you want to leave your pack by the door?"

"Um, no, I'll think I'll hold on to it, thanks," said Shaun, letting himself be dragged inside by her stream of chatter. He politely wiped his feet on the woven straw mat in the doorway. Taking the scanner pack off his back, he put it at his feet as he sat down at the wooden table in the middle of the room. Track plunked himself down on the bench beside Shaun.

The cottage appeared to consist of just two rooms. This room was a combination of living room and kitchen. The table sat near the fireplace, and wooden shelves ran along one wall. Utensils of wood and bone, and bowls of eggs and berries were stacked on the shelves; various dried plants hung from the ceiling. Across the room were two cushioned stools, an animal-skin rug, and what looked like a game or wooden toys scattered on the rug. The floor was smooth wood, and four small windows illuminated the room. The dim glow of a lantern was all he could see through the partially-open door across the room.

"Here you go, nice and warm." Silver set a bowl of stew and a wooden spoon in front of him. "And we're freshly stocked with golden drop berry mead, milk, and long-leaf. What will you have to drink?"

Since he hadn't seen any cows or goats—or reindeer, besides Ávgos'—he could only assume the milk came from a horse or perhaps sheep. The mead was possibly alcoholic, which sounded tempting, but was probably not wise. "I'll try the long-leaf," he said finally.

"Here you go." Silver set down a mug.

"May I have some milk, mother?" said Track.

"All right," said Silver, going back over the shelves. "But no more stew—you've already had your dinner."

She came back over with a mug for Track. "So what's your name?" she asked Shaun.

"My name is Shaun," he said, giving her a polite smile. "And my friends are Lyylia and Ávgos." He hoped they were receiving as warm a welcome.

"Shaun. Well, please do make yourself at home. There's more stew if you're still hungry."

The stew had a strong, gamey flavor, but had more vegetables and seasonings than the stew at their campsite had, and was quite good. Shaun ate quickly, realizing how long it had been since they'd stopped for lunch. The long-leaf tasted surprisingly like unsweetened black tea. He smiled at Silver to show his appreciation.

"What's Kalevala?" asked the little boy, sipping at his milk.

"Oh, Track, you've heard the songs," said Silver. "It's a land of magic at the bottom of the Dark Water Lake."

Track's brown eyes widened. "You live at the bottom of the lake?"

"We don't live at the bottom of the lake," said Shaun, smiling at the little boy. He looked about seven or eight, and Shaun could now see the resemblance with Boots, in the boy's round face. "It's more like…I'm not really sure, actually. We're still trying to figure that out. Something like an inter-dimensional portal, I guess. Maybe it's a wormhole."

Track stared at him.

"It's another world," Shaun then said. "It looks a lot like this one."

"Off to bed, Track, as soon as you've finished your milk," said Silver, ruffling his hair. "And lay out some blankets for our guest, please." Track obediently hopped up and raced through the door into the other room.

"Cute kid," said Shaun with a smile.

"Thank you," Silver beamed. "He is a joy, and so much like his father Boots. Well, when you're finished eating, make yourself comfortable in there. I'm sure you're exhausted from traveling all the way from the Dark Water Lake."

"Yes, I am," Shaun said. "Um, where did you say the outhouse was?"

"The little shed beside the horse paddock. Track stoked the coals earlier, so it should still be warm in there." She gathered up his empty bowl and mug. "More?"

He shook his head and got up from the table. He took his scanner pack to the bedroom before leaving. The small room was dim, lit only by a lantern hanging from a peg on the wall—a heavy curtain covered the one small window. The entire floor was covered with furs.

"Your blankets are over there," said Track, pointing at the far corner. "Do Kalevalans snore?"

Shaun laughed as he put his backpack in the corner. "No, I don't snore."

He'd been hoping for a regular bed tonight. And sharing

a small room with Boots' wife and child felt a little awkward. But at least it was warm and dry.

Outside, Boots was in the paddock, tending to the dog and the horse. The toilet shed was warm, as Silver had promised, and surprisingly clean and odor-free. Shaun was accustomed to the rough camping experience and having to use whatever might be on hand, since most of his science expeditions took him to places far from civilization. Having an actual toilet of sorts was a nice luxury.

Walking back to the house, Shaun looked up to see wisps of red, green, and yellow flickering down through the thick canopy of trees—another impressive aurora display. With all the excitement of finding the reindeer and arriving at the village, he hadn't noticed when they might have begun. Did the aurora start at the same time every night? The probability of that happening on Earth was practically nil, but Boots had implied that the Dancing Lights were as regular as sunset and sunrise.

He was tempted to set up his scanner, but he wanted a better view of the sky than this deep in the forest. And he was exhausted and looking forward to sleeping indoors. Shaun looked down the village path towards the hut where Eider had taken Lyylia, then back up the hill to the shaman's hut with the stone out front. He could see the reindeer in the paddock with the horse. With a final glance up at the bright blue-white light from the star overhead and the colors of the Dancing Lights, he went back inside.

The next morning, Ávgos stood at the back of the village hall, keeping a nervous eye on his reindeer. The animal was behaving surprisingly well, considering that he was being treated more like a pet right now than an outdoor herd animal. Ávgos had borrowed some rope from Shaman Pike to use as a makeshift halter and lead-line.

The village hall was the largest building in the village. The space was filled with long tables and benches, with a circular stone hearth in the center where a warm fire blazed. At the far end was a raised wooden platform. Menninkäinen, both adults and children, filled the benches, and the building echoed with the sounds of chattering conversation. Lyylia and Shaun sat at the table nearest to Ávgos, with Boots and Eider and their families. Ávgos estimated that there were well over a hundred people in the hall.

A young woman sitting nearby stared unabashedly at Ávgos and the reindeer. She held a baby, who was placidly chewing on one of the tie strings of her dress. The baby had dark brown hair and wide blue eyes, and reminded Ávgos of how his little Piijá had looked when she was an infant. He looked away; he didn't want to think about how terrified Sirkka must be feeling right now.

Shaman Pike made his way through the room to the raised platform; his long fur cloak, decorated with tassels of beads and bone, brushed the floor as he walked. His daughter came behind him carrying a small frame drum. She began to strike the drum with her hand in slow even beats as Pike approached the platform. The crowd quieted.

"As everyone already knows, we have guests in the village," Pike began. "Boots and Eider have returned from the Dark Water Lake, and they brought with them visitors from Kalevala. Queen Kuu was correct, as she always is—there is a gateway in the Dark Water Lake that leads to the world of Kalevala, just as the old songs tell us. And the rumors of the Gentle Beasts' return are true as well." He waved to the back of the room at Ávgos and the reindeer. Everyone turned to look at him, and an excited murmur rose.

"This is Lord Oarrbis, and his protector, Ávgos. The legends say that in ancient times, these lords of the wood walked all across Pohjola, and they called the first Menninkäinen shamans 'apprentice', and they called Queen Kuu 'friend.'"

Oarrbis? That was a Sami word. How in the world would Pike know such a word?

"The Kalevalans and their Gentle Beast will be going to see the Queen," Pike continued. "It is a four-day journey to the Mountains of the Moon, if the weather is good. They need supplies for the journey, and companions to show them the way and protect them. As we know, there are hiisi still at large in our land. And we must also send more men to watch at the shore of the lake and defend our borders."

At least a dozen men jumped up and volunteered.

"Fir and Flint will go as guides for our guests," Pike announced over the rising buzz of conversation, and thumped his walking stick for emphasis. "And the rest of you will do our village and all of Pohjola a great service by guarding the Dark Water Lake against any more hiisi." The group of little men all nodded solemnly.

"Eider and Boots—are you willing to take this journey to the Mountains of the Moon and continue to protect our visitors on their way to see the Queen?"

"Absolutely!" Boots shouted. Eider stood up from his seat and bowed deeply at Pike.

"Excellent! It will be a challenging journey with winter just beginning, so all of our brave men will need food and weapons and clothing. Let everything that can be spared be brought to the hall at once. They leave before the day is yet half done."

"Excuse me, Shaman Pike!" Lyylia called, standing up from her seat. Everyone turned to look at her.

"This Gentle Beast is from our world—from Kalevala. And we believe that there are many more of them, kidnapped by the hiisi and brought here. We need to find them."

"Queen Kuu can help you," said Pike. "She has asked for any Gentle Beasts found to be brought to her castle."

"But the men who just volunteered to take us to see the Queen could help us look for the Gentle Beasts instead."

"The Queen can see farther across the land than we could search ourselves," said Pike, cocking his head at Lyylia with a puzzled expression on his face. "But we will ask the Gentle Beast what he believes should be done. My lord Oarrbis! Shall I send my men to search the forests for your kinfolk, or send them with you to meet Queen Kuu?"

The reindeer pricked up his ears as Pike spoke, and then gave a snort and shook his head. Ávgos stared at him, then looked back at Pike.

"Very well, my lord. You shall go to the Queen! For Dream and Queen Kuu!" Pike's daughter beat on the drum again, and that appeared to be the end of the meeting.

Lyylia frowned, and looked over at Ávgos. He just shook his head, and put his hand on the reindeer's back.

The room began to empty, and many Menninkäinen crowded around Ávgos and the others, all talking at once. The reindeer snorted as the crowd pushed closer. Ávgos made soothing sounds, and eyed the door. The animal had been calm during the meeting, but moving crowds was another matter.

"Please excuse us," Lyylia interrupted the crowd, holding up a hand. "The Gentle Beast must rest before the journey."

The crowd obligingly parted and let them exit the hall. Ávgos tossed Lyylia a grateful look.

"What did you just say to them?" Shaun asked when they were outside.

"I said that the reindeer must rest," Lyylia said in English.

"And what did Shaman Pike call the reindeer?" Shaun continued. "Lord something?"

"*Oarrbis*," Ávgos said. "It means 'orphan' in Sami."

"How does he know a Sami word?" Lyylia asked.

"I don't know. And I don't see how Shaman Pike believes that the reindeer answered his question." The Menninkäinen seemed to have an unusual rapport with animals, but there was no way that his reindeer could actually have been *talking* to the man.

While some Menninkäinen were still leaving the village hall, others came bustling back in, bearing armloads of furs, clothing, and baskets of assorted items. A short distance away, two men were hitching one of the small, shaggy horses to a sled. Everyone who walked past the three humans and the reindeer either paused to bow or simply gawk.

The reindeer was nosing around at the edge of the path, so Ávgos led him around the side of the building where the shrubbery was thicker. The reindeer pushed into the brush and began eating, causing a shower of snow from the branches. Lyylia walked around the reindeer and deeper into the brush, pushing brambles aside as she peered at the ground.

"There you are!" Boots came up to them, a little boy beside him. "Come back into the village hall. There's winter clothing—we must see if any of it fits you. You're poorly dressed for a long journey in those Kalevala clothes. And food is being prepared for us to eat before we depart. My son Track will get you settled—I need to help load the sled."

The little boy grinned up at them.

"We'll be along in a moment," Ávgos said, looking down at him. "The Gentle Beast needs to eat."

"All right," said Track. "I'll be in the hall, waiting for you." He trotted off.

"What are you looking for, Lyylia?" Shaun said as Lyylia came back out of the brush, dusting snow off her sleeves.

"Graves," she said quietly. "There is a graveyard just there. One is new—a new mound of rocks, little of snow."

"So?" Shaun said.

Lyylia looked at him and said nothing, a stern expression on her face.

"It's a primitive culture—people probably die all the time from farming accidents and the common cold," Shaun said.

"I know," said Lyylia, glancing back at bushes that hid the graveyard.

Ávgos looked at Shaun; the other man gave a shrug and didn't press Lyylia further. The Menninkäinen probably did have deaths frequently—like any people anywhere, really—and Ávgos did not want to let himself feel disturbed about it. Lyylia was trained to pay attention to death, he reminded himself.

"So," Shaun said quietly after a moment, looking at Ávgos. "Four days, maybe five."

"Yes," said Ávgos.

Lyylia caught Shaun's look, and gave a solemn nod.

Four days until they arrived at the Mountains of the Moon and the home of the Queen. Four days until they learned if they could ever go home again. Four days till they could find out whether Kuu was a real person who could help them, or if they were about to meet an untimely end as some sort of pagan sacrifice to the moon.

Ávgos thought of Sirkka, Piijá, his cousin Mađen, his

mother... He didn't want Piijá and the unborn baby growing up without a father. He took a deep breath to ease the tightness in his chest. If he never made it back home, Sirkka and the rest of his family would never know what happened to him.

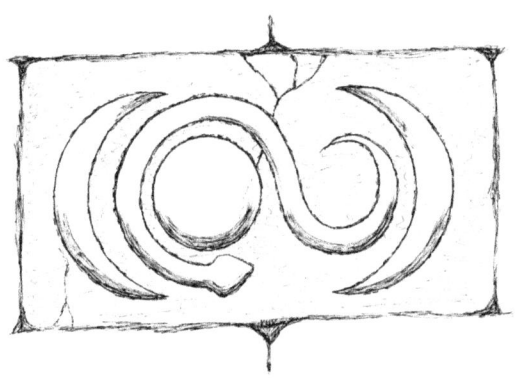

CHAPTER 3: THE MOUNTAINS OF THE MOON

It had been three days since they left Shaman Pike's village, and Lyylia decided that she absolutely hated snow. Snow was, of course, a constant thing during a Finnish winter, but plowed roads, heated homes, and indoor plumbing made it quite bearable. She had never felt so perpetually cold—or so perpetually exhausted—in her life. Twelve-plus-hour days of hiking through wilderness and snow were more rigorous than her police training had been. She wished the Menninkäinen had coffee.

At least they had tents now. And snowshoes for deep snow, and a sled pulled by a pony. Or a small horse; Lyylia didn't know enough about equines to know the difference. She'd seen Icelandic and Norwegian fjord horses when visiting her grandparents as a child—short, stocky animals not much bigger than a reindeer. The Menninkäinen's animals must have been of similar stock. Which made no sense. If they were on some other planet, why did so much seem familiar?

With the little horse pulling their supplies, that left the dog free to help protect them, which was a mild comfort. They'd encountered bear tracks more than a few times, which left Lyylia feeling tense, but the Menninkäinen seemed unconcerned. One night they'd been awakened by wolves howling close by. Thankfully they encountered no evidence of hiisi.

The endless hours of walking left plenty of time for Lyylia to think. She worked hard to never let self-doubt cloud her ability to move forward with a decision and whatever consequences it might bring. Second-guessing decisions could be deadly in police work. But even so, there was often the "should have" or "what if" that came afterwards.

Maybe they should have tried to capture a hiisi for information—if the creatures could even talk. What if they'd stayed at the lake and taken the boat out, searching for this gateway? Would it have been smarter to stay in Pike's village and begin a search for the reindeer instead of traveling further away from the lake to meet this mysterious Queen? Even a career of dealing with the unpredictable hadn't prepared her for this.

"We need a song for our journey on this fine day," Boots announced.

This 'fine day' was certainly better than the snowstorm yesterday. Thankfully they'd come to a village before the snow and wind had gotten too bad. Lyylia was still surprised by the extreme friendliness that seemed to be a Menninkäinen cultural trait; and she wasn't at all used to being invited to spend the night in a stranger's house, no questions asked. She'd been pleasantly surprised by the communal sauna in every village, though.

Today it was still snowing lightly, and the clouds shrouded the light of the perpetual blue star-sun, making it dim like twilight under the trees.

"Do you have traveling songs in Kalevala?" asked Fir.

"I've always liked Willie Nelson's 'On the Road Again,'"

Shaun said.

Ávgos chuckled and Lyylia smiled in spite of herself.

Boots pulled his little wooden flute out of his pocket. "I don't know that one. How about 'The Traveling Companions' Song'?"

He piped a tune on the flute, and Eider, Fir, and Flint began to sing.

'The road is long but the sky is bright
My companions are with me all through the night
Home is calling, I'm traveling home.
Snow is soft, the fire burns warm
My companions are with me all through the storm
Home is calling, I'm traveling home.
Wolves, stay away, Pohjantähti shine down
My companions stay with me till we reach town
Home is calling, I'm traveling home.
Down to the river, across the wild fells
My companions are singing of woodlands and dells
Home is calling, I'm traveling home.
Safe from the wolf, the fox I call friend
My companions are with me till the road reaches end
Home is calling, I'm traveling home."

Shaun clapped enthusiastically when they finished the song, his applause muffled by thick fur mittens. All three of them had taken fur mittens and thick socks from the donations at Pike's village. Lyylia had also accepted a hat and a pair of fur-lined boots. She wished that some of the animal-skin breeches or woven leggings had fit her.

"Do you have songs like that in Kalevala?" Eider asked.

"You mean besides Willie Nelson?" Shaun said. "Yeah, probably. But don't ask me to sing any."

"I can sing Sami *yoik*," said Ávgos. "But maybe later."

"I don't sing," said Lyylia, before anyone could ask her.

They walked for a while in silence. "Do you have a family in Kalevala?" Boots asked Ávgos, looking up at him.

"I do. I have a three-year-old daughter, and my wife is expecting another baby. I miss them."

Lyylia heard the strain in his voice as he spoke. She missed her mother, her sister, and her partner Jassu. She could only imagine the pain and panic that Ávgos must be feeling, wondering how he could ever get back to his spouse and children.

"I'm sorry, Ávgos," Boots said sympathetically. "That must be very hard for you. At least I know I can return to my wife and son in a few days."

"Do you have children?" asked Eider, looking at Lyylia and Shaun.

Lyylia shook her head. "No. But I miss my mother and my sister."

"Nope," said Shaun. "No kids, I don't talk to my parents much, and the guys on my science team are probably glad I'm not around because they'll get to take full credit for all the work. So I'm free as a bird."

Lyylia looked at him. His tone was light and he spoke with a joking smile, but it sounded forced.

He caught her looking at him and flashed her a grin. She looked away. "What's your sister like, Lyylia?" he asked. "Is she a police officer, too?"

"Teija works in Helsinki, works on programs for computers," she said, forcing herself to look at him again. "I haven't seen her since at Easter time."

"So you're not from Helsinki?"

"Helsinki is my home. But I live and work in Kokkola."

Shaun looked over at Ávgos. "I don't suppose you have

a map of Finland in your pocket."

Ávgos chuckled quietly. "Helsinki is on the southern coast, and Kokkola is on the western coast near Sweden. They're not near each other."

Lyylia tuned them out. Teija and her mother would be worried sick about her by this point—more than they usually were. She knew they worried about her every day, just like they'd all worried about her father every day when he went out on the bay in the rescue boat. Lyylia knew that he did what he loved, braving the icy bay to help people. That fire in him had died long before the cancer took over, when that injury kept him from going back out on the boat.

Wolf's Bane gave a sudden bark, bringing Lyylia's attention back. Ávgos' reindeer snorted and pricked up his ears.

"What is it, boy?" Boots said. Eider pulled his bow off his back, and Flint lifted his spear. Lyylia yanked off her fur mittens and unzipped her coat, ready to reach for her gun.

"It's just some other travelers," said Fir, peering into the snowy gloom ahead.

Two Menninkäinen were on the path some distance in front of them. This was only the second time they'd encountered other travelers. Apparently most people here had the sense to stay at home in weather like this.

"Hello there, friends!" Boots called with a wave. "Are you from these parts? Is there a village nearby?"

The two little men continued on down the trail, not acknowledging Boots at all. It was hard to tell at this distance in the gloom, but it looked like neither one wore a coat or hat.

"Fellow travelers! Where are you journeying to today?" Boots called again.

In response the two Menninkäinen quickened their pace and were soon lost in the dimness and filtering snow. Wolf's

Bane gave a quiet growl.

"Strange indeed," said Boots, giving the dog's head a rub.

"Perhaps there is a village nearby and they were returning home from a hunt," said Fir.

"I didn't see them carrying any kill," said Eider. "And they were poorly dressed for this weather. Perhaps they're from the Southern Fens."

"It's warmer in the south?" Lyylia asked.

"A little," said Flint. "The south is very warm in the summer, but they have storms and snow in the winter, just like the rest of the land."

"Well, I hope the travelers fare well," Boots said, "wherever they've come from and wherever they're going."

"Do Menninkäinen from the south come to here often?" Lyylia asked.

"Mostly in the summer," Flint answered. "Summer is an easier time for traveling. I've traveled to the south of Pohjola many times to trade berries and bear pelts for the grain and flax that grows in the Southern Fens."

"This journey is the farthest that I have ever traveled," Eider said. "Besides traveling to the Dancing Ground Island for the midsummer celebration. First the Dark Water Lake, and now the Mountains of the Moon. I will have so many tales to tell my sister and my parents when we return!"

Shaun laughed. "Yeah, who knew we'd be having such a grand adventure!"

"Grand adventure?" Lyylia repeated, staring at Shaun. "This is a game to you?"

He frowned. "Of course not. I'm just excited for Eider that he'll get to see the Mountains of the Moon. And I'm looking forward to it, too."

Lyylia just shook her head, too tired to come up with an

appropriate retort.

After a brief stop for a lunch of dried meat, bread, and dried berries, Lyylia realized that she was now lagging at the back of the group as they walked. And this time she couldn't even blame it on an injury, since the knot on her head had pretty much healed. Ávgos was also walking at the back of the group, leading the reindeer.

"You look as tired as I feel," he remarked.

She gave him a wry smile. "Thanks. Yes, I'm exhausted, and absolutely freezing."

"Like any Sami, I can handle winter weather," said Ávgos, "But I think I got spoiled by living in Turku. I love the north, but I really do miss city life."

"So do I," said Lyylia. "All of this is like nothing I've experienced. Well, I guess it's like nothing any of us has experienced—but I meant the outdoor living part."

Ávgos chuckled.

They trudged in silence for a few minutes. Lyylia stared at the horse and the sled in front of her, and the snow piling up on the animal's shaggy rump. She'd hoped that they would have encountered more reindeer by now. Their theory was that a handful of reindeer had escaped from their hiisi captors and fled to the Pohjola side of the lake instead of being driven into Ice-Dark. Ávgos was confident that any reindeer would have stayed together, since they were herd animals. But the one reindeer they'd found, and the stories—albeit all third-party—that they'd been told by Menninkäinen in villages, indicated that the reindeer found so far had all been solitary.

Ávgos spoke, intruding on her thoughts. "I guess by now you've realized that my cousin Maden had nothing to do with the reindeer disappearing. I know he was your prime suspect."

"Your cousin is no longer a suspect," she said with a dry

smile. "So why did he run to Rovaniemi, in that case?" She turned her head to look him in the face. "That's where he went right after the animals disappeared, isn't it?"

Ávgos sighed. "I told him not to go. I told him it would just complicate things and make him look suspicious, but he didn't listen to me. As usual."

Lyylia waited for him to continue.

"When Sirkka and I were living in Turku, Maðen decided to escape the herder life in his own way and got involved with a gang based in Rovaniemi—they deal in illegal drugs and weapons. When my father fell ill, and Sirkka and I had to leave Turku and move back to the north, we asked Maðen to come back home to help. I think he really wanted to change his life, and really wanted to prove himself to the family, prove that he was an honorable Sami."

"And he did?" Lyylia asked.

"After he came back home, Maðen told us that during a run-in with the police, one of the gang members had been shot and killed. I think Maðen was already having second thoughts about joining the gang, and so when that happened, and then we invited him back home, he wasn't too proud to leave that life behind."

"So he's stayed in Inari ever since?"

Ávgos nodded. "He's a good herdsman. He's helped me tremendously. Managing the family herd is not a responsibility I initially wanted, so I've really appreciated his efforts to clean up his past and become part of the family again. Some people in the village are still wary of him, but our family has welcomed him back."

"So why this sudden trip back to his old associates in Rovaniemi?" Lyylia asked.

"He thought that the gang were the ones who stole the animals from our herd. He was convinced that it was retaliation against him for leaving their organization. And since the animals disappeared right after the separation of the herds, and it was only *my* animals that were taken..." Ávgos looked at Lyylia as they walked. "I agreed with him at the time. It makes sense, right? And I certainly had no other theories."

Lyylia nodded. "Logical."

"Unfortunately, instead of contacting the authorities, Maðen decided to go to Rovaniemi and confront the gang himself." Ávgos sighed deeply again. "I hope he's all right. Maðen didn't want to point those men out as suspects to the authorities, because it would mean revealing the criminal dealings that he'd had with them in the past. And I stupidly, stupidly, decided to help keep his secret by not telling you or your partner about any of it. I'm sorry, Lyylia."

"Well, it would've led us in the wrong direction, as we now know," she said gently. "But if we ever manage to get back home, Ávgos, promise me that you and Maðen will give me all the names that you know. If he has inside information, we can shut the whole operation down." She looked Ávgos directly in the eyes. "I will do everything in my power to ensure that no charges are pressed against Maðen for his involvement, and that nothing is put on his record."

Ávgos nodded solemnly. "I promise."

So that filled in the spots of missing information about Maðen's involvement—or lack thereof—in this reindeer case. Unfortunately, Lyylia had no way of letting Jassu know that. She sighed and stared ahead into the unending forest and lightly swirling snow.

The light snow tapered off during the rest of the day, for which Lyylia was grateful. When they stopped to make camp for the night, the sky was clear. The blue star, the moon, and the rest of the stars were washed out by a pinkish-purple aurora glow that covered the sky. In this land of an unchanging sky she found it disconcerting that the time of greater illumination would be night.

They set up the tents under the trees at the base of a hill. The top of the hill was open and bare, and after the tents were up and secured, Shaun shouldered his backpack and took his computer equipment up the hill.

"What is he doing?" Flint asked.

"He uses that device to listen to the Dancing Lights," Lyylia said, hoping that she was explaining it well enough for the Menninkäinen to understand. She didn't really understand how it worked, but he'd talked about it enough that she was catching on to the basic concept.

"Why?"

"He studies the Dancing Lights in our world, so I guess he wants to study them here, too," Ávgos provided. "To see if they're the same."

"I'd like to see this talisman," said Eider. "Do you think he'd mind if we went up there to see it?"

"I'm sure he'd be happy to tell you all about it," Lyylia said. As tired as she was, an odd curiosity tugged at her. Shaun talked about his life as an aurora scientist, but she had yet to see how the aurora scanning actually worked. She stood up. "I'll go with you, Eider."

Flint joined them. Lyylia regretted having taken off her snowshoes, as the snow was deeper here than on the woodland trail; the powdery snow came to the top of her boots and squeaked as she walked. Shaun was a crouched human form silhouetted against the undulating pink sky as they went up the hill.

"We want to see your magic talisman from Kalevala," said Eider as they approached him.

"Step right up!" Shaun said with a grin, gesturing at the laptop that sat on the empty backpack in the snow. Colored lines zig-zagged across the computer screen. Two small black boxes were attached to the laptop, and wires and cables were spread out, propped up on small branches to keep them out of the snow.

"This helps me study the Dancing Lights," Shaun said as the two Menninkäinen stared down at the computer screen. "This black box is the battery—it stores the electro-magnetic energy from the Lights and powers the computer. And this other black box is the audio recorder. It's recording the sounds that are made by the Lights."

"I don't hear anything," said Eider.

"I know, but aurora—Dancing Lights—make sounds that we can't hear most of the time. That's part of what this machine does—it records the sounds the Lights make, and then converts them into a range that we can hear."

Lyylia stood behind the two Menninkäinen, looking over their shoulders at the computer as Shaun talked.

"This line is a measurement of the wave properties in the visual spectrum," he said, pointing at the screen. "This is ultraviolet and microwaves, this line here is radio waves. See, as the colors of the lights change, so do the sounds they make—that's this line right here. You guys want to hear what this display sounds like? The sounds that you can't hear— changed by my machine into sounds that you can hear."

He adjusted one of the cables that was attached to the machine, and hit a few keys. An eerie electronic-sounding wailing came from the laptop speakers. Both Menninkäinen jumped.

"Amazing," said Lyylia. She wasn't quite sure if she'd fully understood everything he'd said—she wasn't very familiar with scientific jargon in Finnish, let alone in English. But she had to admit she was impressed. "I didn't know so much sounds came from the Lights."

"Pretty cool, isn't it?" said Shaun with a grin.

He stood up and stretched his arms above his head. "You guys can look at that," he said to Eider and Flint. "Just don't touch anything."

The little men moved closer to the computer, and obediently kept their hands by their sides.

"Beautiful, isn't it?" Shaun said, stepping up beside Lyylia. "The first time I saw the aurora as a kid, I was totally hooked." He rubbed at the beard stubble on his chin as he looked up at the colored sky. "We don't get to see aurora very often in Pennsylvania, but it happens occasionally, during peaks in solar activity. During the summer I would spend hours outside at night, just staring at the stars, thinking about the sky—especially when I visited my grandparents, who lived out in the country. I wanted to know every star. The sky was like a great big mystery, and I just had to solve it."

Lyylia smiled at his analogy. "So this is your detective work: to hear a thing that makes no sound, and use it for powering computers."

He chuckled. "That's right. That's it exactly."

They stared upwards in silence for several minutes. The rolling pink-purple light filled the sky above them. Spots briefly flashed a deeper purple, and then settled back into the soft magenta glow. Lyylia suddenly realized that Shaun was now staring at her and not at the sky. She looked back at him. "What?"

He smiled. "Nothing. So, since I confessed my deep childhood dreams, what made you decide to become a police officer?"

"My mother's uncle fought in the Winter War. And my father drove search and rescue boat on the bay at Helsinki," she said, surprising herself with how easily she shared her family history with a relative stranger. "I didn't want to be a soldier, but I want to protect and help people." She thought of her mother and her sister Teija. They still lived in Helsinki; she couldn't protect them living so far away in Kokkola, and now she was even farther away. They both had probably been told by now that she was missing in the line of duty. Her insides clenched at the thought of her mother desperate with worry, of Teija in tears, trying to be strong for both of them.

"The Winter War?" Shaun asked, bringing her thoughts back.

"It happened during World War II," Lyylia told him. "Russia invaded Finland. So many men died, but they gave their lives so Finland could be free."

"Wow. It must be cool to have real heroes like that in your family. Nobody in my family ever did anything special." He sounded sad.

Lyylia looked at Shaun. He'd gone back to staring up at the sky. The magenta color of the aurora was slowly deepening into a more robust purple, and some of the brighter stars winked through the glow.

"The dancing lines on your magic box have changed," Eider suddenly announced. "I promise we didn't touch anything."

Shaun went over to the computer. "It's okay, Eider, you didn't do anything. The lines on the screen changed because the Lights themselves have changed. See, the color is getting darker and they're moving more. These lines here are just showing that change."

"Look!" cried Flint, pointing at the sky away to their left. "The Lights have come to dance on the earth."

Back the way they had come, looking like it was just past their camping spot, purple ribbons of light were plunging out of the sky and into the trees. The forest lit up as the rippling columns of lights meandered through the trees like downward-reaching fingers.

"Oh my God, oh my God, this is astounding," Shaun stammered, kneeling down in the snow and adjusting the microphone cables. "It's off the charts. This is incredible. This has got to be the most beautiful thing I've ever seen." He hit several keys on the keyboard, looked up at the sky again, and adjusted another cable.

The tendrils of magenta and purple light slowly wandered through the forest in the distance. The trees were black silhouettes against the light, and the snow glowed violet. And then, as suddenly as they had appeared, the ribbons withdrew back up into the sky, as if they were ropes let down from some celestial boat. The sky remained aglow as it had been, the color continuing to deepen into a purplish-blue, and the stars shone brighter.

Lyylia let out a breath she hadn't realized she'd been holding. A tingling sensation ran across her skin, and she rubbed her arms through her coat sleeves. "What happened? What was that?"

"Earth-walking Lights," said Eider.

"Does ground-level aurora happen often here?" Shaun asked. "Earth-walking Lights, you called it?"

"I usually see the Lights dancing on the ground at least once every season," Eider said.

"Northern lights on the ground?" Lyylia asked, just to

make sure she was accurately following the conversation. "This happens at our world, too?"

"Occasionally, yes," said Shaun. "I witnessed it once, many years ago, in Alaska. Well, it was actually aurora that came to just above the tree tops, so not quite on the ground. It was amazing, but nowhere near as dramatic as that display. It's a pretty rare phenomenon."

"I haven't seen the Earth-walking Lights in many moons," said Flint.

Lyylia looked back down the hill towards the campsite. Ávgos, Boots, and Fir were outside the tents, staring up at the sky. The animals seemed calm.

"Did you see that?" Ávgos called up to them.

"Yes!" Lyylia shouted back.

"Are you guys okay?" Ávgos asked.

"We're fine. You?"

"We're fine," he called back. "Just amazed."

Lyylia glanced back up at the now-calm sky and rubbed at her hair through her hat. She still felt strange, as if the hair on the back of her neck was standing up.

Shaun looked up at her. "You feel tingly all over? It's the Lights. That much electromagnetic energy, so close to us—I'm glad it wasn't any closer."

"The Dancing Lights don't hurt us, even when they walk the earth," Eider said. "Sometimes we feel prickly on our skin, like you just said." He rubbed his arms.

"I'm glad everyone's okay." Shaun tapped at his keyboard. "I think it overloaded my machine, though."

Lyylia looked over his shoulder and saw that the screen had gone dark.

He hit several buttons, adjusted cables, and then picked up one of the black boxes to examine it. "Hmm. Not good. My equipment's not designed for a display that intense, for sure. Well, I have a repair kit in my backpack—I'm used to doing all kinds of tweaks and repairs out on the field. I'll bring this back to camp and work on it." He began disconnecting the cables.

"Your Kalevala talisman is damaged?" asked Eider.

"It's not bad. I hope. It just got overloaded by the Lights."

The Menninkäinen looked puzzled.

As Shaun picked up the backpack and slid the closed laptop into it, something slipped out of a front pocket and fell into the snow. Lyylia bent down to pick it up. It was the stone necklace that he had taken off of the dead hiisi when they first arrived in Pohjola.

"It's definitely a lodestone," he said, looking at the gray rock in her hand. "My theory is that the hiisi were using magnets to find the portal underwater. I'm not sure how that might help us right now, though."

"What is this talisman?" asked Flint.

"I took it off one of the dead hiisi, when Eider and Boots and the others rescued us from the lake." He took it from Lyylia as she offered it to him, and he held it up for the Menninkäinen to see.

"You kept a talisman of Ice-Dark?" said Flint, sounding shocked.

"It's magnetic," Shaun said. "Do you know anything about what they might have used these necklaces for?"

The two Menninkäinen blinked at him. "What does 'magnetic' mean?" Eider asked.

Shaun gave a quiet sigh. "Never mind. I'll show it to the Queen. Maybe she can help."

"Queen Kuu is full of wisdom, and she sees all the knowledge of Dream our World Serpent," Flint said. "But until we reach her castle, you should put it away. You must not handle such evil magic."

"Sure thing. Putting it away." Shaun slid the lodestone necklace back into the pack.

So the mysterious denizens of Ice-Dark had some basic grasp of magnetism, and the Menninkäinen of Pohjola had never heard the word before. Lyylia was not feeling optimistic about the Queen—if she was real at all—being any more knowledgeable or advanced than her people.

They headed back down the hill towards the tents. "I hope your computer can be fixed," Lyylia said, looking at Shaun. It would be sad to think that one moment could have destroyed his life's work. And even though she didn't understand what he did or how it worked, the computer was almost like having a little a bit of home with them.

"I'm sure I can fix it," he said confidently, giving her a smile. He pulled something out of his pocket—it was a compass. Beneath the clear plastic bubble, the direction indicator was spinning like a top.

Lyylia stared at it for a moment, then looked back at Shaun.

"It hasn't worked since we got here. I don't understand how there can be such powerful aurora displays with no magnetic pole." He shook the compass, but it kept spinning. "It's been just floating, not pointing any direction. After that display just now, it started spinning."

"What does that mean?"

"I have no idea." He shrugged as he put the compass back in his pocket. "Thanks for watching the aurora with me, Lyylia." He grinned at her; she noticed that he had a small dimple in his right cheek, beneath his thin beard stubble. "I'm so excited we got to see the ground-level lights. You should feel special—not many people can say they've seen an aurora display like that. Ever."

Lyylia smiled back at him. Overhead the purple and blue lights washed across the sky.

Ávgos stifled another yawn as he trudged awkwardly on his snowshoes. He used snowshoes all the time—sleek, modern plastic ones, though, not the old-fashioned kind made of wood and wicker. These snowshoes were also designed for Menninkäinen, who overall had smaller feet than the average adult human man.

Boots had energetically roused everyone earlier than usual, explaining that since the weather was good, they should be able to reach the Queen's castle by evening. Adding to Ávgos' exhaustion was the fact that the trek was becoming more difficult. The land grew hillier, and large boulders rose between the trees. More than once he and Shaun had to help push the sled up an incline as it got bogged down in a snow drift.

As the group came over a rise in the land, Ávgos saw a frozen stream off to the left at the bottom of the hill. Several Menninkäinen were standing out on the stream, fishing lines dropped through holes in the ice.

"Greetings, travelers!" one of them called out, giving a wave.

"Greetings to you, friends!" Boots called back. "Is there a village nearby?"

"Yes indeed. Shaman Talon's village, just over the next hill. Where are you traveling today?"

"We're on our way to see the Queen," Boots shouted. "We have with us visitors from Kalevala!"

"Kalevala? We've heard the rumors! So the gateway is real?"

"The rumors are all true!" Boots gestured grandly at the three humans.

The men on the river all waved at them. "Welcome, strangers from Kalevala! Shaman Talon will be pleased to meet you!"

"Word travels fast around here," Shaun remarked as they followed the path down the hill and then back up. The sled managed not to get stuck this time.

"I wish we have traveled a little more yesterday," said Lyylia. "So we could sleep in this village last night."

"But then we wouldn't have had that great view of the ground-level Lights," Shaun said with a grin.

"Is your computer fixed, Shaun?" Ávgos asked. "I know you stayed up late working on it."

"I need more time, but it can be repaired. Nothing major got fried. The battery and the aurora panels got overloaded, but tonight I should be able to start charging it again. And one of my low-frequency receivers melted. I might be able to replace some of the wiring inside it, but if not, I have a back-up."

"Well, I'm glad you'll be able to get it working again." Ávgos wasn't very technically inclined and didn't understand everything Shaun said about his equipment. Impressive, though, that not only was it possible to charge a computer battery by using the Northern Lights instead of sunlight, but that it worked on another planet. Or wherever they were.

At the bottom of the next hill lay the village. Since it was good weather, everyone was outside. Children romped along the snowy paths, men chopped wood, women dumped kitchen scraps into animal pens and chatted over fence posts. Dogs wandered among the trees, horses and ducks and chickens roamed in their pens. A cat sitting on the low roof of a shed stared at them as they went past.

Two young men shoeing a horse were the first to call out a greeting to the group. Almost instantly everyone in sight dropped what they were doing and gathered around the travelers, all talking at once. Ávgos still wasn't used to being welcomed like a celebrity at every village.

"Welcome to our humble village! I am Shaman Talon." An older man wearing a long fur robe came to the front of the crowd and bowed. "You're on your way to see Queen Kuu?"

"Yes," Lyylia said in Finnish. "Were you expecting us?"

"The Queen has told the shamans in every village to watch for you and welcome you," said Talon. "And since this village is less than a day's journey from her castle, I have been especially alert to any travelers in the area. Come, won't you have some food before you continue on?"

"We don't want to linger long, if there's a chance we can reach the Queen's castle before night," Boots said.

"Of course, of course. No, you needn't stay long—but my wife and daughter were just preparing our midday meal, and I would be honored if you would join us."

"Hot food sounds good," Shaun said. Ávgos glanced at him and nodded in agreement.

They followed Shaman Talon through the village; most of the crowd followed them, full of questions about the humans, the hiisi, and the reindeer. At Talon's house, they tied the horse and the reindeer to a fence post, and after giving the reindeer a deep bow, Talon gave both animals some hay. Wolf's Bane stayed outside, as well, and Boots promised him scraps from the lunch table. Ávgos lingered a moment before going inside; the reindeer seemed relaxed and was heartily eating the hay.

Talon introduced his wife Feather and his daughter Rowan. The accommodations were a little cramped, what with the humans' size, plus the other four Menninkäinen. But Ávgos was happy to be off his feet for a little while and eating a hot meal of cooked fish and boiled vegetables.

"Word of your arrival has traveled," Talon said as they ate. "Even to villages where the shaman has no moon mirror. We've been hoping to meet you or hear of your travels. We had some visitors yesterday, but they didn't give us any word of you."

"They didn't give us any word of anything," said Talon's daughter Rowan. "They didn't speak at all. Several people invited them to stay the night, but they went on their way without even a thank-you."

"We met them," Boots said. "Two men, raggedly dressed for winter traveling, who didn't speak to us."

"Yes," said Talon. "They must have been in a desperate hurry to keep traveling through the night, but they wouldn't tell us why."

"Well, no matter," said Feather. "If they were on their way to see the Queen, then you will probably meet them there." She got up from the table. "There is more food, if anyone is still hungry."

"Thank you, but we should go," Lyylia said in English. "You say Queen Kuu's castle is less than one day's traveling from here?"

"Yes indeed," Talon said. "You should be able to reach it by the time the Dancing Lights have begun. Just keep following the road."

"Shaman Talon, you have met the Queen before?" Lyylia continued as they got up and put their coats back on.

"Of course. She often stops by this village if she is travelling. And many of the workers in the castle come here to trade. Queen Kuu is very anxious to meet all of you."

"Why?" Lyylia asked as they all went back outside.

"You have come from Kalevala—the world of legend.

And you have brought a Gentle Beast with you—more legends come to life."

Outside, a crowd was there to see them off. They thanked the family for the meal, and let themselves be led by the crowd to the edge of the village.

"So do you still think this Queen isn't real?" Shaun murmured to Lyylia once they were in the quiet depths of the forest again. "That shaman guy said he's met her, and the Menninkäinen don't seem like the type who would lie to your face."

Lyylia tossed a sideways look at him. "Yes, I suppose she is real. But why is she so eager to meet us and the reindeer? And other reindeer that are found are sent to her castle, too."

"Well, newcomers to a country have to check in with somebody," said Shaun. "Since they don't have border customs, going to see the Queen must be the next best thing. Maybe we should show her our passports."

Lyylia did not smile at Shaun's remark.

Ávgos chuckled quietly. "Then I'm in trouble, because I don't have a passport. I've never left Finland before." Until now.

After walking for a while, they came to another stream— much larger than the previous one where the men had been ice fishing. There was a little wooden bridge for crossing. Or rather, the remains of a bridge. The center of the bridge had been smashed, leaving just each end on the shore sticking a short way out over the ice.

"Well, isn't that convenient," Shaun quipped as they came to a halt.

"What could have damaged the bridge like this?" wondered Eider. "And why haven't the men of the village repaired it?"

"*Perkele,*" Lyylia muttered under her breath as she waded through the snow up to the planks of the bridge that still remained on this bank.

Shaun looked at Ávgos, probably hoping for a translation of the swear word, but then Lyylia switched to English.

"This was recently damaged. Look." She pointed at the smooth expanse of the frozen creek—lying scattered were the splintered boards of the bridge, half buried in snow.

"It looks like the bridge was broken straight down on the middle, like this." Lyylia mimed with her fist, punching straight downwards from above. "Or this." She punched straight upwards. "See, broken pieces are lying on both sides, but near to the bridge."

"But how could that happen?" Boots asked. "Maybe a tree fell across the center of the bridge?"

"No," said Lyylia, shaking her head. "No tree, no marks in the snow. And the bridge didn't break from weighing of heavy snow, neither so—see, the broken wood is scattered, like the bridge was smashed, not collapsed."

"Those two strange travelers," Ávgos said. "Shaman Talon said they were headed the same direction we are, and they seemed in a hurry."

"And word has apparently gotten around about who we are and where we're going," said Shaun. "Maybe somebody doesn't want us to reach the Queen's castle?"

"That makes no sense," said Eider. "Who would do that?"

Ávgos swallowed the sudden lump of fear in his throat. They still knew so little about this place. The Menninkäinen seemed kind and trustworthy—but what if they weren't all that way? Lyylia stood silently by the remains of the bridge, her eyes roaming around the surrounding forest, a slight frown on her face. Shaun pulled out his phone and snapped a picture of the broken bridge.

Ávgos wished he still had his phone. Not that he'd be

able to call Sirkka even if he did. He tried not to think about how distraught and panicked she must be feeling. And what about little Piijá? She wouldn't understand why her father was suddenly no longer there. He wondered if the police were searching for them. He hoped that at this point Maden had had the good sense to come back to Inari.

"Well, we still need to cross," said Flint into the silence. "Let's test the ice." He stood on the bank and plunged the handle end of his spear into the snow until it struck ice. He thumped it down several times, leaned on it, then stepped out onto the creek.

"We should be able to make it across, if we go one at a time. But the horse and the sled, I'm not so sure about."

"I'll pull the sled across, and send the horse across by himself," Boots volunteered. "And I'll go last."

Flint carefully made his way across the creek, tapping and testing with his spear, and made it to the opposite bank without incident. Eider went next, and then Boots commanded Wolf's Bane to cross.

Shaun gestured for Lyylia to cross the ice, and he followed. Then Ávgos joined them; he whistled to the reindeer, and made a sweeping gesture with his arm. The reindeer didn't budge.

"Boots, slap him on the rump," Ávgos called.

"What?" Boots said, sounding shocked.

"Not hard, just a pop so he'll feel it."

Boots looked at the reindeer. "My lord, I would never strike you. Please, we must cross here. It's safe."

The reindeer twitched its ears and headed across the creek. Ávgos shook his head. The Menninkäinen's extreme reverence for the reindeer would be amusing if it wasn't so bizarre.

It was Fir's turn to cross, and then Eider called to the horse. Finally Boots came, huffing as he man-hauled the sled through the snow.

At last they were all gathered on the bank. After re-hitching the horse to the sled, they set off down the road again. Soon they were climbing a very steep hill; Shaun got behind the sled to help heft it over dips and hummocks in the snow, while Fir helped pull from the front.

Boots and Eider, at the head of the group, disappeared over the crest of the hill. "Here we are!" Boots' voice shouted from above them. "The Mountains of the Moon!"

The rest of the group made it to the top, and they all stopped to stare. Despite the workout from getting up the hill, Ávgos felt his breath catch as he stared at the vista. The forest abruptly ended, and in front of them stretched a rolling tundra of hills and valleys. Mountains jutted up from the tundra, startlingly close. The closest peaks were rocky and foreboding and of course covered in snow—but those were just the foothills. Into the distance the mountain range stretched like the Himalayas, violent jagged peaks softened only by thick fog and heavy glaciers.

"Um, wow," Shaun said in a hushed voice. "Those are some mountains, all right."

Packed snow and the grooves of sled runners made the part of the road across the tundra easier to navigate. The mountains grew rapidly closer, all rocks and ice, harsh and beautiful. The blue-white light of Pohjantähti made the landscape all around sparkle like diamonds. And directly ahead, carved into the crags on the wall of the mountains, a castle suddenly lit up with the reflected brilliance of the giant star.

It was almost right in front of them, even though it hadn't been visible until just now. Tall gray stone walls clung to the side of the mountain; turrets and spires looked like they were made of ice. Even the gray stone glinted silver in the light as if polished to a marble finish. The snow-covered peaks surrounded the castle like giant sentinels.

"My God…" murmured Ávgos. Each time he fleetingly thought that maybe he was somehow dreaming of all this, something happened that confirmed that this was reality. His mind never could have imagined a glittering spectacle carved into the mountains like that.

"*Niin kaunis,*" said Lyylia in an awed tone.

"I'm with you, Ávgos," said Shaun, "because I have no idea what Lyylia said."

"Beautiful," Ávgos translated.

"That too," Shaun said.

"The home of our Queen!" cried Boots. "And beauty of her castle doesn't compare to the beauty of Queen Kuu herself! Come, we're almost there!"

Ávgos wondered how they were going to get up to the castle—the closer they got, the taller the mountains looked and the higher up and more inaccessible the castle appeared. But he followed the group along the snowy road, gazing up with continued awe at the vista of the mountains.

Shaun was beginning to wonder if the Mountains of the Moon were some sort of illusion and they were never actually going to arrive at their destination. At least another hour had passed since they first spotted the castle, but each time they glimpsed the castle around a bend in the winding hilly road, it seemed no closer.

Then suddenly they were at the base of a mountain. With

nothing but rock and ice towering all around them, they came to a little hut. A Menninkäinen man, warmly dressed in furs and holding a tall spear, stood outside the hut, and as their group came to a halt, three more men came outside.

"We've come representing Shaman Pike's village," Boots announced. "We have with us the three visitors from Kalevala, and a Gentle Beast."

"Welcome," said the first Menninkäinen. "You're expected. We'll take you to the Queen."

He led the way up a path, and one of the other guards fell into step with them.

"I was hoping I would be on duty when you arrived," he said to three humans, grinning up at them. "I'm very honored."

"Thank you," Shaun said politely.

"Are all the women of Kalevala as beautiful as you?" the little man asked, staring at Lyylia.

She gave a surprised-sounding laugh.

"There are lots of beautiful women in Kalevala, my friend," Shaun said with a conspiratorial grin. "But I can assure you that she is the prettiest of all of them."

Ávgos chuckled quietly. Shaun glanced at Lyylia; she stared straight ahead, avoiding eye contact with him.

The road up the mountain was wide and smooth with packed snow, but winding and steep. They walked and climbed for nearly half an hour, and all of them except their two guides were breathing hard. Shaun kept having to shield his face from the wind as it whipped down the high-walled channel, blowing grit and ice in his face.

Suddenly a gate loomed in front of them—heavy wooden double doors with iron hinges and braces, touched with frost. Two more Menninkäinen guards greeted them, and heaved open the doors.

Inside was a short tunnel lit with torches that opened into a large courtyard, welcoming in its wintry elegance. Smooth paving stones were shoveled free of snow. Trees, leafless for the winter, were planted around, some with stone benches beneath them, others standing in snowy patches that were probably flower beds in the spring. Several statues were also scattered about, on raised stone platforms. All of the statues were carved out of ice.

Shaun stared at the figures as they crossed the courtyard. A bear, an eagle or some similar large bird with wings outstretched, a tree nearly the size of the live ones, all sculpted of ice. Ávgos tapped him on the arm and pointed up at a terrace as they went past. On a small stone platform stood an ice statue of a reindeer.

Two guards stayed outside with the horse and the dog, but they let Ávgos lead the reindeer into the castle. The group followed their guides in silence; Shaun noticed that even Boots and the other three Menninkäinen were gazing around with awe.

The corridors were wide enough for all of them to walk side-by-side if they'd wanted to, the walls all carved of smooth gray stone. Probably granite or something similar, likely the bedrock of the mountain range. The arched ceiling soared at least two stories above their heads, making their footsteps echo as they walked. Tall windows lined the wall on their right, letting in the bright blue-white light from outside.

The interior walls were carved with a swirling motif. Shaun tried to make out the images as they walked—it looked like a repeating pattern of circles and crescents, possibly representing the moon. Thin ribbons of silver were inlayed in the design, and reflected the light from the windows with an almost blinding sheen.

Their escorts led them down several corridors, turned

several corners, and went up a short wide flight of steps. Every passageway looked the same, and Shaun felt more awestruck at each turn. Who had built this castle, and how long had it stood here? Stone masonry of this magnitude was no small feat, and it was a far cry from the wooden cabins of the villages.

He glanced at Lyylia walking beside him. Judging by her studious expression, he figured that she was having similar thoughts. Was this world like a medieval kingdom where the royalty lived in splendor while the common people suffered in poverty? Despite the imposing architecture all around, Shaun didn't feel that was the case. The Menninkäinen seemed happy and healthy, even with their primitive lifestyle, and none of them had ever spoken about the Queen with anything but genuine admiration.

Their guides stopped suddenly at an open door halfway down the corridor. "The visitors from Kalevala, Your Majesty!" one of them announced. Then both men stepped aside, and gestured for the group to enter the room.

The room was small and had no windows, but was warm and well-lit by a blazing fire in the fireplace, and several oil lamps on tall stands along the walls. A brown and white woven carpet covered most of the stone floor, and a large white husky-like dog lay on the carpet in front of the fireplace.

A blonde woman sat at a small wooden table in the center of the room, bending over a rectangle of wood lying on the tabletop; she held several curls of silver wire in her hands. It looked like she was stringing a musical instrument.

The dog looked up from the hearth as they entered the room, and the woman looked up from her work. She smiled brightly, and disentangled her hands from the silver wires.

"Greetings!" she said, pushing her chair back and standing up. "Welcome to Pohjola, guests from Kalevala." Her voice was light and almost melodious, and Shaun felt as if it reminded him of something, even though he knew he'd never heard her voice before.

She came around the table and approached them, and Shaun knew that he was awkwardly staring, but he couldn't help it. She was tall, at least compared to the Menninkäinen; she looked to be at least Lyylia's height, with a slender build accentuated by the simple white dress she was wearing. Her white-blond hair was pinned back with several small elaborate braids, but the bulk of it hung loose, almost to her waist. Her smile was kind and she didn't look a day over thirty.

Though her expression was gentle and she held out her hands in a welcoming gesture, her presence seemed to fill the room. She was beautiful, but more than just an attractive face or body. Shaun immediately felt that he now understood why the Menninkäinen spoke about her with such respect and adoration.

"I am Kuu, Queen of Pohjola," she said, still smiling. "Welcome to my castle. I've been eager to meet you, ever since I heard that you had been brought here from Kalevala."

All the Menninkäinen bowed deeply, and Shaun found himself doing the same. He stared at her again as he straightened up. Despite her aura of regality and beauty, Queen Kuu was dressed very simply. Her floor-length white dress was perfectly plain and she wore no jewelry, nor even a crown. Her eyes, though...

Her eyes were silver. Not just gray irises, as he'd first thought, but truly silver. Her eyes didn't glow, but the silver irises seemed to sparkle of their own accord, like silver rings set with tiny diamonds.

Shaun had to drag his attention away from her eyes as he realized she was speaking again. "I am so sorry that the cursed hiisi abducted you from your world, but I hope that you've found Pohjola to be a pleasant place. My people have treated you well, I hope?"

Shaun merely nodded dumbly, as did Ávgos. Lyylia was the first to break the silence. "*Kyllä, Kuningatar. Kiitos,*" she said, bowing her head at Kuu.

Queen Kuu smiled in response, and her eyes sparkled. "Come, I must have your names," she said. "And the names of these brave men who rescued you and have brought you all this way."

"I'm Boots, Your Grace," Boots began the introductions for the Menninkäinen. "And these are Eider, and Flint, and Fir."

"Thank you, Boots, Eider, Flint, and Fir," Queen Kuu said, and laid her hand on the tops of their heads, each one in turn.

"My name is Lyylia Niiranen," Lyylia said in English. "Your Highness."

"Ávgos Heikkilä, Your Highness."

Shaun had to clear his throat to make sure his voice worked properly. "Shaun Abernathy, Your Highness."

"What elaborate names you have in Kalevala," the Queen said with a smile.

"Um, we usually just go by our first names," Shaun offered.

"Well, welcome Lyylia, Ávgos, and Shaun. And an especially warm and reverent welcome to you, Gentle Lord," she added, reaching out to the reindeer standing next to Ávgos. "And what is your name?"

"We don't give them names—" began Ávgos.

Queen Kuu shook her head. "No, I didn't ask what you called him. I am asking him what he calls himself." She caressed the reindeer's muzzle. "Oarbbis."

Shaun looked at Ávgos. Was that the same name that Shaman Pike had called the reindeer? Ávgos' nonplussed expression told him it probably was.

"There are several of your brothers and sisters here with me," Kuu continued, still talking to the reindeer. "You will be happy to see them."

"How many other reindeer are here?" asked Lyylia.

"Four others are here right now. They look like the forest lords of ancient times—and yet, they do not breathe Pohjola magic. These Gentle Beasts who have been brought to me must be of Kalevala."

"May I see them, Your Highness?" Ávgos asked.

"Of course." The Queen gestured toward the door. "Lead the way to the stables, Stone."

"This way," said one of the guards who had escorted them. He and his companion bowed and then headed down the corridor. Their group followed him, and Queen Kuu fell into step beside them. Her gray fur boots that were just visible beneath the hem of her dress were whisper-quiet on the stone floors. The white husky trotted beside her.

The guard, Stone, led them down one of the windowed corridors, and Shaun glanced out and saw that the aurora had begun. Dancing Lights, indeed—the greens, pinks, and reds all swirled and shimmered across the vault of the sky. Because they were so high up now, he could see for miles across the vast snowy tundra. The white landscape reflected the glow from the Lights and took his breath away.

Belatedly Shaun realized that he'd stopped walking. As he turned from the window, he gave a start as he then realized that Queen Kuu had stopped beside him.

"Beautiful, is it not?" She gave him a warm smile and her silver eyes sparkled.

"Um, yes, Your Majesty. Very beautiful."

"Do you have Dancing Lights in Kalevala?" she asked.

"Yes, we do. I study them every night."

Queen Kuu smiled again. "Then you must tell me, Shaun, the songs that you hear the Lights sing." She glanced over her shoulder. "But another time, perhaps, or else Stone and your companions will abandon us in this corridor."

Shaun saw that the rest of the group had continued on and was about to turn a corner at the end of the hall. The Queen gave him another smile, and set off towards the group. Shaun hurried to keep pace with her, the words she'd spoken ringing in his head. *You must tell me the songs that you hear the Lights sing.* How could she know that his focus was the auditory properties of the aurora?

They went outside briefly to cross another courtyard, and Shaun managed not to get distracted again by the aurora display. They went into another building, and Shaun smelled the distinctive warm and pungent odor of a barn. Two stable workers were busy mucking out a stall, and they paused and bowed as Kuu went past, and stared after the humans with interest.

Most of the stalls housed small horses, stocky animals shaggy with their winter coats, just like in the Menninkäinen villages. Boots' dog Wolf's Bane was snuggled in the straw in one stall, and he lifted his head and wagged his tail as they went past. The horse they'd been traveling with was in the next stall.

At the end of the barn were four reindeer. Queen Kuu introduced each one as politely as if she were introducing people.

"Viehkat, Vuoddji, Chakchageassi, Áhčáš."

Ávgos went into each stall to touch the animals and check their ears. "My earmark on all of them," he said. "They all seem uninjured and well kept." He looked back at Kuu. "Why do you use those words to describe them, Your Majesty?"

"Because those are their names," said Kuu. "Are they not?"

Ávgos pursed his lips and didn't answer.

"Vuoddji was the first one that was brought to me," Kuu continued. "Her fur was so full of briars and nettles that it had to be cut. But she was unhurt. I dislike keeping them locked up in here as if they were horses, but they need to be kept safe, especially now. Suddjet disappeared last night."

"Disappeared?" Ávgos asked. "What happened?"

"We are not sure. The workers believe they must have accidentally left the stable door ajar, although the outer gates of the castle are always closed. None of the other Gentle Beasts—or the horses, either—could tell me anything. They all slept soundly all night, and in the morning, Suddjet was gone."

"Stolen, maybe?" Lyylia asked.

Kuu shook her head. "No one can get past my castle walls. And there are no hiisi in the area—I've had scouts keeping watch in the mountains, and they've seen no hiisi. Unfortunately, none of them has seen Suddjet, either."

"But what if…" Lyylia paused. "A thief inside the castle?"

Queen Kuu laughed lightly. "There are no hiisi inside my castle."

"No, I don't mean a hiisi thief. Maybe someone who lives and works inside the castle."

For the first time Kuu's pleasant expression faded, and she gave Lyylia a firm look. "Menninkäinen do not steal or perform dishonest acts," she said, a hard edge in her voice. "Least of all from their Queen."

Lyylia held her gaze and didn't flinch, but she stayed quiet. Shaun swallowed nervously. The moment passed and Queen Kuu's face softened again. One of the reindeer put its nose over the gate of the stall and whickered.

"What is it, dear Áhcháš?" Kuu said, stroking its ears. "Yes, we've brought another lost brother to you, but Suddjet is still gone. I'm sorry. But now your companions from your world are here. Yes, I know." She turned to Ávgos. "Oarbbis will be well cared for. And I will station guards in the stable to make sure that all of these Beasts remain safe."

Ávgos slowly handed the lead line to one of the stable workers who had come up to them. The little man bowed at Ávgos, and then at the reindeer. "This way, lord Oarbbis." He led the reindeer into an empty stall.

"But now, I'm sure you're all tired and hungry from traveling," Queen Kuu said briskly. "There is food prepared." She gestured toward the guard who had escorted them. "Go with Stone—he will take you to the dining chamber, and I will join you there shortly. I'm looking forward to hearing about your journey and your world."

In the dining chamber, a long table had already been laid with dishes of food when Stone escorted them in. Benches lined both sides, and a straight-backed wooden chair sat at the head of the table. Queen Kuu's chair, Lyylia assumed.

Stone told them that they were allowed to begin eating. Everyone eagerly served themselves from the dishes of food, and Stone positioned himself by the open door like a sentry. For a few minutes, Lyylia focused only on eating. Even with the occasional meal in villages as they'd traveled, it felt like ages since she'd been able to eat her fill of hot food. There was fish and several different kinds of meat, roasted potatoes and vegetable-filled pastries, hot bread with butter, and a pale amber beverage that tasted fruity and mildly alcoholic. The dishes and utensils were metal instead of wood, as they had been in all the village houses where they'd eaten. Drinks were served in tall metal goblets engraved with the same serpentine design that lined the walls of the corridors.

After taking the edge off her hunger, Lyylia scanned the room as she ate. There were no windows, but the space was well-lit with the fire, oil lamps on lampstands, and a chandelier of candles above them. The ceiling—as in the corridors—was nearly two stories high. There was no carpet on the stone floor, but on two of the walls hung large tapestries woven with bright floral patterns. A closed door in the far corner shared the wall with the fireplace, directly across from the open door that led out into the corridor.

Lyylia glanced at Ávgos beside her.

"The names of the reindeer," she whispered to him in Finnish. "Those are Sami words, aren't they?"

Ávgos looked at her and nodded. "But how would the Queen know Sami words?"

Lyylia shook her head. "The Menninkäinen—and the Queen—seem to have this strange ability to understand and speak multiple languages with no prior knowledge. So what puzzles me is why I heard those words in Sami."

Ávgos just shook his head.

Queen Kuu entered at that moment, followed by a young Menninkäinen man and the white dog. Boots, Eider, Flint, and Fir all scrambled up from their benches to bow, but Kuu waved at them to stay seated.

"My apologies for the delay in joining you," Kuu said conversationally as she sat down in the chair at the head of the table. "I hope you have been enjoying the food after your long journey."

Everyone nodded and expressed their thanks.

Stone came over to the table and served up a plate of food for the Queen, then fixed another plate and took it over to the dog, who had sat down in front of the fireplace.

"I would like you to meet Gray," Queen Kuu said, nodding at the young Menninkäinen who had joined them. "He is the son of a village shaman, and he has been living here for several moons, apprenticing with me to learn more deeply the ways of magic."

The young man nodded at the three humans and laid down his fork. "It is such an honor to meet legends from another world!" he said. "And many thanks to Her Grace the Queen for allowing me to be here."

Kuu smiled at him. "I didn't introduce my dog earlier," she said, nodding in the direction of the fireplace. "This is Child of Light. She guards me and protects this castle." The dog looked up from her food at the mention of her name.

Lyylia looked at the dog, and then back at Kuu. A not-so-subtle reminder that the Queen had a bodyguard with her at all times.

"So please tell me about yourselves and your world," Kuu continued smoothly as she began eating. "And how you came to be here."

Lyylia began by recounting the hiisi attack on the shore of Lake Inari, and their arrival in Pohjola. She also explained that they were searching for Ávgos' missing reindeer; and if the animals in Kuu's stable were any indication, then it looked as if the entire herd had been brought to Pohjola. She did her best to tell everything accurately in English, so that Shaun could follow the conversation.

"How many Gentle Beasts have gone missing from your world?" Kuu asked, picking up her goblet.

"One hundred and thirty, Your Majesty," Ávgos answered,

in English.

Kuu took a thoughtful sip of her drink. "Over one hundred Beasts from your world, here in Pohjola. Or, more likely, in Ice-Dark. The ones that have been found in Pohjola may have escaped from Ice-Dark."

"Do you know why the hiisi captured the reindeer?" Lyylia asked. "Or us?"

Kuu was silent for a moment. "Hiisi-Hiisi, the king of Ice-Dark, must have found the gateway. I cannot think why Hiisi-Hiisi should wish to capture creatures from Kalevala, but whatever his reasons, it bodes ill for both of our lands."

Lyylia exchanged glances with Shaun and Ávgos. Both men looked more than a little alarmed at that proclamation. Carefully keeping her own spike of concern from showing on her face, Lyylia looked back at the Queen and opened her mouth.

Kuu spoke before she could form a question. "Earlier this year, in the spring, rumors reached me that hiisi and Näkki had been spotted in the lake and the Dark River. I sent scouts to keep watch at points along the shore, and I had silver nets dropped deep in the lake to guard against Näkki. My aim was to protect the borders of Pohjola. I did not suspect that Hiisi-Hiisi was searching for the gateway."

"What are Näkki?" Shaun asked, before Lyylia could.

"More denizens of Ice-Dark. The hiisi are demons of the land, and the Näkki are demons of the water."

"Your Highness, all we want is to find Ávgos' reindeer and go home," Lyylia said. "Can you help us?"

Kuu's silver eyes locked with hers. "Ice-Dark has lain quiet for so long, but I cannot forget what Hiisi-Hiisi once did. And I will not let him do it again. Together we will find your reindeer, and the gateway to Kalevala."

Next to her, Lyylia heard Shaun exhale quietly. Then Ávgos spoke. "Does that mean, Your Highness, that you don't know where the gateway is? That we can't go back home?"

Kuu looked at him. "I have searched many times for the gateway, and it has eluded me. So at this moment, I must answer no. I cannot return you to your land. Not yet."

Lyylia glanced at Ávgos. His jaw clenched; he gave Queen Kuu a nod, and then looked down at his plate. As much as she missed home, Lyylia could only imagine how desperately Ávgos missed his family.

But at least there was a hope and a chance that his reindeer could be found. And if this King Hiisi-Hiisi had found the gateway, then so could they. Assuming that Queen Kuu was truly willing to help them. She could easily keep them trapped here and keep Ávgos' reindeer to rebuild the population in Pohjola. Or send Menninkäinen to Earth to capture more reindeer, if she was lying about knowing where the gateway was.

Lyylia wanted to believe the Queen. Just like when she'd first met Boots, she felt a strange gut instinct to trust this woman, even though she had no proof yet that Queen Kuu was trustworthy.

"Your Majesty," Ávgos said into the silence that had fallen. "If my reindeer are in Ice-Dark, how do we get them?"

"I must meditate with Dream about this matter," Kuu replied. "I once underestimated Hiiisi-Hiisi's wickedness and cunning, and because of it the Gentle Beasts of Pohjola vanished from the world." A swift flicker shone in her eyes, like a faint wash of violet across the silvery irises. "I will not let that happen again."

"What happened to the reindeer of Pohjola?" asked Ávgos.

"It is a long tale," Kuu said quietly, her tone sounding thoughtful. "It grows late, and I'm sure you are weary from your long journey."

As physically exhausted as she was, Lyylia's mind buzzed with everything the Queen had told them so far. She'd never be able to get to sleep with so many questions still open. She glanced at the two men, and saw her thoughts mirrored in their expressions.

"Please, Your Highness," Lyylia said. "Tell us."

Kuu inclined her head. "As you wish. But not here." She pushed her chair back from the table and stood up. "Come. I will show you."

After following Kuu through a maze of corridors, they came to a hallway filled with light.

Shaun squinted in the sudden radiance. One wall of the long corridor was entirely windows, and the ever-present blue-white sun mixed with the aurora to create a dazzling spectacle. It took him a moment to realize that the brilliance from the windows provided illumination for the opposite wall of the corridor, which was painted with large colorful murals.

"The Halls of Time," Kuu announced. "This chronicles the history of Pohjola."

Shaun stared up at the pictures. They filled the wall, nearly floor to ceiling. He was hardly an art expert, but the paintings seemed primitive and stylized, though the colors were bright as if freshly painted. It reminded him of pictures of elaborately painted ancient Egyptian tombs.

The first panel showed a nearly life-sized depiction of Kuu, dressed in a plain white gown similar to what she currently had on. Beside her was a reindeer. They were painted on a field of green, and above their heads were a blue snake and a full moon.

"Kied-Kie-Jubmel," said Kuu, hovering her hand in front of the image of the reindeer. "My constant companion, and one of the first Gentle Beasts who vanished."

The next mural depicted Menninkäinen building the castle. The stylized, simplistic painting was surprisingly detailed—a collage of men chopping stones and levering boulders, a picture of a half-built tower of the castle, a larger picture of the completed castle, mountains in the background. The next panel showed Menninkäinen daily life—farming, fishing, building homes. The next panel featured Kuu and Kied-Kie-Jubmel surrounded by Menninkäinen, all evenly spaced as if they were dancing or playing a game. On all the murals, scattered all around were reindeer.

Shaun pulled out his phone and held it up to take a picture of the murals. Lyylia put her hand out and touched his arm.

"Not now," she whispered.

Shaun looked at her, then glanced at Kuu, who was gazing up at the next mural and hadn't seen his movement. Looking back at Lyylia, Shaun slid his phone back into his coat pocket. The Queen knew nothing of their technology—such as it was—yet, so Lyylia probably wanted to keep that a secret until they knew more about Kuu and what she could do.

"That was our first encounter with Ice-Dark." Kuu looked up at the elaborate montage as everyone caught up to her. The four Menninkäinen had come along with them, as well as the young shaman Gray, and the guard Stone. There was plenty of room in the wide corridor for everyone to gather and see each mural.

In the center of the mural, portrayed at nearly twice the

size of Kuu and Kied-Kie-Jubmel, was a giant white horse with black wings. Beside him was a black bird. Painted above the horse's head was a coiled white snake with a dragon-like head. Both the snake and the horse were breathing fire.

"Hiisi-Hiisi, the king of Ice-Dark, and his companion, Syöjätär," said Kuu, pointing at the white horse and the black bird. "And Äi, the World Serpent of Ice-Dark." The fire-breathing white snake. Shaun felt a trickle of apprehension as he stared at the images.

At the top of mural were smaller images of reindeer and Menninkäinen facing off with a group of white bear-like creatures and black wolves.

"We had long been wary of Ice-Dark, but curious, as well," Kuu continued. "Hiisi-Hiisi told me of his interest in the Dancing Lights, because Ice-Dark had no such display. He also wished to learn more about the people of Pohjola, and offered to show me the people of his land. So I accepted Hiisi-Hiisi's offer of a meeting. We met on the ice of the Dark Water Lake—the lake and river serve as the border between Pohjola and Ice-Dark. We were not prepared for such violence.

"Kied-Kie-Jubmel and I, with other Gentle Beasts and Menninkäinen, went across the ice. Hiisi-Hiisi met us there, with many Näkki, and an army of lesser hiisi." She paused, a hint of purple glittering in her silver eyes. "There was a battle. So many were torn apart by the hiisi or drowned in the water. Kied-Kie-Jubmel and I had to fight off the magicks of the Näkki shamans and Hiisi-Hiisi himself. Then Äi called the denizens of her world back to Ice-Dark and the army retreated. And never again has anyone crossed the lake, and no one lives near the shore."

The entire background of the mural was a dusty gray color, with the exception of a swath of red across the bottom.

Judging by the images of reindeer and Menninkäinen painted upside down on the sea of red, Shaun assumed it represented blood and death. He shuddered.

After a moment of somber silence, Kuu moved down to the next mural.

This one showed a more peaceful scene. Kuu and Kied-Kie-Jubmel stood on a field of green, surrounded by a blue color, possibly representing an island in water. Above them was a beautiful and surprisingly realistic painting of the Dancing Lights, the colors vivid and swirled across the top half of the mural. Between Kuu and the reindeer a pillar of blue-green rose up from the ground and joined the colors in the sky.

"This is the Dancing Ground Island," Kuu said. "After the battle, Kied-Kie-Jubmel and I went to this island and cast a spell on the Dancing Lights to bring the Lights to the ground. We wanted to study them more closely. If Hiisi-Hiisi had attacked us because he was envious of the Dancing Lights of Pohjola, we resolved to learn what might have intrigued him so."

"We saw some ground-level Lights last night," Shaun put in.

Kuu turned to look at him. "Yes. The Lights often dance upon the earth. And every night at midsummer, the Lights come to dance on this island. Many Menninkäinen travel there for the midsummer celebration and to watch the Lights." Kuu turned back to the painting.

Shaun wanted to ask what she meant by "bring the Lights to the ground." Surely there wasn't actually such a thing as a magic spell that could control ground-level aurora. Aurora didn't work that way, and there was no such thing as magic. Except here he was, on another planet, surrounded by things that defied all logic.

Kuu spoke again before he could continue musing or form a question.

"Some time later, a Gentle Beast named Moon in the West came to Kied-Kie-Jubmel. He said that he had fallen into the lake during the battle with Ice-Dark, but he did not drown— he fell through a gateway below the water, and into another world. He said that he had been trapped there, trying to find his way home, for many seasons, until he chanced upon the gateway again. I knew then that the legend of another world called Kalevala must be real."

Shaun exchanged looks with Lyylia and Ávgos.

"Moon in the West told us tales of the Dancing Lights in that world, and he feared that Hiisi-Hiisi may try to steal the Lights of Kalevala if he could not have the Lights of Pohjola."

The next panel had a background of blue, dotted with Menninkäinen in row boats. Kuu and the reindeer, larger than the other images and with the snake and moon motif above their heads, were also depicted standing in a boat.

"We searched the Dark Water Lake for the gateway," Kuu said. "Moon in the West could not find it again, and we searched for a long time and found nothing. One midsummer's night, when Kied-Kie-Jubmel and I were watching the earth-walking Lights at the Dancing Ground, Moon in the West had a sudden fit of madness and leapt into the column of Lights. He was gone."

"Dead?" Ávgos asked.

Kuu nodded. "Mourning the loss of Moon in the West, Kied-Kie-Jubmel and I continued searching for the gateway." She paused and seemed to gather herself. "And then one day, Kied-Kie-Jubmel did not return from the lake. I assumed that he had found the gateway, and so I waited. But Kied-Kie-Jubmel did not return. As the seasons went by, I heard from fewer and fewer Gentle Beast shamans, and Menninkäinen rarely saw them in the forests any more. And for so long now, there have been none."

The next mural showed the Dancing Ground Island and a shaft of colored light reaching down to the ground, this time surrounded by what looked like five stone pillars.

Then a few murals showed more scenes of daily life: Menninkäinen tending crops, making clothing, playing musical instruments, herds of horses roaming the tundra. There were also some unpleasant events pictured, like a flood and a forest fire, and a mural featuring large boulders and broken huts, which Shaun took to represent an earthquake or a landslide.

As the murals advanced down the hall, the images of reindeer became less prevalent, and eventually stopped altogether. And Kuu, who had been featured in every mural paired with a reindeer, was alone in the last several paintings.

The silence grew heavy in the echoing corridor. Lyylia finally spoke.

"So you believe that all the reindeers—Gentle Beasts— found the gateway? They are at our world?"

Kuu looked at her. "They must be. I would have felt it if they had been killed. When Kied-Kie-Jubmel did not return, and more Gentle Beasts vanished, I continued in earnest to search for the gateway. But my search proved fruitless, and Näkki from Ice-Dark encroached on the lake. So I placed nets of silver rope throughout the water, to deter the Näkki. And I forbade any villages to be built within a day's traveling distance of the border with Ice-Dark."

"Why silver?" Shaun asked.

"Näkki are weakened by silver."

"Did Hiisi-Hiisi know your Gentle Beasts found the gateway?" Lyylia asked. "Is that why the creatures stole Ávgos' reindeer? He thought they were Pohjola reindeer maybe?"

"Perhaps," said Kuu. "But even Hiisi-Hiisi would know that

after all this time, the Gentle Beasts of Pohjola would be dead."

Lyylia raised her eyebrows.

Shaun exchanged glances with Ávgos. He had no idea how long reindeer lived, but something about the way Kuu had told this story, as if it were all ancient history...

"Your Highness," Lyylia said slowly. "How long ago did this happen, this battle with Ice-Dark and Gentle Beasts disappearing?"

"I confess that I have lost count of the passage of time. But it has been at least five hundred winters, perhaps more."

Surely he'd misunderstood that. Shaun looked at Lyylia and Ávgos and saw their stunned expressions. The Menninkäinen, however, all looked merely sad.

"Five hundred years, Your Highness?" Lyylia said, a frown of confusion on her face.

"Yes."

"Wait, all of this happened *five hundred years* ago?" Shaun asked. "How is that possible? Your Majesty, how old are you?" He voiced the question before he realized that not only was it impolite to ask a woman her age, it was probably downright disrespectful to ask a queen.

Kuu's beautiful face remained placid and she didn't seem to take offense. "I am eternal."

"*Mitä?*" Lyylia said.

"You're immortal, Your Highness?" Ávgos said, echoing Lyylia's disbelieving tone.

"Yes," she said smoothly, as if it were the most natural thing in the world. Which apparently, in this world it was. "I have been the Queen of Pohjola since the beginning of time, and I shall remain until the ending of the world. Kied-Kie-Jubmel is like me—he is eternal, as well. And so if he became trapped in Kalevala, he must still be there, even though all the other Gentle Beasts would have long ago perished."

Shaun's mind buzzed with questions. If this battle and the reindeer vanishing had happened five hundred years ago and Hiisi-Hiisi had been the king of Ice-Dark...but Kuu had mentioned earlier that he was currently the king...then he must be immortal, too. And there might be an immortal reindeer running around northern Finland? "Your Majesty," he said. "How can—"

Kuu held up a hand. "It grows late," she said. "I'm sure all of you are weary from your travels. Stone will show you to your rooms. I bid you goodnight and good sleep. Tomorrow we shall begin the search for the Gentle Beasts of Kalevala." Kuu smiled at the group, and then walked off down the hallway, her white dog behind her.

"This way, honored guests," said Stone, gesturing in the direction the Queen had gone.

As they set off back down the hall, Shaun took a last look at the brightly painted murals, feeling a renewed sense of awe. An immortal Queen, and an ancient connection between this world and earth. He hoped that Queen Kuu could help find Ávgos' animals and the portal in the lake, but he had a strange, unsettled feeling that all of this had become much bigger than just some missing reindeer.

Ávgos had slept better last night than he had since arriving in Pohjola. The guest chambers were similar to the bedrooms of Menninkäinen huts—a small room with furs on the floor—but these included several soft pillows made of colorful fabric to enhance the sleeping arrangement. Each bedroom had a fire blazing in the small fireplace, and a lantern on a hook for extra light. Each room also had its own private toilet chamber attached, along with a basin of water on a stand for hand washing and tooth-brushing, and even a sharp metal straight razor for shaving. A first-rate sauna was at the end of the hall, along with a room with an actual tub for bathing.

"So how about these five-star accommodations, huh?" Shaun remarked as they all met in the hall outside their rooms.

"Yes, it's wonderful," said Ávgos. "I'm glad that Queen Kuu is as welcoming as her people are."

"Yeah, sure beats winding up as a pagan sacrifice to the night sky," Shaun said with a chuckle, glancing at Lyylia.

"I am glad I was wrong this time," she said.

They all laughed.

Boots and Eider joined them, and then Flint and Fir emerged. The castle guard who had come to wake them all was waiting patiently at the end of the hall. "This way to the dining chamber for the morning meal, honored guests," he said.

Queen Kuu was already in the room when they arrived, as was the young man they'd met yesterday named Gray.

"Good morning!" the Queen greeted them in a cheerful tone, rising from her chair at the head of the table. Ávgos noticed that the white dress she wore today was more elaborate than the one from yesterday—the sleeves and bodice were decorated with embroidered designs of white and pale blue thread. Her white-blond hair hung loose again, but today she wore a thin circlet of silver on her head. The Menninkäinen all bowed before taking their seats, and Ávgos found himself doing the same.

"Please, join me." Queen Kuu gestured toward the table, which was spread with enough hot food for all of them.

Ávgos' stomach rumbled at the smell of the buttered bread, jam, boiled eggs, and meat pastries.

"You all slept well, I hope?" the Queen asked as they all began eating.

"Very well, thank you, Your Highness," Lyylia said, almost simultaneously with Boots saying "Yes, Your Grace."

"I have instructed my workers to make new winter garments for all of you," Kuu continued. "Your Kalevalan attire doesn't look particularly warm. I hadn't realized that you were so much like I am—my shamans told me that giants had come from Kalevala, so I was imagining people the size of trees." She laughed lightly. "And with the lake turning to ice and your Gentle Beasts missing, you may be here for some time, so you will need adequate clothing."

Ávgos paused in chewing a bite of the savory pastry-wrapped sausage. He knew, of course, that Lake Inari—and therefore the lake in Pohjola—would soon be frozen over as the autumn season advanced. They were trapped, and Queen Kuu knew that. But last night she'd assured them that she would search for the gateway. He swallowed.

"Your Majesty," he said in English. "Is there a way we could begin looking for the gateway? As much as I want to find my reindeer, I also need to return home. We all do. I have a wife and child at home."

Queen Kuu looked at him, her expression sorrowful.

"Oh, Ávgos, I am so sorry. I did not know that any of you had families left behind, though I should have guessed that you did." Her silver eyes glittered as if they were moist with tears. "I wish that I could return all of you to Kalevala this very moment. But as I meditated last night with Dream, he told me that finding your Gentle Beasts is of vital importance, for both of our worlds. We must first find all of your animals, and to do that, I need your help."

That was not the answer Ávgos had been wanting—or expecting—to hear. Queen Kuu had mentioned "Dream" several times last night, but he'd assumed that she was referring to some sort of meditative trance that a shamanistic leader might do. Now it sounded like Dream was a person.

Lyylia asked the question before he could. "Who is Dream?"

"Dream is the World Serpent of Pohjola. He protects this world, and gives me guidance. He has been here since before the birth of the world, before even I was here."

"So, he's like…a god?" Shaun asked.

"If that's your word for it, I suppose," Queen Kuu said agreeably. "Surely Kalevala has a World Serpent?"

Lyylia and Shaun shook their heads.

"Not that we know of," Ávgos said tactfully.

"Dream told me that your world is important. Not just to you, of course, but to Pohjola, as well. Now that we have made a connection with Kalevala, it must not be lightly cast aside. Dream says that he would like to meet you."

Queen Kuu had been eating with her fork in her left hand, and now she laid it down and held out her right arm. She pulled up the embroidered cuff of her right sleeve to reveal a blue bracelet that wound halfway up her forearm. Before Ávgos had time to feel disappointed that the Queen worshipped a piece of jewelry, the jewelry moved.

The bracelet began to uncoil from her arm, and as it slithered onto the table, it became a snake. The tiny creature was no thicker than an index finger, and barely thirty centimeters long. Its entire body was a deep bright blue, but the eyes were red and glittered like rubies. It lifted its tiny head to look at them, and flicked a bright red forked tongue.

Ávgos remembered the paintings in the Halls of Time—

an image of a blue snake and a full moon had been pictured above Kuu's head in every mural. But he hadn't imagined that the blue snake was actually a real living animal.

Beside him, Lyylia made a strangled sound in her throat and scooted away from him on the bench. Ávgos was sitting on the end of the bench nearest the Queen, with Lyylia beside him and Shaun on her other side. Ávgos looked at her; her eyes were wide and she pressed up against Shaun as if terrified.

Shaun put an arm around her shoulder, and she didn't protest. "Lyylia, what is it?"

"I don't like snakes," she replied in Finnish, eyes still on the tabletop.

Ávgos didn't bother to translate. Staring at the little snake, he felt strangely thrilled as he looked at its glittering red eyes. He'd had the same feeling when they'd first met Queen Kuu yesterday and she'd looked at him with her unearthly silver eyes.

"Dream is no ordinary snake," Queen Kuu said. "He is the World Serpent. He will not harm you, Lyylia."

Dream slithered across the table towards them, causing Lyylia to shrink closer against Shaun. Then it raised up, lifting its tiny head as if studying them. Ávgos stayed motionless while Dream stared at him, flicked its tongue, then stared at Lyylia and Shaun in turn.

Kuu laid her hand palm up on the table, and Dream slithered into her hand. "Dream senses great power on all three of you," she said softly. "There is much to be learned from Kalevala and its people." She lifted her hand to be eye level with the little snake, and stared at it in silence for a moment. Then the snake coiled itself up her wrist, and suddenly looked like nothing more than a brightly enameled metal bracelet.

Ávgos let out a quiet breath he didn't realize he'd been holding. Looking across the table at the row of Menninkäinen, he saw their expressions showed awe and reverence, but not surprise. They'd probably all seen Dream before.

Kuu picked up her fork and resumed eating. After a moment, Ávgos picked up his half-eaten sausage pastry. Beside him, Lyylia released herself from Shaun's protective arm and went back to eating, as well.

"In a different matter," the Queen said into the silence, "I'm afraid that I must leave you for a short time. I received word early this morning that the shaman of a nearby village just died. I will return before the evening meal. Please make yourselves comfortable in my castle, and ask any of the workers here should you need anything."

"Thank you, Your Highness," Shaun said.

"Your Majesty, which shaman has died?" Boots asked. "Perhaps it is someone we know."

"Shaman Talon," Queen Kuu replied, looking at him. "Did you know him?"

Ávgos glanced at Lyylia and Shaun, and then at the Menninkäinen. Wasn't that the name of the village leader they'd met yesterday?

"We do know him," Boots said, confirming Ávgos' memory. "We passed through his village yesterday on our way here."

"He seemed in good health yesterday," said Eider. "We ate with his family."

"I am sorry," Kuu said sadly. "His death was a tragic accident. His daughter Rowan told me that he was found caught in the ice of the stream."

"The stream with the broken bridge?" Lyylia asked in English, saving Ávgos from having to translate for Shaun.

Kuu looked at Lyylia. "Yes. Rowan said that her father must have fallen into the stream when the bridge broke. But how did you know that?"

"We saw the broken bridge yesterday," Lyylia said.

The Queen's beautiful face slid into a puzzled frown as she kept her eyes on Lyylia. "How could that be?"

"Your Highness, may I come with you?" Lyylia asked. "Maybe I can help figure how he died."

Kuu regarded Lyylia in silence for a moment, and then nodded. "I should be glad of your company for the journey. My sledge will be leaving soon from the stable courtyard. I will send Stone to bring you."

Lyylia bowed her head. "Thank you, Your Highness."

"And now, I must prepare myself for the journey." Kuu pushed her chair back from the table and stood. "Please, eat as much as you wish," she then said, addressing everyone at the table. "And ask if you have need of anything today. I will see you this evening. Come, Child of Light."

The white dog had been sitting beside Kuu's chair, and she hopped up and followed the Queen out of the room.

"Why are you going back to the village?" Shaun asked Lyylia as soon as Queen Kuu had left. "Shouldn't we all stay together?"

"She will be perfectly safe," Boots put in. "She'll be with the Queen."

Shaun glanced at him. "I know, but..."

"You think Shaman Talon was murdered, don't you?" Ávgos said, looking at Lyylia.

"Murdered?" Shaun echoed. The Menninkäinen all looked confused and horrified, and Ávgos wished he hadn't spoken so bluntly.

Lyylia looked at Ávgos. "Yes, I do," she said, just as bluntly. "Strange travelers, a broken bridge, now a dead shaman. I don't think they are...what's the English word...*sattuma*."

"Coincidence," Ávgos provided, wishing that he didn't agree with her assessment.

"But if you're thinking that someone is after us, why kill Shaman Talon?" Shaun asked.

"I don't know," Lyylia said. "That is why I'm going with Queen Kuu to the village."

"How could Shaman Talon have been killed on purpose?" Boots asked. "Could he have been killed by a wolf or a bear?"

"I don't know," Lyylia said again, her tone softer this time as she looked at Boots and the others. "But I will find out."

The castle guard named Stone appeared in the doorway. "Lyylia?" he said, giving a small bow. "The Queen requests that you join her in the courtyard. I took the liberty of having your outer clothing taken from your room and delivered to the Queen's sledge."

Lyylia rose from the table. "Thank you." She looked back at Ávgos and Shaun. "I'll be fine. And I will find answers." She stepped over the bench and followed Stone out of the room.

After watching her leave, Shaun turned back around on the bench and looked at Ávgos. "I'm sure she'll be fine, and I'm sure she'll find some answers," he said quietly. "I just worry about what those answers might be."

Ávgos nodded solemnly in agreement. He couldn't imagine why someone would be hunting them, or killing anyone, and yet...

He wished more than anything that he could go back home.

The journey from the castle to Shaman Talon's village was much more pleasant than the trek going the other direction the day before. Lyylia sat beside Queen Kuu on the small padded bench in her sledge—a lightweight wood and canvas sleigh pulled by one horse, with the driver on a perch at the back. The canvas roof curved down in front all the way to the floor, providing a nice windscreen. A chilly breeze flowed through the open sides, but it was still better than trudging through deep snow on foot. The horse and driver seemed comfortable even on the steep winding hills, and they sped along at a trotting pace. Barely an hour after leaving the castle, they arrived at the broken bridge.

They came to a stop at the edge of the frozen creek. Peering out the right side of the sledge, Lyylia saw the two ends of the wooden bridge jutting out from each bank, and a Menninkäinen holding a spear standing on the far bank.

"Greetings, Your Majesty!" he called, waving his spear like a signal. "It is safe to cross here! The ice is thick and the snow deep!" He gestured with his spear at the creek.

Kuu leaned her head out the left side of the sledge. "Drive on, Stone!"

Lyylia scanned the area as well as she could as they went past. If there had been any footprints or other evidence left after Talon died, it was long gone; far too many boots had trampled the entire area.

A large group of Menninkäinen were gathered as they pulled into the village. Queen Kuu climbed out of the sledge. The dog Child of Light, who had been sleeping at their feet during the journey and keeping Lyylia's toes nice and warm, hopped out behind her mistress. Lyylia slid out the other side.

"Welcome to our village, Your Majesty," said a young woman, as she and all the assembled Menninkäinen bowed deeply. "I am Rowan, Talon's daughter." Her pretty face was puffy and red as if she'd been crying, but she wore a solemn expression as she bowed for the Queen.

"Dear Rowan." Kuu held out her hands to the little woman. "I am sorry for such a time of sorrow. Your father was a strong shaman and a kind leader. He will be missed. I have brought Lyylia with me—one of the Kalevalans who enjoyed your father's hospitality yesterday."

"I'm very sorry for your loss," Lyylia said.

"Thank you," said Rowan, giving Lyylia a slight bow. "And we are honored to have you in our village once again."

"Where is Talon's body now?" Kuu asked.

"He is being prepared for burial. We all appreciate that you have come for the burial ceremony, Your Grace." Rowan led the way down the snowy path to the shaman's hut.

Talon's body was laid out on the table, wearing the standard Menninkäinen attire of brown tunic and breeches. Several men were in the process of wrapping him up in a large brightly-colored blanket. Lyylia wished she could examine the body, but it would be rude at best to interfere with their traditional burial practices. She had to tread carefully with her investigation.

The Menninkäinen around the table paused in their wrapping to let Kuu lay her hands on the body. After a somber moment, she stepped back and nodded for them to continue. Lyylia scanned the body as quickly as she could from her vantage point before the wrapping resumed. If Talon had been injured, he'd been cleaned up.

"We have finished preparing the gravestone, My Queen," said a Menninkäinen, coming into the hut. "We would appreciate your blessing upon it."

"Of course." Kuu followed him outside.

Lyylia stayed in the hut. The Queen had not asked her to stay by her side, and none of the men wrapping the body said anything about her presence.

"I'm very sorry for your loss," she said after a moment, to the men working. "My friends and I met Shaman Talon yesterday, and he was a gracious host. How did he die?"

"He was frozen in the stream," one of them said, glancing up at her. "His wife and daughter saw that he was missing when they woke this morning, and so all the hunters of the village began a search for him. We found him trapped in the ice of the stream."

"Was he injured?"

"No."

Lyylia paused and tried to think of a tactful way to continue the questioning. If she were on a normal case, the victim's friends and relatives would be expecting to answer detailed questions, if not eager to. But Lyylia was beginning to realize that these Menninkäinen were more than just friendly, peace-loving people—they really had no concept of crime.

Except she was quite sure that a crime had been committed here.

She pursed her lips and scanned the hut, hoping for clues. She spotted Talon's fur robe hanging on a peg on the mantel over the fire. All of the shamans seemed to wear a long ceremonial fur robe, different from the normal fur coats of the rest of the Menninkäinen. The robes were covered with beads and other small objects, sewn on like tassels. She went over to the fireplace. The robe was wet.

"Was Shaman Talon wearing this when he was found?" she asked.

One of the men glanced over his shoulder at the robe. "Yes. It belongs to his daughter now—Shaman Rowan. Ordinarily she would wear it for the burial ceremony, but it's still wet."

Lyylia fingered the little baubles hanging from the robe. An oval-shaped clear glass bead, a vertebrae bone from some animal, a smooth black stone carved with the image of a snake and a crescent moon, a tiny clay whistle in the shape of a bird, a small uneven lump of silver.

One of the threads hung empty. She was no expert on primitive natural fibers, but the broken thread wasn't frayed at all—it looked like it had been cut rather than broken or ripped, and cut very recently. She examined the rest of the robe, and found another bauble-less string, similarly cut.

"What are the objects on this robe used for?" she asked.

"Magic. Only the shamans can use them."

Lyylia wanted to ask more questions, but if only the shamans used the items, then Rowan, who apparently inherited her father's role as village shaman, would be the one to ask. As she examined the cut threads and tried to figure out how she could tactfully question Rowan, a Menninkäinen came to the hut's open door.

"Feather and Rowan are ready for the ceremony," he announced.

"As are we," said one of the men at the table.

They began to haul Talon's wrapped body off the table. Lyylia followed the other Menninkäinen outside, and headed for the crowd that had gathered a short distance away.

The cemetery was a small space crowded with brush, set back under the trees off the main pathway. Grave markers carved with strange angular symbols were scattered around, many of them half-hidden in the snowy brambles. Lyylia wondered if the Menninkäinen placed little importance on the burial site once the funeral was over, or they just didn't die very often.

Lyylia stood at the back of the crowd. Looking over the Menninkäinen's heads, she could see Kuu, Feather, and Rowan standing together at the edge of the cemetery. The softly murmuring crowd hushed.

"Today we mourn the passing of Shaman Talon," Queen Kuu began, her voice carrying easily across the crowd. She had removed her coat, and looked appropriately regal in her long white gown and the silver circlet on her head. "He served his village well. His body will rest in the earth of our beloved Pohjola, but his spirit now dwells in Manala, the land of the honored dead. There he now dwells under the protection of Jambe-Akka and Kontio, and lives with all of the children of Pohjola who have gone on before him."

Manala, thought Lyylia. Another name for Tuonela, the land of the dead in the tales from *The Kalevala*. More strange parallels.

The crowd silently parted as the men carrying Talon's body approached. As they walked slowly with their bundle hefted onto their shoulders, Queen Kuu held up a small frame drum, and began to beat on the drum with her hand in slow, even beats. Feather picked up an instrument—a blunt triangle of wood, five straight strings on pegs, no bridge, no bow. A kantele, a traditional Finnish folk instrument. Feather disappeared out of Lyylia's range of vision as she sat down, either on a log or the ground, and began to pluck a simple tune, keeping time with Kuu's drum beats.

The clear, straight tones were unmistakable. Lyylia hadn't heard the instrument since her school days; every Finnish child learned to play the kantele, and while she'd enjoyed it at the time, playing music wasn't a hobby she'd pursued as an adult. But now here she was, in this strange fantastical place, hearing a tune like an old folk lament, in the bell-like tones of a kantele.

The gateway under the lake. If Kuu believed that the reindeer of Pohjola had found the gateway and gone to earth, then they might have heard the stories and music of ancient

Finland, and brought them back to Pohjola. Or vice versa. Could the ancestors of the Finns and the Sami have found the gateway and come here?

The kantele and drum music went on for some time as the men laid Talon in a shallow grave. After covering him with a thin layer of dirt, they then used large stones from a wagon sitting nearby. Soon the colored blanket disappeared beneath the pile of stones. Lyylia wondered if all Menninkäinen graves were done this way, or if the dead were buried more deeply in the summer when the ground wasn't frozen. It was hard to tell exactly how the rest of the cemetery looked, beneath the brambles and snow.

When the grave was fully covered in stones, a man stepped forward, holding a large flute as long as his arm. He joined Kuu and Feather's instruments—the flute made a droning, two-tone sound as he moved his outstretched hand across the end of the pipe. Then Queen Kuu began to sing.

Her voice was strong and clear, not very high-pitched but not deep, either. Lyylia stared at Kuu, mesmerized, as the rest of the snowy forest all around seemed to fade away.

The long-flute wails, beat on the drum
The song is gone and day is done.
Silence of fish, silence of birds
Stillness walks the forest paths
The long-flute wails, beat on the drum
The song is gone and day is done.
My child weeps in the forest alone
Clouds and snow are my only light
The long-flute wails, beat on the drum
The song is gone and day is done.
Bring milk and furs and lanterns bright
Gather together to mourn those gone

The long-flute wails, beat on the drum
The song is gone and day is done.
The boat carries me far away
Past the mountains and through the Mist
The long-flute wails, beat on the drum
The song is gone and day is done.

Lyylia started, feeling oddly disoriented, as she suddenly realized that the music had stopped. She wanted to cry at the mournful words of the song, but she felt strangely peaceful, as well. Glancing around, she saw the rest of the crowd all silent, many with their heads bowed.

Queen Kuu lowered her drum and spoke.

"Shaman Rowan, daughter of Talon, you now bear the responsibilities of leading your village, protecting your people, and following the wisdom of Dream." Kuu laid her hand on the top of Rowan's head. "May you live long and well."

She began to strike her drum again, this time a faster beat. Feather joined in with a lively tune on the kantele. When the song ended, the crowd began to disperse. Apparently the ceremony was over.

Many people stayed close to talk to Rowan and Feather and Kuu, so Lyylia hung back to wait her turn.

Eventually the crowd of well-wishers dwindled, and Rowan and Kuu went back into the hut. Lyylia approached Feather before she could leave.

"Feather, I want to thank you again for your family's generosity yesterday when we passed through your village. I'm glad that I got a chance to meet your husband, and I'm so sorry for your loss."

"Thank you," said Feather with a teary smile.

"I heard that he died in the stream. When did you realize that he was missing?"

"When Rowan and I awoke this morning, he was gone. We began searching for him, and some men eventually found him in the stream. I have no idea why he would have gone away from the village, especially so early, nor why he would have been crossing the stream."

Lyylia decided not to mention that the bridge had been broken before Talon died. Apparently no one from the village had used that route recently enough to see the damage.

"I noticed that two objects are missing from his cloak," Lyylia then said. "Did Talon use them recently, like for a magic spell?" She never thought she'd be doing a murder investigation involving magic.

Feather looked up at her in surprise. "He hasn't used any of the talismans in many seasons. They must have fallen off when he fell into the stream." She sniffed and hugged the kantele to her chest.

"I'm sorry, Feather—I was just hoping I could help find a reason why he died." She gave the little woman a sympathetic smile.

Feather nodded. "Please excuse me," she said, giving Lyylia a small bow, and then headed for the hut.

Lyylia looked down at the fresh mound of rocks on the grave. The headstone was a rough, flat stone barely twenty centimeters tall, with angular rune-like markings scratched around the edge, like a frame. Kuu had laid her small drum on the grave, and Lyylia bent over to more closely examine the marks. Some of the markings on the gravestone were the same as on the drum skin. So far, it was the only evidence of writing she'd seen here. On the wooden sides of the drum was carved the same snake-and-moon motif that adorned the walls of the castle corridors.

As Lyylia straightened up, she saw Queen Kuu standing a

few meters away, looking at her. Child of Light sat at her feet.

"Your Majesty. I, um, I was just admiring your drum."

Kuu walked over to her; the dog followed, and sat down a few paces away. "This drum has sung at many funerals," Kuu said, bending down to pick up her drum. "But also at many weddings and naming ceremonies. It has performed much magic."

She rubbed her right hand thoughtfully across the frame of the drum as she looked down at Talon's grave. Lyylia glimpsed a flash of the blue bracelet on Kuu's wrist beneath the white cuff of her sleeve. The blue bracelet that was also a magic snake. Lyylia clenched her jaw and resisted the urge to step back. She'd managed not to think about the snake on the ride to the village; Kuu had been wearing a fur coat and thick mittens, making it easier to ignore what was on her wrist.

"You have been asking many questions of the villagers today," Kuu said, looking up from the grave and into Lyylia's face.

Lyylia swallowed and met Kuu's gaze, unnerving as it was to look directly into her eyes. Kuu didn't sound upset or accusatory, so Lyylia hoped that meant that she wasn't in too much trouble.

"Yes, Your Highness. I just wanted to learn more about the circumstances surrounding Shaman Talon's death. I apologize if I was rude or behaved improperly."

Kuu gave a slight smile. "You have not been rude. I understand that our ways must be strange for you. I'm sure life in Kalevala is very different."

Lyylia almost chuckled. "Yes, Your Highness—life in Kalevala is very different. I just...that is, I don't like it when there's an unexplained death."

"Nor do I," Kuu said with a look of sympathy. Her eyes

glittered. "You believe that Talon's death was not an accident."

Lyylia exhaled slowly. She hadn't talked about Talon's death, or anything related, during the sledge ride, so it was a relief to know that the Queen had similar suspicions.

"No, I don't believe his death was an accident. First of all, the bridge was already broken when we came to it yesterday, so Talon couldn't have fallen into the stream from a bridge breaking beneath him." Quickly she told about the two strange travelers they'd met two days ago, furtive and silent and poorly dressed for outdoor weather, who had also passed through Talon's village just ahead of them.

Queen Kuu listened intently, a thoughtful frown on her face. "Menninkäinen would not destroy another village's property," she said at last. "Nor steal magical taslimans from a shaman's robe. And Menninkäinen would certainly not kill another Menninkäinen."

Lyylia doubted that, but she didn't say so. "I don't have any explanations, Your Highness. Or even any good theories yet. But I think we need to be careful."

"Yes. There is a strangeness about, and we must exercise wisdom and caution. Thank you for telling me this, Lyylia." Kuu smiled. "You have a keen mind and a sharp eye."

"Thank you." Too bad her keen mind and sharp eye had gotten her "promoted" away from Helsinki to Kokkola, and then to Inari on this reindeer case. She pushed those thoughts away. She needed to focus on the mystery here if she was ever going to get them back to Finland. She was pretty sure they'd been in Pohjola for over a week now, even though it felt like forever. "I hope I can continue to be a help, Your Highness."

"I'm sure you will." Kuu smiled again. "And Lyylia, you may call me Kuu, if you wish. It is the name given to me by the Creator at the beginning of time. It is the Menninkäinen who created the titles and formality."

Lyylia blinked in surprise. "Um, yes, Your Highness. I mean...Kuu. Thank you."

Kuu laughed lightly. "Come, there is plenty of time for further discussion on our journey back to my castle. But for now, Feather and Shaman Rowan have invited us to dine with them for the midday meal. Let us enjoy their hospitality and remember the life of Talon."

"Yes, of course." Lyylia hoped that Shaun and Ávgos were doing all right by themselves back at the castle. She now felt confident that they would at least be safe there. After glancing back at the grave once more, she fell into step beside Kuu and they walked back to the shaman's hut.

After Lyylia and Stone had left the dining chamber, Ávgos wanted to check on his reindeer, so he asked Gray to show them to the stables. Shaun, Boots, and Eider came along. Flint and Fir asked for an escort to find their way back to their rooms to rest. On the way through the castle, Shaun asked to see the Halls of Time again.

The intense blue-white light coming in the windows brought the colorful murals to vivid life. As the five of them walked slowly down the hall, Ávgos remembered Kuu's chilling story from the night before about the battle with Ice-Dark. He paused at the painting of the battle on the frozen lake, with the strange fire-breathing horse and the dragon-headed snake.

"There's room for many more pictures," Eider said, pointing at the blank wall that extended to the end of the hall.

"The arrival of the Kalevalans will surely become the next picture," said Gray. "Every future generation will come to the Halls of Time to see your story."

"I've never had a painting done of myself," Ávgos said. It would be interesting to be immortalized in the Pohjola history books, as it were. He wished he could tell Sirkka about it.

"Hey, check it out!" Shaun said. He'd moved on down to the end of the corridor, which dead-ended at a wall adorned with a large brown bear pelt, complete with head and paws. "It's a map! And a star chart!"

Ávgos and the others joined him at the end of the hall. One wall panel was painted black, with white stars dotted across it, and lines painted connecting some of the dots into constellations. It was disconcerting how many of the constellations were the same ones that Ávgos saw at home every winter.

"All the stars always circle around the central axis of Pohjantähti," Shaun said, touching the large blue circle in the center. "So there are no seasonal changes in the sky at all? Does the sky always look like this?"

"Yes," said Boots. "At midwinter, Talvitähti rises for ten days, and at midsummer, Kesällätähti." He pointed at two stars at the top and bottom of the painting, respectively.

"So how does that work if none of the other stars rise or set?"

Boots stared up at him. "Those are the seasons, and the motion of the stars."

Shaun sighed and rubbed at his hair. "Nothing here makes sense. The aurora has all the same properties as on Earth, but it's like everything is amplified—the aurora is bigger, brighter, louder, stronger. Aurora is caused by charged particles from the sun hitting the magnetosphere of the planet, but here there's no sun, just that giant version of the north star. It looks too small and far away to send an effective solar wind."

"You say nothing in Pohjola makes sense," Boots remarked, "but what you just said makes no sense, either."

Ávgos had to laugh at that.

Shaun laughed, too, and shook his head. "It's the scientist in me, Boots. I'm a nerd, which makes no sense to most people."

Beside the constellation picture was a map of Pohjola. A mountain range painted in brown ran down the entire length of the right side of the mural. What looked like brown hills or low mountains framed the left side of the picture. The center was a field of green, crisscrossed with blue rivers and small lakes.

"Are we here?" Ávgos asked, pointing up at a small, gray square image, placed in the mountain range near the top of the picture.

"Yes," said Gray. "That is the Queen's castle, and the Mountains of the Moon." He pointed to the left side. "Here are the Western Fells. And the Dark River and the Dark Water Lake that separates us from Ice-Dark." The blue border across the top of the map.

"This is Dancing Ground Island," Gray continued, pointing to a brown circle dead-center of the map. Two large blue rivers converged on it. "It sits at the joining of the Great Eastern and Great Western Rivers. And at the south, the Fenland Sea." A swath of blue, wider than the blue river at the top, was at the bottom of the map. A line of white lay just below it. "And beyond that, the Endless Ice. These are the borders of Pohjola."

Ávgos assumed that the map wasn't to scale. Even so, Pohjola looked like a very large place. What if his reindeer had scattered all across the country? That might make it just as hard to track them all down as if they were all in the mysterious land of Ice-Dark.

"So what's beyond Pohjola?" asked Shaun.

Boots pointed to the top of the picture. "Ice-Dark."

"No, what's beyond it to the east, the south, and the west? What's on the other side of the Mountains of the Moon? What's past the Endless Ice?"

"Nothing," said Boots. "It's endless."

Shaun laughed. "Okay, yeah. But I mean what's outside of Pohjola? Has anyone ever crossed this mountain range? What about the Western Fells? What's beyond it?"

"No one crosses the mountains to the other side," Gray said. "It is the edge of the world, and beyond it is the Mist."

"What's the Mist?" asked Ávgos.

"That which is beyond the edge of the world."

Shaun gave a frustrated-sounding sigh.

"Maybe we'd better ask Queen Kuu these questions, Shaun," Ávgos said.

"Yeah."

Shaun pulled out his phone and took pictures of the map and the star chart. Ávgos felt briefly jealous, absurd as that was. Shaun's aurora-powered computer battery could keep his phone charged, but it's not like he could call home. Ávgos wondered if anyone had found his phone that he'd dropped on the shore of Lake Inari.

"What are you doing?" Gray asked.

"Taking pictures. I'm capturing a small image of these pictures." Shaun turned his phone around and showed the screen to the three Menninkäinen.

"Incredible!" gasped Boots, while Eider and Gray simply stared.

"If we get back home, no one will believe us, even with photos," Ávgos said.

"Probably not. But I still want pictures for myself. I've taken a few pictures since we've been here." Shaun turned his phone back around again. "Here, I'll take a picture of you guys. Smile!"

Boots obediently grinned, but Eider and Gray just looked confused. Shaun tapped his phone, and then laughed.

"Great picture, guys! See?"

Ávgos looked over Shaun's shoulder, and smiled at the picture of an idiotically-grinning Boots and a vaguely stoned-looking Eider and Gray. Shaun showed the phone to the Menninkäinen.

"How…? That is incredible!" Boots exclaimed, staring at the phone. "This magic thing can make an image of anything?"

"Pretty much. It'll do a lot of cool things. Except make a phone call. The signal in Pohjola really stinks."

Ávgos chuckled, and the three Menninkäinen just looked befuddled.

Shaun took a few more pictures of the paintings, and then Gray led them back down the corridor and towards the stables. As they walked across the expansive courtyard and Ávgos was starting to wish he'd brought his coat, a Menninkäinen came hurrying out of the stables towards them.

"Gray!" he called. "I was sent to find you! Ah, and the Kalevalans—good!"

"What is it?" asked Gray as they met in the center of the courtyard.

"You must use a moon mirror to contact the Queen," he said. "I know that she will return by tonight, but I think she should know what has happened. A Gentle Beast has just been brought to us, along with a Menninkäinen who is very ill."

"I have learned some healing magic," said Gray as they all headed for the stable. "Perhaps I can help him. And I can call the Queen and tell her of this."

Inside the low stone building, the smell of hay and the soft whicker of horses greeted them. They walked to the far end of the row of stalls, where the reindeer were kept. Two Menninkäinen stood outside one of the stalls; they were dressed in thick furs with packs on their backs, their boots caked with snow.

"We saw this Gentle Beast yesterday morning, wandering across the tundra," one of them said. "He was headed eastwards towards the mountains, so we followed and soon caught up to him. When we did so, we discovered that a Menninkäinen was traveling with him. He was weak from exposure, and so we traveled through the night to bring them both to the castle as quickly as possible."

In the stall, a reindeer was calmly eating hay. Beside him knelt a Menninkäinen, wearing a tattered leather tunic and breeches that looked far too big for him. He was barefoot. He was also eating hay.

"He hasn't spoken at all. And he refused all food we offered, even though he had no provisions with him. He had no winter clothing and no pack of supplies, only an empty water skin." The man held up the leather pouch as proof.

Ávgos went into the stall, Gray right behind him. Murmuring gently to the reindeer, Ávgos checked its left ear—three notches.

"My earmark," he said, looking over at Shaun.

The Menninkäinen in the stall shied away from Gray's approach, and then suddenly dipped his head down and touched his forehead to Ávgos' hand. As he did, his shaggy brown hair parted and showed his ear. His left ear, and cut into the top of his ear were three very distinct looking marks.

Ávgos felt a strange chill sweep over him. *Impossible.* "It can't be…" he murmured.

"What?" Shaun said.

"Gray," Ávgos said slowly, still looking at the Menninkäinen in the stall. "Or any of you. Is there some kind of magic here that can…can make something change its shape, or its skin?" He couldn't believe he was even asking such a question, but the little man made an oddly reindeer-sounding snort and gathered another mouthful of hay. "A magic…spell, or whatever, that could, for example, make an animal look like a person?"

"We do not know," said one of the travelers.

"The Queen would be powerful enough to do magic like that," said Gray.

Ávgos looked at him. "Could Hiisi-Hiisi?"

All the Menninkäinen shuddered at the name. "Only Queen Kuu would know such a thing," Gray said after a pause.

"Ávgos, what are you getting at?" Shaun asked.

Ávgos bent down and put his hand on the head of the Menninkäinen in the stall, smoothing his hair back from his ear. "He won't speak, he won't leave the reindeer's side, and he's eating animal fodder. And his left ear is marked with my earmark."

"You're kidding." Shaun leaned over the stall gate to get a closer look at the man's ear. "Oh my God. You think…you think this guy is actually a reindeer?"

"I know it's insane, it makes no sense, it's not even possible," said Ávgos. Totally impossible, and yet both the evidence and his gut were telling him it was true.

"So you're saying," Shaun said, staring down into the stall, "that the hiisi abducted your reindeer, and somehow…put a spell on them or something. Which would mean that there could be reindeer all over Pohjola now. And they all look like Menninkäinen."

"I don't know if that's what I'm saying," Ávgos said, his throat tight.

"Reindeer transformed into Menninkäinen. The impossibility of that even happening aside, *why* would anyone do that?"

Ávgos shook his head. "I have no idea. But whatever the reason, it can't be good."

The Menninkäinen all exchanged dumbfounded looks. Ávgos felt just as dumbfounded, and he looked over at Shaun.

"I hope Lyylia is getting her detective skills nice and sharpened on her murder investigation," Shaun murmured. "Because we're going to need every bit of brain power available to figure this one out." He shook his head. "I can't believe this is happening."

"Neither can I," said Ávgos. "And yet, it is."

Missing reindeer, magic spells, a broken bridge, a murdered shaman. It made no sense, but he was now sure they were all connected somehow.

The reindeer and the Menninkäinen continued to eat their hay.

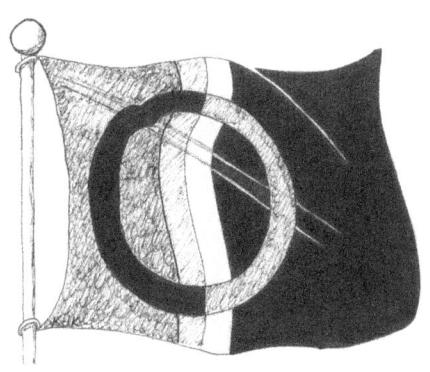

CHAPTER 4: SÁPMI

Detective Jassu Toivonen was not having a good day. Three people missing from Inari village—in addition to that herd of reindeer—and still nothing to go on. He was still waiting on the results of the traces of blood they'd found on the hilltop with Detective Niiranen's discharged bullets. The underwater scanning equipment he was trying to get sent up from Oulu was held up by bureaucratic red tape. Ten men and two snowmobiles were supposed to have arrived that morning to begin a manual search of the perimeter of Lake Inari, but they'd hit a delay and still weren't here.

An American federal agent was also due to arrive this afternoon. Bad enough that three people had been kidnapped— but since one of them was the American scientist, this had now escalated into an international incident. Bierža Syrjälä was still in Rovaniemi, trailing Ávgos' cousin Maden Lahti, but hadn't gotten any new information.

Two National Bureau of Investigation agents from Helsinki had arrived early that morning, and they had ordered a halt on all traffic to and from Inari to make sure no one left the village during the investigation. However, this order also included all the reindeer herders, and so now they had a town of angry

Sami on their hands. At least Kokkola Police Chief Sjöberg had taken it upon himself to do the unenviable task of calling Mrs. Niiranen to tell her that her daughter had gone missing in the line of duty.

And it had started snowing.

Jassu's phone rang—it was the Kokkola office. He stepped out of the bustling hotel lobby and went out into the cold. "Toivonen."

"We got the blood work back from the lab, Detective," said the voice of the forensic officer. "I just emailed you the results, but I thought you'd like to hear it, too. The blood belongs to Detective Niiranen."

"Damn."

"I'm sorry, sir."

"Thanks for the call." Jassu put his phone back in his pocket, then spotted two members of the science group walking down the road towards him.

"Detective Toivonen!" one of the men called to him. "Elias Viiri," he introduced himself as they approached. He was the local Sami guide and translator for the science team.

The other man didn't bother with an introduction or a handshake, and launched into a very huffy-sounding rant in English.

"Mr. Paul Banks would like to know why they are being prevented from leaving the village," Elias translated. "They need to keep up with their work daily—their research is very time-sensitive."

"I'm sorry, Mr. Banks," Jassu said, looking at the man. "But we believe it's safer for everyone if no one leaves the village. We don't want more people disappearing while we conduct our investigation."

After Elias translated, Paul ranted again in English, giving

Jassu his best glower as he talked. Jassu coolly met his gaze.

"All of their equipment is outside the village, he wants to remind you," Elias said. "What if the thieves come to take that, too? They will submit to an escort or a guard, but they need to be allowed to leave Inari village."

"I understand," said Jassu. "I'll take it up with Agent Pelkonen. He's the Bureau officer in charge of the lockdown."

As Elias translated, a small truck, outfitted for winter with snow tires, pulled up under the shelter of the bus depot.

Paul made a sarcastic-sounding comment.

"He was under the impression that no one was allowed to enter the village, either."

"That's probably the American agent, here to help us find your missing teammate," Jassu replied calmly. "I think his flight was delayed getting into Ivalo. I'll speak to Agent Pelkonen about your request. Please excuse me, Mr. Banks. Mr. Viiri."

He left them standing there, the British man ranting again, and headed over to the truck. A young Sami officer bounced out of the driver's side, and introduced himself to Jassu. "Asko Puolitaival, Rovaniemi police," he said briskly, offering his gloved hand to Jassu. "So sorry to keep you waiting."

"Not a problem, Officer Puolitaival," Jassu said.

A bald and very unhappy-looking man climbed out of the passenger side of the truck.

"Jassu Toivonen," said Jassu, extending his hand towards the man. "Welcome to Inari."

"Darrell Chaney," the man replied in a growly voice, shaking his hand, and then said something in English.

"He says he dislikes snow, but is happy to have finally arrived safely," young Puolitaival translated.

"I'm glad you speak English," Jassu said to him. "My translator is the one who got kidnapped. Well, tell him I hate snow, too, but it's October in Lapland. Let's get inside out of the cold."

Puolitaival chattered at the man while Jassu led the way back inside Hotel Inari. He got the American officer checked into a room and had someone go out to the truck to get his luggage, then led them to a table in a semi-secluded corner of the hotel restaurant.

"Okay, I guess this will take a while, but let's get you up to speed on the situation," said Jassu. "I'm sorry, I've forgotten how to pronounce your name…" He looked at Puolitaival.

"Chaney," the man replied gruffly, after the translation.

"Tsei-nee," Jassu attempted to repeat the name. "Okay, so here's what we've got…"

For the rest of the morning Jassu and Chaney laboriously conversed, with the aid of the patient Puolitaival. After Jassu had shared everything he knew, and Chaney had determined his next step was to speak to the remaining scientists, one of the Sami hotel employees came up to them.

"Excuse me, is one of you Detective Toivonen?"

Jassu looked up at her. "Yes, ma'am, that's me."

"A fax just arrived for you, from the Helsinki police department. I've got it at the front desk."

"Thank you." Jassu looked back at the other two men. "Puolitaival, if you wouldn't mind taking officer *Tsei-nee* over to the other hotel and hook him up with the scientists—I need to take care of this."

"Of course, sir," said the younger man, and then spoke to Chaney.

Jassu followed the Sami woman. Behind the check-in desk she pulled several pages off the fax machine and handed them to him.

"Thank you." It was the phone logs for all three of the

missing individuals. Again, something that had taken longer than it should have to get, but better late than never. He went over to a table to sit down and read through it.

Shaun Abernathy's phone had stopped sending a signal at 22:09 on October first, the night before last. The GPS coordinates were listed. Jassu pulled out his phone and did a GPS coordinate and visual map overlay. The last known location of his phone was somewhere out in the depths of Lake Inari.

Jassu swore to himself and looked at the other two records. Lyylia's phone had stopped broadcasting at 22:08, last known location somewhere in the lake between the shoreline and the spot where Shaun's phone had stopped.

And Ávgos Heikkilä's phone was still broadcasting, near the southwest coast of the lake, barely two kilometers from Inari village.

Jassu zoomed in on the map on his screen. Lyylia had told him about going with Shaun to see the equipment that he had set up near the lake not far from the village—the very same equipment that was now missing. There was the hill where Shaun had apparently been with his aurora-scanning device, and for some reason Lyylia had been there, as well. Presumably they were attacked, and she—or someone—fired two shots, and she was injured. Then they were taken down the hill towards the lake, where Ávgos—who had either been with them the entire time, or encountered them on the shore—dropped his phone, either accidentally or on purpose. And then they went into the water.

"Damn it, Lyylia, why do you always have to be right?" he muttered to himself, frustration welling up. First the dead reindeer, now this. The evidence said that the reindeer herd had been driven into the lake. And then the thieves—identity and motive still unknown—had done the same with three people.

Since Shaun's phone had stayed active almost a full minute beyond Lyylia's, Jassu checked the coordinates again, then looked at the surrounding area on the map on his phone. The only islands in the vicinity looked to be nothing but little brush-covered skerries the size of a car. The area was nearly a kilometer away from the region that they had explored with the boat.

Jassu looked back at the fax pages to see the last recorded communication to or from each phone, hoping for more clues. Shaun's last communication had been a text message to Sergei Krechin, one of his co-workers, at 21:22. Jassu read the Finnish translation printed beside the English transcription of the text. *Doing my rounds a little early tonight. I'm starting with site number 1. Later, dude.*

Lyylia's last communication had been a call to her sister, Teija Niiranen, at 21:10 that night. And Ávgos' last communication had been a phone call to his cousin Mađen. Mađen Lahti, their one and only suspect so far, who had fled to Rovaniemi and no one would say why. Ávgos' call to Mađen had been at 20:49 that night, and had lasted six minutes. He wished it had been a text-message conversation so he could see what they'd talked about.

Jassu got up from the table. Now that they had an area pinpointed—something a little more specific than the entire eighty-kilometer-long lake, plus surroundings—he could finally take some action. He could take a boat out to the last known coordinates of the phones, and Agent Pelkonen could send an officer along the shore to find Ávgos' phone. Assuming he could find Agent Pelkonen.

He went outside again, wondering where the two Bureau officers were. Pelkonen had told him that morning that they were going to be making rounds throughout the village, questioning residents. The village streets were just as busy as always. A car went past, towing a snowmobile behind it. Three children and a dog romped in the yard of a house across the street. A man came out of the pharmacy, a large bag in his arms. At the end of the street, a woman rounded the corner, leading two reindeer.

Jassu tucked the phone log papers inside his coat to keep the snow off. He brought up Pelkonen's number on his phone and hit the call button. Maybe now they could find some more answers.

Teija Niiranen hung up her phone and leaned against the wall of the office break room, feeling sick. This could not be happening.

"Hey, Teija."

Jumping at the sound of her name, Teija turned to see her friend and co-worker Johanna headed for the coffeepot.

"I hadn't seen you yet this morning," Johanna said conversationally, "so I was going to ask if you..." She frowned and came over to Teija. "Hey, are you okay?"

"My mom just called," Teija said dully.

"What happened? Is your mom okay?"

"She's fine—as fine as she could be right now." Teija swallowed the lump in her throat. "Johanna, my sister's disappeared."

"Disappeared? What do you mean? Oh my God, that's right, your sister's a police officer. Do you know what happened?"

"She was in Lapland, working on a case," said Teija, fighting back tears. Surely this was a bad dream. "My mom just got the call. Lyylia disappeared night before last. No suspects, no evidence. Two other people disappeared, too." She fingered the thin gold heart charm on its chain around her neck. No wonder Lyylia hadn't replied to the text she'd sent her yesterday.

"Oh my God, I'm so sorry." Johanna set down her coffee mug and put a comforting hand on Teija's arm. "That's awful. Lapland? I thought you said she lives in Kokkola."

"She'd gotten assigned to some special case up in Inari," Teija said. She remembered her sister sharing her frustration about being so far out of her element. Lyylia was a big-city cop; she'd complained that even Kokkola was too small and dull. And now, because Lyylia really had been too far out of her element, she'd paid the price.

Teija didn't think she could verbalize any of that right now without fully breaking down, and the break room would start filling up soon with the first wave of people on lunch. She tucked a wisp of blond hair behind her ear and pursed her lips, feeling tears sliding down her cheeks.

Johanna leaned over and grabbed a napkin from the dispenser on the nearest table. "You should take the rest of the day off, Teija. The boss will understand."

Teija nodded and wiped at her eyes. Her mascara was probably smeared, but she didn't care.

"I'll walk with you," Johanna said. She quickly poured herself some coffee, grabbed a sugar packet, and then walked with Teija back to her desk. "I'll tell the boss you're leaving for the day," she offered, giving Teija's arm an encouraging squeeze. "And I'll call you later."

"Thanks, Johanna." Teija managed a weak smile. She shut down her computer, leaving projects unfinished and emails unanswered. She put on her coat, grabbed her purse, and got in the elevator for the eight-floor journey down to street level. Mechanically she headed for the bus stop, and didn't bother to take a seat in the shelter when she arrived.

Lyylia could not be hurt, she could not be gone, not for long. Miraculous rescues and happy endings didn't always happen in police work—but this was her sister. Lyylia wouldn't have gotten kidnapped without a fight. She'd tracked down kidnap victims and worked on hostage negotiations before, Teija knew. Lyylia could figure out how to rescue herself—and anyone else—from whatever situation they were in.

Everything had to turn out all right. It just had to.

Teija hardly noticed the bus ride or the walk to her apartment building. After trudging up the three flights of stairs and unlocking the door, she was greeted by Niika, her gray tabby cat.

"Yeah, I'm home early today, Niika." Teija rubbed the cat on the head before tossing her purse on the sofa. She should probably go over to her mom's house. She didn't want to. Not that she didn't want to see her mother, but what could they talk about besides rehashing the same conversation? Her mom had promised to call if the police called her with any new information. But when would the police share any updates? It could potentially be days.

A strange, burning resolve washed over her. Lyylia had always been the brave one, the responsible one, the one who followed their father's path of doing something important with her life. If the only thing Teija ever did with her life was to make sure that her sister could continue to make a difference, then that was enough.

She went into the bedroom and pulled her duffel bag out of the closet. After stuffing several days' worth of clothes into it, she went back into the living room and pulled her phone out of her purse.

Johanna answered on the first ring. "Teija? Are you okay? Did you head home?"

"Yeah, I'm at home now. Johanna, I have a huge favor to ask you."

"Anything."

"Can you watch my cat for a few days? I know my place isn't really on your way to work—you can stop by in the evenings, or whenever. Or you can just stay here, if you want. Just as long as Niika has food and water and a clean litter box. I'm going north."

"Teija, are you serious? Look, I know you're upset—but just stay at home for a few days, or go over to your mom's place."

"I'm going to Lapland," Teija said firmly, grabbing her toothbrush, toothpaste, and face wash out of the bathroom.

"I don't mean to sound insensitive here, but I'm sure the police are handling it," Johanna said, speaking slowly. "I know how you feel—"

"Do you?" Teija snapped. "And if you don't want to watch Niika, that's fine—I'll get somebody else to do it." Even as she said that, though, she felt a stab of shame. Johanna had lost both her mother and her brother in the past two years, so she did in fact know the pain of being separated from a family member.

Johanna graciously didn't react to Teija's thoughtless barb. "I can take care of your cat, Teija—that's not a problem. I'm just worried you're making a rash decision you're going to regret."

"Maybe I am, but I don't care." Johanna was probably right, but Teija couldn't stop now. "And you're not going to talk me out of it."

"All right, Teija, all right." Johanna sighed loudly into the phone. "You win."

"Thanks, Johanna. Really. You have a key, right?"

"Yeah, I've got a key." Johanna sighed again. "Just be careful, okay? And stay in touch. Please."

"I will. I promise. Thanks again."

Teija hung up the phone, finished packing, and changed out of her office clothes and into a pair of fleece-lined leggings and a more comfortable sweater.

"You be a good girl, Niika," she said to the cat, giving her head another rub.

The logical part of her mind told her that she was acting rashly out of her grief. She pushed away those thoughts. Closing and locking the door, she slung her duffel over her shoulder and headed down the stairs. It was barely a kilometer to the nearest train station, so she tugged on her gloves and hat and set off at a rapid walk.

Hours later, Teija stood at the ticket window at the bus depot in Rovaniemi, and stared with disbelief at the man behind the counter.

"What do you mean, Inari is closed?"

The man shrugged unhappily. "Look, lady, I'm sorry, but the bus service isn't running to Inari, by order of the National Bureau of Investigation. Something about a big crime up there. The village is locked down. Ivalo is as far as this bus is running right now. And I'm about to close up for the night, so if you want a ticket to Ivalo, you'd best get it now—bus leaves early tomorrow morning."

"No, I'll, um, pass for now, thanks." Teija hefted her duffel bag and wandered out of the bus depot.

She'd had plenty of time to think on the train ride up to Rovaniemi, and had stayed resolved with her decision to go all the way to Inari. She hadn't expected the village to be locked down. Apparently the police hadn't told her mother that. Did that mean that the police were close to figuring out what had happened, close to finding Lyylia and the others? Or did it mean that the situation was even worse than she'd thought? Johanna was right—this trip was not a good idea.

"You weren't trying to get to Inari, were you?"

Teija jumped at the voice. Looking around, she saw a tall man standing partly in the shadows of the overhanging roof at the edge of the building. He was wearing one of those blue four-pointed Sami hats, and had long black hair down to his shoulders. He was smoking a cigarette and had a fierce look in his eyes, but his tone was calm and non-threatening.

"Yeah, I was trying to get to Inari," she answered. "But apparently they aren't running the buses up there right now."

"The police have the whole village surrounded; they won't let anyone in or out. If you're headed there for a holiday, you'd be better off staying here, or maybe going to Saariselkä."

Teija shook her head. "I'm not on holiday. I'm trying to find my sister."

"She lives in Inari?"

"No, but she was in Inari…" Teija trailed off, wondering how much she should be telling this stranger. It obviously wasn't a secret that something bad had happened in the village. The incident very well might have already been on the national news, but Teija hadn't checked TV, radio, or internet news all day.

The man came out of the shadows towards her, an intense

expression on his face. Teija instinctively drew back. "Your sister is one of the people who's been kidnapped?" he asked, his voice low.

Teija nodded.

The man muttered something in Sami under his breath. "My cousin was kidnapped, too. My reindeer are the ones that vanished over a week ago. It seems like we both have the same problem—a missing family member, and no way to get to Inari to try to find them."

Teija nodded in agreement.

The man took a long drag on his cigarette, then tossed it into the slush at the edge of the sidewalk. "Can I buy you a coffee? My name's Maden, by the way."

"Teija."

"Nice to meet you." He jerked a thumb at a row of shops across the street. "Let's get out of the cold and talk for a minute."

Teija hesitated for an instant, but then followed after him as he set off across the street. Since he was actually from Inari, he might have more information.

They ordered coffees, Maden paying for both, then found a small table in the corner. Teija gratefully sipped the hot drink and wondered what she should say.

Maden broke the silence. "I'm going to Inari," he said quietly. "I can take you with me."

She raised her eyebrows. "How? I thought the police weren't letting anyone in or out."

"They can't keep a blockade like that up for long," he said, leaning forward across the table. "The tourist season is starting up. Winter tourism is our biggest source of income. And the herders need to move their animals. And we have to prepare pelts and meat for our distributors. They can't keep the village shut down for too long, crime scene or not."

"So how are you going to get there?"

"I'm leaving tomorrow morning," said Mađen. "Taking the back way. By snowmobile, across the tundra."

Teija paused with her coffee cup at her lips and looked at him. The distance between Rovaniemi and Inari looked far on the map. It was probably even farther than that to be traveling through the wilderness by snowmobile instead of following a road.

"I know the way. I won't get lost," Mađen said. "But if you'd rather wait until the police decide to lift the blockade, that's fine. I won't be offended if you say no."

Teija put her cup down. "Let me ask you a question, Mađen. Why are you doing this? I mean, why are you offering to sneak me into Inari? We don't even know each other."

"Because I know how you feel. You came all the way up here because you need to know what happened. You need to be there." His dark eyes bored into hers, wild and intense. He took a long swallow of coffee. "I know my way across the tundra. You'll be perfectly safe. And I won't hurt you."

Teija figured she should be scared at this point—which she was, a little—but mostly she just felt confused. Confused at the earnest generosity of this man, confused about why her sister and this man's cousin had been kidnapped, confused at her own sudden rash desire to completely trust him.

He took another swallow of coffee. "Like I said, I'm not offended if you say no. Just one thing, though—if you're planning to tell the police that I'll be sneaking into Inari by snowmobile, just don't tell them till after I've left."

"I didn't say I was going to tell the police," Teija said, a bit defensively. "And I didn't say I wouldn't go with you."

Mađen cocked his head at her. "I'm leaving at four

tomorrow morning. I'll show you where to meet me once we get outside."

He stood up and offered to carry her duffel bag.

"There's a Russian pastry shop at the north end of town," he said once they were outside on the sidewalk. "Go up this street a little more than a kilometer, and you'll see it on the left." He gestured toward the road that intersected with the one they were on. "I'll be in the alley behind the shop. And if you need a place to stay for the night, I'd recommend that one." He pointed at a quaint-looking inn diagonally across the street, with reindeer antlers and a Sami flag over the door.

"Thank you," she said.

"If I don't see you by four in the morning, I'll understand—but I'll be leaving anyway. My family needs me, and I've been gone from Inari for too long." He smoothed his black hair behind his ears, and put his four-pointed hat back on. It was starting to snow. "Take care, Teija." He handed her back her duffel.

Teija managed a smile. "Thanks for all your help. And the coffee."

"Sure." He stuffed his hands in his coat pockets and set off down the street.

Teija got a room, then took advantage of the snack machine and the sauna. Exhaustion was finally settling over her, along with a sense of guilt, despair, and a dose of fear. She enjoyed the sauna, but it didn't relax her. Back in her room, she sat down on the edge of the bed and put her face in her hands.

"What are you doing, girl?" she muttered to herself. "This is crazy." It was foolish enough that she'd rashly hopped on a train and traveled farther away from home than she'd ever been. Now here she was, contemplating riding through the wilderness by snowmobile with some man she didn't know, to get to a town she wasn't supposed to be in, to look for someone who might not even be there anymore.

Her phone rang—it was her mother. Teija swallowed and answered the call.

"Hi, honey, I just called to see how you were doing," came her mother's voice. She sounded sad but otherwise calm, so that meant she didn't know that Teija had left town. That was good, at least.

"I'm doing okay, I guess," Teija said. "How are you?"

"I'm managing. I had been planning to ask you to come over for dinner, but then Mikko asked me to come to his place. Dinner tomorrow, then?"

"Um, maybe," said Teija noncommittally. "I took a couple days off work, and I'm...not at home. I'm staying with a friend."

"Oh, that's good, Teija, I'm glad." Her mother sounded happy about that.

"You stay close to Mikko, Mom. And if you hear anything else from the police, call me right away."

"Of course, honey, of course."

"Thanks. Love you, Mom."

"I love you too, Teija." She hung up.

Teija felt guiltier than ever now, having lied to her mother. But if she could just find out something in Inari… Like what, exactly? What was she thinking she could find that the police might have somehow missed? She could hear Lyylia's voice in her mind, admonishing her for being silly and acting emotionally. Right now she'd give anything to hear Lyylia say those things to her, face to face.

At least her mother was with Mikko, which helped mollify her guilt slightly. Mikko had become a good family friend over the past few years, and both Teija and Lyylia were hoping their mother would officially start dating the man and marry him. It had been over seven years since their father had passed away, and their mother had been so lonely, especially since Lyylia had been transferred to Kokkola.

After brushing her teeth and getting into bed, Teija realized that she'd missed a text message from Johanna.

Just hoping you got to Inari OK. Niika is fine. I haven't told anyone where you are.

Teija quickly texted her back. *I'm spending the night in Rovaniemi.* She decided not to mention just yet about Inari being closed and her wild plan to get there. *Thanks so much for everything!*

No problem! Sweet dreams, came Johanna's reply.

Teija hoped so. She set the alarm on her phone, put it on the pillow beside her, and switched off the light.

Maden Lahti stood in the early morning darkness, avoiding the pool of light from the nearest streetlamp, scanning the road that ran past the pastry shop. Soon the owner of the shop would be arriving to begin his morning baking, and Maden needed to be gone by then. Elaborate cakes and puff pastries were displayed in the window. Above the desserts, the windows were draped with a banner of small paper Sami, Finnish, and Russian flags.

Maden was sure she wouldn't come. Why had he foolishly offered to give this strange girl a ride all the way to Inari? She was probably going to the police right now, and that officer who'd been tailing him for days would have the whole Rovaniemi police force after him on snowmobiles.

He'd made one dumb decision after another ever since the herd had been stolen, and it was high time to start putting things right—if he could at all. But lingering in Rovaniemi, trying to avoid the police and his former criminal associates, was definitely not in the realm of good decisions, so it was time to leave. He pushed back his mitten cuff to check his watch. Two minutes after four.

Going around the shop to the alley in the back, he halted when he saw shadowy movement beside his snowmobile. His hand automatically went to the pocket where he kept his knife.

"Mađen?" a timid female voice squeaked.

"Damn, woman, don't sneak up on me like that," he said, trying to keep the startled growl out of his voice.

"Sorry. I got lost and came up the alley," Teija said, her voice thin and frightened sounding. "But then I saw Russian flags and a snowmobile, and figured this had to be it."

Mađen realized that the back door of the shop was draped with the same multinational banner as the front window. "Well, hop on—I'll tie down your bag." He'd come to Rovaniemi with just a backpack. Teija, like most women, didn't seem to know how to travel light, so it took him longer than he would have liked to get her large duffel bag secured on the back of the machine. He climbed on in front of her and started the engine.

"I know we're still strangers," he said, twisting his head around to look back at her. "But you might want to hold on tight to me. I won't be following any roads."

She obediently gripped him around the midsection. "Okay, not that tight," he grunted. "I'm driving—you don't want me to pass out."

"Sorry." She loosened her hold.

Mađen pulled his balaclava mask up to cover his mouth and nose and secured his driving goggles. Between the buildings he saw the glow of headlights coming down the road. Leaving the snowmobile's headlights turned off for now, he took off down the alley. He didn't turn on the lights until they were well out of town.

Several kilometers out into the wilderness it started snowing again—lightly at first, but then getting thicker. That was good—snow would help cover their tracks. Teija's arms around him were firm and unwavering, which was also good—he didn't want to have to stop every twenty minutes because she got tired. He felt a pressure against his right shoulder blade and figured that she'd put her head down to shield herself from the snow blowing in their faces.

It was an hour and a half before Maden stopped for a rest. Teija hadn't loosened her hold on him, but he also hadn't felt her stir at all in some time, and he wondered if he'd succeeded in freezing her to death. He parked the snowmobile in the shelter of some large rocks. A little stream, mostly frozen, wound its way through the stubby brush nearby. The sun still hadn't risen, and the snow, while lighter now, was still falling steadily.

"Toilet and stretch break," he said, turning off the engine.

Teija was not frozen to death, but she looked close to it as she stiffly climbed off the machine. She'd pulled her hat down over her eyes and had covered her mouth and nose with her scarf. She pulled them off and shook off the snow.

Maden dug in his backpack and handed Teija a travel package of tissues, figuring she'd brought no such amenities. Wordlessly she took the package from him and went around behind the tower of rocks. When she came back, he went around behind to relieve himself.

"We should get to Sodankylä village in another hour or two," he said, after coming back around. "We'll stop there to refuel and grab some food."

Teija merely nodded as she rewrapped the scarf around her face.

"Are you still game for this?" he asked.

She shrugged as she paused in her wrapping. "It's a little late for me to back out now."

That was true. "Let's go, then." He climbed back on, revved the engine, and waited for her to get settled.

The sun rose as they neared Sodankylä. Mađen paused at the top of a hill for a moment to admire the view. The snow had dwindled to mere flurries now. The clouds had thinned, and a red-gold glow blazed on the eastern horizon. Wild, sweeping hills stretched in every direction, dotted with little pockets of trees and rapidly freezing ponds and streams. Towers of rock, softened slightly by the fresh dusting of snow, rose up from the tundra. Everything glowed a muted gold in the veiled sunrise.

"It's beautiful," Teija said over his shoulder.

"Sápmi. It's always been the most beautiful thing to me."

"Sápmi?"

"The land of the Sami children. You call it Lapland or Samiland. But my ancestors called it home."

Home—a land of snow and reindeer, rich traditions and dying languages. And because of his stupidity, he'd almost let that life slide through his fingers and be lost to him—again. The gangs of Rovaniemi would never see his face again. He belonged in the north with his reindeer and his family. Somehow he would make sure that Ávgos and their animals were brought back safely. Somehow. He gunned the engine and sped down the hill.

He stopped briefly in Sodankylä for food and fuel. Teija was uncomplaining, though she did purchase a thicker scarf before they left the village. Mađen saw no evidence of pursuit of any sort, either in Sodankylä village or out on the tundra.

The vast, snowy wilderness surrounded them as they sped towards Inari.

Many hours later, long after the thin autumn sun had set and they'd stopped at another village for fuel, Maðen saw the lights of Inari village winking in the distance. A light snow was starting to fall again. He steered the snowmobile to the east of the village, heading towards the lake.

As the trees and brambles grew thicker, he finally pulled to a stop. "We'll park here and walk the rest of the way," he said over his shoulder. "It isn't far."

"Isn't far to what?" Teija asked, climbing off the machine. "Don't you need to refuel again?"

"No, we're here. Inari village." Maðen began unstrapping their luggage from the back of the machine. "Well, the village is about a kilometer that way." He cocked his head to the left.

"Oh, that's good." Her voice sounded brighter. "So we're just walking to the village?"

"Not quite." He hefted his backpack and her duffel bag, and handed her the sack of food he'd bought in Sodankylä. "We're going to an earth hut. It should be empty right now." He pulled some branches and brush around the snowmobile. If the snow kept up, their tracks would soon be gone, and the machine itself well hidden.

"I thought we were just going to sneak into the village," Teija said, following him as he set off into the woods, flashlight in hand. "Wouldn't nighttime be the best time to do that?"

"Probably. You can go to the village, if you want. Like I

said, it's just a kilometer or so that way. But I'm going to spend the night in the earth hut."

"I don't know my way through these woods, and I don't have a flashlight. Mađen, what are you not telling me?"

A lot, he thought, but said nothing.

"What's an earth hut?" Teija then asked.

"A small hut dug into the side of a hill. They're scattered all across the land, and well hidden. But I know there's one in this area." He waved his flashlight at a mound of darkness up ahead—the land rose up in a sudden hill, covered with bushes and small trees. And there it was: the flashlight beam fell on a wooden door in the hillside, half-hidden by scrubby branches and snow.

Mađen kicked away the snow and tugged at the door. It finally opened, and they went into the dark hut. "Sometimes herders stay in the earth huts when they're traveling with their animals," he said, shining the flashlight around. A small wooden table against the wall held two rolled sleeping bags, some cooking utensils, and a kerosene lantern. A stone fireplace and chimney were on the opposite wall, along with a stack of cut firewood and an axe.

Mađen dug in his pocket for his lighter, and went over to light the lantern. "It's customary to leave the hut stocked for the next person who might use it." He gestured toward the sleeping bags, and reached into the cooking pot and pulled out a can of beans and a tin of tea. "The Sami used to use these earth huts to hide in when your forefathers came through, taking our animals and land from us, and taking our children to government schools in the south."

Teija politely didn't respond to the ethnic insult. She went over and put their bag of food on the table. Mađen dumped the backpack and duffel on the floor and set about getting a fire going. He pulled two cans of fish porridge out of their food bag, leaving the beans for the next person who might stay in the hut. He emptied the cans into the cooking pot to heat over the fire, and went outside to fill the tea kettle with snow to melt. Teija cut several slices of the rye bread they'd bought.

They sat on the dirt floor in front of the fire and ate in silence. Maden figured that Teija was having second thoughts about this expedition, especially now. He should just escort her to the edge of the village and part ways with her. He'd promised her a ride to Inari, nothing more.

"So when are you going to tell me what's going on?" Teija's voice broke the silence.

Maden poured more tea into both mugs while he thought about what to say. "When we're done eating, I'll take you into the village," he said finally.

"So I can stay in a hotel? But if the village is locked down, wouldn't it be suspicious if I just showed up and checked into a hotel? Why can't we sneak into the village and go to your house? Unless you're trying to avoid your family or neighbors for some reason."

She was pretty sharp for a blonde city girl.

"My family thinks I'm still in Rovaniemi," he grunted.

"And so do the police, don't they?" Her blue eyes seemed unusually bright in the light from the fire. "You told me yesterday that if I was going to tell the police about you sneaking into Inari, to not tell them till after you'd left Rovaniemi. You're some sort of criminal, aren't you?"

"No," he said. "I haven't done anything wrong." Which was true, technically speaking, but he realized how defensive that sounded.

Teija frowned at him.

"Are you finished?" Maden gestured at the battered tin

bowl in her hands. "We should wash these dishes out before we go to sleep. Bears can smell food kilometeres away."

"Bears?" Her eyes widened in alarm.

Mađen didn't reply; he merely gathered up the cooking pot and other utensils and took them outside to clean them. When he came back in, Teija was unrolling one of the sleeping bags.

"I hope these aren't full of bugs," she said, laying it out on the floor in front of the fire.

"Not in cold weather." He grabbed the other roll off the table and laid it out next to hers.

She dragged her bag away from his before unzipping it and slithering in. Mađen dragged his bag back next to hers again.

"We should sleep back to back, for warmth," he explained, in response to her frown. "Don't worry, I won't touch you. And I may be a primitive Lapp, but I'm not dirty or contagious."

She frowned harder. "I never said anything about you being primitive, dirty, or contagious. If you hate southerners so much, why did you invite me to come with you?"

Why indeed? He was now wishing he hadn't. He didn't need a companion right now—he just needed to find his cousin and their reindeer. "Why did you agree to come with me?" he returned.

She didn't answer as they both got settled in their sleeping bags, their backs against each other. Mađen hoped the smoke from the chimney wouldn't be noticed in the dark. The door had a small bar lock, which was designed more for privacy and keeping bears out than to stop police who were trained to kick down doors.

"I've never been this far north before," Teija's voice said quietly behind him. "Have you ever been to Helsinki?"

"I've never been south of Rovaniemi." Mađen tried to imagine surviving the chaos of a city ten times the size of

Rovaniemi—riding a train just to get across town, bright city lights all night long, crowds of people everywhere...

Again, he wished he'd never offered Teija a ride, but it was too late now. He'd vowed to leave his past mistakes in the past and set things right—and that meant not just for Ávgos and their family, but for this poor lost city girl, too. He'd convinced her that he could help her, so he couldn't just leave her to get herself arrested in a strange town far from home.

"We can't go into the village," Maden finally said to her. "We can't go to my home because the rest of my family thinks I'm still in Rovaniemi. I went to the city when our reindeer disappeared, over a week ago. I have some...friends...in Rovaniemi who, um, well, they're not really friends any more. And I thought they'd stolen the reindeer to get back at me."

"Get back at you for what?" Teija asked.

"For leaving them." He sighed. There was no getting out of it now. "I joined a gang, okay? I made some stupid decisions a few years ago and got in with a bad crowd. But I'd left them for good and moved back home to Inari to help my cousin with our reindeer. So then when half the herd suddenly went missing, I assumed the guys in Rovaniemi had done it. So I went back there to talk to them."

"Did they take the reindeer?"

If only it had been that simple. "No, they didn't. But I've been hiding out in Rovaniemi, trying to stay out of their way, and trying to avoid the police. I'm not a criminal, but because I used to have ties with this gang, and because I left town right after the herd vanished, I'm the number-one suspect."

"Oh." Teija's voice was thin. After a moment, Maden felt her shuddering against his back and figured she was crying. He felt bad about that, but continuing to lie probably would have been just as bad. As always, he was stuck with the dumb decisions he'd made. Maybe he should just take her back to Rovaniemi tomorrow.

The only sound was the crackling of the wood burning in the fireplace. Then Teija drew in a long heaving breath and finally spoke. "So what are we going to do? We came up here to try to figure out what happened to your cousin and my sister. Where do we even begin? Especially if we have to stay hidden from the police."

Maðen felt a flicker of surprise at her use of "we." "I was going to just scout around a bit first—see where the police are searching, how many are here, that sort of thing. Then I want to head for the lake. I think the lake is part of it somehow."

"What do you mean?"

"Ávgos called me the night he disappeared. He told me that they'd found a dead reindeer on one of the islands in the lake. The detective—your sister—thought that the herd had been driven into the water and taken somewhere."

"So wouldn't the police be searching the lake now, too?" Teija asked.

"Probably. We'll just see what we see tomorrow morning." He paused. "So...do you really want to do this? We could both be arrested if we're caught."

He felt her draw a deep breath. "Well, I've come this far."

"All right. Lake Inari tomorrow, then." Another dumb decision, but now they were both stuck with it. "Good night, Teija."

"Good night, Maðen."

Two days later, Teija stared out across the gray water. The lake reflected the overcast color of the sky, the grayness broken by the brown hills of small islands and white pans of ice. Yesterday morning they'd hiked to the shore of the lake—a longer, more challenging trek than she'd been expecting—and then walked some more until Maden found a rowboat moored by some Inari resident. Since no one was allowed to leave the village, the owner of the boat wouldn't be using it, so for two days now, Maden had rowed them from rocky island to brush-covered skerry, staying well away from the sounds of police motorboats.

Teija had totally lost track of where they were—she had no idea that Lake Inari was so big. She felt as if she were out in the middle of the Baltic, past the Åland Islands, far removed from everything. So far they'd found nothing in the way of clues that might tell them what had happened to the missing people or the reindeer.

It was time to call it quits and go back home. Yesterday, with the last of her phone battery, she'd texted Johanna the whole story. She'd also told her mother almost everything. She couldn't keep lying to her mother and let her think that Teija was still in Helsinki, but she didn't mention that she was skulking around with a strange man, trying to stay hidden from the police. Teija just told her mother that she'd gone to Inari, which was more than enough to set her mother worrying. Now her phone was dead, she hadn't had a shower in three days, and discouragement and exhaustion were vying for the top spot in her life. And none of it was helping her to track down Lyylia.

Maden rowed the boat up onto the shore of a larger island, the bottom crunching through the skin of ice that had formed in the shallows. This island looked the same as all the others—rocky, snow-dusted, covered in scrubby bushes that had gone dormant for the winter. Teija had no idea what they should be looking for. Footprints? Another dead reindeer? A message in a bottle? Yesterday Mađen had admitted to being just as clueless as she was, but he still doggedly rowed to the next little skerry, and the next.

"I haven't heard the police engines in a while," Mađen said. "Let's take a break for some lunch." He dusted the snow off a large flat rock and dug in his backpack for protein bars and two apples.

Teija was sure that he was just as tired of protein bars and canned porridge as she was, but she didn't say anything. As she ate, she noticed a large stone off to her left, tall and standing straight upright, as if it had been placed that way on purpose. A weathered-looking set of reindeer antlers lay in the snow at its base.

"What's that?" she asked.

"A *sieidi*," Mađen said. "A traditional Sami sacred site. We don't worship these places anymore, but it's still tradition to leave a gift if you're hunting in the area." He dug in his pocket and pulled out a ten-cent euro coin and tossed it over at the *sieidi*. It hit the rock with a ping and landed softly in the snow at its base.

Teija wondered if it would be insulting for her, as a non-Sami, to leave a gift, or if it would be insulting not to. She didn't ask, though. Mađen had finished his food and stood up to walk several paces away and light a cigarette.

The chilly breeze that had been blowing all day yesterday and today suddenly grew stronger and colder. Teija hurriedly finished her apple so that she could put her gloves back on. She wished she'd packed warmer clothes.

Mađen came back over. "We should probably head back to the hut soon. Looks like a storm is coming." He glanced up at the sky, then tossed his cigarette into the snow and stepped on it.

Waiting out a storm in the dark, chilly earth hut did not sound appealing. Not for the first time, Teija thought about just walking into Inari and giving herself up. Surely she wouldn't actually be sent to jail just for walking into the village. Right? Now that her phone was dead, she had no way to know if the police had called her mom with any updates, or if any news had been posted online.

Thick clouds had blotted out the thin autumn sunlight by the time they reached the shore of the lake, and the wind turned frigid. Teija set off along the path through the snow, back to the hut, while Maden secured the boat. As she approached the hill with the hut, she saw that the door was standing open. Scruffling and rustling noises came from inside. Heart pounding, she turned and ran back through the trees.

"Maden!" she hissed as soon as she saw him. "There's someone in the hut!"

He put his hand inside his coat and pulled out a long knife. "Stay here," he muttered, and then pointed over at an outcropping of towering rocks. "In there."

She scurried over and hunkered down behind the brush and trees, wedged into a semi-secluded spot between the tall boulders. Positioned like this, she couldn't see the hut; all that was visible through the little space in the rocks in front of her was the Inari wilderness. She heard a wordless shout, followed by a loud rustling of bushes. She pressed deeper into her little crevasse. Why had she ever left Helsinki?

An eternity went by as she heard nothing. She held her breath and wished her heart wasn't beating so loudly. Then footsteps crunched in the snow nearby. "Teija?"

Trembling, she scrambled out of her hiding place and

nearly bumped into Mađen. He still had his knife out and quickly pulled it away from her.

"Mađen, what happened?"

"Someone—or something—was in there. At first I thought it was a bear, but..." He shook his head. "It ran off into the woods. Come on—let's see what the damage is."

Still shaking, Teija followed him back to the hut. Everything was in disarray. The table with the cooking utensils had been overturned and one of the sleeping bags had a large gash in it. The bag of food had been dumped out, and the lantern lay cracked on the floor. And Teija's duffel bag had been entirely emptied and the contents strewn all over the hut.

Teija gathered up her belongings while Mađen righted the table and picked up the food. "So much for the noodles," Mađen said, kicking at the crushed box and the dry noodles scattered on the floor. "The rest of the food is still here, I think. Anything of yours missing?"

"Just a sock, I think," she said. "No, wait, here it is. But this sweater's ruined." She held up a sweater that looked like a large dog had been playing tug-of-war with it.

Mađen took the mangled sweater from her and examined it, and then looked down at the torn sleeping bag. "Strange. These long shreds look like claw marks. But a bear wouldn't do this, and that thing, whatever it was..."

"I'm scared, Mađen."

He looked at her, his dark eyes intense. "We'll be okay," he said. "The bolt's still on the door, so we can lock ourselves in and we'll be fine."

Teija nodded. This whole situation was anything but fine.

"We'll be safe," Mađen said, a firm note in his voice. "Now, let's gather some extra firewood before the storm hits, and then we'll lock the door tight and be fine."

Teija swallowed, and nodded again. "Okay."

With fingers going rapidly numb inside her gloves, Teija wandered through the trees, picking up the biggest sticks she could find. She jumped at a rustling noise behind her, but it was just a bird taking off from a branch.

Suddenly a force slammed into her back. She dropped her armload of sticks as she tumbled forwards into the bushes. Before she could reorient herself, something grabbed her ankle. With a yelp, she thrashed and kicked, and saw the briefest glimpse of what looked like a small white bear, except the face was all wrong. She screamed as the creature seized her ankle again and pulled her down into the snow.

She was being dragged. With another wordless yell, she scrabbled at passing tree trunks as she was pulled along the ground. She tried to kick, to roll over, anything—but whatever it was had a death grip on her lower leg and was pulling her at a terrifying speed. She thought she heard Maden's voice shouting nearby.

Teija tried to call out to him, but her breath was knocked out of her at the shock of cold water. Her body went instantly numb, and green-gray lake water filled her vision. In a complete panic she tried to thrash, but she couldn't feel her arms or legs. The pale light above her was fading. She wanted to scream, or cry, but she couldn't.

She'd never see her sister again. *Lyylia!*

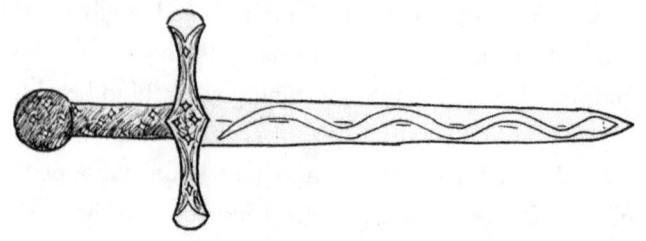

CHAPTER 5:
THE WESTERN FELLS

I n the warm stable, Lyylia stared over the wooden gate into the stall. In the stall stood a reindeer and a Menninkäinen, both eating hay.

When she and Queen Kuu had returned from Shaman Talon's village—now Shaman Rowan's village—they were greeted by a rather flustered Gray, who was babbling something about Gentle Beasts. The Queen's sledge was housed in a different stable from the one where the reindeer were kept, so they'd quickly followed Gray across the wide courtyard to another stable.

Shaun and Ávgos stood by a stall at the end of the row, along with Boots and Eider. After making sure that the two men were safe and fine, Lyylia followed Ávgos' gesture and looked into the stall.

"What's going on?" she asked, momentarily forgetting to speak English for Shaun's benefit. "Why is he eating hay?"

"He is not Menninkäinen," Kuu said quietly.

"I'm afraid not, Your Highness," Ávgos said in English. "He's a reindeer. One of my reindeer." Ávgos opened the gate and went into the stall. Both the reindeer and the little man kneeling in the hay turned their heads towards him, but then went back to their eating.

Ávgos smoothed the hair back from the man's ear. Lyylia could just make out the deep notches cut into his earlobe.

"My earmark," Ávgos said. He indicated the identical mark on the reindeer's ear. "They're both from my herd. Somehow, this man is actually a reindeer."

"Perkele," Lyylia muttered under her breath, then glanced at Kuu beside her. "Sorry, Your Highness." Swearing in front of a queen was probably very improper.

Kuu gave her a mild smile of amusement, then went into the stall.

Shaun stepped up beside Lyylia. "You'll have to teach me some Finnish swear words sometime," he murmured. "I think those might be more appropriate to these weird situations than English ones."

Lyylia managed not to smile at his remark. "Later, maybe," she said.

In the stall, Queen Kuu knelt down in the hay in front of the man and the reindeer. Ávgos stepped out to give her space. Kuu spent several long moments stroking the reindeer's muzzle with one hand and rubbing the little man's scraggly hair with the other.

Then she took the reindeer's head in both hands and pressed her forehead against its head. The animal whickered quietly. "Gentle Lady, I'm so glad that you are here," Kuu said quietly. "Can you tell me what's happened to you and your companion?"

Several more moments passed as Kuu remained kneeling eye-level with the reindeer. The animal flicked its ears and whickered again, but otherwise remained motionless. Lyylia glanced at Ávgos, wondering if this was typical behavior for a reindeer; judging by his perplexed expression, she guessed not.

"Thank you, Arvi," Kuu spoke at last. "Here you are safe."

"Arvi?" asked Ávgos.

"That is her name." Kuu looked over her shoulder at him. "She remembers being separated from her herd and trapped in an unfamiliar place. Then she remembers pain, and she did not feel or smell like herself. She knows that her companion is like she is, even though he does not smell like himself, either."

Releasing the reindeer's head, Kuu turned her attention to the Menninkäinen. "Gentle Lord, can you speak to me?" she murmured, cradling his head in her hands.

He twitched a few times, as if he were attempting to pull away from her, but otherwise made no movement or sound. After a moment Kuu released him. She stood up, and he plunged his head back into the hay and resumed eating.

"He doesn't remember anything," Kuu said sadly, brushing hay from her dress. "He's confused and in pain. Arvi is the only thing that feels familiar to him. He doesn't even remember his own name."

"Two scouts patrolling near the Dark Water River found them wandering the tundra," Gray said. "They knew of the orders to bring Gentle Beasts to your castle; and since the man wouldn't speak or eat, they brought him, too. The men who found them have been shown to guest chambers to rest."

Queen Kuu stepped out of the stall, closing the low gate behind her. "Please invite them to join us for the evening meal, Gray. I should like to speak with them."

"Of course, Your Highness."

Lyylia asked to be shown the way back to her room before dinner, so she could take off her coat and freshen up. She was hoping to be able to talk with Ávgos and Shaun in private, but they didn't go back to the guest chambers. By the time she was escorted into the dining room, the room was already filled with the Menninkäinen they'd been traveling with, plus Gray, Stone, and two others who were probably the scouts who'd found the reindeer. Kuu came into the room a few moments after she did.

Once everyone was seated and had started eating, Kuu asked the two scouts to share their story of finding the reindeer and the man. Then Ávgos explained his discovery.

"Changeling magic is a rare and difficult magic," Kuu said. "If Hiisi-Hiisi has performed such a spell upon all of the Gentle Beasts..." She paused and looked at Ávgos. "One hundred and thirty reindeer were taken from you, yes?"

"That's right, Your Highness."

"Did he, though?" Shaun spoke up. "Put a spell on all of them, I mean. Your Highness, can we be sure that Hiisi-Hiisi transformed *all* the reindeer? You've found several of them, and they've all been animals."

"That is true," Kuu said. "No, I cannot be sure that Hiisi-Hiisi cast spells upon all of them. The Beasts that have been found thus far may have escaped when they were brought through the gateway, or the spell may have faded from them, as it did with Arvi. Likewise, we cannot be sure of Hiisi-Hiisi's true intentions with this subterfuge."

"Murder," Lyylia said in English, before she could stop herself. She wasn't comparing notes with fellow police officers, she reminded herself.

Everyone looked at her. "Murder" was a harsh word for these primitive, innocent people.

Then again, murder was a harsh word for anyone.

"The broken bridge," Ávgos said. "Shaman Talon."

"The strange Menninkäinen who came to the village

before us," Lyylia said. "They weren't Menninkäinen. They were these...changed reindeer. They broke the bridge, and they killed Shaman Talon."

"But why?" asked Shaun. "And how? Reindeer aren't naturally killers, are they?"

"Of course not," Ávgos said, sounding mildly indignant.

"But these are not reindeer," Queen Kuu said. Everyone looked at her. "Hiisi-Hiisi's spell may have changed more than their bodies."

Like turned them into assassins. Lyylia didn't say that out loud, but she knew that Kuu and the men were thinking it.

"I must study this magic," Kuu said. "And I will release the changeling and return him to his proper form." She looked down the row of Menninkäinen seated at the table. "Gray. When we have finished the meal, please bring the changeling to the Moon Tower. I will require your assistance for this spell."

"Yes, Your Majesty," Gray said.

Then Kuu turned her silver eyes on Lyylia and the two men. "I do not often invite newcomers to the Moon Tower, but I would like for the three of you to be present for this spell. Since both you and the changeling are from Kalevala, your spirits may help strengthen his."

"Thank you, Your Highness," Ávgos said.

Lyylia knew she should feel honored, but instead she felt sudden trepidation. Was she going to witness an actual magic spell, whatever that might entail? Murderers she could handle. Magically-transformed reindeer, however...

They finished the meal in relative silence. Gray left for the stables, and the travelers, and Boots and the others, bowed to the Queen, thanked her for the meal, and left. Then Kuu stood up and looked at the three humans.

"Come," she said, her tone solemn. "The Moon

Tower awaits."

They followed Queen Kuu through a maze of corridors and up several sets of stairs, and Shaun tried not to get distracted by the aurora every time they passed a window. He nearly bumped into Kuu when she suddenly stopped at a closed door. He quickly stepped back, managed not to step on the white dog, and bumped into Lyylia, who gave him a reproachful frown. He tossed her a sheepish smile and stuffed his hands into his pockets.

The wooden door was unadorned except for dark iron hinges, the same as most of the other interior doors they'd passed. Kuu laid her hand on the latch, then looked back over her shoulder at them. "Shield your eyes as we ascend," she said. "The light will be very bright at first."

Behind the door was a spiral staircase that wound up inside a tower. Shaun could see bright white light coming from the top of the staircase as they climbed, and by the time they'd reached the top, he found himself squinting.

They'd emerged at the top of the tower under an open sky. The waning moon, just past full, seemed to fill the sky; and yet there was still room for the central blue-white star-sun Pohjantähti, the immense dome of stars, and, of course, the aurora. The light and colors were dazzling, made all the more so by the polished gray marble floor of the tower. Tall columns were scattered about the space—some made of polished marble, some sheathed in silver, others made of solid ice.

Blinking against the stunning brightness, Shaun felt a

brief wave of vertigo as he looked up at the mountain peaks above them. The jagged gray rocks and layers of snow seemed to stretch all the way to the sky, as if the stars might stop to rest on the tops of the peaks. And then vertigo came again as he turned around and saw the mountainside tumbling away below. Lower turrets of the castle jutted out like steps going down the mountain, and far below, the tundra was a rolling ocean of white.

He looked at Lyylia and Ávgos and saw their stunned expressions as they squinted at the view. As his eyes started adjusting to the brightness, Shaun realized that they were not, in fact, under an open sky. The top of the tower was a room, easily two thousand square feet in size, and pentagonal in shape. He could now see the walls—four walls of clear glass, at least two stories high, joined together at their edges by silver columns. The fifth wall of the room was the side of the mountain, rough-hewn but sheer and straight. The tall columns scattered about supported a clear pentagonal ceiling that rose to a point at the center of the room.

"Gray, bring the changeling here." Kuu's voice startled him, echoing off all the stone and glass.

Shaun looked around and saw Gray standing a few yards away; the Menninkäinen-that-wasn't stood beside him, a dull expression on his face, and a rope around his wrist, held by Gray.

Kuu had laid a white blanket on the floor. "Have him stand on this blanket." Gray led him over. "Ávgos. I need you to remove the changeling's clothing. Do not touch him during the spell, but remain close. It will help him to have you where he can see and smell you."

Ávgos hurried over to obey the Queen. Shaun glanced at Lyylia. He didn't really want to watch the poor not-

Menninkäinen get stripped. Kuu had invited them to watch the spell, but hadn't given them any instructions and there was nowhere to sit.

Lyylia looked back at him and gave a slight shrug. Together they moved a few feet away from the top of the stairs—which was merely a hole in the floor with no railing—and stood beside the nearest stone pillar.

Shaun looked past Ávgos and the changeling as Kuu strode across the room towards the wall of the mountain. Five wooden doors, evenly spaced apart and with hinges of silver instead of iron, lined the stone wall. Kuu opened the second door from the left and disappeared, closing the door behind her.

Looking around the spacious area, Shaun saw that this room was more than just an empty tower full of pillars and light. Scattered between the columns were several wooden chests, and pedestals made of ice. On one pedestal sat a silver bowl; on another was perched a large trumpet-like horn carved out of ice. In the very center of the room stood a small table, also carved out of a solid block of ice. The room was chilly, like the corridors and stairwells of the castle, but didn't feel cold enough to be at a freezing temperature.

Kuu emerged from the door, carrying a small silver bowl and some sort of rectangular musical instrument.

"Kantele," Lyylia murmured.

Shaun looked at her. "What?"

"Kantele," she repeated in a whisper. "A Finnish folk instrument."

Interesting. Shaun watched as Kuu knelt down on the floor beside the changeling, who was now sitting on the blanket, so it wasn't quite so awkward to look at him naked. Ávgos had backed away a few feet, holding the bundles of rags the changeling had been wearing. He glanced back over his shoulder at Shaun and Lyylia.

"Gray, begin striking the chimes," Kuu said. "One chime at a time. The order does not matter. I shall be singing and playing the silver-string. Keep the rhythm steady and slow."

Shaun realized he'd lost track of Gray; he now spotted him half-hidden behind a silver pillar. He stood in front of a wooden frame supporting tubular hanging chimes made of ice. Gray struck one with a wooden stick—the clear tone reverberated through the room, unexpectedly loud. Before the echo had completely faded, he struck another chime. Shaun glanced up at the clear walls and roof, wondering how sturdy the huge panes of glass were. Hopefully the glass was designed to withstand cold temperatures and loud sounds.

Kuu dipped her hands in the silver bowl, then stroked wet fingers across the changeling's forehead, shoulders, chest, back, and legs. She put her hands back into the bowl, and began to sing.

There were no words, and no real tune, either. Her clear voice slid from note to random note. Her singing didn't match the chimes at all, but somehow the two sounds didn't clash, either. Then she began to pluck at the kantele that lay on the floor beside her. The aimless bell-like tones rose with the sound of the chimes, her voice weaving with the instruments like a feather blowing on a breeze. Shaun felt frozen in place, as if time had stopped, everything had stopped, except the sound.

Kuu lifted her right hand out towards the little man now slumped on the blanket, her left hand still plucking at the kantele strings. At first Shaun thought it was a trick of the light, but then he saw that her hand was indeed glowing blue. Then he remembered her bracelet that wasn't a bracelet at all.

The little blue snake, glowing brightly, slithered off her wrist and onto the changeling's thigh. Shaun heard Lyylia's quiet intake of breath beside him, and he wanted to look at her or put his arm around her again, but he found couldn't look away.

The ice chimes continued as Kuu stopped playing the kantele and singing, and drew a small silver loop of metal out of the bowl of water. She placed it against her mouth and moved her finger, and a sharp thrum filled the room. A mouth harp. Shaun had seen pictures of the instrument before, but had never heard one.

As the music continued, the blue glow from the snake grew brighter. Shaun had to close his eyes against the blinding light, then cover his eyes with his hand. He heard the sound of the kantele and Kuu's voice again.

Then Kuu gave a loud clap of her hands, and everything stopped. It took Shaun a moment to realize that even the reverberating echo of music was gone, and that the blinding brilliance had faded.

He opened his eyes to see a small brown reindeer lying on the blanket. With a snort, the animal struggled to his feet. He had no antlers; he shook his head and flicked his tail nervously. Ávgos took a step forward and then stopped.

Kuu laid her hand on the reindeer's neck. "I am sorry for the pain, my lord," she said gently. "But you are whole again, and you are safe."

The animal snorted again and stamped a hoof. Kuu stroked his neck. "He calls himself Nuorti, but he's still too disoriented to tell me much else. We should let him rest in the stables with Arvi and the others." She motioned to Ávgos. "You are safe with your friend Ávgos now, Nuorti."

Shaun stared at the reindeer, which moments before had been a Menninkäinen. Magic. Shape-shifting. This was the stuff of movies and comic books, not science and reality. And yet, it had just happened.

"My God," he murmured, and then glanced at Lyylia beside him. Her blue eyes were wide and she looked as stunned as he felt. She looked at him and just shook her head.

Still kneeling on the floor, Kuu laid the kantele and the bowl on the blanket, then reached into the bowl and pulled out the mouth harp. She shook the water from it, laid it on the blanket, then reached in again and drew out the blue snake.

Lyylia made that little strangled sound again, and this time Shaun put a gentle hand on her arm. He wasn't bothered by snakes. In his line of work, bears, moose, and small rodents that chewed on electrical wires were what he had to watch out for.

Gray came out from behind the pillar where the ice chimes hung, and Kuu looked up at his approach. "Thank you for your assistance, Gray," she said. "This was powerful magic we performed here tonight."

"Thank you for letting me participate, Your Highness," he said with a bow. "It was an honor and a privilege."

She smiled at him. "Would you please show Ávgos and the Gentle Beast to the stables? Lord Nuorti must rest."

Ávgos had used the rope to tie a makeshift halter around the reindeer's head. The animal calmly followed him and Gray as they crossed the smooth floor to the stairs. Ávgos glanced at Shaun and Lyylia as he went past, his expression the same as Shaun's thoughts. *Did that really just happen?*

Shaun looked back across the room at Kuu. She was still kneeling on the floor beside the blanket. Child of Light was sitting beside her; Shaun realized that the dog had made herself scarce during the spell. The Queen looked tired. Shaun wondered if he should go over and offer to help her up.

After a moment she stood up and came towards them. As she approached, he saw a flicker of blue as the little snake disappeared up her sleeve. "You have witnessed a powerful spell tonight," she said. She smiled, but now that she was closer to them, Shaun could definitely see fatigue in her face.

"It was amazing, Your Majesty," he said with sincerity.

"Thank you for letting us see," Lyylia said.

"You are most welcome. But now, it grows late. I will show you back to your chambers."

As they followed her towards the stairs, Shaun took one last look at the sky all around. The aurora was every possible color tonight—curtains of yellow and green, with red and purple ribbons weaving across, punctuated with little bursts of blue. He realized that the moon had moved over a full degree from its earlier position. It felt like they'd been up here barely twenty minutes—but it had actually been a good two hours?

He felt a touch on his arm, and saw Lyylia beside him. "Let's go," she said gently. Kuu was already descending the stairs.

"Right." He wasn't sure he'd be able to sleep tonight. The vivid view of the sky was intoxicating, and he could still hear Kuu's ethereal voice in his mind.

The darkness of the winding staircase enveloped him as he followed Kuu and Lyylia and left the Moon Tower behind.

The next morning as a castle guard came to escort them to breakfast, Ávgos asked if he could see his reindeer. He especially wanted to see the one who had, the night before, been a Menninkäinen.

Nuorti, Queen Kuu had called him. *'East.'* The names that his reindeer supposedly chose for themselves certainly were odd. Although not as odd as a magic transformation spell. He could still hardly believe it.

"I will be happy to show you to the stables," the guard said, as Ávgos, Shaun, and Lyylia followed him through the castle corridors. Boots, Eider, Flint, and Fir followed behind them. "But first, Queen Kuu awaits you in the dining chambers."

"Of course," Ávgos said politely. "I didn't mean to imply that I wanted to be excused from dining with the Queen. The Gentle Beasts are my responsibility in my world, so I just want to make sure they're all right."

"You are their guard and protector, yes?" the little man asked.

"Yes, that's right."

The guard smiled at Ávgos. "A kind and noble protector they have, indeed."

"Thank you." It was a comfort that these people loved and respected reindeer, even if it did border on worship.

The Queen was already seated at the head of the table when they entered the dining room. "Welcome! Please join me." She gestured toward the laden table.

"I have news for you," she continued as everyone got settled on the benches and started eating. "I received word early this morning that another Gentle Beast has been found. Hunters from Shaman Wind's village saw it wandering the tundra outside the village."

"Just the one reindeer?" Ávgos asked.

Kuu looked at him. "Yes. I told Shaman Wind about our discovery of the changelings, and he will be sending scouts further away from the village to look for other Beasts or Menninkäinen. I have sent word to many village shamans about the changelings, and will continue to do so until every village is on the alert for strange Menninkäinen travelers."

"Thank you, Your Highness," said Ávgos.

"I also have other news," Kuu said, laying down her fork and looking at all of them in turn. "More Kalevalans have come through the gateway."

They all gaped at her.

"How?" Lyylia was the first to ask. "Who? Are they police?"

"I do not know. They arrived in Shaman Pike's village late last night. A man and a woman, dressed similarly to the way you are dressed. Scouts at the edge of the lake pulled them from the water. They'd been brought through the gateway by a hiisi."

Ávgos exchanged horrified looks with Lyylia and Shaun. "That means there was still a hiisi left on Earth," he said.

"And there could be more still," Shaun said.

"We need to see them," said Lyylia. "I know that police would be looking for us since we disappeared."

"We will rendezvous with them at Shaman Wind's village," said Kuu. "I believe that is where the changelings are crossing the Dark River from Ice-Dark, so I want to search the area."

"We should go to the lake," Lyylia said. "It isn't frozen yet, if more people came through the water. We need to go home, and we need to stop hiisi from kidnapping more people."

"You are not wrong, Lyylia," said Kuu, giving her a solemn look. "But as I told you before, I do not know where the gateway is."

"But we have to do something, Your Highness," Ávgos put in. "There are hundreds and hundreds of people in Inari—the village on the other side of the gateway. If there are still more hiisi there…"

"I know, Ávgos, and I am sorry. But I cannot protect a land that I cannot reach."

She had a point. But they couldn't just sit here waiting until the lake finally froze over. Beside him, Shaun and Lyylia had been whispering to each other, and now Shaun spoke up.

"Your Majesty, may I be excused for a moment? I have something back in my room that I'd like you to see."

She nodded. He got up from the bench, and followed the guard, who was positioned by the doorway as always, out of the room.

Ávgos looked at Lyylia. "What's he talking about?"

"The stone necklace that the hiisi wore," she said.

Ávgos wondered why Shaun thought that was important, especially right now, but before he could ask Lyylia another question, Kuu spoke again.

"After we finish this meal, we will be leaving for Shaman Wind's village. His village is high in the Western Fells, near the Dark River, in an area that is little populated. Scouts from dozens of villages have been positioned along the shore of the Dark Water Lake, and along the River to both the east and the west, but there are no scouts at the far western end of the river. The river crossing there would be difficult, but since it is currently not well guarded, it would be the most likely place for the changelings to cross from Ice-Dark into Pohjola."

Ávgos tried to remember the map of Pohjola from the Halls of Time. "So Shaman Wind's village is even farther away from the lake than this castle is, Highness?" he asked.

"Yes," she said. "But we will be traveling by sledge, so the journey will not be long or difficult. And we will meet the two new Kalevalans there."

"I think it would be wiser to stay here," Lyylia said. "Or go back to Shaman Pike's village to meet the others."

Kuu regarded Lyylia in silence for a moment. "Why?" she finally asked. She didn't sound upset, just curious.

"Every time we travel, we go farther away from the way home. We don't belong here, Your Highness."

Kuu didn't reply. She just continued looking at Lyylia with a neutral expression, though her silver eyes glittered more brightly. The air in the room seemed to grow colder, and a strange stillness settled. Ávgos held his breath. The Queen didn't seem angry; but then, she didn't seem *anything* at the moment. She and Lyylia held one another's gaze in silence, almost as if some sort of mental communication were taking place.

The moment was broken by Shaun's return. He approached the head of the table, and laid a fist-sized lump of gray rock, with a rough line of twine tied around it, beside Kuu's plate.

"I took this off of one of the hiisi right after we arrived here," he said, sitting back down on the bench next to Lyylia. "It's some sort of magnetic ore."

"What does 'magnetic' mean?" Kuu asked, picking up the stone and examining it.

"It's attracted to certain metals, like iron. Or attracted to other rocks of its type." Shaun clapped his hands together to illustrate.

"Ah. Yes, we have stones and metals that do this." Kuu turned the rock over in her hand.

Shaun drew a breath. "My theory is that the hiisi were using the stones to find the gateway in the lake."

Everyone at the table looked at him.

"How might they do this?" Kuu asked.

"Well, the gateway is obviously some sort of interdimensional portal, or a wormhole—like a tunnel that crosses through more dimensions than the regular four dimensions that we live in and observe every day. Therefore, it probably produces energy. Some sort of electromagnetic radiation that, while it may not be detectable to the eye, can be detected with a more sensitive tool, like a magnet."

Shaun's explanation sounded like pure science fiction—

but then again, here they were, on the other side of this "wormhole." Kuu didn't respond right away—she continued turning the stone over in her hand, as if deeply contemplating what Shaun had just said. If she didn't know what 'magnetic' meant, then surely she hadn't actually understood anything he'd just said. Ávgos barely understood it.

But he understood enough to know that a source of electromagnetic energy that could be detected with a magnet could most certainly be detected with high-tech computer equipment.

"How long have you had this idea?" Ávgos asked him. "And why didn't you tell us about it?"

"I thought I'd mentioned it to Lyylia," Shaun said. "And it's just a theory. I'd been mulling it over in the back of my mind for a few days."

Ávgos felt a sudden and surprising flare of anger. "So you've had a potential way of finding the gateway and didn't tell us about it or try to use it?"

Shaun drew back at his tone. "What was I supposed to do? Swim around in a giant freezing lake, waving a rock and hope something happened besides hypothermia?"

Ávgos clenched his jaw, still angry—and feeling angry at himself for feeling angry at Shaun. "You have a computer that reads electromagnetism in the sky. Couldn't you..?" He waved at the air.

"Modify it to scan for a wormhole under water? Maybe, but not without a hell of a lot of work and time. I'm not Scotty from *Star Trek*."

"But if that's the key to getting home—" Ávgos pointed at the rock still in Kuu's hand.

"Maybe it is, maybe it isn't," Shaun said, his voice rising. "We don't know anything about hiisi intelligence or culture.

For all we know it could be a rank insignia or memento from the hiisi's wife when he left home. You didn't make any of these suggestions when we were still at the lake."

"I didn't know!" Ávgos realized he was shouting. "You didn't tell us that you had a theory about electromagnetism!"

"I didn't, not at that moment!"

Lyylia banged her hand down on the table. "Stop, both of you!" She was seated between them, and Ávgos realized she'd been getting the brunt of their shouting. "There's nothing we could do then, so stop arguing. But now...maybe there is something we could do now."

Lyylia looked over at Kuu.

Ávgos felt his anger and frustration wash away under a wave of embarrassment. He was on the end of the bench nearest the Queen, so she got the full show of him behaving like an idiot. Even the times that he and Maden had butted heads, he'd never resorted to a shouting match at the dinner table.

The Menninkäinen across the table had been silent this entire time, and now looked stunned and slightly alarmed. Ávgos avoided meeting their eyes as he glanced sheepishly at Queen Kuu.

She still held the stone in her hand, and looked at the three of them with a thoughtful expression. The silence stretched on, and Ávgos tried not to squirm.

"This stone may indeed be a key to finding the gateway," she said at last. "But it will require meditation, study, experimentation, and time. I will not allow anyone to search the lake at this time."

"But, Your Majesty—" Ávgos began, and Lyylia opened her mouth.

Kuu held up her other hand to silence them. "It is not my desire to prevent you from returning home, but right now it is neither safe nor practical to make the attempt. We have a more immediate problem: the kidnapping and transformation of the Gentle Beasts. We must not only find a way to rescue them, but we must divine Hiisi-Hiisi's reasons for this subterfuge."

She laid the stone down on the tabletop and looked at them with glittering eyes. "Pohjola is in danger—a danger more subtle and devious than the last great battle against Ice-Dark. And Kalevala is also in danger—for Hiisi-Hiisi sent his people to your world to kidnap reindeer for his plans. Finding the gateway will not stop this danger, to either of our lands, because the danger is here. And I need your help."

Kuu picked up the stone again and stared at it a moment, then looked back at the three of them. "You have knowledge that I do not have—perhaps the same knowledge that Hiisi-Hiisi has." She hefted the stone for emphasis. "Together, we can recover your Gentle Beasts and protect both of our lands. If a way to return you to Kalevala presents itself, I will gladly send you back home—but I will not do so at the risk of Menninkäinen lives, or your lives. But first we must focus on the actions of Ice-Dark. To protect Kalevala and your people, Hiisi-Hiisi must be stopped *here*."

Ávgos drew a deep breath when Kuu finished speaking. She was right—their world had become involved in this problem, whatever it was, the moment the reindeer and the humans had been kidnapped. He still wished they could search for the gateway—to send a message home, if nothing else—but the problem was now much bigger than just being stranded in a strange land.

Kuu pushed back her chair and stood up, and everyone scrambled to stand, as well. "We will travel to the Western Fells. There we will meet the newly arrived Kalevalans, and hopefully learn more about how the changelings are entering

Pohjola." She looked over at the row of Menninkäinen. "You four have done a great service and honor by guiding and protecting the Kalevalans thus far. You are welcome to join us on this journey, but you are under no obligation to do so."

They all bowed.

"Make your preparations. We leave before the midday meal." With the magnetic stone in hand, Kuu strode out of the room. Her dog, who had lain quiet behind her chair the whole time, trotted behind her.

Ávgos drew another deep breath. He ached to see Sirkka again, but Kuu's words had left him feeling strangely calm. They would get through this. They'd find his reindeer, stop the evil king, and then safely go home at last.

Maden stood outside the hut. The little man named Hoof had invited him to spend the night with his family, which was a nice change from sleeping outdoors, or even sleeping in the earth hut back in Inari.

Back in Inari... Maden could still hardly believe this was happening. He remembered seeing a white bear-like monster dragging Teija into the lake. He'd gone in after her, and they had surfaced in water that wasn't Lake Inari. Two men, unusually short and dressed in furs, had hauled them from the icy water and informed them that they'd traveled through a magical "gateway" and were now in a place called Pohjola.

Old memories had been stirring in Maden's mind over the past two days as he and Teija followed their rescuers through the forest to the nearest village. His grandmother had told him stories of old Sami myths about double-bottomed lakes, where magical creatures lived in a world below the water and below the ground. And stories from *The Kalevala* of a mystical land in the north full of monsters and magic. Nice fairy tales for children, but not something that mattered in the real world.

Except now it *was* the real world.

Maden turned as Hoof came out of the hut hauling two large leather sacks. Maden went over to help him heft one.

"The rest of our supplies for our journey to the Western Fells," Hoof said, dragging his sack towards the horse and sled that stood waiting outside the hut next door.

Maden helped him tie down the sacks. "You said it's a week's journey to the Western Fells?" he said to Hoof. "And our friends Ávgos and Lyylia will be there when we get there?"

"That's right," said Hoof. "Queen Kuu is headed for Shaman Wind's village high in the Western Fells, and wishes for you to meet her there. The other three Kalevalans are with her."

As bizarre as all of this was, at least these Menninkäinen people seemed fully familiar with humans and Earth—or Kalevala, as they called it, oddly. Apparently word got around quickly with these "moon mirrors" he'd heard mentioned.

And the question of what had happened to Ávgos and Lyylia and the reindeer was finally answered. No wonder the police had gotten nowhere with their investigation.

Unfortunately, it meant that two more people had now been added to the list of missing persons. Well, one person, for sure—Teija would be missed when she never returned to Helsinki or checked in with her friend. Maden had already abandoned his family when he'd gone to Rovaniemi, so the only person who might miss him would be that police officer who'd been tailing him. He wished he had a cigarette.

Tip, the other Menninkäinen who'd been their guide, came out of the hut next door to Hoof's. Teija emerged behind him. She looked surprisingly chipper and more energetic than she had in days. If he'd thought it was bad hauling a city girl around the woods outside Inari village, it was worse trying to keep her calm and motivated while hiking with strangers through the snow on another planet.

"You look like you're feeling better this morning," Maden said to her.

"I had the best night's sleep that I've had in days," she replied. "I'll never take hot food and sleeping indoors for granted again."

"Glad you enjoyed it. It's tent camping for the next week, though." He nodded at the laden sled.

"I know." She sounded unconcerned. She pulled her hood up over her blond hair, and Maden belatedly realized that she was wearing a Menninkäinen-style fur coat. "Tip's neighbor gave it to me," she said. "It even has mittens." She pulled a bulky pair of fur mittens out of the front pocket.

"Nice," he grunted. "The coat you wore to Inari certainly didn't look warm." Teija was petite enough that Menninkäinen clothing would fit her, he mused. Hoof's wife had given him a pair of thick socks, which were long and shapeless enough that they fit, for which he was grateful.

A crowd had been slowly gathering in the snowy pathway through the village, and now an excited murmur rose as the leader of the village, an old man called Shaman Pike, came down the hill towards them.

Maden felt someone plucking at his sleeve, and he turned to look down at a small plump woman and a shaggy-haired little boy.

"Safe journey to you," she said with a smile. "Could you

do me a favor, when you reach the village in the Fells and meet your friends? Please tell Boots that his family loves him and is very proud of him. I'm his wife, Silver, and this is our son, Track."

"You're really tall!" remarked Track, bouncing on his toes.

Maden managed a smile. His own family may not know or care that he was missing, but Ávgos' wife, Sirkka, didn't deserve whatever hell she was living through with him missing. At least this poor woman knew where her husband was. "Boots is his name? Sure, I'll tell him."

Silver grinned up at him. "Thank you. And please tell Eider that his parents and sister send their love, as well. I know they are here somewhere..." She stood on her tiptoes and scanned the growing crowd.

"I'll tell him," Maden said. "I promise."

Shaman Pike arrived, and the crowd quieted.

"It has been an honor and privilege to have Kalevalans in our humble village once again," said Pike. "Tip and Hoof, you do your village and your people proud by guiding and protecting these Kalevalans on their journey to meet their friends and the Queen."

Pike moved through the crowd towards Maden and Teija. "Honored Kalevalans, I have a gift for you." He wore a long fur robe decorated with beads and small objects hanging on strings like tassels. He lifted one of the objects, broke the thread, and held it out towards them.

"Maden, Teija, may this protection stone keep you safe as you journey throughout our land, until you are safely reunited with your loved ones and return home to Kalevala."

Maden carefully took the stone from Pike. It was a lumpy pebble, but as he turned it over in his hand, an opalescent glint of green, blue, and pearly white shone through. Some sort of gemstone ore, perhaps?

"Thank you very much, Shaman Pike," Teija said politely.

Maden nodded his thanks. He held the stone in his hand until Pike turned away, then put it in his pocket as he pulled out his gloves.

"And now, a safe journey!" said Pike. "May Dream be with you all!"

The crowd parted. Tip, leading the horse, headed down the pathway towards the edge of the village. Maden and Teija followed him, with Hoof and his dog Icerunner behind.

"Just a few more days, and we'll finally see Lyylia and your cousin again," Teija said quietly as they walked.

Maden nodded. After everything, he hoped that Ávgos would be as happy to see him as he'd be to see Ávgos. "And we'll get to meet the mysterious Queen Kuu," he said. "She must be a popular ruler—everyone keeps talking about her."

"And we'll meet the other poor person who got kidnapped, too," Teija added. The Menninkäinen had told them that three people had come through the gateway before them. "What kind of a name is 'Sahn?' Is it anyone you know from Inari?"

"Doesn't sound familiar. We'll meet him when we get to Shaman Wind's village, I guess."

They had now left the outskirts of the village and followed a trail through the snowy forest. Maden hoped the good weather would hold. He looked up at the strange, tiny blue sun flickering down through the trees. They had a week to learn more about this place before finally meeting the others. And then maybe, hopefully, they could find a way home.

For three days now, the caravan of four sledges had been gliding through the tundras and forests of Pohjola, and Shaun wasn't bored yet. Stretching and bathroom breaks were brief, and often coupled with a stop in a village, where Queen Kuu spoke with the shaman leader. But even if he would have liked to have more frequent breaks, or to stay in a village for a meal or sleeping, Shaun couldn't complain about the luxurious mode of travel. Cold wind whipped in from the open sides of the sledge, and there wasn't a lot of leg room, but the cushioned bench and back and the canvas windscreen made it very comfortable. And so far, Shaun had been sharing a sledge with Lyylia.

He made a mental note to thank Ávgos and Eider for always riding together. The Queen was in the lead sledge, and the supply sledge brought up the rear of their caravan. They had not encountered anything but wild animals in the woods—no other travelers, no hiisi, and no reindeer. At least the weather had been good so far.

When "night" came and the Dancing Lights began, the sledges continued to travel, the horses still going at a brisk trot through the snow. Shaun leaned out the side of the sledge, gripping the wooden framework of the canvas roof to make sure he didn't slip out. The cold air bit at his face. Pink and red aurora flickered through the tree branches above.

"Dancing Lights?" Lyylia asked.

"Yep," he said, pulling himself back in. "Can you see them?"

"No. But every night you do this—lean outside until you see the Lights."

He laughed. "I'm that predictable?"

"Every person has patterns. I see patterns."

Of course she did. She was a detective, trained to pay attention to things that no one else did. In other circumstances, that might make him uncomfortable, but not here, not with her.

"I see the patterns in the sky, but that's about it for me," he said. "The aurora are pink and red tonight. That means the charged particles are interacting with oxygen at the higher altitudes. And I'll tell you a secret—if you promise not to laugh."

She gave him an expectant look, but didn't crack a smile.

"My favorite color is pink. And I'll tell you why. The first time I saw pink aurora—and I mean really pink, like Barbie pink—I thought it was the most beautiful thing in the world. It's almost that bright shade of pink tonight. I don't often see that Barbie pink color, but it's always been my favorite aurora color."

Lyylia smiled at that.

"Now this doesn't mean I'm going to wear pink shirts, or have pink sofas in my house or anything like that," Shaun added quickly. "Just so you know. I like pink aurora, but I'm still a manly man when it comes to anything else. You know, black, gray, khaki—those are good colors."

This time Lyylia laughed. She leaned her head out of her side of the sledge, just briefly, and not nearly as far out as he always leaned. "I see," she said, pulling back in and looking at him. "Beautiful."

"So, now your turn," he said. "What's your favorite color?"

She was quiet for a moment. "Purple. Light color purple, like flowers."

"Violet?"

"Yes, violet."

Shaun grinned. "Like your scarf?"

Before they'd left the Queen's castle, they'd discovered that the castle workers had modified some Menninkäinen clothing, and given all three of them full Pohjola outfits: lined leather breeches, warm woven tunics, fur coats and mittens, even socks, boots, and underclothes.

Despite being bundled up in full gear, though, Lyylia was still wearing her blue-and-purple scarf. She gave an almost embarrassed little smile, and tweaked at the edge of the scarf peeking out of the collar of her fur coat.

After a while the sledges began to slow, and they stopped at the edge of a small clearing. Boots, who was driving their sledge, hopped down from his perch as Shaun climbed out. A man named Tug was driving Ávgos and Eider's sledge, Stone was driving the Queen, and a man named Falcon had the supply sledge. They had three dogs with them: Child of Light, Wolf's Bane, and another named Long-Tooth.

The dogs began sniffing around the perimeter of the clearing. Shaun felt reassured by having such vigilant dogs with them, as well as the spears and bows and arrows the Menninkäinen carried. They should easily be able to handle any hiisi or murderous changelings they might come across.

Stone and Falcon took bows and arrows, and the dog Long-Tooth, and went into the woods to go hunting. Tug unharnessed the horses. Lyylia began unloading the blankets, while Ávgos and Boots started with the tents. Eider began clearing a space in the snow to build a fire. Shaun picked up a dead branch lying nearby and gave it to Eider, and then headed into the trees to find more firewood.

He spotted Kuu standing a few yards away in the middle of the clearing, her hood back and her face turned up to the sky, holding a silver dish in her hands. A moon mirror. She used it every night when they stopped, using it to communicate with shamans in villages all across Pohjola. Shaun wished he could get a closer look at the thing to learn how it worked, but he was nervous about asking her outright if he could look at it, especially while she was in the middle of using it. A blue glow came from the silver dish, and Kuu lowered her head to look into the light. The pink aurora washed though the trees above her. Shaun turned back to his task of collecting firewood. The sooner they made camp, the sooner he could set up his aurora scanner.

Now that he had well over a week's worth of scans from Pohjola skies, he was noticing more and more differences between Earth's aurora and Pohjola's aurora. Firstly there was the high intensity and the clockwork regularity of Pohjola's Dancing Lights. He also had recorded a unique sound coming from the aurora that he had never observed anywhere on Earth before—an intermittent sound, but with a repeating pattern. He wished he knew more about how the Dancing Lights of Pohjola were produced, since the astrophysics behind aurora didn't seem to apply here.

He stumbled over something in the snow and bent to examine it. A dead branch, which was what he was supposed to be looking for, instead of musing about the Lights. *Firewood first, aurora later,* he told himself. He collected a small armload, then went back to the camp so Eider would have something to start a fire with.

Shaun headed back into the trees in a different direction, gathering more sticks as he went. He crested a rise in the land and began to head downhill, but he could still easily hear the bustle and conversation from the campsite. The sound of gurgling water came from somewhere nearby.

As he snapped a low-hanging dead branch off a tree, it suddenly occurred to him that, in this late autumn wilderness, he shouldn't be hearing running water. Every stream they'd crossed had been frozen solid enough for the sledges to pass over the ice.

Looking down the hill, he saw a wide creek winding between the trees, smooth and white. But a large crack gashed across the ice like a wound. Water flowed briskly through the open space, jostling the chunks of broken ice. Shaun started down the hill, worried that someone had fallen in.

"Stone? Falcon?" he called.

No reply came. But then there was a rustle in the bushes at the edge of the stream, and a large black horse pushed out into view.

Shaun paused in his approach. The animal looked larger than the stocky Pohjola horses, and it had no bridle or harness of any sort. It also looked wet—even at this distance, Shaun could see water dripping from its mane and tail.

"Hello? Is anyone around?" Shaun walked slowly towards it, but saw no evidence of anyone nearby. "Did you fall through the ice?" he said to the horse, though of course he lacked the magical Menninkäinen ability to understand animals. "Where's your owner?"

In response, the horse cocked its head at him and hissed.

Shaun froze. Not only should a horse not be hissing like a snake, but he suddenly noticed the animal's eyes—glittering white like crystals. The horse opened its mouth and pulled back its lips, revealing a mouthful of sharp, jagged teeth.

And then it screamed.

Shaun collapsed into the snow, the world spinning, his vision blurred. The horse's scream, like shredding metal and dying electronics, rang in his ears. He suddenly felt desperately thirsty. How close was he to the creek?

He pushed himself up on hands and knees, stumbled over the pile of sticks that he'd dropped, and collapsed into the snow again, rolling several feet down the hill. He dragged his eyes open, and saw two horse hooves in front of him.

The black horse was standing over him. The horse's legs, with a light feathering of fur around the ankles, were dripping wet; water glistened on its hooves as if they were polished stone. Cold radiated from the creature, a cold more numbing than the night air or the snow Shaun was lying in. His heart was pounding, but he found he couldn't make his arms or legs move.

He thought he heard the barking of dogs, tinny and distant, and faint shouting voices. He tried to call out for help, but all that came out was a cough. The horse's head bent down into his field of vision. Its white jewel-like eyes sent a chill through his mind. The horse seized the bottom of his coat in its mouth and pulled, and Shaun felt himself being dragged downhill. Still dizzy and uncoordinated, he tried to thrash.

Suddenly the horse released him, and a blur of white went past. Child of Light slammed into the horse, and right behind her the other two dogs launched into an attack. All Shaun could do was lie in the snow and watch the scene blur in front of him—the horse kicking and rearing and thrashing, and the three dogs being hurled aside again and again. The horse shrieked, again that metallic demonic wail, and he saw human-shaped figures collapsing in the snow near him.

The horse dipped its head down towards Shaun again, and with a cackling hiss, slammed its head into his torso. The impact knocked the breath out of him, and he felt himself rolling down the hill and then tumbling out onto the ice of the creek. Gasping, all he could do was lie there—he couldn't feel his arms and legs now, and he wasn't even sure if his eyes were open or closed.

He heard shouting all around him, punctuated by the hideous multi-tonal shriek of the horse. Dragging his eyes open, he saw the broken ice of the steam right in front him, the dark water rushing by. The water danced with the reflection of the pink and red aurora overhead. If he could reach the water, he could get away from all this noise, and he could touch the Dancing Lights…

"Shaun!" The shout sounded far away, but he felt hands grabbing his arms and lifting him. Lyylia and Ávgos were dragging him off the ice.

Then all three of them collapsed in the snow as the horse screamed again. A dog lay in the snow nearby, unmoving, a Menninkäinen lying beside it. Boots? Shaun tried to reach for him. At the edge of his vision, he could see the horse out on the ice of the creek, rearing and kicking and lunging at three Menninkäinen with spears. Arrows flew through the air toward the horse, but neither the arrows nor the spear thrusts seemed to slow it down.

Voices were speaking in his ear, a language he didn't understand. Hands touched him, turning him over in the snow.

"Shaun, can you hear me?" This voice he understood. Lyylia's face appeared in his vision. He wanted to hug her, but his arms still wouldn't work.

"Lyylia," he tried to say, but it came out as a groan.

The horse screamed, but this time the cry sounded more like a shriek of pain. Shaun's ears stung with the sound, but vertigo and numbness didn't descend on him.

"It's the Queen!" he heard Ávgos shout.

Twisting his head around, Shaun saw the horse still standing on the ice. Facing off with the creature was Queen Kuu, a long silver sword in her hands, the spear-wielding Menninkäinen behind her.

The horse reared, lashing out with its front hooves; Kuu deflected the strike with the flat of the sword. The horse came down with its head, teeth bared. Kuu skipped to the side and swung the sword across its neck. The horse screamed in pain again, but there was no blood.

Shaun lay in the snow, his limbs still deadweight, staring at the battle as if he were watching a movie. Kuu had worn a white tunic and breeches instead of a dress for the sledge journey; and now with unrestricted movement, she leapt around like a dancer, her knee-high gray boots never slipping on the ice. Kuu struck the horse several times, but still it did not bleed. The sword clanged like a bell every time the horse's hooves struck the blade.

Finally a slash with her sword to its front legs sent the creature tumbling to the ice. It rolled away from her, legs flailing, as she slashed down again. Her sword cut into the ice with an audible crack. The horse rolled back to its feet, but before Kuu could strike again, it leapt for the hole in the ice and splashed into the water.

Leaving the sword stuck in the ice, Kuu dropped down on her knees at the edge of the hole and plunged her right hand into the water. After a moment, she drew her hand back out, and stood up. The horse was nowhere to be seen. As Kuu yanked her sword out of the ice, Shaun saw, even at this distance, that her eyes were glowing a bright purple.

Shaun's head spun as Lyylia and Ávgos lifted him again, pulling his arms across their shoulders so they could carry him. A wave of nausea swept over him. He still couldn't feel his feet.

He closed his eyes, suddenly bone-weary. He tried to push away the memory of the horse's unearthly shrieks. The last thing he thought about before letting unconsciousness take him was the ringing of the silver sword and Kuu's blazing purple eyes.

"Lyylia, you must sleep."

Lyylia looked up from staring into the flames of the fire. Queen Kuu stood outside one of the tents, her small frame drum in one hand.

"I'll be fine, Your Highness," Lyylia said, sitting up a little straighter and tightening the heavy woolen blanket around her shoulders. "I can stay out here a while longer."

Kuu came towards her. "Stone will stand guard for the first watch, and then Tug." Across the clearing, Stone stood facing the forest, a spear in his hand and a bow and quiver on his back.

"I know," said Lyylia. "I...I just didn't want him to wake up alone, I guess."

Shaun lay beside her in the snow, bundled up in blankets and furs. He'd been unconscious since they'd dragged him back from the creek, which was several hours ago now. Kuu wanted him to stay by the fire to keep warm until he regained consciousness.

Kuu gave Lyylia a gentle smile as she knelt in the snow beside her. "You care for him."

Lyylia felt her cheeks warm. "I just want to make sure he'll be all right," she said, keeping her voice cool and professional. "It's my job. That's what I do in my world—I protect and defend the innocent."

Kuu smiled again. "We have much in common, then, as it is also my job to protect and defend."

"Well, you're a lot better at it than I am." Lyylia felt her professionalism slipping, as all the guilt and stress of their time here—and the attack earlier that evening—suddenly dropped onto her shoulders like a load of stones.

"I have had many centuries of practice," Kuu said, a sparkle in her silver eyes. "Do not blame yourself, Lyylia. You have done well, keeping your fellow Kalevalans safe in a strange land. And Shaun will be fine—there is no dark magic left on him."

She leaned over and laid a hand gently on Shaun's forehead; her other hand she placed flat against the skin of her drum in her lap. She then gently touched his throat below his chin, which was just visible at the edge of the blanket. Then she laid her hand on the furs near his stomach, her other hand still resting on her drum.

"He will wake soon, I believe," she said, pulling her hand back. "Make sure he eats some of the stew with the healing moss." She nodded at the cooking pot hanging over the fire.

"I will, Highness," Lyylia said. Kuu had insisted that everyone eat it. Stone and Falcon hadn't been able to hunt anything, so the stew was just a thin porridge made with some of the root vegetables and the reconstituted barley mash that they'd brought with them. Apparently the healing moss was a lichen that was plentiful in the forests of Pohjola. Lyylia remembered that it had seemed to help her head injury when they'd first arrived here.

"How is everyone else?" Lyylia then asked.

"They are fine. Boots is sleeping peacefully now. And Long-Tooth's leg is bandaged and should heal quickly."

While everyone had experienced dizziness, disorientation, and general terror at the monster's screams, Boots had been affected more strongly. Kuu said that he'd been struck with dark magic, the same as Shaun. Boots had spent an hour wrapped up by the fire, just like Shaun, until he'd woken up and had eaten some of the stew. The dog Long-Tooth had apparently been bitten by the monster. Lyylia didn't want to even try to imagine what the outcome might have been if Kuu hadn't driven the creature off.

Lyylia nodded at Kuu in acknowledgement. "That's good.

I'm glad everyone's fine. And I'll be fine, too. I'll just stay out here a little longer."

"Very well," Kuu said with a smile. She picked up her drum and stood, brushing the snow from her breeches. "Good night, Lyylia."

"Good night, Your Highness."

She watched as Kuu went around to the other side of the clearing, spoke briefly to Stone, and then went over to where the sledges were parked and retrieved the moon mirror. Lyylia wondered if she'd be telling shamans about what had happened tonight.

Lyylia still hardly understood what had happened. A shrieking monster that looked like a horse but wasn't, dark magic, Kuu's obvious skill with a sword...

Beside her, Shaun made a quiet groaning noise and shifted around in the blankets. Instantly alert, Lyylia scooted closer to his head. "Shaun?" she said quietly.

After a moment he opened his eyes. He blinked a few times, then his hazel eyes focused on her. "Lyylia?" His voice sounded hoarse.

She smiled. "You're awake."

"Yeah, I guess so." He worked a hand free from the blankets and rubbed at his eyes, then at the beard stubble on his jaw. Then he looked around at the fire and the campsite. "I must have passed out." He looked back up at her. "Lyylia, what happened?"

"We were attacked by a Näkki," she said.

"A what?"

"Remember when Kuu showed to us the battle with Ice-Dark, in the Halls of Time?"

Shaun nodded. "I remember. I went back and took pictures of the murals. You mean those creatures from Ice-Dark that were painted like black dogs?"

Lyylia nodded. "Kuu says they can be horses, too."

"Näkki are evil shamans of the water," came Kuu's voice, and Lyylia looked over to see her coming around the fire towards them. "They are shape-changing creatures that are both cunning and powerful. Näkki can appear as a black horse or a black wolf, whichever form they choose. On occasion in the past there have been problems with Näkki in the Dark Water Lake at the border with Ice-Dark. But never before has one of these creatures come this far into Pohjola."

Kuu knelt down beside them and laid a hand on Shaun's forehead. "How do you feel, Shaun?"

"Okay, I guess. I have a bit of a headache. At least I can move now." He wiggled in the blanket and pulled his other arm out. "I remember I couldn't move, couldn't see straight..." He looked up at Kuu. "I wanted to go into the water. It was trying to drown me, wasn't it?"

"Perhaps. Or kidnap you."

Kuu had said the same thing to Lyylia and the others earlier. So they were in fact being hunted. Lyylia also realized that the broken bridge and the death of Shaman Talon had probably been the work of a Näkki and not reindeer changelings, after all. She hadn't mentioned that theory to Kuu yet, but she figured that the Queen had come to the same conclusion.

Shaun shifted around in the blankets, and Lyylia and Kuu helped him to sit up. Lyylia picked up the small wooden bowl lying beside the fire and spooned the remainder of the porridge into it.

"Eat it all," Kuu told him. "There is healing moss in it, and it will refresh you. When you are feeling strong enough, please return to the tents to sleep." She looked at Lyylia. "Both of you."

"Yes, Your Highness," Lyylia said. "I'll get some sleep, I promise."

Kuu smiled, laid a hand on Shaun's shoulder, and then rose and returned to her spot across the clearing over by the sledges.

Lyylia looked back at Shaun. He sipped at the porridge and met her eyes. "Well," he said, lowering the bowl. "This is scary as hell."

She nodded in agreement. She sat with him in silence while he finished the bowl of porridge. Then she helped him stand up and disentangled him from the heavy fur outer blanket so he could walk. She led him over to the nearest tent where Boots and Falcon were sleeping. She had the next tent, with Eider and Stone, who was still standing guard. Tug and Ávgos were in the next tent, with Kuu in her own tent at the end. Kuu had taken the injured Long-Tooth into her tent after the fight with the Näkki; Child of Light was presumably in there, as well. Wolf's Bane lay in the snow outside Boots and Falcon's tent.

Lyylia pulled the flap aside and held it open for Shaun. He paused and looked at her. "Thank you. I know that you and Ávgos pulled me off the ice. I...I don't even want to think about what might have happened if you guys hadn't showed up when you did."

Lyylia smiled at him. "It was Kuu who saved us."

"I remember that, I think. She fought it. I didn't know she'd brought a sword with her."

Lyylia hadn't known that, either, but she was glad to know that the Queen was both armed and capable.

Shaun started to say something else, but then shut his mouth. Lyylia raised her eyebrows, but he just smiled at her. "Nothing," he said. "Well, good-night, Lyylia."

"*Hyvää yötä,* Shaun," she replied in Finnish, returning his smile.

He smiled again, then ducked down to enter the tent. Lyylia took one last look around the quiet campsite—the dwindling fire, the tethered horses dozing at the edge of the trees, Stone standing alert, and Kuu standing with the silver dish in her hands, her face upturned to the Dancing Lights overhead. Lyylia let out a breath, and then crawled into her tent to get some sleep.

"Fair travels to you, strangers!"

Teija looked up from her meal of bread, cheese, and hard-boiled eggs. Two Menninkäinen hunters were coming down the woodland trail towards them. One carrried two dead rabbits, and the other had a cluster of birds tied at the feet slung over his shoulder.

"Good day to you!" Tip returned the greeting. "Rest a moment, and join us for some food!"

"Thank you," they said, sitting down. "And greetings to you, visitors from Kalevala."

"Nice to meet you," said Teija politely. Maðen merely nodded.

It was pleasant, if a little disconcerting, how friendly everyone was. Teija almost felt like a celebrity, since everyone they met had heard of their arrival and was excited to meet them. For a place with no telephones or mail service, news traveled awfully fast. Everyone had also heard of Lyylia and the others, though no one they'd encountered since leaving Pike's village had met them face to face, and therefore had no current information about them. Teija hoped that they were safe with the mysterious but apparently much-adored Queen of Pohjola.

"Are you on your way to Shaman Berry's village?" asked one of the hunters, as they helped themselves to some of the cheese that Tip offered.

"Our journey's end is at Shaman Wind's village, high in the Western Fells," Hoof said, tossing a peeled egg to the dog Icerunner who was resting beside him. "At least another day's travel away, I believe. Is Shaman Berry's village close by?"

"Oh, yes," said the other man. He pulled a pouch of dried fruit and nuts from his coat pocket, and offered it to everyone. "If you're traveling down the road that direction, you will arrive there well before night. That's where we're from—we went out hunting early this morning, and are on our way home."

Indoor sleeping tonight, at least, which was nice. Although the leather tents and fur blankets they'd been camping with were surprisingly warm.

Everyone finished eating and gathered up their gear. The four Menninkäinen chatted cheerfully, and Maden and Teija walked along in silence. Teija found herself lagging behind the group again, as she had been for most of the trip, despite her best efforts to keep pace. Even in places with deep snow where they all put on snowshoes, she had trouble walking with any speed on the awkward, old-fashioned snowshoes.

Maden dropped back to walk beside her.

"I'm fine," she groused at him before he could say anything.

"Just trying to be polite and make sure you're all right," he grunted back. "You don't have to be rude."

"Sorry," she said, a bit more gently. "But if you wouldn't keep calling me 'city girl' as if it were a curse word…"

"I didn't say anything."

"Not this time."

Maden frowned at her. "Women," he muttered with a shake of his head, and strode ahead, leaving her to trail behind.

Voices sounded up ahead, and they came to a frozen creek where a bridge-building project was underway. Menninkäinen were busy sawing a downed tree into planks, while others were lashing the planks of wood together with ropes.

"Greetings!" said a man holding a tall spear. "You're headed for Shaman Berry's village, yes? Just a moment—wait right here."

He turned and marched towards the stream. "Roll the tree out, men—we have people who need to cross! And weapons at the ready—we must be prepared at any moment!"

The little men stopped what they were doing and rushed to pick up spears and bows and arrows. Several others began rolling another felled tree towards the creek. With a lot of heaving and grunting, they slid it across the stream at a point where the bank was fairly level with the surface of the ice. More Menninkäinen on the other side grabbed the end of the tree as it came across. All of the weapon-bearing men stood at attention with their spears and arrows pointed at the tree-trunk bridge.

"What's going on?" Teija asked. Winter seemed like an odd time to build a bridge across a narrow, frozen stream.

"We've received a word and warning that the water may be possessed by a Näkki," said the spear-wielding Menninkäinen who seemed to be in charge.

"A Näkki?" Tip said incredulously. "But those are just stories, creatures of songs and the old myths!"

"Just like Gentle Beasts and giants from Kalevala, my friend?" replied the other man in a good-natured retort.

"What's a Näkki?" asked Maden.

"An evil spirit that lives in water," said the spear-man.

"Shaman Berry received a message from Queen Kuu herself, saying that she had encountered a Näkki and that everyone should be wary of the water. That's why we're building a bridge. The stream is shallow here and normally we wade across in summer and cross the ice in winter. But we dare not do that now, in case a Näkki is living here. Once the bridge is built, there will be armed guards posted day and night, to make sure travelers are kept safe."

"Thank you for the warning," Hoof said. "Since we've been traveling, we hadn't heard any of this. We will be cautious of the water now." He set off across the tree-bridge, Icerunner right behind him.

Teija hesitated at the end of the log. It wasn't a huge tree, and the bark was peeling in places. *Come on, girl,* she told herself. Walking across a narrow log was hardly the most challenging thing she'd done in the past week or so.

"Want me to carry you?" Maden said from behind her.

She tossed a glare over her shoulder at him, and hurried across the log. Maden came behind her, then Tip, then the two hunters.

The Menninkäinen around them kept their weapons trained at various points on the ice until they were all safely on the other bank.

"Safe travels, friends!" the man in charge called after them as the others busied themselves hauling the log back to the bank and resuming their work.

"So what is this Näkki thing they were talking about?" Teija asked, trying not to sound nervous.

"It's a story told to children to teach them that water can be dangerous," Tip said.

"Now comes winter's wind and chill,
Ice on the river and fog on the hill,

The Näkki rages like a wolf alone.
Beware of storms, heed the water's song,
The river rages like a wolf alone."

"I've heard that song, as well," said one of the hunters.

Maden frowned, and Teija tried not to feel worried.

They received the typical warm welcome when they arrived at Shaman Berry's village. After being divided up to different homes for dinner, they all gathered together again outside Berry's hut, at her request. Most of the village had turned out, as well, and they'd all brought wooden skis, which lay in a huge pile beside the upright stone that marked Berry's hut as the shaman's residence.

"Please, take whatever you find that will fit you," Berry said to them. "By midday tomorrow, you will have reached the Fells, and skis will make your journey easier."

Teija had noticed that the forest was growing thinner and the ground hillier as they'd traveled this afternoon. She was better at cross-country skiing than snowshoeing, but these skis all looked dangerously short and narrow.

Eventually she selected a pair, along with a set of poles. The others selected skis, as well, and they all thanked Shaman Berry and the villagers. On the way back to the huts for the night, Teija noticed that the green aurora that had been rippling overhead all evening suddenly seemed brighter. The snow and the trees all around seemed awash in a greenish-yellow glow.

"Look, earth-walking Lights!" said Hoof, pointing.

She and Maden turned to stare where he was pointing. Off in the distance, beyond the village where the trees grew sparse, the curtains of green looked like they'd fallen out of the sky and were trailing the ground.

Maden muttered something in Sami.

"They're really…touching the ground?" Teija asked. Her

skin felt prickly.

"Yes," said Tip. "Several times a year, the Lights come and walk the earth. Just briefly—see, they're going back to the sky again."

In the distance, the snow was glowing green, but then the veil of moving light faded back up into the sky, like a window shade being pulled up. The green curtain blended back in with the rest of the Lights in the sky and resumed its meandering ribbons of shifting yellow and green.

"I've seen the Northern Lights all my life, but I've never seen anything like that," Maðen said, sounding impressed.

"Every year on midsummer's night, the Dancing Lights come to the earth on an island we call the Dancing Ground," Tip said. "The old songs say that in the ancient times, the lord of the Gentle Beasts went to the Dancing Ground and called the Lights to the earth on midsummer's night."

"Wow," was all Teija could say.

Outside her host's hut, she paused to look up at the Lights once more. The calm ribbons of green stayed in the sky. She glanced over at Maðen and saw that he was looking at the Lights, too.

"I wonder if Lyylia and Ávgos saw that where they are," she said.

Maðen looked over at her. "Shaman Berry said that Shaman Wind's village is less than two days away."

Teija smiled. "That's good. So we'll see them soon."

"Yep." He looked back up at the sky.

"Thank you, by the way."

Maðen turned back to her. "For what?"

"I don't think I ever said thank you for rescuing me," Teija said. She felt a bit embarrassed that she hadn't said anything before now. "When that hiisi grabbed me...well, you went after me, not knowing what had happened or anything."

"I'm not a fan of people being forcibly drowned," he said. "Especially in my home lake." He actually cracked a slight smile. "It's not like I really rescued you, though. I was just swimming after you and the monster, and then we were cracking through ice here. Tip's the one who killed the hiisi."

Teija had lost consciousness shortly after being dragged into the water, and didn't remember anything until she'd woken up bundled in furs by a campfire. "Well, thank you anyway." She smiled.

"You're welcome, I guess." Maden gave her another almost-smile. "Sleep well, Teija. See you in the morning."

"You too, Maden. Good-night."

They arrived in Shaman Wind's village early in the day, and Ávgos was disappointed that the other people from Finland weren't there yet. He was anxious for an update, any sort of update, from home. Shaman Wind informed them that he'd spoken with Shaman Berry via moon mirror the night before, and the newcomers had stayed the night in her village and would arrive here by the evening. Ávgos wanted to stay to meet them, but Queen Kuu had other ideas.

"The Dark River and the border with Ice-Dark is a few hours away," Kuu said. "The weather is mild, and we should be able to reach the border before night. I am certain this is the area where the changelings are crossing from Ice-Dark. We will camp on the tundra and return here tomorrow morning."

Ávgos wondered what sort of proof Kuu was hoping to

find, but he decided not to ask. Her mood had changed, ever since the Näkki attack four days ago. She seemed more...*intense*, somehow, yet also more withdrawn. She no longer ate with everyone whenever they'd made camp in the evenings, instead standing off by herself with the moon mirror in her hands. He wondered if she'd gotten any sleep the past several nights.

While the villagers prepared a sled of supplies for the trip to the border, Ávgos followed the Queen and Shaman Wind to a paddock behind Wind's house. A horse was there, standing under the roof of a run-in shelter, eating hay. Beside it was a reindeer.

Kuu entered the paddock, Ávgos behind her.

"My earmark," Ávgos said, looking at the animal's left ear.

Kuu touched the reindeer and spoke quietly to it for a moment.

"Iiđeed is her name," Kuu said as they exited the paddock. "Please keep her here, Wind, until we return from the river. I would like to take her back to my castle, where she can be kept safe with her companions."

"Of course, Your Majesty," said Wind.

A short time later, they set off north towards the river. Kuu had requested that both Ávgos and Lyylia accompany her; Stone was also with them, along with two men from Wind's village, and a horse pulling the supply sled. Child of Light went with them, of course, and another dog from the village.

They were all given skis. For the first several hours, Ávgos enjoyed the exercise and the wide open snowy tundra all around. He hadn't used old-fashioned wooden skis since he was a child, but these skis were surprisingly smooth and sturdy.

After a short rest and some food, they continued on. The clear weather started to turn—the brisk breeze became an icy wind, and a thin layer of clouds blanketed the stars. The light of Pohjantähti became a hazy glow and bands of fog settled on the hills.

It was so quiet in the snow and the fog, despite the wind and the swish of skis. The only animals they saw was a herd of wild horses, stocky shadows in the foggy distance. In this land so much like home, Ávgos kept expecting to see a herd of reindeer.

At the head of the group, Kuu slowed to a halt, and turned to face the little caravan. "We will stop here and set up a camp. I don't want our camp to be in sight of the river."

The Menninkäinen began unloading the sled.

Lyylia slid to a stop and leaned on her ski poles. Ávgos halted beside her. "Are you all right?" he asked her.

"Just exhausted," she said. "And I thought I was in good shape. I love skiing as much as the next Finn, but my God..."

Ávgos gave a wry smile. "I know how you feel. My legs are starting to ache."

Together they slid over to the sled to help unload it. "So why do you suppose the Queen wanted the two of us on this trip, but not Shaun?" Ávgos mused aloud, as they dragged a heavy blanket roll off the sled. "He seemed a little annoyed about being left behind."

"Well, she considers you the reindeer expert," Lyylia said. "Which you are. And I assume she wants my deductive reasoning skills. I wouldn't worry about Shaun—he probably set up his aurora scanner the minute we left the village."

"I'm sure you're right," Ávgos said with a chuckle.

After they'd set up two tents and built a fire with the fuel they'd brought, Kuu left the camp in the care of the two men from the village. The horse and the dog stayed, as well. With Ávgos, Lyylia, Stone, and Child of Light, Kuu set off north again into the fog.

They skied on for at least another couple of hours—or at least what felt like it. Ávgos' sense of time had abandoned him here, with no familiar routine of tending to reindeer and tending to his family. Shaun, who had been tracking the count of days on his computer, had told him the other day that they'd been here for two weeks. It felt longer than that.

Finally Kuu slowed again, and Ávgos saw that they were coming to the edge of a cliff. They halted about a meter from the edge and took in an impressive sight. A rocky foreboding wall plunged away below, the bottom a dizzying distance away; a gray-white thread of a frozen river lined the bottom of the gorge. Wisps of icy fog floated through the air below. No birds flew, no hardy bushes or moss clung to the walls of the gorge. It was entirely lifeless.

The other side of the gorge was a cliff just as tall and sheer, and it didn't look all that far away—relatively speaking. But it seemed oddly darker and out of focus, even though the fog here was thin. It was almost as if the perpetual overhead light of Pohjantähti just didn't quite reach that far.

Beside him, Stone muttered, "Dream protect us!"

"He will, Stone," Kuu said. "And Äi, the World Serpent of Ice-Dark, cannot reach across this river and harm us, no matter how close we stand to her land. But Hiisi-Hiisi's subtlety has managed to reach across, and it will be stopped."

"So that's Ice-Dark on the other side?" asked Ávgos.

"Yes." Kuu's voice was tight.

"Is the gorge this steep for the entire length of the river?" Lyylia asked.

"This is the steepest part of the gorge. But the walls remain high on both sides until the river widens near the Dark Water Lake," said Kuu. "That is many days' journey in that direction." She pointed eastwards, away to their right.

"How far does it go in that direction?" Lyylia asked, pointing to their left.

"Less than a day's journey. We are very near to the edge of Pohjola."

"So that's where the river begins?"

"No, that is where it ends. The river begins at the eastern edge of Pohjola, high in the Mountains of the Moon."

"Okay, so what about past the end of the river? Wouldn't Hiisi-Hiisi be sending the reindeer changelings over at an easier crossing than this?"

"The terrain is like this across the Western Fells. The easiest crossing is near the lake, but I have scouts posted along the river there," Kuu said.

"But what's past the edge of Pohjola?" Lyylia pressed.

"Nothing."

Lyylia sighed. "It can't be nothing. The river has to end in another lake or an ocean or something."

"There is nothing past the end of the river," Kuu said. "It simply ends. Mist surrounds all of Pohjola—past the Mountains of the Moon in the east and the Endless Ice in the south, and here in the Fells of the west. None can venture through the Mist, not even Hiisi-Hiisi or changelings from Kalevala. To enter the Mist is death."

Lyylia didn't seem to know what to say to that, and Ávgos couldn't come up with a reply or a question, either. Kuu certainly ought to know the borders of her own land, but her answer didn't make logical sense. Nothing made logical sense here, though...

"Is it actually possible for anyone or anything to climb that?" Lyylia said finally, looking down into the gorge.

"It's possible," said Stone. "A strong climber with an ice axe and arrow tips on their boot soles could scale these walls.

But it would be very dangerous."

"But would a barefoot Menninkäinen who used to be a reindeer be able to do that?" wondered Lyylia.

Kuu and Stone looked at Ávgos.

"I have no idea," he said helplessly. "In my world, reindeer stay reindeer their entire lives."

"And normally, they would here, as well," said Kuu.

"This still seems like an unnecessarily difficult crossing," Lyylia said.

"This is true, but it is also the most unobserved crossing," Kuu said. "Ever since hiisi were spotted in the lake back in the spring, I have had scouts patrolling the borders of the lake and the river." She looked out over the gorge, at the shadowy bank on the other side. "I did not have scouts monitoring this far western edge of the river, however, because I knew the crossing was the most forbidding, and there are few villages in the Western Fells. I sought only to protect villages from pestering hiisi—there was no indication of changelings or Näkki or any other threat at that time."

"So you believe that Hiisi-Hiisi would know this?" Ávgos asked. "That this part of the river was unguarded?"

"He must," said Kuu, turning her head to look at him. "If he has been preparing for this mission of subterfuge, then he would have been spying on the movements at Pohjola's border as he made his plan." Very briefly, a blush of violet light flashed across her silver eyes. "If our positions were reversed, it is what I would do."

No one said anything. The wind tugged at them, and made an eerie whistling sound as it swept down the gorge. Overhead, a diffuse greenish glow flickered through the clouds as the Dancing Lights began.

Kuu glanced up at the sky, then back at the gorge. "Stone,

Ávgos, you two ski to the east, and see if you find anything. Lyylia, you and I will head west. I believe we still have some time before the weather worsens, and then we will return to the camp."

Ávgos obediently followed Stone as they turned to the right and skied along the edge of the gorge. He wasn't sure what they should be looking for. Footprints? A line of Menninkäinen scaling the cliff face?

"I have found something!" Stone's voice shouted. He had ventured a short ways ahead of Ávgos. "My Queen, I have found something!"

Ávgos skied over to him, and looked down into the gorge. Lying on the narrow, rocky shore on the other side of the frozen river was a dead reindeer.

"I think we just found where they're crossing the river," Ávgos murmured. He didn't know whether he'd been hoping to find evidence to support Kuu's theory or not. He looked across the gorge at the shadowy shore of Ice-Dark and felt an uncharacteristic swell of fury and hatred at the mysterious King Hiisi-Hiisi.

Kuu and Lyylia arrived.

"I don't want to try to climb down that," said Lyylia. "But I wish we could see from here if it's got your earmark."

"It would have to be mine, wouldn't it?" Ávgos said. "There are no more Pohjola reindeer. Right?"

"That is correct," said Kuu. She squatted down at the edge of the cliff, the tips of her skis hanging off the edge as she peered over. Stone put out a hand towards her.

"Please use caution, my Queen."

"Thank you, Stone. Look, do you see that lying beside the Gentle Beast? It looks like fur, but it is not big enough to another reindeer."

Lyylia squatted down next to her, laying her ski poles in the snow. "It's clothing. See, that brown lump lying across its front legs—it looks like a shirt."

Ávgos squinted down into the foggy depths and wished he had his herding binoculars with him. "And that other brown lump over near the bottom of the cliff looks like a bundle of rope," he said, and sighed. "I guess that confirms it, then. This reindeer, transformed and dressed as a Menninkäinen, probably fell while trying to repel or climb down the cliff, and then shifted back after it died. I hate to just leave it there, but…"

Kuu stood up and put a hand on his shoulder. "I am sorry, Ávgos. No living thing should be treated this way, least of all a Gentle Beast. Come—it grows late, and we are all weary. We have learned what we came here to learn—let us return to the others and camp for the night."

The return trip to the campsite felt longer, colder, and more exhausting than the trip to the river. The clouds dimmed the light from Pohjantähti, the moon, and the aurora, making Ávgos feel even more tired. He began to worry that they'd overshot the campsite in the foggy gloom, or had set off from the gorge too far to the east or the west.

"We should be nearing the campsite," Stone said. He then gave a loud wailing sort of call. Ávgos jumped at the sudden piercing sound. After a moment, a faint reply came from ahead, a similar high-pitched wail.

"Yes, we are nearly there," Stone said. He looked over at Ávgos and Lyylia. "Fells-cry. It is a call that can be heard across a great distance."

Eventually the campfire came into view. The two Menninkäinen had hot porridge and warm long-leaf brew waiting for them. Ávgos realized that he was famished, as well as exhausted. Kuu joined them for this meal.

"Now that we know where the changelings are being sent across, we could send a scouting party across into Ice-Dark," Lyylia said as they began eating.

"No," said Kuu. "It is too dangerous. We do not know what might lie on the other side. And with the complication of Näkki in Pohjola…I can only hope that no Näkki lay under that ice as we looked down into the gorge. Hiisi-Hiisi is trying to move in secret—otherwise he would not be using such an elaborate scheme as changelings from another world. If we send scouts into Ice-Dark, he will know that we have discovered the changelings."

She set down her bowl of porridge and looked at Ávgos and Lyylia. "Tomorrow morning, we will return to Shaman Wind's village. Stone, I am placing you in charge of scouting out locations for other guard posts. No closer to the Dark River than this—if there are scouts on Ice-Dark's border, I don't want these camps to be seen from that side." She looked at the other two Menninkäinen. "It is much to ask of you, but I need you to stay here as guards until more Menninkäinen from other villages can arrive to man other posts."

"We will gladly stand watch, Your Grace," said one of them. "We brought three days' worth of food and fuel, and we can make it last longer, if needed."

"You will not be left alone that long," Kuu said, giving them a gentle smile. Ávgos realized it was the first time he'd seen her smile in days.

The clouds grew thicker and it began to snow, blocking out what little they could see of the Dancing Lights. Stone volunteered to keep first watch, but Kuu shook her head.

"You need your strength, Stone, for the task I have given you. Sleep. I will keep watch through the night."

"But, my Queen—" Stone started to protest.

"Sleep," she interrupted him. "All of you." She went over to the sled, now unhitched from the horse, and rummaged in the small pile of bundles still on the sled. Then she straightened up and turned around, and held up a long sword in a smooth leather sheath. White and blue gemstones glittered in the gold hilt.

Ávgos still vividly remembered her fight with the black horse, her graceful, almost easy movements as she swung her sword and avoided the Näkki's strikes. He felt suddenly confident that they'd be safe tonight and that everything would eventually turn out all right.

In the snowy twilight everyone crawled into the tents. Ávgos wondered what Sirkka was doing. He knew she'd be staying strong through her worry, staying strong for Piijá. He wished he could talk to her. He hoped Maden had returned home and was looking after her.

As he bedded down in the furs between the two Menninkäinen from the village, he thought of the Queen, standing guard outside in the storm, armed only with a gold and silver sword. But it was enough, and he quickly drifted off to sleep.

Lyylia crawled out of the tent, feeling her sore muscles complaining with the movement. Even after all the walking they'd been doing in Pohjola, the skiing yesterday had brought her to a new level of exhaustion.

It was as dark as a winter twilight back home—the thick clouds diffused only the faintest glow from Pohjantähti, and the snow was falling more heavily than the day before. The campfire still blazed heartily in the snowfall, and Lyylia joined the others around the fire for a quick breakfast of hardboiled eggs and dried fruit. She glanced around at Ávgos, the three Menninkäinen, the horse, and the dog.

"Where's Kuu?"

"The Queen returned to the edge of the Dark River," Stone said. "She left as soon as I awoke, earlier this morning. She will return soon."

A few minutes later, Kuu appeared out of the snow and fog. She slid to a halt at the edge of the campfire. Child of Light sat down and shook herself, sending snow scattering in every direction.

"Any changes at the river, my Queen?" Stone asked her, taking her ski poles from her.

"No, nothing new that I could see." She pulled off one of her mittens and accepted the mug of steaming long-leaf that one of the other Menninkäinen handed her. As Kuu downed the beverage, Lyylia realized that she had her sword strapped across her back. The gold hilt caught the firelight as Kuu turned and handed the empty mug back. "Thank you." She looked at Lyylia and Ávgos. "We should leave soon, before the storm worsens."

Stone came over with a small pack as they strapped on their skis. "Here is food for the day," he said. "Have a safe journey."

"I'll carry that," Ávgos volunteered. Stone handed him the pack.

"Thank you, Stone," Kuu said. "Men from other villages will be arriving soon."

"We will watch and protect the border, my Queen. And send word immediately if we should see anything or capture any creature crossing from Ice-Dark."

"Thank you," Kuu said again. "Dream be with you."

All three of the Menninkäinen bowed.

Lyylia, Ávgos, and Kuu set off into the snowy gloom. Trying to ignore her aching muscles, Lyylia doggedly followed Kuu as the endless tundra marched past. Ávgos puffed beside her. The white blurry forms of Kuu on her skis and Child of Light trotting beside her consumed Lyylia's focus.

They stopped for only the briefest rests and quick bites of food. The wind and biting snow stung at Lyylia's face with equal vigor whether she was moving into the wind or sitting still. Her scarf that she had wrapped across her nose and mouth was stiff with ice. Despite her wool-lined fur mittens, her fingers had gone numb.

At last, Lyylia saw what looked like deep tendrils of fog up ahead, but then realized it was curls of smoke from chimneys. Soon the little collection of snow-laden stone huts came into view, with lantern lights glowing warmly from tiny windows.

As they drew closer, she saw Shaun and several Menninkäinen coming out of houses to greet them.

"Welcome back!" Shaman Wind boomed as the three of them slowed on their skis. He was one of the tallest Menninkäinen they'd met, with a deep-chested voice.

"Greetings, Shaman Wind," Kuu replied, halting in front of him.

"It was a successful journey, my Queen?" Wind asked as he took her ski poles and bent down to help her off with her skis.

"I believe so," Kuu said.

Lyylia handed her poles to an eager-to-help Menninkäinen, and gratefully let Shaun unstrap her boots from the skis.

"Good to see you made it back safely," he said, smiling up at her. "There's a surprise waiting for you in Shaman Wind's hut."

"Surprise?" Lyylia repeated with a frown. More "surprises"

was not what any of them needed right now. Shaun just grinned, that irritating, cocky smile that highlighted the dimple on his cheek beneath his beard stubble. "What surprise?"

"You'll see," he said cryptically. "So what was the Dark River like?"

"Frozen. And difficult for a crossing. But they are crossing from Ice-Dark anyway—we found a reindeer."

"You did?" Shaun gathered up her skis and stood up.

"It was dead," Ávgos put in, stepping off his skis and nodding a thanks to the Menninkäinen who helped him.

"Was it a changeling?"

"I'm sure," Lyylia said.

"The newcomers from Kalevala arrived yesterday evening, Your Highness," Wind was saying as he took Kuu's skis and stood back up. "They arrived safely and said that they did not encounter any Näkki on their journey."

"That's good news," Kuu said. "I am anxious to meet them."

As much as she wished that more people from Finland hadn't gotten trapped here, Lyylia was also anxious to meet them. They could give her an update on the investigation, on what the police were doing to try to find them. If only they could find the portal here and communicate with Earth...

As the group followed Shaman Wind through the snow towards his hut, a tall human man came out of one of the other huts. Since Shaun and Ávgos were beside her, the sight of another human briefly startled her—she didn't realize how accustomed she'd gotten to seeing people who were all a good head shorter than she was.

"Oh my God…" said Ávgos, and slowed in his walking. "It can't be… Maden?"

The other man raised a hand at Ávgos in greeting and came towards him.

Lyylia's brain kicked into gear. Mađen—Ávgos' cousin who had been the primary suspect for the disappearance of the reindeer, and who had been in Rovaniemi when they were still in Inari. But how—

"Lyylia!"

Lyylia's heart skipped a beat at the familiar voice. Another human had come out of the hut and was running towards her. She could only gape in stunned silence as her sister threw her arms around her.

"Oh, Lyylia, I thought I'd never see you again!"

"Teija…" Lyylia embraced her sister, her thoughts and emotions in a whirlwind. "Teija, how can you even be here? What…?"

"Come inside out of the cold!" said Shaman Wind, pushing open the door of his house. "There is food prepared for everyone."

The table was barely big enough for six human-sized people to squeeze onto the benches. Wind's wife served hot bread and roasted meat and potatoes in a creamy sauce, then retreated to a chair across the room to nurse her baby. Wind pulled a stool up to the table, since the benches were full.

"I welcome you to Pohjola and the Western Fells," Kuu began conversationally, once they'd all started eating. "I seem to be at a disadvantage here, since Shaun was here to welcome you to the village, and clearly you already know Ávgos and Lyylia. We were not told your names—only that more people had come from Kalevala. I'm Kuu, Queen of Pohjola. It's an honor to meet more Kalevalans."

"My name is Mađen, um, Your Majesty," said the younger Sami man. "Ávgos is my cousin. It's an honor to finally meet you, Your Highness." He gave a nodding bow to her across the table.

"And you as well, Maðen," Kuu said with a smile, and then looked over at Teija.

Lyylia was seated between Kuu and Teija, so she leaned back slightly so that the two of them could see each other.

"I'm Teija, Your Majesty—Lyylia's my sister."

"I thought so, the moment I saw your face—you two look so much alike."

"And now I'd like to hear how she got here," said Lyylia, looking at Teija. It felt surreal, seeing her sister sitting next to her in a Menninkäinen hut. "The lake where the gateway is, on the Finland side—in Kalevala—is nowhere near where she lives."

Teija sighed and looked at her. "Your boss called Mom and told her you'd disappeared. We were both so worried... It was a stupid decision, I know—but I went up to Inari, just hoping that somehow, some way, I could find out what had happened to you. I just…I just had to do something."

"But how did you get *here*?" Lyylia asked.

"Our hut was broken into and ransacked by something," Maðen said. "Now we know it was a hiisi. I saw Teija being dragged into the lake by this furry monster, so I dove in after her. And we wound up here."

"'Our' hut?" Ávgos said, raising his eyebrows.

"One of the earth huts, along the lake," Maðen said. He then launched into a tale of his chance encounter with Teija in Rovaniemi and their journey up to Inari. As he talked, Lyylia looked at her sister and couldn't decide if she felt impressed or horrified. Teija had always been prone to flights of fancy, but something as brash and dangerous as taking a snowmobile journey across Lapland with a complete stranger…

Lyylia pulled her attention back to what Maðen was saying. "You're sure you saw National Bureau officers?" she asked him. "Not just local Sami police or officers from other jurisdictions?"

"I think so," he said. "We didn't get close enough to any of them to read insignia on their uniforms."

"If the police had quarantined the village after we disappeared," Lyylia said. "And then you two disappeared, too..."

"Except nobody knows we disappeared," Teija put in. "Mom and my friend Johanna knew I'd gone to Inari, but no one else knew we were there."

"So that means no one is even looking for you," Ávgos said, and looked at his cousin, an odd expression on his face.

Lyylia tried not to think about how distraught her poor mother must be at this point, with both of her daughters now out of touch and missing. "It also might mean that by this point the police have lifted the lockdown on Inari," she said. "Which could be good, because it might mean that fewer people are actively searching the lake. So if there's still another hiisi there, it might not capture anyone."

"Or it could be bad," Ávgos added. "Because now the locals can move around, and the tourists can come in, so there are more people it could potentially attack."

"If there are any hiisi still there at all," Lyylia finished. Which they had no way of knowing. They should be prepared for the possibility, though, that yet another person or two might arrive from Finland in the next few days, before the lake froze over completely.

She exchanged somber looks with Ávgos. Mađen frowned and worked his jaw. Teija stared down at her plate. Shaun was quietly eating, and didn't look up when the conversation paused. Lyylia belatedly realized that they'd all been talking in Finnish, so of course he had no idea what was going on.

"May I interject one question?" Kuu said into the pause.

"Of course, Your Highness," said Lyylia.

"I realize that you are discussing places and things of your world that I would know nothing about. But…what is this word 'police?' I don't understand what that means."

"The police are the guardians and protectors of society," Lyylia explained. "They keep people safe, they…investigate mysteries that are hurting people. They help to enforce the law and keep things organized. I'm a member of the police. That's what I do in my world—I solve mysteries and try to keep people safe."

"Ah," said Kuu, her silver eyes widening with understanding. "That makes sense. That is why you are always asking complicated questions."

Everyone at the table laughed, Lyylia included. "Yes. That's what I do for a living, Highness—ask complicated questions."

"One of our questions was answered at the Dark River," Kuu then said, her face growing serious. "Changelings are indeed crossing at a point not far from this village." She looked at Maden and then Teija. "Have you been told of the changelings from Ice-Dark?"

"Yes," said Maden. "I think so. Shaman Wind told us about an evil king who stole our reindeer from Earth."

Kuu nodded. "Hiisi-Hiisi, the king of Ice-Dark. He captured your beasts, and is now casting dark spells upon them to transform them into the appearance of Menninkäinen. We do not know how many might be in Pohjola, nor do we yet know why he is doing this. We found a dead reindeer in the river gorge."

Shaman Wind bowed his head in a sorrowful manner, and Maden frowned.

"Stone and the others remained at the border to stand watch," Kuu continued, looking at Wind. "More guard posts will be set up along the border, as I told you last night, Wind."

"Yes, Your Grace," Wind said. "Today I had everyone begin collecting supplies in the village hall. Any supplies that arrive from other villages will be stored there and sent out as soon as possible. I am honored to help organize this effort in protecting our land."

After the meal, everyone was divided up between different homes to sleep for the night. What with the exhausting day and no visible Dancing Lights, Lyylia had no idea what time it was, but she was more than happy to have a warm place to sleep out of the storm. She wished that she and Teija could have stayed together, but she knew it would be impractical and rude to ask a family to host two guests.

Teija...she could still hardly believe her sister was here. Lyylia wished her sister *wasn't* here—Teija wasn't cut out for difficult and dangerous situations, and she needed to be at home in Helsinki to look after their mother, especially now. And yet, Teija had braved the difficult and dangerous to find her.

Lyylia wanted to be angry with Teija, but as she bedded down in the furs in her host's bedroom, she felt hot tears slipping down her cheeks. Foolish, selfish, happy tears. She rubbed at her eyes with her tunic sleeve, and turned over so that the Menninkäinen family couldn't see her face when they came into the room. She shouldn't be happy that the hiisi had terrorized more people in Inari, or that her mother had probably gone from panic to deep depression at this point.

She wasn't happy about those things, but to see Teija, to have her sister here with her... She let herself silently cry until she fell asleep.

Shaun hurried through the blowing snow, using his sturdy laptop case to shield his face from the wind. The storm had gotten progressively worse during the night—he was glad that Lyylia and Ávgos and Kuu had made it back from the river yesterday afternoon. Shaun had cobbled together a little lean-to shelter of sorts with a donated ladder and a tent skin to keep the snow off his computer during the past two nights. But with this wind, he wasn't sure that the microphones would be catching very accurate auroral recordings.

Shaman Wind's village—appropriate name for the leader of this remote, unsheltered tundra village—had a large community hall, like other Menninkäinen villages where they'd stayed. All of the travelers had gathered there this morning, since it was the only building large enough to accommodate five humans and the Menninkäinen who had come with them.

A fire blazed in the pit in the center of the room—the flames flared and danced in the wind as Shaun slammed the door behind him. Ávgos and Maden were sitting at the table nearest the door, along with Boots, Eider, and three other Menninkäinen. Across the room, Kuu and Shaman Wind sat at another of the long tables. Lyylia and Teija were standing by the fire and looked up as Shaun came in. Another table across the room was piled with blankets, food, tools, and other supplies for the groups of guards who were to be stationed along the river border.

Shaun put his case down at the other end of Ávgos and Maden's table and unpacked his laptop. Boots was the first to come over, with the other Menninkäinen close behind him. "Tip and Hoof and Falcon wish to see your magic talisman that lets you speak to the Dancing Lights," he said.

"Well, I don't speak to the Lights," Shaun said. "But the Lights speak to me." He scrolled through the recordings from last night. Despite the storm, it looked like there was some usable data. "See, the Dancing Lights make all kinds of sounds that we can't hear with our ears. This device reproduces the sounds so we can actually hear them."

Shaun felt rather proud of himself for having gotten good at explaining his work in not only layman's terms, but explaining it to a pre-industrial mindset. "The lines that show up here and move across the screen like this, that's just a visual representation of the sounds. See, this is a high-pitched sound. This one's much lower and more intermittent." He pointed at the computer screen as whistling static and low popping noises came from the speakers.

"The Dancing Lights make all those noises?" said Hoof. "I've heard sounds before when the Lights are especially bright, or sometimes when the Lights walk the earth, but never like that."

"Right—these are the sounds that you can't hear. Can dogs sometimes hear things that you can't?"

"Yes."

"It's kind of the same thing," Shaun said. "This machine can hear the sounds that Menninkäinen—and even dogs—can't hear."

Shaun noticed Ávgos whispering to Mađen, probably translating for him what Shaun was saying. When Mađen and Teija had first arrived in the village, Shaun had quickly figured out that while Teija's English was as good as Lyylia's, Mađen spoke almost no English. Their getting-to-know-you session, that had taken place while Lyylia, Ávgos, and Kuu were gone, had been a little slow, with Boots doing the translating, since the language barrier didn't exist for him.

Waiting for one of his analysis programs to load, Shaun looked over at Lyylia and Teija standing by the fire. He'd recognized Teija as soon as she and Maðen had arrived in the village. Her blond hair was longer and less curly than her sister's, and she was several inches shorter, but her eyes and her voice were the same as Lyylia's.

He pushed away a wave of loneliness. Both Lyylia and Ávgos had people who loved them enough to leave jobs, homes, and families and face the unknown to find them. Shaun was sure that the other three guys on his science team were missing his computer equipment more than they were missing him right now. And if his family even knew that he'd gone missing, they were probably muttering amongst themselves about how he should've just stayed at home in Pennsylvania, working in the steel factory like everyone else.

Shaun let himself stare at Lyylia and Teija a moment longer. When he looked back down at his computer, he saw Eider at his elbow, also blatantly staring at the two women.

"Teija is even more beautiful than her sister," Eider murmured, then looked at Shaun with an embarrassed smile.

Shaun grinned at him. "How lucky are we? We get to travel with two incredibly hot women." He caught himself before saying "three hot women," figuring that calling Queen Kuu "hot" would be disrespectful at best.

"Hot?" repeated Eider.

"Kalevala slang," Shaun explained. "It means incredibly beautiful, when you're describing a woman."

Eider smiled.

The other Menninkäinen were all absorbed with watching the laptop screen and seemed to be ignoring their exchange. But Shaun glanced up and saw Ávgos across the table, trying to hide a smirk.

"Oh, come on, Ávgos. I know you're a married man, but you have to agree that they're hot."

"I am staying out of this conversation," Ávgos returned mildly.

Shaun chuckled and turned back to his laptop. He put the recordings from last night through a sound scrubber to get rid of the ambient noise of wind, and then ran the sound files through the analysis programs that compared each wavelength to all the previous recordings. There it was again—that frequency that he'd never encountered anywhere on Earth. The microphones recorded the repeating collection of tones almost every night, though they'd been the strongest and most frequent on the night of the ground-level Lights.

Shaun glanced up to see Queen Kuu and Shaman Wind approaching the table.

"I was just telling Wind how you bring out this glowing box every night during our travels," Kuu said conversationally. "It listens to the Dancing Lights, is that right?"

"That's right, Your Highness." Kuu hadn't asked him about his computer at all. He wasn't even sure if she'd noticed it, since she was usually removed from the group and busy with a moon mirror when they'd made camp in the evenings. Despite the news about the changelings crossing into Pohjola, Kuu seemed more relaxed now than she had in several days.

"Does your talisman tell you the songs of the Lights even during a storm when you can't see them?" Kuu then asked.

"Yes, it does. I get some interference from the wind, but I did capture some recordings last night. Would you like to hear them?"

"Certainly," said Kuu. She and Wind came around the table to stand behind Shaun with everyone else.

"Fascinating," said Wind, peering at the graphs and scrolling numbers on the screen.

Shaun played one of the recordings from the previous

night. Electronic warbling and popping came from the laptop.

"This one is interesting," he said, selecting the next recording. He glanced up briefly as Lyylia and Teija approached the table to join in. "I've listened to the Dancing Lights every day for years in Kalevala, but I've never heard this particular sound until I came to Pohjola."

Instead of low warbling or high chirping like most aurora sounds, this recording covered the range of low and high frequencies. Normally each sound was different based on altitude of the aurora, ambient electrical charges in the air, and other factors. But this series of sounds formed a distinct pattern and did not appear to be associated with any other unusual factors—at least that Shaun's microphones and sensors had been able to pick up so far.

Kuu leaned forward and put her hands on the tabletop. "Let me hear that again," she said, when the recording finished.

Shaun played it again. Kuu leaned closer, a strange, intense expression on her face. Headphones would give greater clarity to the sounds than the laptop speakers; Shaun thought about getting them, but they were in the equipment backpack, which was at his host's house.

Suddenly Teija gave a yelp, and both she and Lyylia backed away from the table. Shaun looked down and saw a bright blue snake head appear under Kuu's sleeve cuff. He jumped in spite of himself as Dream slithered across the back of Kuu's hand and onto the tabletop. An awed murmur swept through the Menninkäinen.

Dream glided over to the laptop, and then raised up as if he were looking at the computer screen. His red eyes glittered. Kuu sat down on the bench next to Shaun.

"Once more, please, Shaun—let me hear those sounds again."

Keeping an eye on the little blue snake, Shaun hit the play button again. The pattern of low whistles and multi-pitched clicks came from the speakers. Dream remained in his raised position, nose pointed at the laptop, and flicked his tongue.

"I know these sounds," said Kuu. "Dream, can it be?"

The little blue snake turned his head to look at her, then turned back to the computer screen.

"You know these sounds?" Shaun repeated, looking down at the snake and then at Kuu. "What do you mean?"

"The sounds are different, but the pattern and the tones… it is a spell I once sang." She leaned towards the laptop, close enough that Shaun could see her silver eyes reflecting the light from the screen, and her long hair brushed against his arm.

"Long ago," Kuu said, still focused on the laptop, "after the battle with Hiisi-Hiisi and his army on the Dark Water Lake, Kied-Kie-Jubmel and I cast a spell on the Dancing Lights to bring them to the ground."

"You told to us this story at the castle, yes?" said Lyylia, approaching the table again. She stayed on the opposite side from where Kuu was sitting. Teija remained several steps back.

"Yes," said Kuu. "The story is painted on the walls in the Halls of Time."

"Kied-Kie-Jubmel, my Queen?" Wind put in. "The king of the Gentle Beasts, lord of the woods and the first shaman of Pohjola?"

"Yes, Wind—the same. Kied-Kie-Jubmel, who has become a mere legend in your songs. At the beginning of time, together we shared the wisdom of Dream with the first Menninkäinen who wanted to become shamans." She pointed at the laptop screen. "And these sounds that you, Shaun, have captured from the Dancing Lights—these sounds are the song that we sang that night at the Dancing Ground."

"Um, are you sure, Your Highness?" Shaun asked carefully. If he remembered the story correctly, that happened some five hundred years ago. Surely her memory of the incident wasn't that clear.

"I am quite sure," Kuu said in a tone of finality.

Maðen asked a question in Finnish.

"Yes, I suppose you and Teija would not have heard the story," Kuu said. "I will tell you the full tale later, but to put it briefly, hundreds of seasons ago, the reindeer of Pohjola vanished. Neither Dream nor I have ever been able to figure out what happened to them. I thought that they had found the gateway and traveled to Kalevala, but..." She trailed off and shook her head.

Then Kuu looked at Shaun, an intense look on her face. Shaun tried not to feel swallowed up by her eyes. "You said that you have heard this song in the Lights ever since you arrived in Pohjola?" she said.

He nodded. "Yes, Your Highness. Almost every night that I've been able to record the Lights. Sometimes my recorders catch it only once during a night's display, sometimes multiple times. It was the strongest on the nights when we witnessed the Lights coming down to ground-level."

Kuu bowed her head and covered her face with her hands. "Oh, Kied-Kie-Jubmel, my most beloved friend!" Kuu muttered into her hands. "So many endless seasons I've missed you and searched for you, and all this time you have been calling for me. Dream, forgive me!"

The room was uncomfortably silent. Shaun wondered if Kuu was crying. He shifted on the bench beside her, wondering what to do. The little blue snake remained in front of the laptop.

Then Kuu lifted her head; her eyes were moist, but she wore a determined expression. "We must go to the Dancing

Ground," she said, her voice strong again. "Kied-Kie-Jubmel and I cast our spell on the Dancing Lights on that island—this spell." She pointed at the laptop. "Only Kied-Kie-Jubmel would know that song. I must cast another spell there, to bring him down from the Lights."

"What do you mean, Your Grace?" Wind asked.

"*Mitä?*" Lyylia said.

Kuu looked across the table at Lyylia and Teija, then glanced around at everyone else huddled behind her looking at the computer. "Kied-Kie-Jubmel never left Pohjola," she said. "He is in the Dancing Lights."

Shaun stared at Kuu. There was absolutely no way that a reindeer could actually be part of the aurora; the aurora was electromagnetic energy, not a physical place. Not only was this a completely absurd idea, but…

Kuu met his gaze, and he could see it in her eyes. She was completely serious. Then he remembered the Menninkäinen transforming into a reindeer, and the black horse that came out of the ice and nearly killed him, and the little blue snake on the table in front of him. This was a world where science and logic were not the ultimate authorities.

"Wind, please carry on with the plans of distribution of men and supplies to guard the edge of the river, as we discussed," Kuu said, standing up. She stepped over the bench, then laid a hand on the tabletop. Dream coiled into her palm.

Wind bowed. "Yes, Your Majesty."

Kuu looked at the rest of the Menninkäinen gaping up at her. "Make ready to depart. We will leave as soon as the storm lessens. We head for the Dancing Ground Island."

Shaun felt a strange shudder of anticipation. He wasn't sure if he could believe Kuu's idea that the reindeer was *in* the Lights. Or that there was such a thing as a magic spell that could control ground-level aurora. But he was eager to find out.

Dream coiled himself around Kuu's right hand, then slithered up inside her sleeve. Shaun pulled his eyes away from the snake on her wrist as Kuu spoke again.

"There I will once again join Kied-Kie-Jubmel in song. Pohjola has been without its reindeer for far too long."

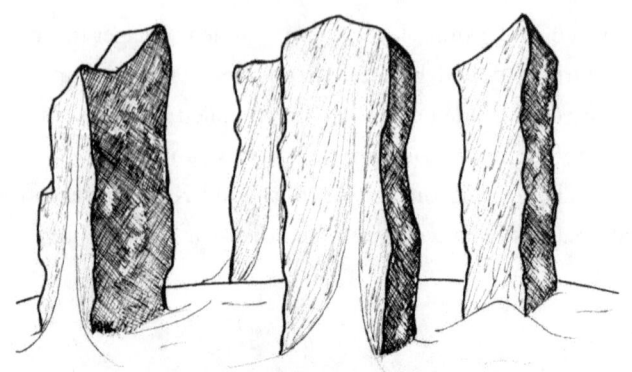

CHAPTER 6:
THE DANCING GROUND

Maden never minded hiking, regardless of weather, but he had to admit that traveling by horse-drawn sledge was a nice luxury. They'd been traveling for the past three days, and had picked up another sledge from a generous family in one of the villages where they'd stopped.

They'd left the open tundra behind them, the windswept hills gradually replaced by trees and more level terrain as they traveled. Shaun, who had waterproof cases on his technology and was the only one of them with functioning phone, had showed him a picture of a map of Pohjola. Painted on a wall in the Queen's castle, according to what Ávgos explained to him. Maden wondered if he'd get to see Queen Kuu's castle.

With Shaun's photo of the crudely painted map as a reference, Maden determined that they were heading south and east, to a large island in the north-central area of Pohjola. Since he'd done nothing but travel since he'd arrived here, he judged Pohjola to be a good bit smaller than Finland. At least the northern parts. Who knew how far away the Southern Fens actually were?

Beside him, Ávgos made a grunting sound and shifted around on the bench. They were sharing a sledge, and Ávgos had been dozing off and on all morning. Mađen wished he could doze during the long hours of travel, but his mind was still churning with everything that had happened in the past few days.

He'd been so focused on finding Ávgos that now he wasn't sure what to do. It's not like he could bring his cousin back home, because no one in Pohjola knew how to find the gateway. Mađen was apparently the only one of the five of them who had remained conscious during the entire trip from Inari to Pohjola. Except that he didn't remember any "gateway." He'd explained to Queen Kuu that all he saw as he swam after Teija and the hiisi was shifting light and shadows and murky shapes of water plants and fish.

Mađen looked over at Ávgos as his cousin came awake.

"Good nap?" Mađen asked him.

"I suppose." Ávgos pushed his hood back and rubbed at his neck.

Mađen stared out the side of the sledge for a few moments, then looked back at Ávgos again. "I'm sorry, cousin."

He'd never been good at apologizing, but this was at least the third time he'd apologized to Ávgos in as many days. There really wasn't anything else he could do right now.

"Mađen, please stop apologizing," Ávgos said, meeting his eyes. "It's okay. None of this is your fault."

"If I hadn't run away to Rovaniemi..." Mađen trailed off and shook his head. "I'm sorry I didn't check on Sirkka. I should have gone straight home to look after her and Piijá the moment I heard you'd disappeared."

Ávgos didn't say anything. Mađen figured his cousin was still hurt that he hadn't gone home right away. Sure, Sirkka could take care of herself, and she had Ávgos' sister and brother-in-law to rely on, but still... Mađen should be in Inari right now, looking after the family, not riding around in a sledge in a magical world.

Looking back out into the snowy wilderness, Mađen saw that they were approaching a village. When the sledges stopped, he was glad to get out and stretch. The Menninkäinen sledges weren't designed for tall people with long legs.

A crowd gathered around them, the Menninkäinen jostling one another as they all pressed closer towards the Queen. The atmosphere of the crowd seemed tense.

"Welcome to Shaman Petrel's village, Your Highness," said a young man wearing the bead-and-talisman-covered robe of a shaman. He gave an awkward-looking bow. "Formerly Shaman Ice's village."

"Formerly?" Queen Kuu asked.

"My father, Shaman Ice, died two days ago, Your Highness." Petrel lowered his head. "He was found trapped under the ice of the pond."

"A Näkki." Kuu's voice was tight.

A nervous murmur swept through the crowd.

"We suspect so, my Queen," said Petrel. "We received your message of warning, and no one has been ice fishing. And no one leaves the village alone—the hunters are always in pairs. I awoke in the morning to find my father missing from our hut. We eventually found him frozen in the pond." Petrel lowered his head again. "I don't know how he was stolen away from the hut without me waking."

"I am sorry for your loss," Kuu said gently. "Has Ice been buried yet?"

"He has, My Queen. We share a moon mirror with Shaman Char's village, on the other side of the pond, which is why I had not been able to contact you yet about my father's death."

Kuu nodded. "I understand. We must not linger long here, but I will bless your father's grave."

Petrel bowed. "Thank you, Your Grace."

Kuu looked out across the tightly-gathered crowd. "I understand your fears," she said, her voice strong as she addressed the villagers. "A cursed Näkki has robbed you of your leader, and I share in your sorrow at his loss. But know this—no matter what these invaders do to sow fear or pain into your hearts, you are children of Pohjola, and no creature from Ice-Dark can hold sway in our land. Dream and I will protect you."

The tension faded from the air as the crowd murmured a happy thanks, and Shaman Petrel gave another bow. Maden wasn't big on platitudes and pep talks, but he had to admit that he felt encouraged by what the Queen had just said.

"We would be honored if you and the Kalevalans would stay long enough to eat the midday meal with us," Petrel said. "Whatever we have is yours, and everyone would be pleased to share with you."

Kuu smiled at Petrel. "We would be honored to join you for a meal, Shaman."

The travelers were divided up between several houses, since there were too many people in their party to fit into one Menninkäinen hut. Maden found himself invited to Shaman Petrel's home, along with Lyylia, Falcon, and the Queen.

Eating hot food indoors was another nice luxury. As he ate, he tried to focus on his plate and not on the fact that he was squeezed onto the bench between Falcon and Queen Kuu.

He was seated on Kuu's right, and every time she lifted her mug, he caught a glimpse of blue wound around her wrist. After the blue snake had suddenly appeared when they were all looking at Shaun's computer, Ávgos had explained that it was a magical creature called Dream. Maden had no fear of snakes in general, but the idea of wearing a magical snake as a piece of jewelry... It left him feeling both awed and uncomfortable—a feeling magnified right now by the fact that Kuu was sitting so close to him, he could feel her body heat and smell the lightly floral scent of her blonde hair.

He understood now why the Menninkäinen always spoke of her with such reverence. But she was also a stunningly beautiful woman, which was a little distracting, especially right now. He frowned at his plate as he speared a bite of meat and tried to focus on the conversation instead of Kuu's leg, which had just bumped his under the crowded table.

"I'm afraid I have no vanishing stone, Your Grace," Shaman Petrel was saying. "I have a ruby protection stone, but I recently lost my fire stone. It was tied to the robe, but that string now hangs empty. It must have been lost when my father was trapped in the pond."

"Keep your protection stone, Petrel," Kuu said to him. "Place it outside your hut in the moonlight—it will help to keep your village safe from Näkki."

"I will, Your Grace. Thank you."

"I also have need of a mouth harp, and a drum striker made of metal."

"I believe I have a metal drum striker, Your Grace," Petrel said. "You are welcome to use it for as long as you need it."

When they finished eating, everyone went back outside, while Petrel rummaged around in his house looking for his drum striker. Falcon went over to where the sledges were parked to tend to the horses. Maden wasn't sure what to do, so he stood behind Lyylia and Kuu.

"Your Highness, Petrel's robe was missing a talisman,"

Lyylia murmured quietly. "Just like Shaman Talon's robe right after he was killed."

Maden had heard something about another shaman who'd been killed, probably by one of these mysterious monsters called Näkki. He stepped closer to Lyylia. "So what does that mean?" he asked in a low voice.

"It means that the Näkki are specifically targeting the shamans," Kuu said, looking up at him.

"I agree," Lyylia said. "Kuu, I think the Näkki are stealing talismans—either to prevent shamans from using the talismans against them, or to use the objects themselves. What do a vanishing stone and a fire stone do?"

"A fire stone, like its name says, can be used to create a flame where there is no tinder."

"Like a flint?" asked Maden.

"No—flint creates a spark and ignites tinder. A fire stone will burn by itself."

"Interesting," said Lyylia. "That could potentially be used as a weapon. What about a vanishing stone?"

"That is a rarely used magic," Kuu said. "But one that could greatly aid us at this moment. With it you can vanish from one place and immediately appear in another."

Lyylia pursed her lips. "So if a Näkki stole a vanishing stone and knew how to use it, it could transport instantaneously to any part of Pohjola."

Purple light flickered briefly in Kuu's eyes. "Yes."

Shaman Petrel emerged from the hut and approached them. "My drum striker, Your Majesty," he said, handing Kuu a small silver stick. "And my sword. It has been in my family since my grandfather's grandfather was young. Please, take it."

Kuu took the fur-wrapped bundle from the little man. She unfolded the furs to reveal a short sword with a leather-wrapped hilt. It was plainer than the sword she'd worn on her back the day Maðen met her, but it glinted brightly in the light and looked very sharp.

Maðen shifted his weight as he watched her delicate hands rewrap the furs. Delicate hands that could wield a sword. Ávgos and the others had told him about the encounter with the Näkki, and how Kuu had single-handedly driven it off. He wasn't sure if he should feel reassured or intimidated that this mesmerizing woman could fight off magical monsters with nothing but a sword. He hoped they wouldn't encounter another of these Näkki creatures.

Maðen looked around the village at the cozy wooden huts, the simple little people milling around and chatting with each other and the humans. Ávgos was over by the sledges, talking with Shaun and two Menninkäinen men. In some ways, this place felt like home—the forests and tundras and the close-knit communities. But now these innocent people were threatened by an evil king in another land—and so was his home. Maðen wished that one day he could tell the mysterious King Hiisi-Hiisi exactly what he thought of someone who kidnapped people and stole reindeer.

Abruptly he realized that Queen Kuu was staring at him. Lyylia and Shaman Petrel had wandered off, and he was alone outside Petrel's hut with the Queen standing beside him. He looked down at her radiant face, and felt momentarily trapped by her eyes. Her silver irises seemed to shimmer like starlight reflected in water.

She gave him a gentle smile. "Tell me your thoughts, Maðen."

Had he been talking out loud to himself? He shoved his hands into his coat pockets and tried to look away, but found he couldn't.

Finally he cleared his throat. "Um, what do you mean,

Your Highness?"

She smiled again. "You seem conflicted. I am sure much of this is strange and overwhelming for you."

"A bit, yeah." He shifted his weight again.

"Your cousin Ávgos is blessed indeed to have someone so loyal and true," she said.

Maden raised his eyebrows as he stared at her. "Loyal and true?" he scoffed, his tone harsher than he wanted. "I don't think so. You wouldn't say that if you knew anything about me." He grunted in his throat and frowned at her. "Your Highness."

Kuu was silent for a moment, and he suddenly worried that he'd overstepped himself just then. He'd never been good with authority figures.

But then she smiled again, which both relaxed and unnerved him. "Then perhaps we both have much to learn. Come, Maden. I must bless the grave of Shaman Ice and his journey to Manala, the land of the honored dead. And then we must be on our way to the Dancing Ground."

She turned and walked away. Her white dog, who'd been sitting nearby, trotted after her. Maden stared after the Queen for a moment, then pulled his hands out of his pockets and followed her.

Loyal and true, she'd said. No, the very fact that he was here instead of in Inari taking care of the family and the rest of the herd proved that he was neither of those things. Kuu might be beautiful and smart and good with a sword, but she was wrong about him. So very wrong indeed.

It was unfortunate that one of the sledges had a cracked runner, but Lyylia was grateful for the opportunity afforded by the repairs to enjoy a hot meal in a Menninkäinen home. After four days of traveling by sledge and camping out in the woods, it was nice to be indoors for a few minutes. This village had not been troubled by Näkki, thankfully, but the nervous villagers had greeted the Queen with relief and joy.

While some men of the village worked on the sledge's runner, several Menninkäinen families had invited the travelers into their homes for food and rest. Lyylia and Teija and Tug had been taken in by a woman named Vine.

Tug had finished eating, and he and Vine's husband went back outside to help with the repairs. Vine came over to the table to collect Tug's empty bowl.

"There's plenty more stew, if either of you would like some more," the little woman said.

"No, I'm fine, thank you," Teija said politely.

Lyylia felt almost guilty as she held out her bowl, even though Vine had offered. "I'll take a little more. It's delicious—thank you."

Vine smiled and dished up another bowlful. The peppery meat porridge tasted surprisingly like Karelian hot pot. It was nice that so much of the food here was familiar. If only coffee existed in Pohjola, though...

While Lyylia finished her food, Teija went outside to the toilet shed. She came back a few minutes later with a strained look on her face.

"Not good," she whispered to Lyylia as she sat back down at the table. "My monthly cycle just started."

"Damn," Lyylia murmured back. She hadn't even thought of that being a problem—but in another week or so, it would likely be a problem for her, too.

"I wonder if the Menninkäinen have the same biology and physical processes as we do," Teija said.

"We could ask, I guess," Lyylia said, glancing over at Vine, who was sitting on a stool across the room digging through a basket on her lap.

"They're not the sort of people who get offended by talking about something like that, are they?" Teija said anxiously.

"One way to find out." Lyylia got up and went over to Vine. "I have a question for you, Vine. Do you, uh, do Menninkäinen women have a monthly…ah, that is, once every moon, do the women here…" She trailed off, feeling suddenly awkward.

"Oh, your woman's cycle has come," said Vine. "It always happens when you're traveling, doesn't it? Most inconvenient. I can help you." Setting her basket on the floor, she got up and went into the bedroom.

Lyylia glanced over at Teija and saw her relieved expression.

"Here you are," Vine said, coming back. She handed Lyylia a small cloth bag. "Is that enough, or do you need more?"

Lyylia glanced into the bag, and saw a narrow belt and several rolled pieces of cloth. Uncomfortable and inconvenient, probably, but better than nothing.

"Um, maybe a few more, if you have them. We're not sure when we might stop at another village. Thank you so much, Vine."

Vine went and got another cloth bag. Lyylia thanked her again, and handed one of the bags to Teija.

Teija went back outside, and Lyylia sat down on the bench at the table while Vine returned to her basket. Lyylia watched as the little woman pulled a wad of wool out of the basket, and a long wooden stick with a flat stone at one end. Lyylia had seen old fashioned drop spindles at museums, but had never seen one used. Vine held the stick upright, twirled a small piece of wool around it, and then set it spinning. Lyylia watched, feeling oddly soothed by the rotating spindle and Vine's fingers smoothly pulling the wool into twine.

Teija came back into the hut. "They've finished fixing the sledge, so I think we're about to leave."

Lyylia stood up and retrieved her coat from the hook by the door. "Thank you so much, Vine," she said, after pulling the coat on over her head. "For the food, and the, uh, other things."

Vine looked up from her work with a grin. "You are most welcome. Have a safe journey! Dream be with you!"

Outside, Lyylia looked at the newly repaired sledge. Shaun and Eider were just climbing in. Shaun met her eyes and gave her a grin and a thumbs-up sign. She smiled back at him.

Lyylia and Teija got settled in their sledge, and the caravan set off. Lyylia watched the snow-laden evergreen trees sliding past and listened to the lulling swish-swish of the horses's hooves and sledge runners in the snow.

"I miss Mom," Teija said after a while.

"I know," Lyylia said softly. "It was bad enough getting reassigned to Kokkola last year and leaving you two in Helsinki, but there's no way I can protect Mom when I'm literally a world away." She paused and swallowed the lump in her throat. "I miss Dad."

Teija said nothing, and leaned her head on Lyylia's shoulder. All those years ago they'd watched their father die a little each day when he was forced into early retirement after his accident on the boat. And then when the cancer came, he'd lost the will to fight.

Lyylia looked at Teija, and saw her fingering something at her throat. "You're still wearing that little heart necklace he gave you?"

Teija straightened up and smiled at her. "I never take it

off. Mom still sometimes wears the bracelet he got her that last Christmas."

"He gave me a wallet," Lyylia said. The only jewelry she ever wore were the plain gold studs in her ears, and her father had known that. "I stopped using it last year, because it had started to rip. I didn't want it to completely fall apart. It's in my bedroom closet." She wondered if she'd ever see her apartment, or that old wallet, again.

The sledge began to slow, and Lyylia leaned out the side to see what was happening. They were coming to a frozen creek. Kuu had been stopping the caravan at every stream of water, no matter how wide or narrow, to determine if the water was safe. Kuu climbed out of the lead sledge and approached the creek's edge.

Lyylia pulled herself back into the sledge, but a strange flicker of movement caught her eye, and she leaned out again. Her heart suddenly leapt into her throat.

Standing on the opposite bank, directly facing the Queen, was a huge black horse.

Teija looked at Lyylia, hearing her sharp intake of breath. Then she leaned out her side of the sledge.

Her eyes froze on the horse standing on the other side of the creek, its glistening black fur a shocking contrast to the white of Kuu's clothing and the snow all around. She was about to ask Lyylia what was happening when the horse spoke.

"Cross if you wish, Your Majesty," it said in a deep gravelly voice. "But know that water and ice are my domain."

"Run!" Kuu shouted, and at the same moment the horse tossed its head and gave an ear-piercing shriek.

Teija slid off the seat, her head spinning, and she suddenly felt desperately thirsty. She collapsed beside Lyylia in the snow.

"Run!" Lyylia hissed, tugging at Teija's arm.

"I need water…" Teija panted, struggling to her feet.

"No, you don't," Lyylia said. "Cover your ears."

Together they stumbled through the snow. Chaos had erupted around them. One of the dogs launched itself at the big black horse, but the horse tossed the dog off with no difficulty, slamming it into one of the other dogs. The sledge horses were panicking, rearing and stamping in their traces, and suddenly two of them bolted. Teija hit the ground and rolled as the horses stampeded past, the sledge swinging wildly behind them.

"Lyylia!" she shouted, frantically looking around. Someone grabbed her arm, and Eider dropped down in the snow next to her.

"Teija, come on, let's run!"

Teija struggled up again, and together they ran, Eider with his mittened hand firmly holding onto hers. She had no idea where the stream was, and she'd forgotten why they were supposed to be avoiding it.

Then suddenly the black horse was in front of them, so close that she could see water running down its legs. It reared, and she and Eider dove out of the way of its slashing, razor-edged hooves. And then that hideous scream came again, making her head hurt and her eyes hurt, and she sank into the snow, every muscle numb.

The gunshot sound of cracking ice snapped some clarity into her head, and she struggled up again, Eider still beside her. She saw the frozen creek, very close by, with shattered ice floating in the water. Another black horse was climbing out of the water. Still clutching Eider's hand, she turned—but then she saw a third horse.

Three Näkki had them surrounded. Teija pressed against Eider as the three huge black horses, all glistening wet and with eyes like lumps of glowing ice, encircled the group, forcing everyone into a tight cluster. She looked around and swallowed hard as she didn't see Lyylia. Hopefully she'd gotten away. Mađen was also missing, and Shaun, and at least one of the Menninkäinen.

"Please, don't try to fight," said one of the Näkki, in a harsh deep voice that sounded like grinding ice. Two of the Menninkäinen had spears pointed at the horses. "And the same goes for you, Majesty," the Näkki continued. "Perhaps your magicks could turn back one of us—but we are three and you are one. And I am a shaman of greater power than that little man I killed a few days ago."

"Then you severely underestimate me if you think my power is equal to that of one of my shamans," Kuu replied. She held her unmittened hands out in front of her in a defensive pose. Teija wished Kuu had been able to grab her sword. As Kuu turned her head to follow the pacing Näkki, Teija saw her eyes glowing such a bright purple, it was almost too bright to look at.

"Threats, little moon goddess?" the Näkki retorted, tossing its head. Its black mane showered water across the group. "I'm not here to fight you, Majesty. I'm here to warn you."

"Warn me of what, ice demon?"

"Please, be seated and rest," the Näkki sneered. "You won't be going anywhere."

Everyone hurriedly sat down in the snow. Teija huddled between Eider and Ávgos. Kuu remained standing.

"Sit," grated the Näkki. "Your Majesty."

Kuu knelt down in the snow and leaned back on her heels. The Näkki seemed satisfied with that.

"So speak, ice demon," Kuu demanded.

"I bring a warning from the lord of Ice-Dark. The creatures you call Gentle Beasts that have been wandering your land are not yours, and never will be, so don't try to claim them." Ávgos shifted around, but didn't say anything, and the Näkki didn't seem to notice him. "And don't try to fight us or drive us from Pohjola—we are already too many for you to count."

"That is no warning—that's a threat," Kuu returned. "I do not take kindly to threats. And neither does Dream. My World Serpent will not allow such an evil to come against Pohjola and survive."

"Ah, but he already has. The eyes of your World Serpent have missed us, and now we are here in numbers greater than you can know. King Hiisi-Hiisi has magicked the Beasts of Kalevala into Menninkäinen, and they have all crossed into Pohjola bearing Näkki with them."

"Why?" Kuu said. "What interest does Hiisi-Hiisi have in polluting the waters of Pohjola?"

The Näkki snorted, blowing steam from its wide nostrils. "Many reasons, little moon goddess. He still remembers well the hurtful blow you dealt him on the ice of the lake centuries ago."

Kuu rose up on her knees. "Hiisi-Hiisi attacked us first!"

"That is not how he remembers it, Majesty. But he has not forgotten, and he will repay in kind." The Näkki lowered its head until Kuu could have reached up and touched the horse's nose. Its unearthly icy-white eyes glittered and glowed. "And Hiisi-Hiisi also desires your light."

Teija had no idea what the Näkki meant by desiring the Queen's light, but it sent chills through her anyway. Kuu sat back on her heels again, and glared defiantly up at the horse.

It gave a gravelly sort of laugh, harsh and not at all humorous. "Ah, come, little queen—save your anger for when you might need it more. Not that it will do you any good—Pohjola is already under our control."

The other two Näkki had been slowly circling the group this entire time. Teija abruptly realized that the other two Näkki were no longer horses—two large, wolfish dogs were now pacing around them. Their eyes were the same—shining and solid white, and water, still unfrozen, dripped from their long and matted black fur. One of the creatures paused in front of Teija and bared its fangs. She shrank back against Eider and Ávgos.

"We didn't stop you here to harm you, Majesty," the Näkki continued. "Merely to warn you." It tossed its mane again, spraying more water. "But I did not say I wouldn't harm the others." It turned its head to one of the other Näkki. "Several of the party escaped. Go and hunt them down!"

One of the dogs gave a hiss, and took off into the woods. Teija glanced at Eider, feeling panic swelling up again. His expression was surprisingly calm, and he caught her eye, and then glanced down at the snow where Kuu was sitting. She looked and saw that Kuu had her hands resting in the snow beside her legs. Teija caught the briefest flicker of blue on Kuu's wrist. She wasn't sure of all of the capabilities of the little magic snake that Kuu wore, but Eider seemed reassured by it.

"So tell me, demon," Kuu said. "Why bring people here from another world, only to hunt them down and kill them? Surely your king has more sense than that, if he's put together this grand scheme."

"*My* king is no one," the Näkki snapped, its ears flattening against its head. "The Näkki *choose* to serve the lord of Ice-Dark. The hiisi were sent through the gateway to bring back the Beasts. Why they brought back those things—" the horse gestured with its nose at Teija and Ávgos "—I know not. The lesser hiisi are foolish creatures of base instincts; they serve Hiisi-Hiisi with a loyalty unto death, but they lack enough thought to obey his commands properly."

The horse stomped a hoof in the snow, shaking off water. "The Näkki should have been the ones to go through the gateway, as water is our domain. But Hiisi-Hiisi forbade it and cast a spell to bar us from it. So to answer your question, Majesty, Hiisi-Hiisi did not bring these creatures here from the other world, and therefore it does not matter whether they live or die." The Näkki lowered its head towards Kuu again. "Except that we Näkki feed upon fear, and it is our nature to wound and kill. And since we won't be doing that to you, Majesty, we might as well feast upon them." It laughed again, that sickening sound like ice and gravel.

"They are under my protection, demon."

"Then killing them shall strike you a sore blow indeed."

"You said you were not here to fight," Kuu said darkly. "But you have killed Menninkäinen, and I will defend my people. We will fight you."

"Not if you cannot find us. Farewell, for now, Your Majesty." The Näkki reared and let out a blinding scream, echoed by the wolf-Näkki. Teija clapped her mittens over her ears as the world spun. Her vision blurred, but she could still see Kuu, sitting tall and resolute in the face of the Näkki's scream.

Then the horse and the dog turned and raced into the creek, splashing beneath the icy water and vanishing from sight.

"Keep going, keep going!" Shaun panted as he and Lyylia raced away from the raging Näkki. He heard ice cracking and water splashing, and panicked shouts fading behind them.

"Teija!" Lyylia stumbled in the snow as she turned around.

Shaun grabbed her shoulders. "I saw her and Eider running. She's okay. We've got to get away, Lyylia." He tugged at her arm, and they started running again.

Stumbling through the deep snow, they dodged between the trees. Suddenly Shaun stopped short, grabbing Lyylia's arm again, as they came to the top of a steep hill.

Then the cry of the Näkki shot through the air like lightning, making Shaun's head spin and his feet suddenly feel like lead. He wanted to scream, but couldn't.

"Jump!" Lyylia shouted, and threw herself into him. Together they tumbled over the edge and landed in a dense thicket of brambles and bushes.

Shaun kept his eyes screwed shut, waiting for the dizziness from the fall and the Näkki shriek to fade. His left knee hurt—but at least his legs weren't numb.

"Don't let me get up," he whispered at Lyylia through clenched teeth. "I'm not following that thing again."

"I won't let you go," she murmured back, and he felt her hands pressing against his shoulders, holding him. "Just stay quiet."

They lay there for several tense moments, not moving. No more bone-chilling screams came, and no sounds of crunching snow or rustling underbrush. Perhaps Lyylia's jump off the top of the hill had put enough of a break in their tracks so the Näkki wouldn't find them. As Shaun's heart rate slowly returned to normal, he could still see the Näkki's water-slick black hide and glittering white eyes in his mind. He took a deep breath, trying to clear his thoughts, and finally opened his eyes.

Lyylia's face filled his vision. Abruptly his brain switched tracks as he realized that he was lying on top of her in the deep snow, their faces mere inches apart, and her arms were still wrapped around his shoulders.

"I don't think the Näkki seen us here," she whispered, her breath warm on his face. "You are okay?" She studied his face with concern in her blue eyes.

He nodded. The Näkki had all but vanished from his mind now as he stared at her, watching her mouth as she spoke. "Yeah, I'm okay," he finally managed.

Lyylia gave a short nod of acknowledgement, then her eyes wandered to the snow-covered brambles around them as she listened for sounds of pursuit. They lay fully enclosed in a dense thicket of bushes at the bottom of the steep hill. The snowy forest around them seemed quiet and serene now. Before wasting any more precious time contemplating the situation or wondering if he was making a wise decision, Shaun bent his head and kissed her.

She didn't hit him, which was good, or even try to pull away. After a moment he released her and lifted his head and waited for her knee in his gut or possibly a string of Finnish profanities. Even though he had her somewhat pinned in the snow, as a police officer, she should have the training to toss him off without much difficulty.

When she did none of those things, he decided to take the moment while he had it and kissed her again. This time she responded by kissing him back, and tightened her hold around his shoulders.

Eventually they parted again, and Shaun found that he was short of breath and feeling very warm and his leg no longer hurt. He stared down at her beautiful face and mesmerizing blue eyes and the little curls of blonde hair escaping her hood.

He felt like he ought to say something, but nothing came to mind except "Wow, what a kiss." She'd probably appreciate something more sagacious than that, though.

Another Näkki scream shattered the moment. Shaun winced and buried his head in Lyylia's shoulder. Her arms tightened around him.

The numbing dizziness of the scream passed quickly. Lyylia shifted beneath him, releasing her arms from around him. "Get up," she whispered. "I need my gun."

Shaun rolled off of her, his left knee throbbing again where he'd probably twisted it in the fall down the hill. Lyylia was on her feet before he'd even managed to sit up. She reached under her coat and pulled out her handgun.

No more demonic screams came. Shaun slowly stood up, testing his knee to make sure he could still walk. The thicket of bushes they'd landed in was tall and dense enough that they could both stand and still be hidden from view. However, it made it challenging to see what might be in the forest nearby. The sound of footsteps crunching in snow came from somewhere, and they both froze. Lyylia lifted her gun.

"Shaun! Lyylia!" a voice shouted. One of the Menninkäin-en—Hoof or Tip, probably. "Maden! Boots!"

"We're here!" Lyylia called. She holstered her gun under her coat as they pushed through the brambles and emerged in the fresh deep snow at the bottom of the steep hill. Shaun looked up to see Tip peering down at them.

"Dream be praised!" he said. "Are either of you injured?"

Lyylia shook her head. "We are fine." Then she glanced at Shaun and raised her eyebrows at him.

Was his gimpy knee that obvious? "I'm fine," he said. He was pretty sure nothing was broken or even sprained, but he was glad that they had sledges to ride in.

They began the difficult climb back up the hill. Tip offered to get some rope, but there were enough small trees and bushes that they could pull themselves up.

They followed Tip back to where the caravan had stopped at the stream's edge. Shaun scanned the area, noticing the trampled snow, missing sledges, and everyone huddled together. Everyone except Boots and Maðen. And the Queen.

"Lyylia!" Teija called. She pulled away from the group and ran to Lyylia, throwing her arms around her sister and babbling in Finnish.

"Where's everyone else?" Shaun asked, looking at Ávgos. "Where's Kuu?"

"I am here," Kuu's voice answered, and she appeared between the trees at a bend in the stream. Her eyes blazed purple, and she had her sword in her hand. "The Näkki have well and truly fled, for now—this stream is clean." She looked at Shaun, then at Lyylia and Teija clutching each other. The purple in her eyes softened. "I am glad to see you two safe. Boots and Maðen are safe, as well. Dream is with them. The Näkki that pursued them has been killed. And so when the other two Näkki realize that their fellow is dead, we should be far from this place."

"Wait, there were *three* Näkki?" Shaun said, feeling a flush of horror.

"Yes," Kuu said. "And they spoke of many disturbing developments, not all of which were lies, I believe."

Shaun remembered the chilling, gravelly voice of the Näkki speaking right before Kuu told them to run. He'd been hoping he'd just imagined that it talked. Apparently not.

Shaun heard a shout, and through the trees he saw Maðen and Boots coming towards them, Maðen leading two horses and their sledge. One of the dogs was with them.

"You made it!" Ávgos said with a relieved smile.

"Yes, thanks to the Queen and Dream," Boots said as they approached. "We saw a great black wolf running towards us, and we couldn't move...but then in a flash of blue light it fell to the snow, and we could move and think again." He bowed at Kuu.

"*Kiitos, Kuningatar,*" said Maden, and held out his hand toward Kuu. "*Hän pelasti meidät.*" The little blue snake was curled up in his palm, and it slid from his hand back onto hers.

Kuu smiled as Dream curled himself around her wrist. "Thank you, Maden."

"We found Icerunner on our way back," Boots said, glancing at the dog. "This is the only sledge we could recover, Your Highness. We also saw that two other horses had dragged their sledge onto the creek and the ice broke. They...they're dead."

Maden added something in Finnish.

"Well, thank you for trying," said Kuu. "We'll have to carry on with just four sledges. At least we still have the supply sledge. We're almost at our destination, but we mustn't linger."

Everyone busied themselves tightening up the horses' traces and rearranging supplies to make room for passengers on the remaining sledges. Shaun wanted to ride with Lyylia, but he saw Teija climbing into the sledge with her.

"Shaun," Kuu said, paused beside her sledge. "Ride with me."

"Yes, Your Highness." He cast one last glance in Lyylia's direction, then scrambled in after Kuu.

Child of Light was curled up on the floorboard, so Shaun carefully arranged his feet to avoid kicking her. His knee twinged with the movement.

"Shaun, you are injured," Kuu said as the sledge

began to move.

What was it with women being able to see right through him? He hadn't even been limping. "Just twisted my knee, is all. I'll be fine, Your Highness."

Kuu laid her hand on his left knee. Her touch felt hot through his lined leather breeches—far hotter than any woman's touch should. The ache faded.

"It is no serious injury," Kuu said. "I will make a poultice of healing moss when we make camp. A night of rest with a warm poultice on your knee should fully restore you."

"Um, thank you, Your Highness. It feels better already."

Kuu gave him a gentle smile. All traces of purple were gone from her eyes now.

Shaun noticed that her sheathed sword lay on the furs in her lap. Also in her lap was a moon mirror.

"Your Highness, can you tell me how a moon mirror works?" he asked. There'd never be a better time than this.

Kuu handed him the silver dish. "To speak with someone else, both moon mirrors must be filled with water."

"Why water?"

"Water is the lifeblood of the land. Water is the simplest form of magic, and without it, nothing can live. And so with the moon mirror, the water brings to life the words of those who use it."

And water was also an excellent conductor of electricity, Shaun mused as he examined the object. From a distance, when Kuu used it, it looked like she held up a silver plate or a small bowl to the sky. It was more of a flat dish or pan with straight sides, a perfect circle, just the right size to balance on the palm of one hand. The bottom half of the dish was filled with what appeared to be broken pieces of glass or chunks of clear crystal, creating a jagged pattern of prisms and reflections from the silver backing. Covering the shattered pieces was a smooth surface of glass. Delicate, angular symbols were engraved on the underside of the dish.

"Does it have to be used only at night?" he then asked. "Or do you use it then because it's more convenient than using it while traveling?"

Kuu smiled. "Since the mirror must be filled with water, it is easier without the motion of a sledge, yes. It can be used any time, but it is more effective and can reach farther if the Dancing Lights are in the sky."

He turned the dish over in his hands. Water...electromagnetism in the sky...what if this object was more of an "aurora mirror" than a moon mirror? His mind started buzzing with ideas and questions.

"What's it made out of?" he asked.

"Silver. Mined from the Silver Caves deep within the Mountains of the Moon."

"And are the crystals in the bottom quartz? Or just shards of glass?" Shaun tapped the smooth layer of glass in the bottom of the dish.

"They are a rare crystal of ancient magic," Kuu said. The somber tone in her voice made him look up.

Her expression was sad. She took the dish from him and held it up between them. "The crystals in the moon mirrors hold the memory of the songs sung before the birth of the world. Dream still remembers the songs. These crystals are but a poor copy, but they are all that is left of the music."

Shaun had no idea what to say to that. He looked at Kuu's face. Her silver eyes reflected the moon mirror, but her gaze seemed far away. In that moment he was reminded that Kuu had lived for thousands of years, and she was likely remembering a time in history eons ago. The weight of that realization settled on Shaun's mind. Kuu was not merely a beautiful woman—she was an ancient being possessed of more knowledge and power than he could hope to understand. Suddenly the world—both Pohjola and Earth—seemed very far away.

Kuu lowered the moon mirror and set it down in her lap. Shaun blinked and shook himself.

"I have something for you," Kuu said briskly, the sadness and memory gone from her voice. "As the threat of Näkki grows, we all must be prepared to defend ourselves and others." She rearranged her sword and the mirror in her lap, and handed him a bundle wrapped in furs.

He unfolded the wrappings to reveal a sword.

"This belongs to Shaman Petrel," Kuu said. "He has given us leave to use it. I hope that his village will not be plagued by Näkki again, but I am certain that we will be, and we will need every weapon available. This is yours for the duration of this quest."

Shaun carefully picked up the sword. It was shorter than Kuu's sword, and surprisingly light—the leather-wrapped hilt fit comfortably in his hand. He probably should have felt excited or honored to be given a shaman's sword, but all he could do was stare at the smooth blade and try to imagine himself killing something with it. He wasn't a violent person, and he'd never used a weapon besides his fists for anything in his life.

"Um, thank you, Highness," he said finally. "It's… I'm honored."

"I wish that it were not needed," Kuu said gently. "I do not like to kill, either. But to protect ourselves and Pohjola, I'm afraid it will be necessary."

Shaun nodded and laid the sword gingerly on his lap. He'd be happy to have every last Näkki dead—he just wasn't sure that he was strong enough to help make that happen.

He thought of Lyylia. If he had to protect her with this sword, that he could do, he decided. He had to.

"The water is clean!" Kuu's voice called out. "It is safe to cross."

Lyylia leaned out the side of her sledge to see Kuu climbing back into the lead sledge. The ice of a wide river stretched smoothly into the distance. This was the junction of two rivers, Kuu had explained, and here at their joining was the Dancing Ground Island. Hilly and heavily forested, the island sat surrounded by the ice, connected to the shore by a long stone bridge.

Lyylia pulled her head back in as the sledge began to move. They crossed the bridge single file, though the bridge was easily wide enough for two sledges side by side. The walls of the bridge were solid stone as high as a Menninkäinen, but were weather-worn and cracked in places.

"This bridge feels ancient, and special somehow," Teija said quietly beside Lyylia. "Like a lot of history has happened here. Look—those carvings are almost worn smooth."

Lyylia saw patches of the intricate swirling motif of snakes and the phases of the moon. "That's the same design that's on the walls of the hallways in Kuu's castle."

"Really? Wow. I hope I get to see Kuu's castle."

After crossing the bridge, the sledges followed a pathway into the trees. Rocky slopes rose on both sides of the path, with vines and brush clinging to the rock walls and hardy trees growing in every available crevasse. Lyylia tried to keep an eye out on both sides of the sledge. This was a good place for an ambush.

But no ambush came, and soon the land opened up into a clearing, and the sledges came to a stop. An open field smooth with snow spread out before them. Over to the left, scattered amongst the trees at the bottom of a cliff, were about twelve huts. At the far right side of the clearing, the land sloped upwards. Four tall stone obelisks stood at the top of the hill.

Kuu pushed back her hood, and surveyed the area with a smile on her face. "Welcome to the Dancing Ground!"

"Who lives here?" Lyylia asked.

"No one," said Kuu. "Those huts were built for the purpose of the celebration at midsummer. Every midsummer, this entire island, and much of the land on either bank of the river, is filled with Menninkäinen who have journeyed from their homes to celebrate and feast and watch the Lights. These huts are usually used by families who have brought the elderly or infirm with them. There are more huts on the other side of the island. We can use these huts tonight, since no one else is here."

Everyone began unloading the sledges, putting the supplies in several of the huts. Lyylia was glad for any indoor sleeping opportunity, and was pleased when she saw that the huts were all stocked with a complete array of cooking utensils, and even firewood. Tucked further back under the trees against the edge of the cliff were three outhouses and a sauna.

"This is practically civilized," Teija remarked as they lugged blankets and food satchels into the huts.

Back outside, Kuu addressed the group. "I shall begin the spell once the Dancing Lights begin. During the spell, I will not be able to stop and fight, should any Näkki appear."

"We will protect and defend, Your Grace," said Boots.

"I need to build a fire made of alder wood," Kuu continued. "I must light the fire before the Dancing Lights begin. There is a stand of alder trees in the forest that direction, near the bank of the river."

Tug pulled an axe off the supply sledge. "We will bring you alder wood, My Queen." Tip stepped up next to him.

Kuu nodded at them. "Be mindful of the water, both of you."

They bowed and headed into the woods.

"We need to set up a defensive perimeter," Lyylia said, looking around the clearing. "Kuu, where will you be performing the spell?"

"At the top of the hill by the standing stones. The Dancing Lights will touch the earth in the center of the stone circle, as they do every midsummer, and as they did when Kied-Kie-Jubmel and I cast the first spell upon the Lights. That is where I will stand to bring him home."

"Maden and Eider, climb to the top of that cliff overlooking the huts," Lyylia began. "If that vantage point gives you a good view of this clearing and the stone circle, that will be your post. Maden, get a spear from the supply sledge, and Eider, make sure you're fully stocked with arrows."

Maden gave a grunt of acknowledgement and Eider bowed.

"We should have men and dogs spaced evenly around this clearing," Lyylia continued. "And at least one guard posted on the far side of that hill. There mustn't be any gaps that a Näkki could slip through without being seen."

"I will stand watch at the far side of the hill," Falcon volunteered, loading a bow and quiver onto his back.

"Wolfsbane and I will join you," said Boots, picking up a spear. The two men and the dog walked up the slope to the stone circle and disappeared down the other side.

Lyylia looked at Ávgos and the remaining Menninkäinen. "The rest of you, space yourselves out around this clearing. We need eyes on every part of the surrounding forest."

This defensive strategy would be totally useless, however, if the Näkki attacked with their scream. After the Näkki attack two days ago, Lyylia had cobbled together makeshift earplugs for everyone from little scraps of fabric and a tiny amount of beeswax from a candle in one of the lanterns. There were three lanterns packed on the supply sledge, which they never needed to use unless it was completely overcast and snowing hard. Lyylia wasn't confident that these waxy little blobs would be enough to stop the debilitating effects of the Näkki screams, but it was the best they could do.

She looked over at Shaun. He was standing next to one of the sledges that had been parked under the trees near the huts, probably setting up his laptop and scanning equipment. Lyylia knew that Kuu had given him Shaman Petrel's sword. Since a sword was a close-range weapon, unlike the spears and bows and arrows that everyone else would be using, he would be most effective placed close to Kuu as a bodyguard.

Lyylia slowly made her way across the clearing towards Shaun. She'd managed to avoid talking to him, except for the most basic of communication, for the past two days. The memory of their kiss was still fresh in her mind, as was her embarrassment and frustration.

Why in the world had she let him kiss her? And worse, why had she kissed him back? The emotional adrenaline high of lying together in the snow, afraid that they were about to die, was no excuse.

Shaun looked up and smiled as she approached. Even with her aloof behavior, he still acted like he was happy to be around her. Which just made it that much more awkward.

"For recording the spell and the Lights?" she asked, keeping her voice cool and businesslike.

"That's right," he said. The laptop sat on the seat of the sledge, microphone wires trailing out the open sides of the sledge. "I hope it won't get fried, like the last time we saw ground-level Lights." He placed a small black box on the canvas roof. "But I can't *not* record this."

"I'm making defenses, in case Näkki come during the spell," Lyylia said. "I will stand near the stones on the hill, to protect Kuu. You can stand with me. If any Näkki get through my bullets, you can use the sword for close fighting."

Shaun licked his lips. "Right. Close-range fighting, protect the Queen…" He cleared his throat. "I've never used a sword before. Lyylia, I don't even know how to fight. I realize that makes me very unmanly, but I'm a scientist—I don't know how to fight off a magic horse with a sword."

"No one of us knows how to fight a magic horse," Lyylia said matter-of-factly. "I don't know if bullets will kill it."

"That's a huge comfort, thanks." He quirked a grin, that cocky smile on his face that annoyed her so.

She looked back out across the clearing. "I'll tell Kuu we have defenses as good as we can."

"Lyylia." Shaun came around the sledge and stopped a few paces from her. "About, you know, the other day… I'm sorry. I just…I mean…" He looked at the ground, then back at her face. "I'm sorry if I offended you."

She pursed her lips as several replies went through her mind all at once. *Thank you for your apology. Don't worry about it—let's just pretend it never happened. Apology accepted—now let's focus on what's important, like staying alive.* Instead, she found herself saying the worst reply of all. "I wasn't offended."

He gave her an annoying little half-smile. "Well…that's

good to know." He gestured toward the sledge behind him. "Give me another minute to finish setting up my scanner, and I'll join you at the top of the hill. With the sword."

She nodded, then turned away and headed for the hill with the standing stones. She saw Kuu and Teija at the top of the hill, building a fire with the alder branches Tug and Tip had cut down. Child of Light sat nearby, her ears alert.

Lyylia forced all thoughts of Shaun from her mind. It was time to work now. She would put Teija in one of the huts during the spell—she'd be safe there.

Approaching the top of the slope, Lyylia saw that the stone pillars were as big around as she was, and a good two meters high. The arrangement had once been a full circle of five stones, she realized. One stone obelisk lay fallen in the snow. Lyylia squatted down and brushed the snow off a section of the stone. Ice was caught in the rough surface, revealing a weathered but still visible pattern of lines and angular markings. A large crack, smoothed by the seasons like the rest of the stone, ran across the width of the stone. It had probably fallen centuries ago.

Lyylia stood up as Kuu and Teija came over to her. "We've got the area as secured as possible, Your Highness," Lyylia said. She gestured out across the clearing. "Guards are posted all around the clearing, with two scouts at the top of that hill above the huts. Boots and Falcon are on the other side of this hill. And Shaun and I will stay close to you."

"Very good," Kuu said. "But you and Shaun will have to remain outside this stone circle. Only Teija and I can be inside the circle."

"Teija?" Lyylia raised her eyebrows.

"Yes. Teija will be helping me with the spell."

Lyylia looked at her sister. Teija's blue eyes were bright

with excitement. "How is that possible, Your Highness?" Lyylia finally managed. "We aren't, uh, shamans."

"To be a shaman, one must know how magic works, why it works, and to discipline one's mind as Dream teaches. But none of these are required for the role that Teija will perform. Kied-Kie-Jubmel and I together first cast the spell upon the Lights. I have changed some parts of the spell, since it is a different magic that must be brought forth tonight; but two are still needed. I was not alone for the first spell, and I cannot do it alone now."

"It's okay, Lyylia, I think I can do this," said Teija. "Queen Kuu explained everything. All I have to do is play the mouth harp." Teija held up the tiny instrument.

Lyylia stared at the little loop of metal in her sister's hand. She wanted to protest, but she couldn't. And why should she, anyway? This was probably the safest place for Teija, besides the huts. Lyylia could protect her here.

"I'm sure you'll do fine, Teija," Lyylia finally said. As she turned to step back outside the circle of stones, she saw Maðen coming up the hill.

"Everyone's in position," he said to her. He'd removed his gloves, and had a spear clutched tightly in his right hand. "Eider and I have a good view from the top of the cliff. We can see this clearing, the other side of this hill, and a lot of the surrounding forest."

Lyylia nodded. "That's good."

Maðen then looked at Kuu. "Your Highness, I heard you talking sometime earlier about needing a protection stone. I, um, I think I can help." He pulled a pebble out of his pocket.

Kuu took it from him. "An opal protection stone," she said, turning it over in her hand. Lyylia saw the rough stone shimmering with glints of pearly colors in the light. "I was given an emerald protection stone from one of the villages we passed through, but this will be a welcome addition to this spell. Where did you get this?"

"Shaman Pike gave it to me. It was the first village we came to after we arrived here from the lake."

Kuu smiled. "Pike's gift to you will serve all of Pohjola well tonight. Thank you, Maden. I will return this to you after the spell is completed."

Maden gave a small nodding bow. Then he looked at Teija, then Lyylia, and headed back down the hill.

Lyylia saw Shaun headed up the hill, the short sword in his hand. He wore a determined expression, and held the sword upright in front of him as if he were prepared to use it at any moment. Lyylia looked away before she smiled at him.

Kuu directed the two of them where to stand, and then went back inside the circle of stones. Ripples of green and yellow and violet flickered in the sky overhead. Lyylia glanced at Teija, standing beside Kuu. Then she looked past them at Shaun, standing on the far side of the stone circle. He hefted his sword and smiled at her. This time she let herself smile back at him.

Then she turned around to face the clearing, and reaching under her coat and tunic, she pulled out her handgun. She'd put the shoulder holster on over the short-sleeved undershirt that was part of the Pohjola-made ensemble she'd received at Kuu's castle. This way, the heavy woven over-tunic still hid the gun whenever she took off her coat.

She still felt reluctant to tell the Menninkäinen or Kuu about her weapon, since a police officer didn't go around revealing their concealed firearms to anyone and everyone. Although at this point, standard police procedure meant nothing.

If any Näkki appeared, then she'd have to explain her gun

to everyone. Assuming they all survived. If Näkki did attack, she had no idea if arrows, spears, or even bullets would stop it.

She looked back at Teija and Kuu at the top of the hill. *Stay strong, Teija,* she thought.

Overhead, the green and gold aurora washed across the sky. Lyylia drew a breath, and pushed her earplugs in. They were as ready as they'd ever be.

Teija stood where Kuu had positioned her near the small fire in the center of the circle of stones. She held the mouth harp in one hand, and a moon mirror filled with water balanced in the other hand. She kept her breathing shallow so as not to jostle the water over the edge of the silver pan.

Kuu stood on the other side of the fire. Her unsheathed sword and her small frame drum lay in the snow at her feet. She had her face upturned to the aurora overhead; her lips moved as if she were speaking, but Teija didn't hear anything. She wondered if the spell had officially begun or not.

Then Kuu lifted up a little wooden flute and began to play. Teija recognized the flute as the one that Boots sometimes played in the evenings after they'd made camp. Kuu played a slow simple melody.

After a few moments, Kuu laid the flute in the snow beside the fire and picked up her drum. With a silver stick in her other hand, she began a slow rhythm on the drum, and sang the tune that she had just played on the flute. There were no words.

The aurora rippled overhead as Kuu continued to sing the wordless tune. So far all was quiet, except for Kuu's clear voice.

Then Kuu, still singing, approached Teija. She took the moon mirror from Teija and placed it in the middle of the fire. The flames waned and smoldered, and didn't appear to burn Kuu's hands.

Teija stared for a moment at the fire dancing around the edges of the silver dish, then remembered that was her cue. She put the mouth harp to her lips and began to play. She didn't have to play a tune, Kuu had told her—which was good, because she had no idea how to do that. All she had to do was make slow, even beats in time with Kuu's wordless song. Placing the long part of the mouth harp against her teeth as Kuu had showed her, she kept her lips open and her tongue motionless as she thrummed the little metal tab.

Kuu picked up her sword, and stabbed it downwards into the snow beside the fire. It stayed upright, and Kuu picked up her drum again. Slowly beating the drum and singing, she paced a slow circle just inside the ring of standing stones.

Teija continued thrumming the mouth harp, and watched the firelight reflecting off the sword. She wasn't fond of weapons, but she had to admit that it was a beautiful sword. Gems like diamonds and sapphires were set into the gold hilt, and the silver blade was engraved with the delicate design of a snake. Thankfully the head of the snake was at the tip of the sword, and therefore currently hidden by the snow.

Kuu finished her circle and came to the center. She held the drum over the moon mirror and the smoldering fire. A faint sheen of blue light surrounded her hands. That was Teija's other cue—she lowered the mouth harp and backed out of the circle of stones. She walked a few paces away to where Kuu had cleared a small patch in the snow and laid the opal protection stone on the bare ground.

Maðen had told her that Shaman Pike had given it to him,

but she'd completely forgotten about it, since she'd had no idea at that point what a protection stone might do. She still wasn't sure, but she trusted Kuu's assurance that the little rock would keep her safe from Näkki or magic spells or whatever.

Teija glanced over at Lyylia, who was just a couple of meters away. Lyylia met her eyes, then looked back out into the clearing again. She had her gun in her hands, but had the barrel angled towards the ground.

Now Kuu added words to her song.

Return to the earth
Son of Dream, lord of silver
Kin of light, master of song
Return, return
Kied-Kie-Jubmel, lord of the land
Son of Dream
Return to the land of your birth

She repeated the song as she walked out of the circle. There was a bright flash of light overhead, and wave of green light came down and licked at the top of the standing stones, like a flame trying to catch. Electricity pricked the air. Then a blinding shaft of golden-green light hit the ground in the center of the circle. Teija staggered back a step, holding up a hand to shield her eyes. A faint roaring sound filled the air, like far away thunder or the distant rumble of a train.

The light faded almost as abruptly as it had appeared, and Child of Light began to bark. Squinting and blinking, Teija looked around, but the bright flash had made everything seem suddenly dim.

Looking back at the circle of stones as her eyes adjusted, Teija saw a large grayish-brown animal with antlers lying next to the moon mirror and the extinguished fire. The creature roused itself and stood up. It was a reindeer.

This animal was larger than any reindeer Teija had ever seen, in pictures or in real life—it was nearly the size of the Menninkäinen's small horses, with dozens of prongs on its sprawling antlers. It turned its head to look at its surroundings, and then pricked its ears towards Kuu. She went towards the animal.

"My Lord Kied-Kie-Jubmel," Kuu said in a solemn tone, and bowed at the reindeer.

Teija glanced down the hill at the clearing and saw that all of the Menninkäinen had dropped their weapons and were bowing deeply.

"My Queen," the reindeer spoke, a deep rumbling voice that seemed to come from the ground up. "You have found me at last."

For some reason, Teija was not surprised that the reindeer could talk. She stared at the animal's eyes; they were a deep grayish-blue color, but seemed to glitter and sparkle the way Kuu's eyes did.

Kuu reached out a hand, almost tentatively, and touched the reindeer's gray-white muzzle. He briefly closed his eyes, and when he opened them again, the blue color glittered even brighter.

"My Lord," Kuu said. "Come and let these loyal Menninkäinen who have risked their lives to help me behold you properly."

"Of course, My Queen." Together they walked down the hill into the clearing.

Teija started down the hill after them, but then paused when she saw that Lyylia hadn't moved. Boots and Falcon had come over the crest of the hill and were headed down to join the others.

Shaun came over the hill and joined Teija and Lyylia.

Finally Lyylia holstered her gun under her coat, and then the three of them walked down the hill.

All the Menninkäinen clustered together in the center of the clearing, and, as one, fell to their knees in the snow in front of the reindeer. Ávgos stood behind them off to the side, looking a little uncomfortable. Lyylia led Teija and Shaun over to stand with him. Teija saw movement in the trees at the edge of the clearing, and saw that Eider and Mađen had made their way down from the top of the cliff.

"Beautiful children of Pohjola, I am so glad to see all of you," rumbled Kied-Kie-Jubmel. "We have long missed the songs of the Menninkäinen, the scent of the forests, and the face of our Queen. Rise, please, all of you."

"We?" Kuu said. "Oh, Kied-Kie-Jubmel, no… All of the Gentle Beasts…?"

Kied-Kie-Jubmel lifted his nose towards the sky. "Yes, Kuu. We are all up there."

Teija looked up at the Dancing Lights, a calm wash of green, yellow, and violet once again. All of the reindeer of Pohjola had been living in the aurora for centuries? How was that even possible?

"Who are these people?" Kied-Kie-Jubmel then asked, angling his head at the group of humans. "They are not Menninkäinen."

"They are Kalevalans, My Lord," said Kuu. "It is a long tale."

"Kalevala?" He snorted and stomped a hind foot. "Kuu, how can you trust them?"

"As I said, it is a long tale. But they are the ones who led me to you. I would not have learned that you were in the Lights if not for them. This one especially." She pointed at Shaun.

Shaun, still clutching his sword in one hand, bowed

awkwardly at the reindeer.

Kied-Kie-Jubmel looked at Shaun and blew a steamy cloud of breath from his nostrils, but said nothing. He turned his head to look around the clearing and the hill, his large gray-brown ears moving back and forth.

"I count four stones on the hill," he said. "I thought we had five placed there."

"The fifth stone lies buried in the earth and the snow," Kuu said. "It fell centuries ago."

Kied-Kie-Jubmel snorted and swung his head back around to look at her, his massive antlers sweeping dangerously close to Kuu's face. "Centuries ago? Kuu...how long has it been since the Gentle Beasts left Pohjola?"

Kuu pursed her lips and didn't answer right away. "Over five hundred winters, My Lord."

"Five hundred...?" Kied-Kie-Jubmel flared his nostrils and stomped a hoof. "Dream preserve me! I knew that many seasons had passed, but..." He trailed off, and lowered his head. "Forgive us, My Queen!"

Kuu reached out and rubbed a hand across one of the branches of his antlers. "There is nothing to forgive, My Lord. It is I who must beg your forgiveness, for not figuring out sooner how to find you."

The reindeer blew more steam from his nostrils, though this time it didn't sound like an angry snort. "I see that everyone carries weapons," he said. "Kuu, what is happening?"

"Pohjola has been infiltrated by Näkki. Somehow Hiisi-Hiisi has found the gateway to Kalevala—"

"Surma must have told him of it," Kied-Kie-Jubmel interrupted her.

"Who is Surma?" Kuu asked.

"The Näkki who escaped."

"What Näkki?" Kuu frowned. "Kied-Kie-Jubmel, I'm afraid I do not know what you are talking about."

Teija glanced at Lyylia and the others. She was the latecomer to this world, but she and Maden had been told about the last battle with Ice-Dark and the strange disappearance of Pohjola's reindeer. Shaun had shown them pictures on his phone of murals in the Queen's castle depicting the story. She wondered if she'd missed some details, but judging by everyone's stunned and puzzled expressions—including Kuu's—apparently Teija wasn't the only one who was confused.

"Didn't Moon in the West tell you of Surma?" Kied-Kie-Jubmel said, looking up at Kuu.

Kuu reached out and touched the reindeer on the side of his neck. "Moon in the West is dead, My Lord."

"No, he is not. He is in the Lights along with all of us. He was the first."

"The first? I do not understand."

"It would seem that we both have a long tale to tell," said the reindeer.

"Perhaps you should be the first to tell us of yours," Kuu replied.

The Menninkäinen all sat down in the snow, looking up at Kied-Kie-Jubmel expectantly. Teija looked at Lyylia; she returned Teija's glance, then looked at the others, and shrugged slightly. They all sat down.

"It begins with the battle against Hiisi-Hiisi on the ice of the Dark Water Lake," said Kied-Kie-Jubmel. Kuu remained standing beside him, her hand resting gently on his back. "Many Gentle Beasts and Menninkäinen died that day. But two Menninkäinen and two Gentle Beasts fell through the ice and sank through the magic gateway into Kalevala. A Näkki pursued them. The two Gentle Beasts were Moon in the West and his son, Earth Beneath. In Kalevala, they fought to stay alive. Moon in the West told me frightening tales of a land torn between seasons of blackness like Ice-Dark and seasons of constant burning light like fire, and of the savage giants of Kalevala, who hunted Gentle Beasts and murdered them. And he said that the two Menninkäinen betrayed him and joined a roaming tribe of these Kalevala savages."

Teija glanced at Lyylia, then at Ávgos and Mađen. The ancient Sami peoples, like their modern descendants, herded and ate reindeer. If this was all that Kied-Kie-Jubmel knew about humans, then no wonder he had balked at them.

"They were trapped in Kalevala for many seasons," the reindeer continued. "Eventually the savage Kalevalans killed Earth Beneath. The Näkki, called Surma, after terrorizing the Kalevalans and Moon in the West for many years, found the gateway again and returned to his own land. It was many more seasons, nearly half a century, before Moon in the West found the gateway and returned to Pohjola. The Menninkäinen remained in Kalevala."

"I remember this," said Kuu. "I remember when Moon in the West came to us, then calling himself Night-Fire Desolation. He was wild and full of mad tales of how Hiisi-Hiisi had stolen the Lights of Pohjola and sent them to Kalevala. He did not mention anything at that time about a Näkki, though."

"Yes, he was quite mad with grief and from the violence he endured in Kalevala," said Kied-Kie-Jubmel. "And he did not believe us when we said that Hiisi-Hiisi had not stolen the Dancing Lights, even though he could see it for himself."

"And it was that summer," Kuu continued. "That we were at the Dancing Ground for midsummer, as had become our custom, to watch the Lights dance upon the earth. Moon in the West came to us, and just as the Lights touched the earth, he leapt into them. He was killed by the magic of the Lights."

Kied-Kie-Jubmel slowly shook his head. "That is the part of my tale that you do not know, Kuu. Moon in the West did not die when he leapt into the Lights. He joined the Lights and was taken up into the sky. Many moons later, when we were searching again for the gateway in the lake, the Lights danced on the earth again, and I was taken. Across the seasons, the Lights danced on the earth as they had always done, and each time, they brought another Gentle Beast back to the sky."

Kuu folded her hands together and pressed them against her mouth. Her silver eyes glittered. "Oh, Kied-Kie—I thought that you had found the gateway and had gone to Kalevala. I continued to search the lake, but then so many more seasons passed, and the Gentle Beasts began to vanish from Pohjola… I knew by then that it could not be the gateway, but I did not know where to begin to search."

"And we had no way to tell you that the Dancing Lights were now drawn to the magic of the Gentle Beasts. And then, after a time, we no longer cared so much. We knew that we had left Pohjola, but we could not act. It was as if we were half asleep, or in a waking dream. Only when more Gentle Beasts suddenly began joining us again did I try to wake myself. I could not use my magic—all I could do was sing the spell that had accidentally caused the Lights to take me in the first place. Several more Gentle Beasts have joined us recently—and yet, they are not like us."

Teija saw Mađen and Ávgos shift around. Kuu looked over at them.

"The Gentle Beasts of Kalevala," she said. "Reindeer, they are called. That is our tale that you have not heard, but it is all due to Hiisi-Hiisi."

Kied-Kie-Jubmel exhaled loudly and put his ears back. "Yes, there is much that I have missed. Five hundred seasons… We will talk, Kuu, but I think that these loyal men and women should sleep. The Dancing Lights have been awake for some time now, so the night grows late."

"Yes, of course." Kuu smiled at the group. "Please, all of you go and take your rest. Thank you all for your help tonight, especially you, Teija. Tomorrow there will be much to do."

Teija stood up with the others and joined them in bowing at Kuu and Kied-Kie-Jubmel before heading across the clearing towards the huts. She had helped Kuu bring this talking reindeer back to earth from the sky. Impossible as it seemed, she had helped perform a real magic spell. She fingered the mouth harp in her pocket as she trailed behind Lyylia and Shaun. Kuu would want it back, but she supposed it could wait until tomorrow.

Shaun stopped and looked back up the hill; Teija stopped beside him and Lyylia. None of them spoke. They watched Kuu and the reindeer walking side by side up the hill towards the stones. Kuu walked with one hand on Kied-Kie-Jubmel's back; her dog trailed behind them. The fire had gone out, but Kuu's sword still stood upright in the snow, reflecting the aurora.

At the top of the hill, with a backdrop of the standing stones and the golden-green Dancing Lights, Kuu dropped to her knees in the snow and wrapped her arms around Kied-Kie-Jubmel's neck. The reindeer bent his head and rubbed his nose against her long hair.

Teija smiled, but felt a strange wave of homesickness as she watched the reunion. She felt Lyylia take her hand and squeeze it.

Together, the three of them turned away and went towards the huts.

After a night's sleep indoors, a hearty breakfast, and a good scrubbing and shave in the sauna, Ávgos felt more refreshed than he had in days. He helped Maðen and Hoof clear out the hut they'd used for the night, loading food and blanket rolls back onto the sledges. Kuu had said that she wanted to return to her castle.

Looking up the hill to the standing stones, Ávgos saw Kuu and Kied-Kie-Jubmel standing inside the circle, with Child of Light sitting a few meters away. The reindeer lowered his head at Kuu in what looked like a bow, then disappeared down the other side of the hill.

"A giant talking reindeer," remarked Maðen from the other side of the sledge as they secured ropes around the stack of rolled tents and blankets. "When I woke up this morning, I kept wondering if everything that happened last night was a dream or something."

"I know what you mean," Ávgos said, looking at him. "Each time I get used to some unbelievable thing happening here, something else even more unbelievable happens."

"What did he mean about other Gentle Beasts joining them?" Maðen asked. "Our reindeer are part of the Dancing Lights now?"

"I think that's what he meant," said Ávgos. "When we first met Queen Kuu and she showed us several reindeer that had been brought to her, she said that one of them had recently disappeared. We all assumed it was a hiisi. I guess it could have been a Näkki, though we didn't know about them at the time. But if it was actually a magic spell..." He shook his head. "I don't know."

Suddenly one of the dogs began barking, and the horses snorted and stamped. Hoof pulled a spear off the back of the supplies sledge. "Icerunner, what is it?"

With a loud rustling of underbrush, Kied-Kie-Jubmel burst into the clearing. "Menninkäinen, arm yourselves!" he thundered. "There are Näkki in the river!"

Everyone dropped what they were doing and scrambled for weapons. The Menninkäinen gathered in a loose cluster with their backs to the huts, and pushed Teija and Lyylia to the center of the group. Ávgos grabbed a spear off the sledge and tossed it to Maden, then grabbed one for himself. He noticed that Shaun had pulled out the sword. Kuu was still at the top of the hill. He fumbled in his pocket for his earplugs.

Then the scream came. The hideous discordant shriek echoed off the huts and the rocky cliff behind them. Ávgos dropped his spear and sank to his knees in the snow, his head spinning. Another scream came from a different direction, and he saw a huge black shape streak past his vision.

Shaking his head and fumbling for his spear, Ávgos saw a shaggy black wolf, dripping wet, standing over Falcon. Boots and Tip thrust their spears into its side; it gave a loud hiss and lurched backwards, away from Falcon. Ávgos hurled his spear at it, though he felt weak and unsteady; the spear pierced the creature's side near the other two spears, and clear water gushed out of the wounds.

Tip wrenched his spear back out of the Näkki and thrust it again; with another hiss, the wolf jumped back out of range, and then twisted its head around to pull the other two spears out of its side. Water spurted down its fur like clear blood, and with a growl it backed away several more paces.

Ávgos tried again for his earplugs, finally getting them out of his pocket and into his ears. He started towards the spears lying in the snow, but the wounded wolf-Näkki opened its mouth in another shrieking wail. Ávgos didn't collapse this time, but his vision blurred and his legs felt weak as he lunged for the nearest spear. By the time he managed to grab the spear and ready himself to attack again, the wolf was no longer there in front of him.

Three huge black horses were pacing around the clearing. Apparently the wolf had turned back into a horse, but Ávgos couldn't spot which one they had wounded, because all the creatures were glistening with water and leaving little pools of ice in every footprint in the snow. Everyone had been scattered from their original defensive circle. A few meters away, Maðen stood protectively over Falcon and Tug, who were both collapsed in the snow, spear in one hand and his boot knife in the other hand.

"Näkki, stop!" Kuu's voice rang out across the clearing. "Cease your attack, or your leader will die!"

Kuu and Kied-Kie-Jubmel stood in the center of the clearing; the reindeer's antlers were lowered against a Näkki's side, and Kuu had her sword tip pressed under the horse's chin. Child of Light stood beside Kuu, fur bristling and teeth bared.

The Näkki hissed and put its ears back. "Näkki do not fear death, little moon queen. But if you wish to save everyone here, you will release me. Or the female Kalevalan dies."

"Teija!" shouted Eider.

Ávgos looked around and his heart thudded as he saw Teija lying in the snow at the edge of the trees; a Näkki stood over her, with a front hoof on her chest and its nose centimeters from her face, jagged teeth bared. Ávgos glanced over at Lyylia—she had her gun out, but she made no move.

Kuu pulled her sword away from the Näkki's neck but did not lower it. Ávgos could see a strange blue glow forming around her hands. Kied-Kie-Jubmel took a step back, but kept his antlers leveled at the horse.

"Name yourself, demon!" Kied-Kie-Jubmel bellowed. "I

will know the name of the creature who dares to attack us and threaten the Queen!"

The Näkki gave a loud gravelly laugh. "You can't beat me that easily, little Beast-shaman. A Näkki's name is his power. I am the spirit of the deepest water, and I shoot the arrows of infirmity into all who would cross me."

"Tell your Näkki to let her go, demon," said Kuu. The glow around her hands was growing brighter.

Suddenly Lyylia stepped forward, heading for Kuu and Kied-Kie-Jubmel.

"No!" Shaun lunged after her.

Ávgos tried to snag his sleeve but was out of reach. "Shaun, no—wait," he said. He had no idea what Lyylia might be planning, but if they all just charged forward, the other Näkki would certainly kill Teija—and the rest of them. "Just wait."

The Näkki facing off with Kuu and Kied-Kie-Jubmel turned his head at Lyylia's approach. "You wish to fight me, little Kalevalan?"

Ávgos took a careful step closer to Shaun. "Just wait, Shaun," he murmured. "Don't worry about Lyylia. Or Teija. They're too far away. If the Näkki move to attack, let's both of us go for that one there. It's the closest." He inclined his head to the right.

Shaun glanced at the nearest horse and nodded, then looked back at Lyylia. Ávgos tightened his hand around his spear.

Lyylia walked towards the Näkki with slow even steps, her gun out in front of her. She stopped a few meters away and leveled the gun at the creature. "Iku-Turso!" she shouted.

The horse gave a loud hiss and put its ears back. The Näkki standing over Teija hissed as well; the other three horses had been moving slowly around the group, and they all froze. *Iku-Turso*, Ávgos thought. Why did that name sound vaguely familiar?

"Iku-Turso," Lyylia repeated. "Leave now, and take all of your demons with you."

"And why should I do that?" the Näkki grated, stomping a hoof.

"You don't know what Kalevalans are capable of, Iku-Turso." Lyylia stepped closer. "Let her go, and leave us. Now."

Ávgos held his breath, glancing quickly around at the motionless Näkki, Maden and the Menninkäinen tense and ready with their weapons, and then back at Lyylia. Kuu had lowered her sword, but her hands glowed with blue light, and her eyes shone violet as she watched Lyylia. Kied-Kie-Jubmel stood still, only his tail twitching, his antlers still lowered at the Näkki.

The Näkki gave another hiss. "I concede to your greater power—for now," he said. "But beware the enemies you've made this day, little Kalevala shamaness. You haven't seen the last of us, and our numbers are greater than you know." With that, he threw his head back and screamed.

Ávgos dropped his spear and covered his ears. He gritted his teeth and willed himself to remain standing; through blurry vision he saw the Näkki gallop past, bellowing out a harsh barking sort of cry. The other four Näkki scattered into the forest. In seconds, all was silent.

Lyylia had stayed standing during the Näkki's scream, but as soon as they were gone, she crumpled. Kuu caught her around the midsection and eased them both down into the snow.

"Teija!" Eider ran across the clearing, with Maden on his heels. Shaun dropped his sword and ran for Lyylia.

Ávgos left his spear where he'd dropped it and stumbled after Shaun. His head was still ringing from that last scream, despite the earplugs, and his feet felt numb. He made it as far as Kuu and Lyylia and Shaun in the center of the clearing, and had to let himself kneel down in the snow to rest. Across the clearing he saw Maden and Eider helping Teija sit up. Kied-Kie-Jubmel headed towards them.

Shaun was cradling Lyylia, with Kuu kneeling beside them. Kuu laid a hand on Lyylia's head, and then on her chest. The blue light had faded from her hands, but her eyes were still purple.

"Lyylia, you spoke that Näkki's name," Kuu said. "How did you know its name?"

"My God, I can't believe that actually worked," Lyylia said. Her face was pale and she was breathing hard. "I've had gun fights with drug dealers that weren't as terrifying as that." She looked at the Queen. "It was a wild guess, Kuu—a gamble and a hunch. It's from *The Kalevala*, our old stories." She drew a breath, still visibly trembling in Shaun's arms. "During World War II, my great-uncle served on the *Iku-Turso*—it was one of the few submarines we had before Russia took them all. My father told me about it. He said the submarine was named after a water monster from *The Kalevala* who was the father of the nine diseases. That Näkki said he was a 'spirit of the deepest water' and 'shoots arrows of infirmity'—sea monster and the nine diseases. Like I said, a gamble and a hunch."

Ávgos pulled his earplugs out and shook his head, impressed. "I thought the name sounded familiar, but even if I had remembered that specific monster from *The Kalevala*, I never would have come to that conclusion."

Lyylia shifted around in Shaun's arms. "Teija. Is she—?"

"I think she's okay," Ávgos said, looking back over at Maden and Eider. The two of them were helping her to stand. Boots and Kied-Kie-Jubmel were with her.

"Truly wondrous, the magic of Kalevala," Kuu said, the

violet light now fading from her eyes. She picked up her sword in her right hand, and with the other picked up Lyylia's gun that had fallen in the snow.

"It's not really magic, Kuu," Lyylia said. "I tricked the Näkki. You know that we're not shamans."

"Perhaps." Kuu gave a small smile, and held up her hand, the gun lying flat in her palm. "A different sort of magic, I believe."

Ávgos held his breath. This was the first time that Lyylia had so blatantly brandished her gun, and certainly the first time that someone else had handled it. He wasn't sure if Lyylia had been purposefully trying to keep her gun a secret, but it wasn't a secret now. He almost wished she'd shot Iku-Turso. It would be good to know if bullets could kill a Näkki, since the spear-thrusts had hardly slowed it down.

"This is a Kalevala weapon," Lyylia said, taking the gun from Kuu's hand. "It's dangerous, and shouldn't be used except at the utmost need."

Kuu looked down at the weapon in Lyylia's hand, then back at her face. "I understand."

Lyylia reached under her coat to put the gun away.

"Lyylia!" Teija called. She was coming towards them, Eider holding her arm, with Mađen and Boots close behind her.

"Teija!" Lyylia struggled to stand; Shaun helped her up, and released her to Teija's embrace. "Oh, Teija. Are you all right?"

"She is unharmed by injury or magic," said Kied-Kie-Jubmel, who had approached, as well.

"Your Highness!" called out Hoof. He and Tip were bent over two Menninkäinen still lying in the snow. "Falcon and Tug have been injured!"

Kuu stood up. "I will see to them."

"I will make sure that no dark magic lingers on anyone,"

said Kied-Kie-Jubmel. "And then I shall join you, My Queen."

The reindeer stopped in front of Ávgos and placed his nose against his chest. Oddly more disconcerting than Kied-Kie-Jubmel's ability to talk was his size. He looked just like any reindeer and had the same musky scent, and his warm breath and velvety nose brushing past Ávgos' forehead was a familiar sensation. But he was nearly twice the size of an ordinary reindeer, and had more tines on his antlers than Ávgos had ever seen, even on the oldest males.

"You bear no wounds from the Näkki or their magic," Kied-Kie-Jubmel rumbled.

"Thank you," said Ávgos. He finally stood up, and then bowed at the reindeer. His feet were no longer numb and his headache was gone.

After he pronounced everyone fine, Kied-Kie-Jubmel headed for the nearest hut. Kuu had already taken Falcon and Tug inside.

Ávgos looked at Maðen, then exchanged looks with Shaun. Lyylia and Teija were still holding each other, Teija with her head buried in her sister's shoulder. No one said anything, but Ávgos knew they were all thinking the same thing.

Now what? They'd survived another encounter with the Näkki—maybe even "won" this time. But what about next time? They'd won with a bluff, but Lyylia's gun and Kuu's sword wouldn't be able to take out multiple Näkki all at once if they showed up in a group again.

Hoof and Tip came out of the hut, their faces distraught.

"What is it?" asked Boots. "What's happened?"

"Falcon is dead," said Hoof. "The Queen says that Tug will recover, but Falcon...neither she nor Lord Kied-Kie-Jubmel could save him."

Everyone exchanged horrified looks. Ávgos felt suddenly

exhausted, as the terror and adrenaline of the encounter left him and cold fear settled in. *Falcon is dead.* That easily could have been him, or Mađen, or any of the others.

Teija started crying quietly. Lyylia tightened her hold on her, and Shaun put a hand on Lyylia's arm. Ávgos looked at Mađen; his cousin looked more angry than scared. Ávgos wanted to be angry, at the Näkki and the whole situation in general, but this very moment, he felt like joining Teija in tears.

He thought of Sirkka. *I'm sorry, Sirkka,* he thought despairingly. At this point, getting back home safely seemed like the most unlikely thing in the world.

A wide stone bridge, as ancient and weathered as the first one they'd crossed onto the island, connected the far end of the Dancing Ground Island with the opposite bank of the river. Lyylia stood at the head of the bridge, her heart pounding and the cold wind tugging at her hair. Kuu had decided that a spell was needed to ensure their safe passage across the river. And because Lyylia had been the one to guess Iku-Turso's name and drive the Näkki away, Kuu wanted Lyylia to perform the spell.

All she had to do was sing. She thought of Teija playing the mouth harp during Kuu's spell on the Dancing Lights. As if being in this magical land wasn't strange enough, now they were casting spells.

Storm clouds were rolling in this morning, and Kuu wanted to travel as far as possible towards her castle before the weather slowed them down. They'd spent a second night in the huts on the island, for which Lyylia was grateful. Everyone had needed the warmth and rest after the Näkki attack; especially Tug, who'd suffered several bite wounds.

Yesterday afternoon they'd buried Falcon under a mound of stones. Kuu had chosen a spot at the foot of the cliff near the huts, and she and Kied-Kie-Jubmel had sung over his grave. A small flat rock with angular markings crudely scratched on it served as the headstone. Lyylia wasn't sure how Kuu had managed to make the carvings on the rock, but she didn't ask. Maybe one of the huts was stocked with a hammer and chisel, or other metal tools.

Kuu had contacted the shaman of Falcon's home village to give his family the news. Apparently Falcon's wife had considered it an honor to have him buried at the Dancing Ground by the Queen. At least they didn't have to worry about getting his body back home. Lyylia prayed that this was the last time they'd have to think about transporting or burying a body.

Kuu came up behind Lyylia, a lump of emerald ore in one hand and a mouth harp in the other. "The spell is simple, Lyylia," Kuu said, holding out the stone. "Just sing the words I told you. This spell will not keep the Näkki at bay for long, but it is enough to protect us as we cross the water. The Näkki are likely still nearby, and seeing you singing this spell will remind them that we are strong enough to fight them."

Lyylia nodded and took the protection stone from Kuu. Behind them the four sledges were waiting, horses harnessed and everyone inside, ready to go. Kied-Kie-Jubmel stood a few paces behind Kuu, and he inclined his head slightly as Lyylia looked at him.

Kuu lifted the mouth harp to her lips, and Lyylia faced the river and held the protection stone out in front of her. Kuu had told her that the tune for the spell didn't matter—she just needed to sing the words rather than speak them. Lyylia had finally settled on "Kylä Vuotti Uutta Kuuta," an old folk song that she remembered her grandmother singing. She'd never known all the words to it, though based on the title of the song it had something to do with a village waiting for the moon to rise. It was the only tune she could think of that seemed appropriate; an older folk song fit better in this world than the latest Eurovision hit.

Iku-Turso, I banish you
You cannot touch us here
We are protected from the water
Iku-Turso, I banish you, I banish you

As she sang, Kuu played the mouth harp. Lyylia had practiced the song several times while the sledges were being loaded, and that was enough for Kuu to memorize the tune and thus play a harmony of sorts. A mouth harp wasn't the most tuneful instrument, but Kuu matched Lyylia's pitch and rhythm perfectly.

Lyylia stared out over the ice of the river as she repeated the lines, then repeated them again. *Sing the words three times and hold the protection stone towards the river,* Kuu had told her. As she finished, she lowered the stone and looked back at the Queen.

She wasn't sure if she was supposed to have felt anything during the spell—though what magic might "feel" like, she had no idea. There was no glowing light or rush of energy, so she had to assume that the spell had "taken," despite the apparent lack of results.

"Well done," Kuu told her with a smile. "We are now ready to depart."

Lyylia handed the lump of ore back to Kuu, and went and climbed into the second sledge. She was riding with Shaun today. She'd wanted to ride with Teija, but Kuu had requested that both Tug and Teija ride in her sledge. Teija would be safe with Kuu, so Lyylia didn't protest.

The sledges began to move, with Kuu's sledge in the lead and Kied-Kie-Jubmel trotting beside it. They crossed the bridge without incident, and soon were gliding through the forest on the other side.

Lyylia looked at Shaun out of the corner of her eye and noticed that he was staring at her, a strangely stunned expression on his face.

"What?" she finally asked.

"That spell was amazing," he said. "You were amazing. You have a beautiful singing voice."

She gave a dry chuckle, to try to hide the blush she felt creeping across her face. "Magic," she said, shaking her head. "I never imagined I would do a magic spell."

Shaun grinned. "Well, you handled it like a pro."

She smiled back. They settled into silence, and Lyylia peered out the side of the sledge. The dense forest slid past in the dim overcast light, the only sounds the hiss of snow beneath the runners and the creak of the horses' harness. It was starting to snow. No sign of Näkki. So far.

She leaned back against the seat, and realized that Shaun was staring at her. Still, or again. Granted, there wasn't much to look at besides the monotonous snowy trees or the canvas roof of the sledge in front of them, but still… She raised her eyebrows at him.

"What do you miss most about home?" he asked.

The question surprised her. Whenever she and the others talked about home, he'd never contributed much to the conversation. She regarded him for a moment; his hazel eyes were serious, almost sad.

"I miss the sun," she said finally. "Real light that changes—sunrise and sun setting. I miss my mother. And I miss coffee. A lot."

Shaun laughed. "Yeah, me too. The food here is good, and that long-leaf stuff isn't bad, but it's not coffee."

"What do you miss from home?" she returned the question, since he'd brought up the subject.

He didn't answer right away. "I miss being able to carry on a really in-depth scientific conversation with someone who knows as much or more than me about aurora, magnetism, astronomy, physics, technology." He looked at her. "I don't mean to sound condescending. That sounded like I was calling everyone else stupid—that's totally not what I meant."

"I know," she said gently. "You miss other scientists."

"Yeah. I miss being able to talk to my peers, I guess. But to be honest, I don't miss the other scientists on my team."

"You don't like them."

He gave a lopsided smile that highlighted the dimple in his cheek. "Not really. And they don't like me, either. I'm the youngest on the team, and I'm always coming up with crazy ideas—like aurora-powered batteries and stuff." He chuckled. "I've sometimes imagined how Paul or the other two would manage here if they'd been captured by those hiisi creatures instead of me. No aurora-powered computer to find Kied-Kie-Jubmel in the Lights, that's for sure."

Lyylia smiled. "Do you have family?" she then asked him. The question was more personal than she probably should be asking, but in all the time they'd been in Pohjola, he'd never mentioned any family he might have left behind.

"Yeah—they're all in Pennsylvania, where I'm from," Shaun said. "Working in the steel plants or bussing tables at the diner. I love them because they're my family, but we don't really get along. None of them have ever approved of what I do. They think science is silly—and have told me so my entire life. I'm the first person in my family who's ever been to college—but instead of congratulating me on the achievement, all I ever got was flack about how I thought I was 'too good' to work in the factory like everybody else. So I call the family on Christmas, and I call my mom on her birthday—but I haven't been home in years."

He looked away from her, staring down at his backpack and Shaman Petrel's sword on the floor of the sledge. "Sorry," he said, glancing back up. "That's more than you bargained for. I didn't need to subject you to my family issues."

"It's okay," Lyylia said. Now she understood. All he had in life was his love of the Lights, and a dream. And here, not only were both of those accepted and appreciated, they were needed. No wonder he seemed to have so little interest in getting back home.

She had no idea how to express these thoughts to him, though, especially in English. She felt a sudden urge to hug him. She couldn't quite bring herself to do that, but she reached out and touched his hand that was resting on the bench between them.

Neither one of them were wearing their mittens. Shaun's hand felt surprisingly warm as she slid her fingers over his. He turned his hand over and entwined his fingers with hers. She looked back up into his face.

He locked his gaze with hers, an intense look in his eyes. *Please don't kiss me again,* she thought, even as he leaned forward and pressed his lips to hers.

This was not the time or place for a romantic entanglement. She was a police officer—she needed to stay focused on her work, even when she wasn't trying to keep people safe in dangerous alien territory. A police officer didn't get swept away by a lonely guy with rugged good looks and an irritating sense of humor...

Even as she argued with herself, she realized she was returning his kiss, and wrapping her arm around his neck to pull him closer. She felt his arm around her, and his other hand now gripping the back of her head as he continued to kiss her.

I should stop this, she thought. But she didn't want to. She gave herself up to it as they kissed and held each other close, and the sledge continued on in the gently falling snow.

Shaun had spent most of the last two days working on his scanner. Riding in the sledge didn't offer much in the way of workspace to spread out equipment, but Lyylia gamely helped him by holding wires and tools in her lap. She'd also offered him her long-dead cell phone to cannibalize for parts.

Several microphones and receiver boxes had gotten fried during Kuu's spell that brought the Dancing Lights and Kied-Kie-Jubmel to the earth. The computer itself had sustained only minimal damage this time. He was glad that he had developed the habit of always carrying a well-stocked field repair kit in the scanner pack.

He'd been able to set up the scanner last night when they stopped to make camp, and even with only two microphones instead of the usual five, it had gotten some good readings from the aurora. Most noticeable was the distinctive frequency that indicated ground-level aurora. Shaun had recorded that sound enough now to easily recognize it.

Last night's recording had been a little different, though. There was an odd energy spike that Shaun had recorded only once before: three days ago, when Kied-Kie-Jubmel had appeared. Kuu had explained that the spell had reversed the effect of the earth-walking Lights, meaning that now every time they touched down, a reindeer would be returned. As unbelievable as that sounded, his recordings indicated that was already happening.

As Shaun packed up his repair kit and the remains of the innards of Lyylia's phone, he glanced over at her. Lyylia had dozed off, her head lolling against the frame of the sledge and her hood partly obscuring her face. Too bad she hadn't dozed off against his shoulder instead. He'd have gladly sacrificed the last of his computer repairs to have her sleep in his arms.

Lyylia gave a sudden start and opened her eyes.

"You okay?" Shaun asked.

Her blue eyes flicked around the tiny confines of the sledge and then settled on him.

"I'm okay." She sat up straighter and tightened her scarf.

She looked tense. Shaun wondered if she'd been dreaming about Näkki. He had dreams about them sometimes—just jumbled imagery of black horses with horrible fangs, and ice everywhere, and that shattering wail like an electrified demon. He shook his head to push away the thoughts and finished latching his equipment cases and fitting them into the backpack.

Glancing back at Lyylia, he saw that she was fully composed now and staring out at the snowy forest. Shaun wished he could hear her sing again.

When they stopped to make camp, a thin haze of clouds was deepening across the sky. The Dancing Lights, blue and green tonight, glowed through the clouds and the trees. After helping to set up the tents, Shaun unboxed his laptop and the newly-repaired receivers.

He spotted Kuu over by the sledges; she had a moon

mirror in one hand, and a mug in the other, probably filled with melted snow for the moon mirror. Shaun tucked his laptop under his arm and went over to her.

"Your Highness, I'd like to show you something, if I may," he said.

"Of course, Shaun." She turned and placed the mug and the moon mirror on the roof of the nearest sledge, then turned back to look at him. "What is it?"

He opened his laptop and showed her his scans from last night, explaining his theory that the ground-level aurora were different now because of the reindeer.

"Your talisman hears true indeed," said Kuu with a smile. "Kied-Kie-Jubmel said he felt several Gentle Beasts return to Pohjola last night."

"He felt them?"

"The Dancing Lights still flow through his blood."

"Um, okay." Before he could figure out a question to ask, Kuu put a hand on his shoulder.

"Thank you, Shaun, for everything you have done. Your Light-listener is truly a great magic, and you have blessed all of Pohjola with it."

"You're welcome, Your Majesty."

Kuu smiled again, her silver eyes sparkling in the dim light.

Shaun finished setting up the microphones and the computer on the trunk of a fallen tree, and put the waterproof laptop case upside down over it to protect it from snowfall during the night. Hoof and Tip had returned from hunting, and he joined everyone else around the fire for dinner.

The scream came just as he was crawling into his tent behind Boots. He tumbled forward into the blankets, searing pain in his ears and his mind. Blindly fumbling in the blankets, his hand hit something smooth and hard. The sword. They all slept with weapons in the tents now. With a surge of adrenaline, Shaun yanked the sword out of its fur wrappings and staggered out of the tent.

Outside, the campsite was chaos. The central fire illuminated five black horses, trampled tents and overturned sledges, and people desperately trying to fight. Eider lunged at a horse with a spear, but the creature reared and deflected the spear thrust with its hooves, knocking Eider backwards into the snow.

Anger flared through him, and Shaun charged at the horse. His sword grazed its side as the Näkki twisted out of the way, snapping at him with jagged teeth. Shaun stumbled to the side and collided with Teija, nearly landing them both in the snow.

"Shaun!" She clutched at his arm.

"Get behind me, Teija," he said. He looked around, trying to find Lyylia, but then there was another Näkki in front of him. He slashed wildly with the sword. This time his thrust bit deeper and sent water streaming down the creature's flank.

The Näkki shrieked, and Shaun's head exploded with pain again. His legs crumpled and he collapsed in the snow, dimly hoping that he hadn't landed on Teija. He struggled to lift the sword as the Näkki loomed over him.

Then a pair of gray boots scattered the snow next to him, and he heard the clang of a sword. He rolled over and saw Kuu with her sword, driving the Näkki back. It hissed and reared, hooves meeting the blade with a ring. As it reared again, she ducked and thrust her sword into the creature's chest, right between its front legs. With her left hand she grabbed one of the Näkki's flailing legs and twisted. The horse toppled into the snow, water gushing from the wound. She gave another slash to its neck, and the creature lay still.

Kuu turned and held her hand down to Shaun, her eyes a blazing purple. He took her hand; her strength startled him as she pulled him to his feet.

"Are you hurt?" she asked.

"No." Shaun looked around and saw Teija lying in the snow at his feet. "Teija." He knelt back down. She didn't look injured, but was curled into a fetal position with her hands over her ears. He dug in his coat pocket for his earplugs and pushed the waxy wads of cloth into his ears.

An explosion slammed him from behind. He collapsed on top of Teija, head spinning. His first thought was that his laptop had blown up, but that explosion was too big for that. He rolled off Teija, coughing, and heard Kied-Kie-Jubmel shouting.

"Pursue them! Don't let them get away!"

Another hand extended down to help him; this time it was Boots. Shaun scrambled up, and then bent down to haul Teija to her feet.

The Näkki had apparently scattered. Shaun had no idea why they were chasing the Näkki instead of just letting them go, or what had caused the explosion. But he grabbed his sword in one hand and Teija's hand in the other and set off after the Menninkäinen as they ran into the forest.

Suddenly there was a flash of light through the trees—a burst of bright green, and a strange whooshing noise like wind through a tunnel. *Ground-level Lights?* Shaun wondered. He didn't feel electricity pricking the air. He doggedly continued forwards, his head aching and his legs still feeling rubbery. Teija stumbled behind him.

They came to where the Menninkäinen were gathered, weapons still raised, all looking around in confusion. The four dogs were wading through the snow, sniffing frantically. No sign of the Näkki—or Kuu and Kied-Kie-Jubmel, or the other humans.

"What happened?" Shaun panted.

"I don't know," said Boots, sounding equally out of breath. "The Näkki took Lyylia and Ávgos and Maðen, and we were in pursuit, and then there was a flash of light—"

"The Näkki captured them?" Shaun said, a sick feeling washing over him.

Child of Light started barking. The Menninkäinen all turned their weapons towards a rustling sound, and Shaun hefted his sword.

Kuu and Kied-Kie-Jubmel appeared between the trees, with a body draped over the reindeer's back—it was Ávgos.

"*Missä on Lyylia?*" Teija asked breathlessly. "*Ja Maðen?*"

"Take Ávgos back to the camp," Kuu said by way of an answer.

Shaun handed his sword to Tug, who was still recovering from the last attack but had made it out here with the others. Shaun stepped forward to help the other Menninkäinen haul Ávgos off the reindeer.

"I've got him," Shaun said. Ávgos was a few inches shorter than he was, but he still surprised himself by hefting the weight of another man over his shoulder. He must still be on an adrenaline high.

"The Näkki have taken Lyylia and Maðen," Kuu said. "That flash of light was a vanishing stone. They will be headed for Ice-Dark, probably straight across the Dark Water Lake. Guards are posted all along the shore, but they will be no match for four Näkki intent on breaking through."

"We have no vanishing stone," said Kied-Kie-Jubmel. "Dream, give me speed."

Kuu reached out a hand and touched him on the chest, on the white fur between his front legs. "The speed of summer lightning and the strength of the moon," she said, as her hand glowed with a pale blue light against his fur. "Go, Kied-

Kie-Jubmel."

She pulled her hand away and he leapt between the trees, disappearing from view.

"Back to the camp," Kuu instructed.

The campfire was still blazing brightly, but the remains of their tents and blankets were covered with soot, and one of the sledges was charred beyond use. All of the horses had broken their tethers and scattered. The only horse that remained was a dead Näkki lying in the snow.

Eider and Hoof gathered some blankets and laid them by the fire so Shaun could put Ávgos down. Kuu knelt beside him, laying her sword in the snow. Her hands still glowed blue, and she touched Ávgos on the forehead, the chest, and then tugged at the neckline of his coat to touch him on the throat. She sang quietly under her breath. Then with her hands on Ávgos' chest, she leaned over and put her mouth against his, as if doing CPR. He stirred, and then coughed and opened his eyes as Kuu sat up. Shaun let out a breath he didn't realize he'd been holding.

"A Näkki sleep spell," Kuu said, and helped Ávgos to sit up. "Your strength will return quickly, Ávgos."

She picked up her sword and stood. "Is anyone else injured?" she asked, looking around at the group. Everyone shook their heads, except for Hoof, who had a bleeding gash on his forehead.

"A small cut only, My Queen," he said.

Kuu went over and examined his head. "I will make you a bandage to stop the bleeding, Hoof," she said. "But yes, it is a minor wound only." She looked at the group. "Pack everything that is salvageable, and try to find the horses. There will be no more rest tonight—time is even more of the essence now. We must reach my castle."

As the Menninkäinen bustled into action, Shaun pulled out his earplugs and knelt down by Ávgos. The other man looked groggy and disoriented.

"You okay, Ávgos?"

"I think so." Ávgos rubbed his head. "What happened?"

"Näkki," said Teija, dropping down beside them. "Ávgos—Maden and Lyylia are gone."

"What?"

"The Näkki took them," said Shaun tightly. "Just rest for a minute, Ávgos, while we pack up. Stay with him, Teija." He laid his sword beside her, and got up to help the Menninkäinen gather what was left of their supplies.

He found his laptop. It had not exploded, and miraculously had been knocked off its perch and into the bushes on the other side, so it had been entirely out of the battle zone. He brushed off the snow and put it back in its case, then dug around till he found the backpack. That was undamaged, as well.

He helped Eider to roll up one of the tents. He looked over at the charred and splintered sledge; Kuu was poking around in the smoldering remains.

"Kuu, what was that explosion?" Shaun asked.

"A fire stone," she said, turning to look at him. "A talisman that is used to start a fire without flint or fuel. With a simple spell for enhancement, it can create a burst of fire such as that." She pulled at the harness at the front of the sledge; the leather traces cracked and crumbled in her hands. "And the vanishing stone is a talisman that can move one a great distance in an instant. Both are stolen Pohjola magic, likely taken from one of the shamans who the Näkki killed."

"So Lyylia and Maden are long gone, then," Shaun said, feeling sick. He stayed kneeling in the snow as Eider lugged the tent over to the supply sledge. He spotted the smooth wooden handle of a spear lying in the snow; he reached out and picked it up. Spears and swords hadn't been enough.

Kuu squatted down beside him, and rubbed her hands in the snow to clean off the soot from the burnt sledge.

"We will find them," she said quietly, the angry violet light still flickering faintly in her eyes. "If the Näkki wanted Lyylia and Maden harmed or dead, they would not have captured them."

That was not as comforting as it should have been. Shaun nodded resolutely anyway, and clutched the spear as he stood up.

All eight horses, and most of the blankets and food, had been recovered. Since they were now short another sledge, Boots and Tip crafted make-shift bridles out of rope so that two horses could be ridden.

"We must dispose of this Näkki," Kuu said. "It must not be left here poisoning the land."

The big black horse lay sprawled like an eyesore in the snow. No one had mentioned it as they'd gathered up the camp, as if talking about it might suddenly bring the thing back to life.

"Skin it," she said. "Burn the skin, and leave the body to fade."

Shaun didn't want to watch that gruesome task, so he helped Ávgos and Teija into one of the sledges and made sure they were comfortable.

When he turned back around, he was surprised to see that the Menninkäinen were already finished. The black horsehide ignited like dry paper as they hefted it onto the fire. The body of the Näkki was nothing but ice.

Shaun stepped closer to get a good look. Except for its sprawled position in the snow, it could have passed for a piece of ice statuary like in the courtyards at Kuu's castle. And it was already starting to dissolve. Or evaporate, was more accurate, maybe. It wasn't melting—just slowly shrinking and losing its horse shape, like dry ice minus the fog. He didn't know whether to be horrified or furious that a creature made of nothing but water and ice could terrorize them so.

The Näkki skin burned quickly, and Eider and Hoof kicked snow onto the remains of the fire.

As he walked over the sledges, Shaun looked up at the Dancing Lights, faintly visible through the trees and clouds. *We're coming for you, Lyylia*, he thought. *Somehow.* His stomach clenched at the thought of her in the clutches of the Näkki.

The light snowfall had stopped, but the thin clouds remained as the horses set off through the forest. Somewhere to the north lay Kuu's castle, Lyylia and Maden, and Ice-Dark.

Chapter 7: Ice-Dark

Maden awoke with a start, coughing and gasping. He tried to get his eyes to function, but all he could see was blackness and swirling patches of color like fire.

As he caught his breath, he realized that he was wet and lying on a hard rocky surface, but it was pleasantly warm, and helped bring feeling into his cold aching limbs. Guttural snarling sounds echoed, but he couldn't tell if the sounds were far away or close by. He then became aware of a smell—a hot, briny sort of odor, like some kind of smoke.

Finally his eyes started adjusting to the low level of light. He was lying on the stone floor of a cave. A glow like firelight came from an opening some distance away. He heard water gurgling, and rolled his head to see a wide stream running through the cave. A human form lay on the cave floor near the stream. He sat up with difficulty, and squinted at the figure. It was Lyylia.

Forcing his muscles into action, he shakily crawled across the floor towards her. The surface was hard, of course, and scattered with loose gravel that he couldn't see till he put his hands or knees on them. Grunting in pain, he finally made it over to Lyylia's side. The only thing that made the trip easier was the fact that the floor was warm.

He put his hand on Lyylia's shoulder, and she turned her head to look up at him. She put a finger to her lips to shush him, and then gestured toward the floor. When he just stared at her in befuddlement, she tugged on his arm and whispered, "Lie down. And be quiet. If they think we're still unconscious, they might keep talking."

Obediently he let himself collapse back onto the floor of the cave. The sounds, he realized, were Näkki voices. Now that his brain was starting to clear, he could understand the words through the guttural, rasping tones.

"And you think that none will notice?" came one of the voices.

"He is not searching for us," returned another voice. "We should take them to her—she would want shamans from another world."

"Do not presume to tell me what she wants!" the first voice snapped. The conversation dissolved into hissing and snarling.

There was a splashing sound. Maden looked over at the stream that flowed past them, but nothing disturbed the surface. The stream must flow into the other room of the cave. The red fire-like glow through the jagged opening was still all that he could see. Even though his eyes had adjusted to the light, it was still hard to judge the size of the opening or how far away it was.

"We must go," said a third Näkki voice. "He knows that the border has been crossed. He sees all that Äi sees."

"That is a lie that only the weak believe," came the hissing reply.

Maden had heard only one Näkki speak before, but now that he was hearing three of them conversing, he realized that they all had individual voices. And the angry one who had just spoken sounded like the one and only Näkki—up till now—that he'd heard.

"Iku-Turso?" he mouthed at Lyylia.

She nodded.

"Go," Iku-Turso's voice instructed. "Tell the others. And you, believer of lies, go with him."

"I believe no lies, and Näkki serve no master!" shouted the other Näkki, and the conversation died again amid hissing and growling and what sounded like a physical tussle.

"They were talking earlier about what to do with us," Lyylia whispered to Maðen. "We're in Ice-Dark. I think they put some kind of spell on us to take us through the water. I'm pretty sure that we're the only two who got captured, so everyone else must still be in Pohjola."

"That's good."

A deep rumbling sound, almost too low to hear, trembled up through the floor of the cave. A puff of air, warm but sulfuric smelling, blew past as everything vibrated. The Näkki were still engaged in their argument, still not speaking in words that he could understand. What sort of magic were they doing?

"I think we're inside a volcano," Lyylia whispered again, as the trembling subsided. "That's what that smell is, and why the floor is warm."

"Is that what that shaking was? Did the volcano just erupt?" Maðen suddenly felt eager to take his chances on meeting Hiisi-Hiisi face to face, rather than dying inside a volcano.

"Probably nothing so dramatic. Just regular geo-thermal activity."

"How do you know all that?"

She gave tiny shrug with the shoulder that she wasn't lying on. "Just a guess."

The Näkki's argument seemed to have stopped, and there

was the sound of more splashing, then padding footfalls on the stony floor. Maden shut his eyes and lay perfectly still.

"And so we travel again, to meet the ruler of Ice-Dark," said Iku-Turso's voice, directly above them. "Consider it an honor, Kalevalans. And you are not asleep, shamaness—you cannot fool me."

Maden heard Lyylia roll over. He stayed where he was, completely still and focusing on breathing slowly and rhythmically. Even if Iku-Turso knew that he was awake, too, he seemed to be more interested in Lyylia.

"Iku-Turso," Lyylia said.

The Näkki laughed, that harsh grinding sound that Maden hated. "Yes, now that you know my name, you seem to want to speak it all the time. Well, you are now in my domain, and your magicks will not work here."

"You don't know that, Iku-Turso," Lyylia calmly returned.

"I may have to freeze that skillful tongue of yours to the inside of your mouth."

"But then you'll never know my name," Lyylia countered.

Still focusing on keeping his breathing slow and steady, Maden carefully opened one eye a tiny crack. He couldn't see much except for Lyylia lying beside him, but he did catch the movement of a black dog as it leaned over her. Everything in him wanted to jump up and attack the creature, but he knew that would be suicide at best. He wished that he'd been awake enough before to check and see if the small knife in his pocket or the long knife in his boot were still there. He couldn't feel them in the position he was lying in right now.

"I will know your name soon enough, little shamaness. But first, we go to the water." The Näkki put his nose down and breathed on them—the breath was both hot and cold at the same time, and smelled vaguely like salt water. Iku-Turso thrust his head into Lyylia's shoulder, shoving her into Mađen.

Mađen rolled over, intending to get up, but Iku-Turso slammed his head into them again. The impact of the wolf's head was shockingly forceful, and sent them both skidding across the gravel. The cave floor sloped slightly at the water's edge, and before Mađen could try to stop his momentum, they rolled into the stream. Warm water closed over his head, and he lost consciousness.

Teija stared out the side of the sledge, gaping in awe at the imposing mountains. She hadn't done much traveling before and so had never seen large mountains in person—but this mountain range was surely taller than any in Scandinavia. The tops of the tallest peaks were shrouded in mist, even though the weather was clear. And even more impressive than the landscape was the glittering castle built into the rocky side of one of the mountains. Briefly Teija let her fear and despair fade into the background as she gazed around at the majestic scenery. The Mountains of the Moon were aptly named.

The scenery became much less exciting as they began ascending a snowy mountain trail. High rock walls on either side of the narrow twisting channel made her feel suddenly claustrophobic. She looked at Eider sitting next to her; he gave her a smile and squeezed her mittened hand in his. She felt a little better.

They went through a set of huge wooden doors in the mountainside, and emerged in a broad open courtyard. After the sledges came to a stop, Teija climbed out, staring around at the bare-branched trees and statues carved of ice, the long stone buildings that were probably stables, and the walls and spires of the castle above them.

Teija fell into step behind Shaun, Ávgos, and the Menninkäinen as they all followed the Queen towards the castle doors. The doors opened and a Menninkäinen clad in a plain white tunic and brown breeches came out, carrying a spear.

"Welcome back, Your Majesty!" he said with a bow.

"Stone!" Kuu greeted him. "I am glad to see you returned from the Western Fells."

"I bring news on our defenses at the Dark River," Stone said.

"I am anxious to hear updates. Has Lord Kied-Kie-Jubmel arrived?"

"He has, My Queen. He arrived with three other Gentle Beasts late last night, and he wishes to speak with you."

Kuu and Stone strode into the castle, and everyone else followed, since the Queen hadn't told them what to do or where to go. Teija was anxious to see Kied-Kie-Jubmel again—he'd gone after Lyylia and Maden when the Näkki took them two days ago, so hopefully he had some news.

Two days. Their caravan had been traveling non-stop day and night, with only the briefest pauses for food and toilet breaks, and a few stops in villages to change out horses. The trip had thankfully been uneventful, but that had left plenty of time for Teija to sit in the sledge in silence and worry. Now that Queen Kuu was back at her castle and the magic reindeer were returning, hopefully they could figure out how to rescue Lyylia and Maden.

The carved walls and palatial windows of the castle corridors were just as Lyylia had described, but Teija couldn't study the design very closely, because she had to focus on keeping pace with Kuu. Stone abruptly halted in front of an open door in the middle of a corridor and stepped to the side, positioning himself like a sentry beside the doorway. Kuu pulled off her coat and draped it over her arm before entering the room.

A long wooden table with benches took up most of the space in the center of the room. Standing over by the fireplace were four reindeer.

"My lords," said Kuu, halting just past the end of the table, her dog at her heels. She inclined her head at the reindeer.

The Menninkäinen jostled each other and nearly toppled over with their deep bows. Teija and the others bowed, as well.

The largest of the reindeer came forward. "My Queen," Kied-Kie-Jubmel greeted her. "The Näkki vanished themselves and their captives too far for me to catch up to them. The Menninkäinen guarding the lake fought valiantly against the Näkki, but they were no match for them." Kied-Kie-Jubmel's ears lowered.

"How many Menninkäinen were killed?" Kuu asked quietly.

"One. And three were injured, but I was able to heal them. I sent one of them with two uninjured companions back to the closest village. They took the deceased Menninkäinen with them to be properly buried. They will leave the injured man to his rest, and return with further reinforcements. I went out onto the ice of the lake for some distance, but I could not see the Näkki—they were in Ice-Dark by that time."

They were in Ice-Dark. The words pounded in Teija's head and she felt tears pricking her eyes. She was determined not to cry in front of everyone. She glanced over at Shaun and Ávgos; Shaun clenched his jaw, and the Sami man was staring at the floor.

"Excuse us, Your Majesty," a Menninkäinen interrupted

from the doorway. He and another man stood there holding large serving trays with slices of bread and steaming mugs. "Food will be ready in time for the evening meal, but in the meantime we thought you and the others would like some warm refreshment after your long journey."

"Thank you," Kuu said. She gestured for them to enter, then gestured for everyone to sit down on the benches.

Warm buttered bread was a welcome treat, and Teija gratefully helped herself to the food and a mug of hot long-leaf.

Kuu remained standing and addressed the other three reindeer.

"My lords and lady, I'm so happy to see you. Pohjola has missed your presence for far too long. I'm sorry that you have returned to find your land so distraught, but your wisdom and strength has never been needed more than now."

One of the reindeer lowered his head at Kuu and said: "It is an honor, My Queen, to serve you and Pohjola once again. I am Silence of the Sky."

The other two reindeer introduced themselves. Son of the Mountains was the other male, and the female was named Rain Upon Ice. Teija hoped she wouldn't have to remember such elaborate names. All the reindeer looked the same to her.

"Lord Kied-Kie-Jubmel has told us of all that has happened in our absence," said Silence of the Sky. "And most recently, that two of the shamans from Kalevala have been abducted by Näkki and taken to Ice-Dark."

"Yes. And we must devise a means to rescue them. These are their companions: Shaun, Ávgos, and Teija."

Teija followed the two men in turning around on the bench and giving nodding bows to the reindeer. The three reindeer all bowed their heads to the humans.

"It's an honor to meet you," Shaun said politely.

"The honor is ours," said Silence of the Sky.

Kuu finally sat down at the table and helped herself to a beverage. "First of all, Stone, please tell us of the situation at the border."

Stone was standing over by the door, and he stepped forward. "Guard encampments have been placed along the river, just out of sight from Ice-Dark. No fewer than three men per encampment, and all camps are spaced apart so that each one can just see the next camp. There are no blind spots now that changelings or Näkki can slip through. Several of the encampments have moon mirrors, so messages can be relayed quickly should anyone capture invaders from Ice-Dark."

"Very good," Kuu said. "Thank you for organizing that, Stone."

He bowed deeply.

"The spell upon the Dancing Lights is working, My Queen," Kied-Kie-Jubmel then said. "Many Gentle Beasts have returned every night."

"Soon we will have enough numbers for an army," said one of the other reindeer. Teija had already forgotten his name.

"Sending an army blindly into Ice-Dark would not be wise, Son of the Mountains," Kied-Kie-Jubmel said. "Hiisi-Hiisi would have an army of his own waiting for us."

Teija felt a flutter of fear—on top of the general worry and terror she'd been carrying for two days now. Armies. They were talking about war.

"We also have no knowledge of the land or where Lyylia and Maden might be," Kuu said.

"I wish we had a map of Ice-Dark," murmured Shaun. "That would help. Have any of you—" he looked at Kuu and the reindeer "—ever been to Ice-Dark?"

Kuu shook her head. "I cannot leave Pohjola, nor can

Kied-Kie-Jubmel. We are bound to the magic of our land, just as Hiisi-Hiisi is bound to the magic of his land. We can both cross the water of the lake, as it belongs to both of our lands, but we cannot enter another land. And no Menninkäinen or Gentle Beast has ever crossed the border into Ice-Dark."

"But we've got to do something," Shaun insisted.

"And we shall." Kuu gave all three of them a gentle smile. "We shall not abandon your fellow Kalevalans. However, we must plan and prepare."

She looked over at Stone. "Please show the Kalevalans and these Menninkäinen to guest chambers, Stone." She looked back at everyone at the table. "Please, rest and refresh yourselves after our long journey. We will continue this discussion at the evening meal. I have many things I must discuss with Kied-Kie-Jubmel."

Everyone got up and followed Stone out of the room. While Teija was happy to have an opportunity for a nap indoors lying down, instead of dozing sitting up in a chilly sledge, she would have rather continued a discussion about how to rescue Lyylia and Maden. Not that she had any useful ideas to contribute. She'd had two days to think of ideas, and had come up with nothing. Surely Kuu had some ideas, at least.

Teija glanced at Shaun and Ávgos as they walked. She hadn't had much of a chance to talk to anybody besides Eider during the trip, since they hadn't camped in the evenings. Shaun slowed and peered around a corner as they went through an intersection of corridors. The blue-white light coming in the high windows seemed brighter down that hall.

"I think that's the Halls of Time down that way," Shaun said quietly.

"I think you're right," Ávgos agreed.

Teija wanted to see the murals in person, but now was probably not the best time. "But no map of Ice-Dark there," she said, remembering the picture of the Pohjola map on Shaun's phone.

"No." Shaun shook his head. "I would have taken a picture of it if there had been."

They arrived at the corridor of guest rooms, which looked like every other hallway, with the polished stone floor and high ceiling and the snake-and-moon designs carved all over the walls. Each small room had its own fireplace and private toilet room, and furs and blankets on the floor for sleeping. Teija was pleased with the cozy setting, but wished she could share a room with someone. After weeks of sleeping in tents packed together like tinned fish, having a whole room to herself felt strange. She really wished she could share with Lyylia.

She found a sauna and a bathroom at the end of the corridor, and gratefully took advantage of the bathtub. The room had a small vent in the wall to let heat in from the sauna next door, and a hand pump to fill the metal tub. Filling the tub was a lot of work, but the water coming from the pump was hot. She wondered why the Menninkäinen didn't bother with running water in their villages if the technology existed in Pohjola. Maybe they hadn't figured out how to keep their pipes from freezing in uninsulated wooden huts.

Teija felt guilty enjoying the luxury of a hot bath while Lyylia and Maden were suffering who knew what sort of hellish experiences. The logic that King Hiisi-Hiisi wanted the humans alive—and hopefully, relatively unharmed—was of very little comfort. While Teija scrubbed herself with the soap and let the hot water ease her chilly muscles, she finally let herself cry.

Shaun felt refreshed after using the sauna, but he was too antsy to rest. He paced around his small guest room, skirting the edge of the bed furs on the floor. Now that Kuu was back in her castle, presumably with weapons and magical talismans at her disposal, then surely they could figure out how to mount a rescue. Or maybe talk to Hiisi-Hiisi to negotiate Lyylia and Maðen's return. As Kuu had said, he must want them alive or else they wouldn't have been captured. And holding them hostage for some sort of exchange was the most logical reason that Hiisi-Hiisi would want live captives.

At least, it seemed logical to Shaun. That's how it worked in the movies, but this was real life—real life in a setting far more fantastical than even a movie. He sighed and rubbed his hand through his hair as he continued to pace.

There was a knock at his door. He opened it to find Stone there, along with Ávgos.

"The Queen requests your presence in the Moon Tower," Stone said.

Shaun stepped out into the hall, closing his door behind him. "What about Teija?" he asked, looking at Ávgos.

"Her Grace requested only the two of you," said Stone.

Ávgos returned Shaun's look and gave a slight shrug.

Shaun fell into step with Ávgos and Stone. Walking through the wide echoing corridors brought on a strange sense of déjà vu. For the first time since arriving in Pohjola, they had returned to someplace familiar.

Soon they were climbing the narrow winding staircase to the Moon Tower. Even though Shaun was prepared for the light, the brilliance at the top of the stairs made him stagger. The Dancing Lights had not yet begun, but the stars, the crescent moon, and Pohjantähti produced more than enough light to shine through the clear walls and ceiling and reflect off all the ice and silver.

Kuu and Kied-Kie-Jubmel were standing by a small table of ice in the center of the room, along with six Menninkäinen. Shaun recognized Gray, the young shaman living at the castle, and belatedly recognized the tallest of the Menninkäinen as Wind, the shaman of the village in the Western Fells. One of the two remaining Menninkäinen held a spear and was dressed in the plain leather breeches and white tunic of Kuu's castle guards, and the other wore outdoor furs and had caked snow on his boots.

"Thank you for coming," said Kuu. "Ávgos, I need for you to confirm for me that these two Menninkäinen changelings are from your world." She had her hands resting on the shoulders of two of the little men, who were dressed in shabby rags and were barefoot, and stared straight ahead with expressionless faces.

Ávgos went up to them and gently pushed back their hair to check their left ears. "My earmark," he said. "These are my reindeer."

Kuu nodded. "I thought as much. Thank you, Ávgos. I will transform them back to their proper form, but first, I must question the Näkki."

"Näkki?" Shaun asked in alarm. "There's a Näkki here?"

"Yes," Kuu said. "The guards patrolling the border in the Western Fells captured these two changelings just after they crossed the river gorge. I knew that the changelings were somehow smuggling Näkki into Pohjola, but until now, we were not able to catch them in the act."

The fur-clad Menninkäinen beside Shaman Wind held up a full water skin. Silver thread was wound around the stopper.

The Näkki could apparently appear and disappear quickly via the water, but they could also change size when in water?

It was a terrifyingly brilliant plan—no one would question a traveling Menninkäinen carrying a water skin.

Kuu looked at Shaun and Ávgos. "Since both of you have experience fighting Näkki, I would like to have you present."

Shaun wished he'd known that—he would have grabbed his earplugs out of his coat pocket. Now he knew why she hadn't asked for Teija.

Kuu went over to a nearby ice column and rummaged in a wooden chest on the floor. Shaun realized that she was wearing her sword across her back. She had changed clothes from the traveling attire she'd been wearing for the past couple of weeks; she now wore a form-fitting white dress, and a surprising amount of jewelry. She had a narrow silver circlet around her head, several jeweled rings on her fingers, and a long silver chain around her neck. Shaun wondered why she'd gotten so dressed up for an interrogation.

She came over with two long daggers in her hands, and handed one to Shaun and one to Ávgos. "I don't believe these will be needed, but I want you armed, just in case."

"Thank you, Your Highness," Ávgos said after a pause.

Shaun merely stared at the light glinting off the blade and nodded mutely.

Kuu took the water skin and headed across the room towards the rock wall of the mountain, and they followed behind her. Gray and the castle guard came, as well; Kied-Kie-Jubmel brought up the rear. Wind and the other Menninkäinen stayed with the changelings.

Five wooden doors, all closed, led into the mountain, and Kuu opened the one on the far right. The passageway was already lit with lanterns. Kuu's dog sat down just outside the door as they all went into the passage. Kied-Kie-Jubmel tugged the door closed behind them.

The passageway grew quickly narrow, as well as low. After just a few steps, Shaun and Ávgos were walking stoop-shouldered, and Kied-Kie-Jubmel had his head lowered so that his antlers would clear the ceiling. The lanterns along the walls, all hung at about waist height, illuminated the walls and ceiling that were carved much like the walls of the castle corridors. The swirling snake-and-moon designs, inlaid with silver, glittered in the lantern light. Shaun tried not to feel claustrophobic in the low tunnel.

The passage sloped downwards, and then suddenly opened up into a small room. Shaun breathed a sigh of relief and stood up, rubbing at his aching neck. They were in a small round room, carved directly out of the mountain. The floor was rough-hewn rock, but the walls and ceiling, like in the tunnel, were smooth and carved with the silver-inlaid design. The ceiling was still low—Shaun could have easily touched it, but it was better than the tunnel.

Kied-Kie-Jubmel positioned himself at the mouth of the passageway, and Kuu gestured for everyone else to gather in a circle around the walls of the chamber. Then she lifted the water satchel and began to sing. Her voice was as beautiful as always, but the wordless tune she sang sounded oddly sharp and discordant. Shaun felt chills and tightened his grip on his dagger.

As Kuu sang, she untied the piece of silver twine from the mouth of the water satchel, then handed the satchel and the thread to Gray. The dissonant melody continued, and now she added words.

Silver, show your strength, entwined forever be
Until my words release you.
As the light of the moon, silver, show your strength.

Still singing, she pulled off her long silver necklace. Holding it out in front of her, she wove the slender chain between her fingers, as if making cat's-cradle figures. After singing the words three times in a row, she stopped and held the long chain out, dangling towards the floor.

"Gray," Kuu said, nodding at him.

The Menninkäinen stepped forward, opened the water skin, and poured it out onto the floor. At the same moment, Kuu dropped the silver chain into the stream of water.

As the water splattered on the floor, the necklace hit the puddle and a black wolf appeared—no magical flash of light, no warning scream. It was just suddenly standing there. Shaun grunted in surprise and lifted his knife.

The creature stood still, dripping into the shallow puddle of water, its icy white eyes glinting. Shaun realized that Kuu's silver necklace had become a harness of sorts, wrapped around its head and snout.

"Name yourself, demon," Kuu commanded.

The dog pulled its lips back to reveal jagged teeth. "You will need more than this simple harness spell to draw my name from me," it rasped. The silver harness kept it from opening its mouth very far.

"Very well. We don't need to know your name, for now— you are still captive here. And you will answer my other questions, or you will die."

The Näkki hissed at her.

Kied-Kie-Jubmel stepped forward. "Tell us why your master has sent you here."

The Näkki flattened its ears and bristled at the reindeer. "Näkki serve no master!"

"Really?" Kuu said calmly. "I was under the impression that Hiisi-Hiisi had sent you."

The Näkki hung its head, but bared its teeth again. "He did."

"Well, then either you are a very poor liar, or you are

greatly confused," said Kied-Kie-Jubmel.

The Näkki hissed at him.

"What did your master send you here to do?" Kuu asked.

The Näkki opened its mouth as far as the harness would allow. Shaun braced himself for a scream, but Kuu's hand flashed out and grabbed the thin silver halter. She squatted down next to the wolf, holding its head at arm's length, her fingers entwined in the halter and the creature's shaggy black fur.

"Tell us what your master sent you here to do," Kuu repeated.

"He is not my master!" the Näkki shrieked. "Pohjola is ours—we've taken it and we are keeping it. Hiisi-Hiisi wants your light, and he can come and take it himself. We are not here to serve him or help him."

"Our light?" said Kied-Kie-Jubmel with a snort. "Does he not have starlight on his side of the lake?"

The Näkki hissed, and tried to turn its head to look at him. "The lights of color that move in the sky. He thinks the lights have power; he craves power, above all else and to the ruin of all."

Kuu twisted her fingers tighter into the Näkki's fur. Tilting its head back, she closed her other hand around its throat. The Näkki tried to squirm, but she held it stationary.

"If I kill you, there is one less Näkki in Pohjola," she said, her voice dark. "But if I send you back to your king whom you claim to hate so, I will make sure that all other Näkki contaminating my land know about it. I don't like using killing magic, so I would just as soon send you back to your master."

The Näkki seethed and hissed through its teeth, glaring at Kuu; she matched its gaze, her own eyes glowing purple.

"You admit that your people did not come to Pohjola of

your own volition," Kied-Kie-Jubmel said into the silence. "Hiisi-Hiisi sent you here. Your reward for subduing Pohjola and leaving it open for his attack was to live here and govern yourselves?"

The Näkki growled low in its throat. "Yes," it finally grated.

Kuu released the Näkki's head and stood up.

"We are finished here, for now." She looked down at the wolf. "You will remain in this prison of silver until I have decided whether to kill you or return you to Ice-Dark." She turned and led the way back up the tunnel; Kied-Kie-Jubmel brought up the rear. Shaun glanced back over his shoulder before the slope of the passage fully obscured the room. The wolf stood in the center of the little room, making no move to try to follow them.

Prison of silver… He could see the lantern light flashing off the closed door up ahead. The door was wood, but the inside was lined with a sheet of silver. Näkki were weakened by silver, Kuu had said, and so this tiny compartment, all decorated with silver from floor to ceiling, truly was a prison for such a creature. And the jeweled silver rings she'd worn hadn't been just for decoration.

He also abruptly realized why this passageway had such a low ceiling. A Näkki would be unable to shift into horse form. A wolf Näkki was no less deadly than a horse Näkki, but at least in wolf form it was smaller. Kuu had probably built this room after the first big battle with Ice-Dark, all those centuries ago. Shaun figured that he should feel relieved or encouraged that she had prepared defenses such as this, but instead he felt more frightened than ever.

After everyone had left the passage, Kuu closed the door and locked it with a large silver key hanging on a hook beside the door. She turned to the Menninkäinen castle guard who'd been with them.

"I want a guard outside this door at all times. After I transform the changelings, I will speak with Stone about arranging a rotation of guards for this post."

"Yes, My Queen." The little man hefted his spear and positioned himself in front of the door.

"Gray," Kuu continued. "Please begin the preparations for the changeling transformation spell—the same talismans and instruments we used before. Although there are two changelings, Kied-Kie-Jubmel is with me this time, so the spell should not take as long. We should be finished before the evening meal."

"Yes, Your Grace." Gray hurried over to a chest across the room.

Kuu pulled her sword scabbard off over her head. "Ávgos, I would like you present for this spell, since these creatures know you. Shaun, you may return to your chambers and rest, if you wish."

"I'll stay, actually—if that's okay, Your Highness," Shaun said. He didn't want to be alone right now.

"That is fine." Kuu took the two daggers back from Shaun and Ávgos, and carried the daggers and the sword over to the nearest chest. She laid the weapons inside and started to close the lid, then stopped. Reaching back into the chest, she pulled out a different dagger.

It resembled her sword, with a shiny silver blade and gold hilt. The blade was smooth, though, with no engraving of a serpent. Like her sword, there were jewels set into the hilt; but instead of just a few small diamonds and sapphires, the hilt of this dagger was encrusted with gems of every color, some large, some small. The jewels flashed like aurora in the light as Kuu held the dagger flat on her palms.

"I remember that knife," Kied-Kie-Jubmel rumbled quietly. "It has a companion sword. A different sword from the one you use now."

"Yes." Kuu's tone was somber. "That sword is long gone." She offered no explanation. Holding the dagger almost reverently, she walked over to the square table made of ice in the center of the room.

"Shortly after the Gentle Beasts first began to disappear from Pohjola," she said, "myself and some of the older Menninkäinen who had been in the battle on the lake believed that somehow Hiisi-Hiisi was behind the vanishings. We discussed ideas and strategies around this very table." She laid her hand on the smooth surface. "Since that day, no weapon has ever touched this table."

With a swift motion, she plunged the dagger into the tabletop. Tiny ice shards went shattering in every direction as the blade drove into the table almost to the hilt. Her eyes flushed violet. "This knife will stay here until every Näkki is driven from Pohjola's waters and our land made safe. Hiisi-Hiisi will not have our land, our people, or our Lights. Or the Kalevalans."

Shaun felt chills that had nothing to do with the cool air or the ice constructs all around. He stared at the glittering dagger imbedded in the ice table. He tried not to feel despairing—Kuu's proclamation seemed like an impossibility right now.

But he'd witnessed so many impossible things here, he reminded himself. Not the least of which was a table made of ice that had apparently not thawed in the past five hundred years. Or the woman in front of him, who had immobilized a Näkki with her bare hands and just thrust a blade into the ice table as if it were a hot knife in butter.

Shaun drew a deep breath as Ávgos went over to the

changelings and Gray bustled around arranging blankets and musical instruments. They'd made it this far. Somehow, some way, they could win this and rescue Maden and Lyylia.

Lyylia landed on a hard surface, and snapped out of her semi-conscious, probably magic-induced, stupor. She smelled smoke again, and felt heat at her back, and assumed they were still inside the volcano. She was completely drenched—either still or again—but realized that she was quite warm. Almost hot, actually, which was an unusual sensation. A chilly breeze swept past her face, and it felt refreshing.

Before she could get her eyes open and focused, hands with claw-like grips grabbed her arms and hauled her up into an upright position on her knees. Shaking her head to get her wet hair out of her eyes, she finally was able to look around.

The first thing she saw were the clawed white-furred hands gripping her arms. She tried not to yelp out loud at the little grotesque face mere centimeters from hers. The hiisi opened a mouth full of sharp jagged teeth in either a snarl or some attempt at a wicked grin. Hiisi were on either side of her, holding her still, and she could feel at least one more at her back. She saw Maden kneeling a few meters away to her left, also surrounded by hiisi. Three black wolves sat between them.

They were in a large stone chamber. It was hard to gauge the actual size—huge columns of slate gray stone were scattered all around as far as she could see, and stretched up to a ceiling out of sight in the darkness overhead. The chamber was full of hiisi, scampering around like mice or crouching behind stone columns.

The only light came from torches attached to the columns, and a few stone bowls sitting on the floor, filled with burning oil. In the distance across the room, an elaborate fountain sent water cascading down several tiers of rock, ending in a large bubbling pool. Steam rose from the water. Lyylia squinted at the fountain—either there was some sort of light source behind the falling water, or the water itself was glowing a pale greenish-blue color. A steady cold breeze flowed through the chamber. The floor, like in the previous cave, was warm.

"So these are the shamans of Kalevala," came a deep voice.

The rumbling voice echoed around the chamber, and the floor seemed to shudder. The scampering hiisi all quieted and hunched down.

"Yes, My Lord," rasped one of the dogs. It sounded like Iku-Turso.

"Foolish little hiisi, bringing them here, thinking them merely curiosities from another world," rumbled the voice, almost gently. "But I forgive my earnest servants, because they only meant to stop troublemakers from interfering with my plans. They had no idea they had captured mighty shamans, instead of mere meddling fools."

"Shamans or fools, which shall it be?" cackled a higher-pitched voice, also echoing from every direction at once. "Fools or shamans, we shall see!"

Lyylia held her breath as she felt the floor shudder again. The faint rhythmic trembling felt more like heavy footfalls than seismic activity, but she heard no footsteps.

"I especially commend the loyal Näkki," continued the deep voice. "For stealing the shamans away from the moon queen and bringing them to me."

Iku-Turso lowered his head in a bow, his nose nearly

touching his paws.

"And now, I wish to finally speak with these shamans myself. Release them!"

The hiisi claws gripping Lyylia's arms released. Away to her left, Maden scrambled up, pulling a knife out of his coat pocket as he stood. She tried to catch Maden's eye. One little knife in a room full of hiisi and Näkki was only going to antagonize them. Maden swiped at the nearest hiisi, which hissed at him and scuttled out of reach. Lyylia stood more slowly, trying to look non-threatening.

"Welcome to Ice-Dark, worthy Kalevalans." A shadow moved between the pillars. "I am Hiisi-Hiisi."

A giant horse stepped into the light. It was white—or really, almost milky and translucent, as if it were made of ice and snow. But the eyes were red, glowing like hot lumps of coal, and when the mouth opened, the blood-red tongue was forked.

The horse approached them, the huge icy hooves making no sound on the stone, even though the floor vibrated with its steps. The creature had to be at least the size of an elephant. Trying not to tremble, Lyylia craned her neck to look up at its head as it came closer.

"You are my guests," rumbled the horse, the forked tongue moving, a shocking red against the icy-white face. "And you bring a weapon into my throne room?" Hiisi-Hiisi swung his head towards Maden.

In a blur of black, Iku-Turso lunged at Maden and snapped the knife out of his hand. Maden yelped and grabbed at his hand as Iku-Turso tossed the knife onto the floor at Hiisi-Hiisi's feet.

Gritting her teeth, Lyylia remained still. There was no way she could defend him with mere physical force.

"Shamans and fools, shamans and fools!" came the cackling

again. Lyylia finally saw the speaker of the shrill voice—a large black raven was perched on Hiisi-Hiisi's back. The bird's eyes blazed red.

Hiisi-Hiisi regarded the fallen knife for a moment, then turned his head away from Maðen to look at Lyylia. Iku-Turso remained standing by Maðen's side, looking up at him with jagged teeth bared.

"You are the shamaness I have heard about," Hiisi-Hiisi said. "The Kalevalan who can see the unseen and divine the names of the Näkki. Come, tell me your name."

With difficulty, Lyylia met his gaze and said nothing.

"I have no wish to kill you. However, I cannot say the same about your companion. Tell me your name, or I will give him to my Näkki for them to feast upon."

"You don't want to do that," Lyylia said, trying to keep her voice from shaking. "Word of my powers has spread, but that's only because he hasn't displayed his true powers yet. He's a greater shaman than I am."

Hiisi-Hiisi took a step towards her, which brought his head directly above hers. Hot dry breath poured down on her, and she shuddered despite her best efforts not to. That horrible red snake tongue flicked out, almost touching the top of her head.

"I think you are lying."

Craning her neck, she stared up at the giant white horse head above her. "My name is Jaana."

Hiisi-Hiisi snorted, blasting her with hot breath that smelled of sulfur. "Now I know that you are lying. Very well, Jaana, you may keep your name and your shaman companion, for now. But be reminded that no matter the scope of your powers, you are now in my domain. My magic comes from Äi herself, and you are far from Kalevala and your World Serpent."

"The shamans are fools, and lies they tell!" squealed the

raven, cocking its head as it looked down from its perch on Hiisi-Hiisi's back.

"Take them away," Hiisi-Hiisi said, and suddenly both Lyylia and Mađen were surrounded by white furry creatures again, grabbing at their arms and legs with their claws and holding them still. "We will speak again soon."

The swarm of hiisi half pushed-half pulled them between the stone columns. The voice of the raven followed them down a wide stone corridor. "Shamans and fools, fare thee well!"

The corridor walls were a dark gray, with only the occasional torch sconce to light the way, and Lyylia quickly lost track of the twists and turns. Then they were tossed into a small cave-like chamber. A metal gate clanged shut behind them.

"You okay?" came Mađen's voice. His hands gently took her arms and helped her up off the hard stone floor.

"I'm okay," Lyylia said, brushing her damp hair out of her eyes again as she stood up. "Are you all right? How's your hand?"

"Fine," Mađen grunted. "Iku-Turso just grabbed the knife out of my hand. He didn't bite me."

The only light came from a torch on the wall of the corridor directly across from their cell. Lyylia went over to the gate and tested it. The gate wedged tight against the rock around it, but the lock was primitive; they might be able to pick it with something.

She turned back around to examine the rest of their prison. A little trickle of water ran through the center of the room, but the entrance and exit points of the stream weren't even close to being large enough to provide some sort of escape. The ceiling was low enough that Mađen could reach it with his arms above his head.

Mađen pulled a small flashlight out of his coat pocket and

swung the narrow beam around their cell. It was a small cave dug directly into the rock, with no seams between walls and floor and ceiling. Most of the rock was dark gray, but veins of light gray and reddish-brown minerals showed up in the light. The only object in the cave was a clay pot against the back wall.

"A chamber pot, I guess," Lyylia said. "How considerate of them."

Mađen switched off the flashlight. A faint greenish glow shone in a narrow band across the ceiling. They both stared up at it.

Mađen reached up and ran his hand along the vein of glowing rock. "It feels like rock, just like the rest of the ceiling," he said. "I wonder what makes it glow like that?"

"It could be radioactive, I suppose," Lyylia said. She wished she knew more about minerals and geology. Not that that would necessarily help them, though. For all they knew, it could be magic rock native to Ice-Dark.

Mađen jerked his hand back. "Damn. Well, let's stand over on this side of the cave, just in case."

"That's amazing that your flashlight still works, after going through all that water," Lyylia then said, kneeling down next to the little stream in the middle of the room.

"My coat has waterproof inner pockets," said Mađen. "I wish I'd had more stuff in my pockets that day on Lake Inari. Everything was in my backpack."

Lyylia dipped her hand in the water, and then yanked it back. "It's scalding. This whole place must be built on a geothermal vent or something."

"No wonder I'm roasting." Mađen pulled off his coat.

Lyylia likewise was still feeling warm, in addition to wet, and wet clothes were uncomfortable, warm or cold. She pulled off her coat, scarf, tunic, boots, socks, and breeches. Her

Pohjola-made outfit included a short-sleeved undershirt and knee-length long underwear, so she kept those on. She'd long ago gotten rid of her bra, as it was getting uncomfortable, and at this point seemed pointless for both function and propriety. She still wore her own camisole, though, under the short-sleeved shirt.

Maden removed his flannel shirt and undershirt, along with his coat, and pulled off his boots and socks. He kept his trousers on. They laid out their clothes on the warm floor to dry.

Lyylia sat down and field-stripped her gun.

"I'm glad they didn't find that," Maden said. "They also didn't find the other knife I keep in my boot. I wonder why they didn't search us?"

"Maybe Hiisi-Hiisi wants to test us," said Lyylia. "He thinks we're shamans—he's probably hoping we'll try to fight, so he can see what we're capable of."

"And I fell for that ploy, didn't I?" Maden growled. He squatted down by the gate lock, knife and flashlight in hand. "That's just the way I react when I'm scared out of my mind. Not all of us can be as perfect and competent as you."

"I'm far from perfect or even competent," Lyylia said, pausing in the reassembling of her gun to look up at him. "And I'm scared too."

Maden looked back at her. His glower softened, then he turned back to the gate lock.

Lyylia's gun was as clean and dry as it was going to get, so she finished reassembling it and loaded a bullet into the chamber. On second thought, she pulled the magazine back out and stuffed it into the pocket of her coat. If they were searched later, she didn't want the hiisi getting ahold of a fully loaded gun. Hopefully they wouldn't be able to figure out that the pistol and the magazine went together.

Maðen sighed and switched off the flashlight. "I don't think this is going to work. This knife blade is too big for that lock. I don't suppose you have a hairpin on you."

Lyylia shook her head. Her hair clip had disappeared somewhere during the trip through the water. She wished she had it, or at least had a rubber hair tie, to keep her curls under control.

The air was cool, and despite the heat from the floor, Lyylia felt chilled. Her woven tunic was mostly dry already, so after sliding her underarm holster over her shoulders, she put the tunic back on.

"Well, we've survived this long," she said. "Maybe that protection stone actually works. Kuu gave it back to you, right? The little opal stone you gave her for the spell at the Dancing Ground."

Maðen came over and picked up his undershirt and put it back on. "Kuu gave it back to me. But, uh, I don't have it anymore. I, um, I gave it to Teija, after the Näkki attack, when that Näkki had her trapped. I didn't want that to happen again."

Lyylia stared up at the big Sami man and felt a lump come to her throat.

"Thank you," she said finally. "Thank you for taking care of my sister." She swallowed. She could only hope that Teija was still safe with Kuu and the others. "I still can hardly believe she went all the way to Inari to look for me. I…" She swallowed again, and then looked down, focusing on tying the laces at the neckline of her tunic.

"Well, um, you're welcome," Maðen said. "You know, Teija's pretty hardy for a city girl."

Lyylia looked back up at him and smiled.

"Ávgos and Shaun will take care of her," Maðen then said. "And Kuu will, too."

Lyylia managed another smile. "I know." She prayed that everyone else was safe in Pohjola. And that somehow she and Maðen could get back there. She just had to keep them both alive long enough to figure out how.

Ávgos sat between Shaun and Boots at the dining table, as their entire traveling party enjoyed a hot meal indoors for the first time in days. Gray, Wind, and the other Menninkäinen who'd brought the changelings and the water satchel had joined them. As Kuu had promised, she'd finished transforming the changelings back into reindeer long before Stone summoned everyone to dinner.

Kuu had not appeared for the meal yet, though Stone said everyone could eat. Ávgos wondered if she'd taken a nap after the transformation spell. Seeing his reindeer standing where two people had stood was no less astounding this time than the first time he'd watched her transform a changeling. But like the previous time, he'd noticed that she seemed exhausted after the spell.

Everyone had just about finished eating when Kuu and Kied-Kie-Jubmel finally entered the room. Three other reindeer accompanied them—probably the three that had been with Kied-Kie-Jubmel earlier. Not only was Ávgos going to have to get used to the idea of talking reindeer; he was going to have to adjust to seeing them indoors.

Stone served up a plate of food for the Queen.

"My apologies for keeping you waiting," Kuu said, taking a bite of food. "We were discussing strategies for rescuing

Lyylia and Maðen from Ice-Dark."

Everyone sat up a little straighter. Ávgos pushed his empty plate away and leaned forward a bit to look down the table at Kuu.

"Hiisi-Hiisi captured them most likely for one of two reasons. He either believes them to be powerful shamans and hopes to use them to access magic from Kalevala. Or, he took them believing that I would treat with him for their safe return."

Kied-Kie-Jubmel spoke, while Kuu ate a few bites of food. "The Queen and I shall go to the Dark Water Lake and demand an audience with Hiisi-Hiisi. We will not bow to his wishes or his threats, but we will hear what he has to say."

"It is possible that we can come to an agreement about the return of the Kalevalans," Kuu said. "However, we must be prepared should his answer be unreasonable."

After all the work Hiisi-Hiisi had gone to, stealing reindeer and smuggling Näkki into Pohjola, Ávgos very much doubted that he would give a reasonable answer and just hand over the captives. He had a cold, sinking feeling that a battle was inevitable.

"The time may come, very soon, when all of Pohjola must stand and fight," Kied-Kie-Jubmel said solemnly. "We must begin—"

"Excuse me, Your Majesty," interrupted a Menninkäinen in the doorway. "Please forgive the interruption, but there is a Gentle Beast who wishes to speak with you."

"By all means, show him in," said Kuu.

The man gave a quick, nervous bow. "He…he told me to tell you that he refuses to enter your castle until it is free from the contamination of the Kalevala savages. His words, as he instructed me to tell you, Your Grace."

Kuu pursed her lips. "Did this Gentle Beast give you

his name?"

"Night-Fire Desolation."

Kuu exchanged looks with Kied-Kie-Jubmel. "Please tell Moon in the West that his Queen requests his presence immediately."

The little man bowed deeply. "Yes, Your Majesty."

A tense silence hung in the room. Kuu finished eating. Ávgos exchanged nervous looks with Shaun and Teija. He remembered Kied-Kie-Jubmel's story about Moon in the West, the mad reindeer who had been trapped on Earth and was accidentally responsible for the spell that had caused the Dancing Lights to take the reindeer in the first place.

The sound of hooves on stone echoed down the hall, and a reindeer appeared in the doorway.

"Welcome!" said Kuu, lifting her hands. "Please come in and join us, my lord. All of Pohjola rejoices to see another Gentle Beast."

The reindeer remained in the doorway. Even though he was smaller than Kied-Kie-Jubmel, his massive antlers branched out so widely that Ávgos wondered if he could fit through the doorway without careful maneuvering. His ears and tail were flicking nervously.

"Your Majesty," the reindeer finally said, in a voice that sounded far more calm and staid than his body language indicated. "Why have you betrayed us?"

Kied-Kie-Jubmel snorted, but Kuu remained calm. "Much has happened in your absence," she said. "Ice-Dark has made moves against us, and the Kalevalans—"

"Lies and treachery!" the reindeer bellowed, and suddenly bolted into the room and leapt up onto the table. Everyone seated on the benches scrambled up and away as the animal thundered down the table, trampling plates and dishes. He skidded to a stop at the end of the table in front of Kuu. "How dare you betray us!" he shouted down at her.

"How dare you speak to your Queen in such a manner!" roared Kied-Kie-Jubmel.

"Moon in the West, calm yourself!" Kuu said, standing up to face him.

"Moon in the West is dead!" the reindeer said with a snort, pawing at the tabletop. "Night-Fire Desolation I have become! I was cursed by the Kalevalans, and now you bring them into your home!"

"This is my home, and I will invite in whomever I please!" Kuu returned. "Night-Fire Desolation—if that is what you wish to be called—please, step down and let me explain. So much has happened since the Dancing Lights—"

"They stole the Lights!" he interrupted her. "Thieves, murders, invaders!" He reared up, hooves flailing.

Before Ávgos even realized what he was doing, he dashed forward and shoved Kuu out of the way. As he pushed her against Kied-Kie-Jubmel, he stumbled over her chair and a sharp pain shot through his left shoulder.

Grunting with the impact of the reindeer's hoof, he stumbled again and hit the floor, then frantically rolled out of the way as Night-Fire Desolation jumped down.

"Murderers! Tuonela torment your souls!" The reindeer lunged with lowered antlers.

Ávgos felt hands grabbing him, and Shaun and Boots dragged him backwards. The other three reindeer and Kuu's dog had surrounded Night-Fire Desolation, and Kuu had been pushed back and had a protective barrier of Menninkäinen between her and the reindeer. Teija had retreated to the absolute farthest corner of the room.

"Are you okay?" Shaun said to Ávgos as he and Boots

helped him up.

Ávgos nodded. "He got my shoulder. It's just bruised, I think." He moved his left shoulder around, feeling pain, but no restricted movement. Reaching inside the neckline of his tunic, he felt a raised welt on the skin, but no blood.

Kied-Kie-Jubmel faced off with Night-Fire Desolation. "Calm yourself." His rumbling voice was commanding, but not angry. "The world has changed since we last lived in it, but your Queen has not. No one here is your enemy."

Night-Fire Desolation still had his antlers lowered and was restlessly twitching his tail. "We were one with the Dancing Lights," he said finally.

"Yes," Kied-Kie-Jubmel said.

"I still see the Dancing Lights in my eyes, hear their song in my thoughts."

"As do I," said Kied-Kie-Jubmel.

"And now we are flesh once again."

"Yes."

"Flesh can die." Night-Fire Desolation's ears twitched.

"No one here is going to die."

Night-Fire Desolation relaxed from his defensive posture, and the other three reindeer slowly backed away, releasing him from their circle. "I have been to Kalevala," Night-Fire Desolation said, his voice calmer now. "These beings are savages, as bad as any denizen of Ice-Dark."

"These Kalevalans are not the same as the ones that you once knew," Kuu said, stepping forward.

"That one is," said Night-Fire Desolation, swinging his head to stare at Ávgos. "I will never forget the scent. You are *noaidi*."

"No, I'm not a shaman," Ávgos answered him.

"But you are *Sámit*."

"Yes." It was strange to hear this otherworldly creature speaking Sami words with such clarity.

"Your Highness, you do not know what you have invited into your land," Night-Fire Desolation said, looking at Kuu as she approached him. His voice was steady, and his ears and tail had calmed. "The *Sámit* of Kalevala—do you know how they treat Gentle Beasts?"

"Yes," said Kuu. "Ávgos is a guardian and protector of the Gentle Beasts in his world."

"Protector!" Night-Fire Desolation snorted. "Yes, they protect them from wolves so that they may kill the Gentle Beasts themselves. They eat them, Your Majesty. They murder Gentle Beasts, they wear their skins like wolf pelts, their shamans use their bones for their hideous rituals, and they devour their flesh."

There was silence while Ávgos listened to his heart thudding in his chest. When no one said anything, Night-Fire Desolation took a slow step towards Ávgos. "Answer truly before the Queen—do your people wear the skins of Gentle Beasts and eat their flesh?"

Ávgos drew a long breath and frantically tried to think of a good way to answer. "Yes," he finally managed.

There was a quiet gasp from several of the Menninkäinen. Kuu looked at him with a confused expression on her face, a mixture of disbelief and revulsion. Ávgos swallowed and felt himself starting to sweat.

"I didn't hide anything from you, Your Highness," he said, trying to keep his voice calm. "It's just that…things are so very different in Kalevala from the way they are here. The Gentle Beasts of my world—they're not like them." Ávgos gestured toward the reindeer in the room. "They're not shamans—they're just animals, livestock, like horses or sheep."

"You eat them, you murder them," Night-Fire Desolation growled.

"Yes—and we eat fish and rabbits and bears, just like the people here do. But the reindeer—they're special. Every time we kill one, we thank it and honor its spirit. The reindeer…choose to give themselves to us, just as we choose to give ourselves to them by protecting them from danger." Personally, Ávgos didn't say a prayer of thanks to his reindeer at slaughtering time, but he knew his father and grandfather had, and the underlying sentiment was there in the heart of every Sami.

"In Kalevala, they're not Gentle Beasts—they're just reindeer," Ávgos continued hurriedly, looking at Kuu as he spoke. Her expression was unnerving—the shock had faded from her face, and she looked more hard and impassive than he'd ever seen her. He saw no hint of purple in her silver eyes, so he hoped that was a good sign. "To my people, the reindeer are life, and livelihood, and what gives us our identity. We guard them and protect them, because without them, we…. we would cease to be Sami."

Kuu still gave no reaction at all, but Kied-Kie-Jubmel moved subtly closer to her, as if ready to protect her—or perhaps, himself.

"And now you are here to devour us," Night-Fire Desolation said.

"No! I came here to get my reindeer and bring them back to my world." Ávgos wished his heart would stop pounding. "Actually, I didn't mean to come here at all—the hiisi kidnapped my reindeer, and then kidnapped us."

"You have not heard their story, Night-Fire Desolation," Kuu finally spoke. "If you are suggesting that the Kalevalans have come here with the intention of harming anyone in Pohjola, I can assure you this is not the case."

Ávgos breathed a quiet sigh of relief, and he heard Shaun beside him do the same. At least Kuu still trusted them that much, after his confession.

"Lies!" the reindeer roared suddenly, rearing up. "They've bewitched you, Your Majesty. This man lies—he must indeed be a powerful *noaidi* to have woven such a spell to blind you. To blind all of you! If you let them stay here, you will all die!" He spun on his hind hooves and galloped out of the room.

"Stop him!" Kuu shouted.

All four of the reindeer ran out of the room after him.

Kuu went for the door, then paused to look back at the humans and Menninkäinen. "All of you, please stay here. I will return." Then she hurried out of the room, her dog beside her, and closed the door behind her. It shut with a heavy clank, and Ávgos wondered if she'd just locked them in.

"Let's see your shoulder, Ávgos," said Shaun, breaking the silence that fell.

Obligingly, Ávgos pulled off his tunic, and sat down on the bench at the table. It looked like his earlier assumption had been correct—he had a huge red welt that was fast turning into a bruise, but nothing felt broken and he wasn't bleeding.

"It looks painful, but it will soon heal," Gray said, coming up beside Shaun to examine Ávgos' shoulder.

Ávgos nodded in agreement as he put his tunic back on.

"So is it true?" Boots said, a hesitation in his voice.

Ávgos looked him in the eyes. "Everything I told the Queen was true."

"I know you're not cruel savages and all those things that Night-Fire Desolation said. It's just…it's just a little hard to understand that you could really…eat Gentle Beasts."

"Because they're not Gentle Beasts in my world," Ávgos said gently. "You were with us, Boots, you and Eider, right after you'd rescued Shaun and Lyylia and me, and we found that reindeer in the woods. That animal was nothing like Kied-Kie-Jubmel or Silence of the Sky or any of your Gentle Beasts."

"He's right," said Eider. "Kalevala must just be…so different from Pohjola, so different that we can't even imagine it."

"You're completely about that, Eider," Shaun said. "After all, my Light-listener scanner is proof of that, isn't it?"

Both Boots and Eider gave a little chuckle, and the tension in the room eased. Everyone gathered back around the table and sat down. Ávgos idly righted the toppled empty pitcher of long-leaf that the reindeer had knocked over. Everyone had eaten and drunk their fill, so at least there was very little spilled food on the table.

"I hope Kuu and other Gentle Beasts are okay," Teija said after a while.

"They're probably talking to Night-Fire Desolation, so that he understands that you're not savages here to hurt him," Eider reassured her.

"I hope she believes we're not savages," Ávgos said quietly. He was tempted to try the door to see if Kuu had indeed locked it, but he stayed seated. He noticed Shaun eyeing the door, and wondered if he was thinking the same thing.

Just then the door clanked and swung open, and Kuu came in, with two Menninkäinen guards behind her. "My apologies for leaving you," she said. "And for locking you in this room, but I wanted to make sure that no one would be hurt."

Was she making sure that Night-Fire Desolation wouldn't hurt them, or that the humans wouldn't hurt anyone in the castle? Ávgos carefully watched her face. Her expression was solemn, but if her trust in them had been damaged, she gave no indication.

"Please, take your rest while you can," she said. "We have much work ahead of us." She turned and left the room, Child of Light at her heels.

The two guards bowed at the group. "This way, honored guests." Ávgos, Shaun, and Teija fell into step with the other Menninkäinen as they followed the guards back to their sleeping chambers. Ávgos saw Kuu ahead of them down the corridor. She rounded a corner to head up a wide flight of steps, and didn't look back.

Maden had finally given up on picking the lock of their prison cell. He wished he hadn't pulled out his smaller knife when they first met Hiisi-Hiisi—that was the multi-tool knife. The screwdriver or the nail file might have fit better than the long wide blade of his boot knife. He even tried using his snowmobile key, which was in one of his coat pockets, but that wasn't long enough.

"What I wouldn't give for a good set of lockpicks," he muttered, sheathing the knife back in his boot. They'd both gotten fully dressed again, minus their coats. Lyylia was still barefoot, though.

He looked at Lyylia as he slid down the cave wall to sit next to her. "Not that I own a set of lockpicks, by the way," he added. "Or have ever used them before." He cleared his throat.

"Ávgos told me why you left Inari and went to Rovaniemi after the reindeer disappeared," Lyylia said after a moment. "You technically didn't break the law, even if you were evading police questioning. If we ever get back home, I will make sure that nothing is put on your record."

Maden regarded her in the dim light from the torch across the hall. He doubted that she, as a big-city cop from a southern jurisdiction, would have the authority to do that, but he appreciated her offer.

"And if you have any names," she continued. "Please tell me. With your help, the authorities could shut down the whole weapons and drug trafficking ring. And protect you against potential retaliation."

He was quite sure she didn't have the power or authority to do that. If any of those guys ever got locked up, they always managed to get their sentence shortened and were out on the streets again in no time. He looked away, staring out through the bars of the gate. "Sure," he said finally. "If we ever get back home."

The sound of something scampering down the hall was startlingly loud, and they both scrambled up as a lone hiisi halted in front of the gate. It pushed two small bowls between the bars, hissed, and hurried off.

"Our rations, apparently," Maden said, picking up the bowls. One had several small raw fish in it—freshly killed, and complete with scales and eyes. The other bowl contained a dark liquid that smelled pungent and sour.

Maden sat back down and pulled out his boot knife again to scrape the scales off the fish.

"We don't know what could be in that," Lyylia said, a look of mild disgust on her face.

"If Hiisi-Hiisi wanted us dead, he could have killed us earlier. As you pointed out, he probably wants to know more about us. Why bother poisoning us?"

"It's not intentional poison I'm worried about." Lyylia squatted down next to him. He offered her a chunk of flesh on the tip of his knife, and she reluctantly took it. "I just hope we don't catch some bizarre disease from this."

Mađen wasn't excited about raw fish, either, but as soon as he started eating, he realized how famished he was. They finished off the fish quickly, then Mađen took a sip of the dark-colored drink. He spit it back out immediately and cursed in Sami, wiping his mouth. "It tastes like vinegar, only worse."

"Here, I have an idea," said Lyylia, taking the bowl. She poured the vile liquid into the chamber pot, then rinsed the bowl in the little stream and filled it with clear water. "We can let this cool for a minute until we can drink it."

"You sounded exactly like your sister when you complained about the fish just now. She fussed about diseases and organisms in the water—first in Samiland, then in Pohjola."

Lyylia gave a wry smile. "We're both much too civilized to have had any experience with drinking outdoor water out of strange streams. Until now."

Mađen shook his head and almost smiled. "City girls, the both of you."

Soft footfalls and claws on stone sounded out in the passageway, and two black wolves approached the gate.

"You, female," grated the larger dog. It was Iku-Turso. "Hiisi-Hiisi commands your presence."

Mađen and Lyylia both stayed where they were. "Why just me?" Lyylia asked.

"Hiisi-Hiisi commands it," the Näkki snarled. "Come."

The other Näkki scraped its paw across the edge of the gate, and with a clank it swung open.

"You, stay," it hissed at Mađen.

Mađen glanced at Lyylia, wondering if they should try to rush the two Näkki. He opened his right hand, prepared to reach down and grab his boot knife.

She gave him a tiny shake of her head, and stepped out into the corridor. The Näkki pushed the gate shut behind her. She was probably right. One knife between the two of them was no match for two wolves with sharp teeth. Not to mention their scream. His earplugs were in his coat pocket, a couple of meters away, and the gun was in the shadows at the back of the cave, farther away than that.

Out in the corridor, Iku-Turso suddenly reared up on his hind legs and slammed Lyylia into the wall. Standing on his hind legs, with his paws pinning her shoulders, he was taller than she was. His sharp jagged teeth hovered centimeters from her face.

"No!" Maden shouted, grabbing uselessly at the bars of the gate. "Iku-Turso, let her go!"

The other Näkki hissed at him.

Maden yanked his knife out of his boot.

"Before I take you to Hiisi-Hiisi," Iku-Turso said, his voice low and gravelly, his face level with Lyylia's. "I shall tell you what he intends to do with you. Hiisi-Hiisi wants your powers for his own. Beware his spells that can ensnare your mind and alter your will. You are clever, and you see beyond what is in front of you. If anyone could withstand Hiisi-Hiisi's mind-magic, it would be you."

"Why are you telling me this?" Lyylia asked. Her voice sounded surprisingly calm and strong.

"Because," Iku-Turso rasped, lowering his voice further. "I despise Hiisi-Hiisi."

"And you want my power for yourself," Lyylia said.

Maden reached through the bars and swiped at the other Näkki. The wolf ducked back out of reach of his knife and gave him a snarling hiss. He looked back at Iku-Turso, still pressing Lyylia against the wall. It didn't look like she was even trying to fight him, probably because he was talking. Which meant that he was focused on Lyylia, not him. Mađen adjusted his grip on his knife. He'd never been very good at throwing knives, and this was the wrong sort of blade and handle for a good throw, but if he could just hit Iku-Turso without hitting Lyylia...

Iku-Turso put his ears back. "Hiisi-Hiisi has no respect for the Näkki who loyally serve him. It was we who finally found the gateway beneath the lake, it was we who traveled to your world and found it populated by the beast-shamans who once lived in Pohjola."

Mađen stayed motionless, his hand poised to throw the knife. So the Näkki had traveled to Finland before? The thought of a Näkki loose in Inari was even more frightening than the potential that a hiisi could still there.

"So you stole our reindeer?" Lyylia said.

"No," Iku-Turso said with a hiss. "Our King, in his arrogance, decided that he did not trust even his loyal Näkki to capture the beasts, so he sent the lesser hiisi to do the deed. And when the foolish creatures could not find more reindeer, as you call them, they captured whatever they could find, which turned out to be you and your companions. A foolish mistake, but one that could benefit the Näkki if you can keep your magic from him."

"I won't let Hiisi-Hiisi take my magic from me," Lyylia returned darkly. "But not for the sake of benefitting you. You've killed Menninkäinen, you've tried to kill me and my people, you've invaded Pohjola. Rot in hell, Iku-Turso—you and all your Näkki."

He gave a loud, hissing snarl. Lyylia squirmed against the wall and slammed her knee up into Iku-Turso's stomach. Mađen hurled his knife.

The other Näkki lunged at Maden's outstretched arm, its teeth just barely missing him as he yanked his arm back through the bars. The knife hit the wall right next to Lyylia and clattered to the floor.

Iku-Turso hadn't budged with Lyylia's kick, and he turned his snout towards her right arm, outstretched against the wall where he still had her shoulders pinned with his paws. Her tunic sleeve had been pushed up past the elbow, and Iku-Turso raked his tongue along her forearm.

Lyylia's scream echoed off the stone walls. She writhed against the Näkki, but he kept her pinned to the wall.

"Stop it!" Maden hollered. "Damn you, Iku-Turso, stop!"

The Näkki completely ignored his shouts, and slid his tongue along Lyylia's arm again. She shrieked and tried to thrash.

Maden dove for the back of their prison cave. Frantically fumbling in the dark, his hand finally found Lyylia's gun. A few quick steps brought him back to the gate.

Iku-Turso had released Lyylia, and she lay in a heap on the corridor floor. Iku-Turso loomed over her, and Maden didn't wait to see what the Näkki was about to do next. He leveled the gun at Iku-Turso's midsection and fired.

Iku-Turso lurched back and slammed against the wall with a very dog-like yowl. The other Näkki screamed.

His head exploding with pain, Maden grabbed at the bars of the gate as he felt his knees give out. He slid down to the floor, and saw the gun lying just outside the bars where he'd dropped it.

With supreme effort, he pushed himself to his hands and knees, and reached through the bars for the gun. As his hand closed around the grip, he realized that the gun was missing the magazine. He'd just fired his one and only shot.

Across the corridor, Lyylia still lay motionless on the floor, Iku-Turso partly on top of her. The other Näkki filled his vision, shaggy black fur and hard white eyes. Maden slammed the barrel of the gun into its head, but his thrust was weak and the creature didn't even flinch. It opened its mouth, jagged teeth mere centimeters from his hand, and screamed again.

Maden collapsed on the floor, his entire body numb. As his vision blurred, he could still faintly see Lyylia, lying beneath Iku-Turso. He hoped she wasn't dead. If she wasn't, she probably would be soon—as would he. He wondered where the gun was, but he couldn't see it, couldn't move his arms to reach for it. He felt his eyes closing as unconsciousness took him.

Teija spent a restless night, despite the warm fire and cozy furs in her bed chamber. After a series of anxious dreams and waking up for the third time, she gave up on sleep, and visited the sauna. She was wide awake and dressed when castle guards came to wake everyone for breakfast.

Tired of being cooped up in her room, she stood out in the corridor with the two guards. They both gave her cordial bows but were not very chatty. After a moment Eider emerged from his room, and greeted her with more enthusiasm.

"Good morning, Teija. Did you sleep well?"

"Not really," she confessed. "I kept having weird dreams and waking up."

Eider frowned with concern as he came and stood beside her. "I'm sorry. This morning I'm sure Queen Kuu and Lord Kied-Kie-Jubmel will divulge their full plan for rescuing your sister and Mađen."

"I'm sure," Teija said non-committally. If the Queen still liked them or trusted them after Ávgos' revelation that humans on Earth ate reindeer. She tried not to feel nervous about facing Kuu at breakfast.

One of the guards offered to go ahead and escort them to the dining chambers while the other guard waited for the others. As they walked through the wide echoing corridors, they passed that intersection again with the brightly lit corridor.

"Is that the Halls of Time?" Teija asked their escort.

"It is."

"Can we stop for just a moment and take a look? I've heard so much about it, but I haven't gotten to see it yet."

The guard nodded and turned the corner.

The hallway was so bright, Teija realized, because one entire wall was nothing but windows. It afforded a dizzying view of the mountain and tundra below. The light illuminated the giant murals on the opposite wall.

"Wow," Teija murmured as she and Eider wandered slowly down the hall, staring at the paintings. She'd seen all the pictures on Shaun's phone, but they were far more awe-inspiring in real life. She saw everything that she'd learned about Pohjola—Menninkäinen building the castle, earth-walking Lights at the Dancing Ground, the battle with the Näkki and the hiisi on the lake. And as the pictures advanced down the hall, no more building, no more fighting, and no more reindeer.

Past the map of Pohjola and the chart of constellations, the hallway ended at a wall. A large bear skin, complete with head and claws, hung on the wall. The blue-white light from the windows shone on the brown fur, brightening it to a bronzed sheen.

Teija touched the coarse fur of the bear skin, absently

wondering if this, like so many other things here, was centuries old. Her fingers brushed something metal as she stroked the edge of the pelt. She pulled the skin back; instead of a stone wall behind, there was a wooden door. Unlike the rest of the doors she'd seen, this one was locked with a complex series of latches—more like a puzzle than a simple lock-and-key mechanism. She pressed the cold iron of one of the levers, but it didn't budge.

This wasn't the entrance to the dungeon, because Shaun and Ávgos had told her about the prison for the Näkki up in the Moon Tower. Something about this door seemed sorrowful, and more ancient even than the rest of the castle. Laying a hand on the door, the wood felt cold—colder than the metal of the latches.

She gave a little shudder, suddenly feeling like she'd intruded on someone's private moment of grief. She let the bear skin slip back over the door.

Turning back around, she saw Eider about halfway down the corridor, looking up at one of the paintings. He turned his head and smiled at her. His sandy hair looked almost silvery-blond in the light from the windows. Suddenly anxious to distance herself from the hidden door, Teija hurried back down the corridor to join him.

"Ready to go?" he asked her brightly.

She nodded, and walked close to him, trying to shake the strange sense of sorrow and loneliness that seemed to cling to her.

The warm smell of food in the dining chamber lifted her spirits a bit. The table was laden with hot bread and sausages and boiled eggs and yogurt with honey. Everyone else was also just arriving. Shaman Wind and the man who'd brought the changelings had left to return to their village, so it was just

Boots, Tip, Hoof, and Tug around the table with them, and Shaun and Ávgos, of course. Teija wondered if Kuu would be joining them.

Everyone started eating, and after a few minutes, Kuu entered the room. Child of Light, and the young Menninkäinen named Gray, were with her.

"Good morning," Kuu greeted everyone as she sat down. Teija wasn't sure if it was her imagination, but the Queen looked tired, and more somber than she usually did.

"Lord Kied-Kie-Jubmel will be joining us in a moment," Kuu continued as she began eating. "We discussed many strategies late into the night, and we have arrived at a decision. I will explain everything once he arrives."

Teija glanced at Shaun's and Ávgos' apprehensive expressions. That sounded promising. She hoped.

The room was silent, except for the sounds of forks and spoons on metal plates, and the dog chomping on her plate of sausages behind Kuu's chair. After a moment, Kuu laid down her fork and looked at the three humans. "Shaun, Ávgos, Teija."

They all froze and looked up at her. Teija's heart skipped a beat, and she let her spoon slip down into her bowl of yogurt.

"Take courage, all of you," Kuu said gently, and her stern face relaxed into a warm smile. "Have no fear of the words Night-Fire Desolation spoke to you yesterday, nor of the words you spoke to me. You have no enemies here."

Teija let out a breath, and beside her, she heard Shaun do the same. The pallor of tension and gloom that she'd been feeling ever since she woke up evaporated. She exchanged looks with the two men—their expressions of relief mirrored hers. Shaun smiled at her.

Glancing at Eider on her other side, Teija saw him give her a little "I told you so" smirk. She was grateful that the

Menninkäinen's view of them had not changed after yesterday's revelation about the reindeer, and was even more grateful that Kuu's view was the same as her people's.

As everyone finished eating, Kied-Kie-Jubmel entered the room, with three reindeer behind him. Teija hoped that Night-Fire Desolation wasn't one of them.

"All has been made ready in the Moon Tower, My Queen," said Kied-Kie-Jubmel.

"Thank you," Kuu said. She introduced the other three reindeer as Forest Wanderer, Silence of the Sky, and Child of the Southern Snow, then looked back at Kied-Kie-Jubmel.

"Please tell everyone what you have learned about the Dancing Lights."

"For those of us who have returned to the earth," rumbled the big reindeer, "we have discovered that our eyes can still see as the Lights see. We are still connected to the Lights. At night, we can see as they see, perhaps even do as they do. Last night, I was able to observe all of the northern part of Pohjola, from the Mountains of the Moon to the Dark Water Lake, and all along the Dark River to the Western Fells."

"I could see this, as well," put in Silence of the Sky. "And I could see the Dancing Ground, and the rivers as they flow southward to the Fenland Sea."

Kied-Kie-Jubmel nodded and continued. "I could also see the Dark River, and the opposite bank, in Ice-Dark. But beyond that, my vision faded, as did the Lights. Armies of lesser hiisi patrol the edge of the darkness. There are some spaces in their ranks, but anyone who crossed the border at any point would very likely be seen."

So Ice-Dark was guarding their border as diligently as Pohjola was guarding theirs. Teija's heart sank.

"As we Gentle Beasts have been discussing our experience

with the Lights," Kied-Kie-Jubmel said, "I have started to realize that perhaps the Lights are not really part of Pohjola. If they are not fully bound to Pohjola, then Hiisi-Hiisi could truly steal them."

Teija had no idea how that could be possible, but it was a terrifying prospect. Shaun shifted around on the bench next to her and opened his mouth, but the reindeer continued talking.

"This, of course, we will not allow Hiisi-Hiisi to do. We will defend our land and our Lights, and send every Näkki back to Ice-Dark."

"To that end," Kuu then spoke. "Kied-Kie-Jubmel and I will demand an audience with Hiisi-Hiisi. While our desire is to treat with him peacefully, we must expect his answer to be one of violence. I have spread the word to every village shaman that every able-bodied man and Beast willing to fight should join us at the shore of the Dark Water Lake.

"This should serve to draw the majority of Hiisi-Hiisi's armies to the lake. Hopefully this will grant safer passage to the scouts we will send into Ice-Dark to search for the Kalevalans."

The room was silent for a moment, while the enormous danger of that idea sank in. Teija swallowed hard.

"To further protect our scouts," Kuu continued. "I shall be casting on them a spell of invisibility. Like changeling spells, this is a rare and difficult magic, but I believe it will provide the best possible protection."

Beside her, Teija heard Shaun mumbling in English under his breath, something about how it was impossible to turn people invisible. Impossible, yes, but if anyone actually could do it, Kuu could.

"Silence of the Sky has already volunteered for this task," Kuu said, glancing at the three reindeer beside Kied-Kie-Jubmel. "I cannot command anyone to take this journey. Even unseen by the denizens of Ice-Dark, it will be dangerous. None of us know what lies in the land of Ice-Dark, nor do we have any idea where Lyylia and Maðen might be."

Teija saw Shaun squirming in his seat, but then Eider jumped up. "I volunteer to go, Your Majesty."

Teija stared at him, feeling suddenly cold. She could see that he was trembling as he stood there, and she slid her hand over to grab his under the table. His hand was clammy.

"I volunteer, as well, My Queen," said one of the reindeer.

Shaun stood up. "Me, too. I volunteer to go."

Kuu looked at him. "While I commend your valor, Shaun, I do not want to risk another Kalevalan in Ice-Dark. And I have a feeling you may be more needed here."

"But Your Majesty—"

"Forest Wanderer and Eider will accompany Silence of the Sky," Kuu interrupted him. She gave him a firm, but not unkind, look. Shaun clenched his jaw but sat back down.

Eider bowed, and then sat back down on the bench, still clutching Teija's hand.

For a moment everyone at the table looked at each other in silence. Teija's heart pounded. A battle? Eider going to Ice-Dark? Even protected by invisibility, how could they ever find Lyylia and Maðen?

Boots leaned across the table and looked at Eider.

"Are you sure about doing this, Eider?" he asked.

"I'm sure."

"I won't try to talk you out of it," said Shaun, leaning around Teija to look at Eider. "Even though I wish Kuu was sending me. But I guess I'll be joining Kuu's army at the lake."

Teija looked at Shaun and Ávgos. "You're going to fight, both of you," she said in English.

"Yes," said Ávgos. His face was grim but determined. "We've got to."

"I cannot command you to go to battle," Kuu said from the head of the table, looking at the two men. "There is no shame if you decide to remain here. However, your knowledge and skills would be most welcome in the days to come."

The two men looked at each other, then back at Kuu. "It's our fight, too, Your Highness," Shaun said. "Hiisi-Hiisi dragged us into this when he stole Ávgos' reindeer. And we need to do whatever we can to help get Lyylia and Maðen back."

Kuu gave a small smile and nodded at them. Then she looked at Teija. "You will be safe here in my castle, Teija. There will still be guards and workers here."

Teija nodded and looked down at the tabletop. She certainly didn't want to go to battle—and she wouldn't know what to do even if she did—but she still felt like a useless coward just staying behind while everyone else risked their lives.

Kuu pushed back her chair and stood. "Eider, Forest Wanderer, and Silence of the Sky please join me in the Moon Tower. We must begin at once. The rest of you who wish to join the battle, please report to the stable courtyard."

Teija had been holding Eider's hand under the table this whole time, and she gave it a final squeeze as he slid off the bench. Her throat felt tight as she watched him march stoically out of the room behind the Queen.

"He'll come back," Shaun said quietly after they'd left. "We all will."

Teija wanted to agree, but she couldn't even bring herself to nod. Lyylia had to come back, they all had to come back... but they were going to war. What if no one came back?

Lyylia jolted awake, instantly aware of the blinding pain in her right arm. She was lying on a warm stone floor, and could see nothing but darkness. She tried to move, which sent a sharper pain searing through her arm, and she gave a yelp.

She felt something touching her shoulders and back. "Lyylia," she heard a familiar voice say. "Are you all right? Can you move at all?"

She shifted around more carefully this time, and felt hands helping her to sit up. Her head spun as she finally opened her eyes. Maden crouched next to her, his hands supporting her. They were back in the cave with the pillars and torches and the glowing fountain. She saw white-furred shapes moving around in shadows between the pillars.

"Maden, what happened?" she asked. Her mouth felt dry.

"Iku-Turso attacked you. I thought he was killing you."

It all came rushing back: the cold damp weight of the wolf pressed against her body, jagged teeth and salty breath centimeters from her face, his tongue... She looked down at her right arm—a red oozing blister like an acid burn streaked all the way down her forearm. *Näkki saliva is toxic, apparently,* the analytical part of her mind observed, kicking her brain back into gear. She also remembered what Iku-Turso had said—about Hiisi-Hiisi's magic, and his own hatred of his king. That could be potentially useful information...

"Kalevalans!" thundered a voice from all directions at once. Hiisi-Hiisi appeared out of the shadows, eyes blazing red in his icy-white face. The black raven that had been with him before flew in from a different direction, and circled around the pillars. "I show you hospitality, and this is how you return my good graces? By wounding one of my Näkki?"

"Nothing you've shown us has been what we'd call hospitality," Maden snapped back. "Look what your precious

Näkki did to her!" He pointed at Lyylia's arm.

Hiisi-Hiisi gave a loud hiss, his blood-red forked tongue slithering out from between his teeth. "I see," he said, his voice calmer but no less grating. "Then I commend you for protecting your own. I did not order my Näkki to harm either of you."

He lowered his giant white head to look at them more closely. Lyylia willed herself to stare into his burning eyes, and Maden slowly stood up.

"Perhaps you spoke the truth after all, Jaana," Hiisi-Hiisi said, his voice calmer still. "That your male companion is a powerful shaman of hidden strengths." Black smoke-like shadows lifted from his back, and wings swept down in front of him.

Like a solid shadow, pitch black yet not quite opaque, the wings dipped down to nearly touch the ground in front of his icy hooves. At the ends of the wings were huge, clawed talons. In one set of talons, he held Lyylia's handgun.

"This is the talisman that you used to wound my Näkki," he said, looking at Maden. "Kalevala magic it must be, because I know that nothing of the sort exists in Pohjola."

"How can you be so sure of that?" Lyylia countered. Maden had shot Iku-Turso? She didn't remember that—she must have passed out by then. She was relieved to see that the magazine was still not in it.

"You are not the only one who can see beyond what is seen, Jaana." Hiisi-Hiisi swung his head back to Maden. "What do you call this?"

Maden hesitated a moment. "Gun," he finally said.

"And what is your name, master shaman of the gun?"

"Maden."

Lyylia looked up at him with a frown. Why was he telling Hiisi-Hiisi this?

Hiisi-Hiisi slowly extended his shadowy wings towards Maðen and opened up his talons. "Take your gun talisman, shaman Maðen. And your knife." He opened his other clawed wingtip to reveal Maðen's multi-tool knife. "An honored and worthy guest you are indeed, and no more Näkki shall harm you here."

Maðen reached out and took the gun and the knife, and put them in his trousers pocket. Hiisi-Hiisi raised his wings up and folded them against his back; they disappeared like smoke vanishing in the wind, and his back stayed icy white.

"Come, I will restore your arm," Hiisi-Hiisi then said. He walked over to the bubbling fountain. "Dip your arm in this water. It will restore you, not harm you further."

Lyylia made no move to get up, but Maðen took her shoulders and helped her to stand. "Have no fear, Jaana," Hiisi-Hiisi rumbled, his voice almost gentle. "I know how to combat the magicks of my Näkki."

Lyylia didn't want to believe him, but the way her arm was throbbing and burning, it was hard to imagine how it could hurt much worse than it did right now. As she approached the cascade of glowing water, she saw a black swan floating in gentle circles in the large bottom basin of the fountain. The swan had bright red eyes.

"Syöjätär's magic can wound or heal," croaked the bird. "Come to the water, come and kneel."

Lyylia wasn't about to kneel before an obnoxious shape-shifting bird that talked in rhyming couplets, so she sank down to a sitting position at the rocky edge of the pool. Taking a deep breath, she plunged her arm into the bright turquoise water.

Instantly the burning pain vanished. She stared at her arm through the bubbling water, and saw the red blister fading. After a few moments, she pulled her arm out. The pain was gone, she could move her arm and her fingers properly, and all evidence of the wound had disappeared.

"Restored, as promised, Jaana," rumbled Hiisi-Hiisi. "Now tell me, Jaana is not your true name, is it?"

Lyylia said nothing as she got to her feet and pulled her tunic sleeve down over her arm.

"Tell me, Maðen, what is her true name?" Hiisi-Hiisi asked.

"Lyylia," he answered.

She stared at him, and he looked back, his expression the same as what he usually wore, bland with a hint of a perpetual frown. She raised her eyebrows at him; his eyes seemed to look past her, and then he turned back to Hiisi-Hiisi.

Hiisi-Hiisi chuckled, a hoarse grating rumble. "Lyylia. Welcome to Ice-Dark, shamaness Lyylia of Kalevala."

Lyylia met his gaze and said nothing. Could Iku-Turso's warning actually be true? Was Hiisi-Hiisi exerting some sort of mind control power?

"I know that the Beast-shamans of Pohjola have returned," Hiisi-Hiisi continued. "After an absence of many centuries. Tell me, Maðen, do you know where the moon queen has been hiding them?"

"She didn't hide them," Maðen said, staring straight up at Hiisi-Hiisi. "They were caught—"

Lyylia kicked him in the leg.

He looked at her and frowned. "What was that for?"

Hiisi-Hiisi laughed. "Ah, Lyylia, you are truly sharp of mind and quick of judgment. I shall enjoy your magic."

"Don't you dare hurt her, Hiisi-Hiisi," Maðen said, anger flushing into his voice. Whatever influence Hiisi-Hiisi might have had over him, Lyylia's kick apparently had been enough to break it. For now.

"Maðen, just stay calm," she said, looking at him, then

turning her head up to the giant horse head looming above her. "Hiisi-Hiisi won't be getting anything from either of us."

Hiisi-Hiisi gave another rumbling laugh and flicked his red tongue. "Come, Maden, Lyylia, I wish to show you something." He walked past them, passing close enough that Lyylia could have touched his icy translucent leg if she'd wanted to. His underbelly just cleared her head, and the giant white hooves, big as car tires, still made no sound on the stone floor.

Maden fell into step behind him, and Lyylia followed. The chilly breeze that constantly flowed through the chamber suddenly increased as they stepped outside onto a balcony. The floor was warm on her bare feet, even out on the balcony, but she shivered in the cold air.

All around them arched a black sky filled with stars. Like in Pohjola's sky, the stars were larger than the night sky on Earth, as if the heavens were merely a curtain pulled closer to the ground. There was no moon, no aurora, and no central sun-like star. But there was enough light to see a harsh and austere landscape far below—jagged cliffs and deep canyons, and rocky barren plains.

Directly below them were the black stone walls of the fortress. Above and all around were steep spires of rock like giant teeth, with snow on the higher peaks. Much like Kuu's castle, this place was high and inaccessible, carved directly into the mountainside. Water flowed down some of the nearby outcroppings and walls of rock, sending steam rising into the air. In the near distance, smoke and a faint glow came from a lower peak.

"These mountains that breathe fire and smoke are called the Spine of Äi," said Hiisi-Hiisi, his booming gravelly voice startling after the stretch of silence. "And there, that highest peak, that is the Mouth of Äi." In the far distance, as high as the snow-covered mountain tops, was another volcano, this one blazing red and sending rivers of lava down its side like trickles of blood. "Äi the World Serpent lives there, and it is a sacred place and the center of all magic in this world. If you approach it, you will die."

Lyylia had no desire to go near a giant erupting volcano, whether it was the home of a deadly magic snake or not. The wind tugged at her hair, and brought a faint smell of sulfur and smoke from the distant volcano. Looking towards the other end of the balcony, she saw a long tube of glass and metal mounted on the stone wall and angled up towards the sky.

She walked towards that edge of the balcony. "What is this?"

"A star-eye," Hiisi-Hiisi replied, his abrasive voice holding an almost conversational tone. "I created it myself, with the wisdom and guidance of the World Serpent. I use it to study the sky."

Maden joined Lyylia at that end of the balcony and they looked at the telescope. This was the most advanced piece of technology she'd seen so far, here or in Pohjola. How much more advanced were the people of Ice-Dark than the Menninkäinen of Pohjola? Looking out over the balcony edge, she saw that the land was flatter in that direction; and in the sky in the far distance, hanging just above the horizon, was a bright blue star. The telescope was pointed directly at it.

"That," rumbled Hiisi-Hiisi, his voice harsher than before, "is the light of Pohjola."

"My God, it's Pohjantähti," Lyylia murmured. Were they so far away that the brilliant mini-sun that was always directly overhead was now just a bright dot on the horizon? Her mind reeled at the thought. How far had they come, and how long had it taken to get to where they were now? And how could they ever get back?

With a rustling of wings, the black swan flew out of the chamber and wheeled overhead, before landing on Hiisi-Hiisi's broad back. "Star-eye, star-eye, it sees all of earth and sky," rasped the swan, blinking its bright red eyes.

Movement far below caught Lyylia's eye, and she peered over the stone wall. On the bare, dusty plain, dozens of long black shapes crawled across the landscape. Squinting and trying to focus on the distant shapes, she thought she could make out tiny clusters of white moving amongst the larger black shapes. Hiisi, perhaps? Were the black things some other creature of Ice-Dark? They were too big to be Näkki.

"Those are the fire-mouths," said Hiisi-Hiisi. "More magicks of my own design, made from stone and metal and treasures dug from deep within the Spine of Äi. I realize now that Ice-Dark cannot be such a different world from Kalevala—for you, Maðen, held a fire-mouth in your hand."

Lyylia looked back over her shoulder at the monstrous horse.

"I think I shall rename them," Hiisi-Hiisi continued. "Giving them the Kalevalan word and thus the power of magic from another world." He tossed his head, his white mane blowing back in the wind, and his fiery eyes blazed even brighter. "Behold the guns of Ice-Dark!"

Lyylia looked at Maðen, seeing his horrified expression. Her heart thudded in her chest as she leaned over the balcony again. Everything below snapped into clear focus. Hiisi by the hundreds were pulling cannons, giant cannons as big as military tanks, and they were heading towards the blue star on the horizon. Towards Pohjola.

CHAPTER 8: THE EDGE OF THE DARKNESS

"You're sure this is going to work?" Maden said.

"No, I'm not at all sure," Lyylia said. "But we've got to try something."

Maden squatted down to take a swallow of cool water from the bowl beside the steaming trickle of water in their jail cell.

"But what if Hiisi-Hiisi doesn't summon me?" Maden asked. "What if he asks for you?"

"Then I'll take the flashlight, and make the same proposal, like we discussed."

They'd been in this prison for close to two days, Maden guessed. Lyylia claimed to have an excellent internal clock, and she agreed with him. They had taken turns keeping watch while the other slept, though Maden had dozed only fitfully during his allotted hours. They'd been fed at regular intervals, though each meal was a meager serving of raw fish and the vinegar-like drink.

Lyylia was convinced that Hiisi-Hiisi would want to talk to Maden alone at some point soon, because of the mind control he'd been able to exert over him. Maden was still frustrated by that. He didn't remember telling Hiisi-Hiisi anything important, nor did he remember feeling coerced or have any gaps in his memory. The concept of mind control was terrifying, to say the least. Maðen ached for a chance to plunge a knife into Hiisi-Hiisi's face.

Lyylia had given him a mental exercise to try when he was in Hiisi-Hiisi's presence. She said that she had learned it as part of her police training, to keep the mind focused with chaos all around or during a threatening situation. This wasn't quite the same thing, since there was actual magic involved, but it was worth a shot. Find one thing to focus on, she had told him—a person, or place, or even a concept that gave him peace and a sense of inner strength.

"Kalevalans," grated a voice. A wolf stood outside the gate, with two hiisi behind him. "King Hiisi-Hiisi commands the presence of the one called Maðen."

Maðen glanced at Lyylia. Of course she'd been right. There was a reason she was a police detective. He hadn't even been a successful criminal. He just hoped her idea about making a deal with Hiisi-Hiisi would work, too.

Maðen came towards the gate. "Why me?"

"Hiisi-Hiisi commands it," the Näkki hissed. "Come willingly, or we will drag you."

Lyylia nodded at him. "Just remember what we talked about," she murmured.

As he followed his escorts down the corridor, Maðen thought of his little cousin Piijá, Ávgos and Sirkka's daughter. She was a happy and gentle child, and was adjusting well to living in the north even though she'd been born in a southern city. She was going to grow up to be a reindeer herder like her parents, and she needed her father there to teach her.

He checked his pockets, even though he knew what was

there: the multi-tool knife, a lighter, his snowmobile key, and the flashlight with the batteries removed. With the image of Piijá's round face and big brown eyes fixed firmly in his mind, he followed the Näkki into Hiisi-Hiisi's chamber.

"Welcome, Shaman Mađen," boomed Hiisi-Hiisi's voice, the sound echoing off the stone columns. The giant white horse stepped out of the shadows. "Have my servants been treating you well?"

"Not really," said Mađen.

Hiisi-Hiisi cocked his head and peered down at Mađen. "Have they given you cause to fight them, or use your magic against them?"

Mađen started to say "no," but then thought about what Hiisi-Hiisi was saying. He brought Piijá's face to mind before answering.

"If we'd used our magic against the Näkki, you would know about it, so you don't really need to ask me that." He stared defiantly up at the giant icy horse head looming above him. "You want us to use our magic, don't you? You have no idea what we're capable of."

Hiisi-Hiisi gave a quiet hiss and flicked his tongue. "So enlighten me, Mađen," he said in a patient tone. "What are you capable of?"

"More than you'll ever know."

Hiisi-Hiisi gave an abrasive chuckle. "A wise and fair answer, Mađen. For all I might know, you and Lyylia have lain quiet thus far, simply preparing for your moment to tear my castle apart from the inside out."

Mađen thought of Piijá again and said nothing.

"So do you feel that Queen Kuu was a more gracious host than I?" Hiisi-Hiisi then asked.

"Perhaps."

Hiisi-Hiisi gave another grating chuckle. "And did you try such stubborn and manipulative tactics on her?"

"No, just different ones."

"Is that so? And what sort of magic did you perform to aid Queen Kuu and to defend Pohjola against my plans?"

Maden tried to think of a way to answer that. He certainly wasn't going to talk about Shaun and his aurora-scanning computer. He fixed the image of Piijá in his mind.

"What makes you think that we had anything to do with defending Pohjola or helping Queen Kuu at all?" Maden said, looking up at the horse and forcing himself to stare into those fire-red eyes.

"My Näkki told me otherwise," Hiisi-Hiisi rumbled.

"No offense to your precious Näkki, but Lyylia figured out Iku-Turso's name, and none of them knew about my gun talisman, so clearly they're not as all-knowing as you think they are. And just because we hate the Näkki doesn't mean we've sworn allegiance to Kuu."

"And just where do your allegiances lie?"

"Not with her. And not with you, either, in case you were wanting to win us to your cause. We swear our allegiance only to Kalevala."

"I commend your loyalty, but you are no longer in Kalevala."

"No, we're not, and it's all your fault," Maden said. "Your servants brought us here from Kalevala, and our reindeer, too."

"Reindeer? The beasts from Kalevala that the people of Pohjola worship?"

"Yes. In fact, that's where our real magic is. If you really want to see what sort of magic we're capable of, take us to the reindeer." This was the biggest gamble of all—betting that Hiisi-Hiisi still had some of the reindeer, and that he'd be willing to let them see the animals.

"Why should I believe any of what you say?" Hiisi-Hiisi demanded.

Maden forced a nonchalant shrug. "Well, you can keep us locked up here indefinitely, or you can take us to our reindeer and we'll show you what our magic can do."

"Or I can simply kill you now." That red tongue flicked out again, and Maden tried not to think about going for one of his knives. *Piijá*, he thought instead.

"You could," Maden said, struggling to keep his voice slow and casual. "But you'd be losing a powerful ally. Honestly, though, I don't really care. We don't want to help you, any more than we want to help Pohjola. We just want to return to Kalevala. With our reindeer."

Hiisi-Hiisi exhaled putrid smoke from his nostrils and tossed his head. "What makes you think I need an ally to defeat Pohjola?"

"Then why did you capture us?" Maden returned.

Hiisi-Hiisi snorted again. "Prove to me that what you say is true."

"We need our reindeer."

Hiisi-Hiisi laughed, a deep grating rumble. He began to pace in a slow circle around Maden, those giant icy hooves silent on the floor. "I cannot be so easily fooled. You did magic in Pohjola without your reindeer."

Maden opened his mouth to answer, but then stopped. *Piijá. Ávgos. Sirkka.* "You see this?" Maden reached into his pocket and pulled out the dead flashlight. "This is a powerful talisman from Kalevala. Just press this stone on the side, and it can blind your enemies. This end shines clear like starlight, and this end is as red as the color in the Dancing Lights. But it won't work without the magic of the reindeer. Its magic has run dry, and I need the reindeer to fill it back up again. Otherwise I would have used it against your Näkki a long time ago."

Hiisi-Hiisi's shadowy wings materialized as they lifted from his back, and he swept them down to take the flashlight in one of the talons. "This seems a frail talisman," he grated.

Maden held his breath, hoping that Hiisi-Hiisi wouldn't break the flashlight. He brought Piijá's face to mind again.

"I do not believe you," Hiisi-Hiisi said finally.

Maden took a deep breath. "Okay, look—to prove my goodwill, I'll give you this talisman." He dug in an inside pocket of his coat, where he still had his lighter. His cigarettes had gotten ruined on the trip through Lake Inari, because they hadn't been in a watertight pocket. He surprised himself as he realized that this was the first time in ages that he'd even thought about a cigarette.

"This isn't a very powerful talisman, I admit, but it doesn't need the magic of the reindeer to work." Maden knew that the lighter still worked, even though he hadn't needed to use it in a while, and he held it up for Hiisi-Hiisi to see. He flicked it on.

Hiisi-Hiisi snorted. "A fire-starter. A common magic, and a talisman of no value to me."

"Sorry, but it's all I have," Maden said. "The powerful stuff needs the magic of the reindeer. But here—I'm giving it to you as a gesture of good faith."

Hiisi-Hiisi laughed again as he took the lighter. "A pathetic gesture." He folded his wings and they disappeared, along with the lighter and the flashlight. "If you wish to extend me a more meaningful gesture and perhaps delay your death, you can tell me about the magic of this talisman."

The shadowy wings reappeared, this time with another object clutched in one set of talons. Hiisi-Hiisi swept his wings down to Maden and held out a wide collar with a large boxy attachment secured on the strap.

Maden slowly took the reindeer GPS collar from Hiisi-Hiisi's talons and tried to think of a miraculous story to spin. He finally settled on the truth. "It's a tracking device—talisman. It helps us know where our reindeer are, even when we can't see them. It only works in Kalevala, though." He pressed the power button, but the collar was completely dead.

"And why is that?" Hiisi-Hiisi asked. "If your reindeer are the source of your magic."

Because Ice-Dark doesn't have orbiting satellites, Maden thought, but he didn't say that out loud. He thought of Piijá again. "Because this talisman is tied to the magic of Kalevala," he said finally.

Hiisi-Hiisi snorted again, and swished his long white tail. The translucent hairs, like gossamer icicles, caught the light of the torches and seemed to glitter and sparkle. The effect was far too beautiful for a creature as evil as Hiisi-Hiisi.

Just then a flapping of wings echoed through the chamber and the black bird, a large raven again, flew in from the balcony.

"Winds from the south, the tempest it grows," screeched the bird, circling the room before landing on an unseen perch high up on one of the columns. Only its bright red eyes were visible in the darkness as it peered down at Maden. "Shamans and fools, Syöjätär knows."

"Indeed," Hiisi-Hiisi rumbled. His talons pulled the GPS collar out of Maden's hands and his wings folded and vanished again. "You speak the truth, Syöjätär—this shaman is a fool. Return him to his chamber!"

A Näkki and two hiisi appeared out of the shadows and surrounded him, and the Näkki gave him a not-so-gentle nudge with its nose. Maden stumbled forwards, then obediently began walking after the little white creatures.

Back in the prison cave, after the Näkki and hiisi secured the gate and left, Mađen told Lyylia everything. "So he kept the flashlight and the lighter, and I have no idea if he's going to take the offer."

"Well, you did what you could," Lyylia said. "The lighter was a good idea. Maybe it will intrigue him enough to get us to the reindeer."

"If there are any reindeer left here."

"It's the only plan we've got right now. If it can get us out of this fortress—or even just out of this jail cell..." She shook her head. "And if this does nothing more than buy us a little more time, that's worth it, too. I know Kuu is doing everything she can to try to rescue us."

Mađen hadn't thought about anyone from Pohjola trying to mount a rescue. He was so used to being on his own and not trusting anyone. He realized with surprise that he agreed with Lyylia. He'd come to trust Kuu and the Menninkäinen—even like them. And he wanted to believe that Ávgos would try to have them rescued.

He sat down in the back corner of the chamber, letting the darkness envelope him. Lyylia stood near the gate, staring out into the dimly-lit corridor. Mađen ran a hand through his hair, and then leaned his head back against the wall, feeling suddenly tired. He thought of Piijá again.

Shaun looked out the side of the sledge as the horses pulled up to a bustling war camp, set up at the edge of trees a few hundred yards from the shore of the lake. After a solid two days and a night of traveling—stopping in villages only long enough to change out the horses—they'd arrived at the lake. The sledge that Shaun and Ávgos were riding in was one of a caravan of fourteen sledges that had left the castle, carrying weapons, food, supplies, and Menninkäinen ready for battle.

All around were campfires and tents, tethered horses and wandering dogs, and hundreds of Menninkäinen—more than Shaun had seen gathered anywhere at once. Reindeer milled amongst the crowd. The air was filled with the busy noise of voices talking, metal clattering, dogs barking.

A reindeer approached the disembarking group. "Set up your tents over there, in that space under the trees," it instructed. "You have brought weapons from Queen Kuu's castle?"

"We have, my lord," said a Menninkäinen. "As well as earplugs and other supplies."

"Once everyone in your party is armed, please distribute the remaining weapons to anyone here who needs one, along with the earplugs. Many men here could bring only knives and farm tools from their villages."

The Menninkäinen bowed, and everyone got to work. Shaun joined Ávgos and Boots in hauling the tent skins off one of the sledges.

"Look at the strength of our numbers!" Boots said. "The Näkki of Ice-Dark will tremble when they see our forces!"

"It's an impressive gathering on such short notice," Ávgos said diplomatically.

Shaun nodded in agreement, but couldn't bring himself to feel as optimistic as Boots. He had zero battle experience, but he knew enough about the general concept of war to know that a few hundred farmers did not make an impressive army. Unless the opposing army numbered in the fifties or so, they were severely outmatched.

The spears they had brought from the castle all had silver tips. Shaun still had the sword from Shaman Petrel that Kuu had given him, but he wondered if he could use a spear instead. The sword was so short that a Näkki would literally have to be on top of him before he could use it—at least a spear provided a reach of a few feet. Too bad he'd never learned archery. Kuu had given him a scabbard and belt; the sword was heavy against his left leg as he dragged a rolled tent through the snow.

At least they all had earplugs. Kuu had had her castle workers make hundreds of little wax blobs, which were packed between sheets of cloth in a large wooden crate on one of the sledges. Shaun knew from past experience that earplugs weren't a complete guarantee against the effects of Näkki screams, but they certainly helped take the edge off the dizziness. He wondered, though, how effective earplugs would be against potentially hundreds of Näkki all screaming at once. He tried not to shudder at the thought.

As the three of them worked to set up the tents, Shaun listened to the energetic buzz of conversation all around. Everyone seemed to be in high spirits—probably because the last big battle with Ice-Dark was only a legend in the minds of the Menninkäinen and they had no real concept of war. A few yards away, three men sat around a campfire playing music. One was piping away on a little flute, one was twanging a mouth harp, and the third one played a stringed instrument sort of like a primitive violin or lyre; the bow scratched energetically across the two strings. Shaun wished he could feel encouraged by their cheer.

At least Teija was safe back at the castle. He'd given her a hurried crash course in aurora science and how to set up his scanners and microphones before they'd left. As much as he wished for the comfort and distraction of his computer equipment, he knew the front line of a battle was not the best place for it. At least this way the computer could still record nightly displays, and if Teija retained any of his rushed explanations, she could even monitor the continuing return of the Gentle Beasts.

It might give her something to do besides just sit and worry. He tried to distract himself from his own worried thoughts by trying to understand, not for the first time, how Eider and the two reindeer were able to see anything while they were invisible. If their eyes were invisible, then how could the lens refract light and enable them to see? He hadn't had a chance to witness the spell or talk to Eider afterwards, since he was already in a sledge headed for the lake. He hadn't been able to talk to Kuu, either, though he doubted that he'd get a satisfactory scientific answer from her about how her magic spell worked. Nothing here made scientific sense.

As he tugged at one of the tent poles, jamming it down into the snow, he noticed that Ávgos had paused in his work and was staring out across the camp.

Shaun straightened up. "What is it, Ávgos?"

"Do you recognize this place?" Ávgos said quietly. "This is where we arrived in Pohjola."

Shaun looked around, at the forest behind them, the snowy ridge in front of them, and the lake in the distance, the blue ice like a frosted mirror, reflecting the bright sky. Somewhere beneath all the ice and water was a magical portal that led back to Earth. And somewhere on the other side of the lake, out of sight on the opposite shore, were Lyylia and Maden.

"You're right," Boots said. "We had our camp just on the other side of that ridge when we saw you and the hiisi in the water."

"So close to home, and yet so far away," Ávgos murmured.

"I was just thinking the same thing," Shaun said.

"Shaun," Ávgos said, his voice even quieter. "If you get through this, and you and the others make it home, but I don't——"

"You'll make it, Ávgos," Shaun interrupted him. "We're all going to make it."

Ávgos nodded, not meeting Shaun's eyes. "Just promise me that, if for some reason I'm not with you, when you get home, find my wife and…"

"You're going to talk to Sirkka yourself."

Ávgos finally looked at him, and nodded silently.

Shaun returned to his work on the tent pole. If he was going to survive this mess—somehow—then everyone else was going to, too. There was no way in hell he could go back to Earth and tell someone that their family member had died on another planet at the other end of a magical wormhole.

"I promised Silver and Track that I would return to them soon," Boots said. "They know that I'm here with the army. But I told them I'd come back, and I intend to do so."

Shaun looked down at Boots, wishing he had such an eternally positive attitude. Boots' dog Wolfsbane was beside him, and Shaun felt oddly comforted. That dog had been through as much as any of them had.

"It'll be just like shooting wolves, right, Ávgos?" Shaun said, as the three of them moved on to set up the next tent. "Didn't you tell me that you've killed wolves before, when they attacked your reindeer?"

"Yes, I have, many times," Ávgos replied. "But that was with a rifle, from the back of a snowmobile."

"I've never killed a wolf," said Boots, sounding impressed. "But myself and two other men did kill a bear one time when it came into our village and killed a sheep."

"Well, it's more than I've done," Shaun said. "I've killed small rodents when they get into the scientific instruments out on the field. I think I'm the least qualified of anybody to be out here in the front line of an army."

"But you are here to help save your beloved," Boots said. "That gives you a strength beyond what others have."

Shaun paused and looked at Boots. He hadn't told anyone about his feelings for Lyylia—or the brief romantic moments they'd shared—but he supposed it was no secret that he cared about her. He didn't want to fight—and yet, the thought of Lyylia imprisoned in Ice-Dark made him want to violently kill every last Näkki with his bare hands. He wondered if Boots was right, and hoped that when the time came, he'd be able to fight like he wanted to.

Ávgos gave a mild chuckle. "But really, we're all out here to save our beloveds, aren't we? Protecting Pohjola will protect Silver. And eventually enable us to get back home, I hope, so that I can see Sirkka again."

Boots smiled. "You're right, Ávgos, you're absolutely right."

Shaun smiled too, but he felt a wave of shame. If he was really trying to save his beloved, he should be on the other side of this lake looking for her, instead of letting Eider risk his life for such a task.

The background noise of conversation and preparations suddenly shifted, a murmur going through the crowd like a breeze, and then everyone grew quiet. Shaun looked up from the tent skins and saw everyone standing at attention.

Kuu rode on horseback through the crowd. She wore white breeches and a tunic rather than a dress; but she also had on a leather breast plate, and leather arm braces from wrist to elbow. Her pale blond hair was pulled back in a tight braid, and her sword was in its scabbard across her back. As she wound through the crowd, Shaun saw that she also had leather shin guards on top of her boots. Her frame drum rested across the saddle in her lap, and she had a dagger on her hip. Child of Light trotted behind the horse.

The horse, small and shaggy like all Pohjola horses, was light gray, and its bridle was made of silver rope. Kuu, though she had no helmet, had a circlet of silver around her head. A strange shudder of hope went through him. Kuu looked every bit the warrior queen. She looked down at him as she rode past and smiled. He drew a deep breath and stood up a little straighter.

Kuu had come to the lake ahead of their caravan, to make her announcement to Ice-Dark, and to send Eider and the two reindeer across the border. Thus far, there had apparently been no response from Ice-Dark—though with the forces Kuu was gathering, she obviously expected a response soon.

Shaun's chest tightened again at the thought of an all-out battle. But as he watched the Queen ride through the crowd, tall and straight and the hilt of her sword glinting in the light, the fear ebbed away. Pohjola may not have a proper army with actual soldiers, but with Queen Kuu to lead them, they might just survive this after all.

Shivering and wiping her wet hair out of her eyes, Lyylia looked around. They were in another cave, but this one was more of just a sheltered cove in the side of a hill. A rough wall of loose stones, about a meter and a half high, had been constructed around the opening of the cave, making the area into a run-in shelter and corral of sorts. A fierce cold wind, gritty with dust, blew in from the barren tundra outside the corral. But the discomfort was worth it because she and Maden were now out of Hiisi-Hiisi's castle.

Sixteen reindeer milled around the space. Right now they were stamping and snorting in alarm because two Näkki and two humans had just appeared in their midst, emerging from the narrow stream that ran through the back of the cave.

At least, Lyylia assumed that's how they'd arrived, since they were wet again. The last thing she remembered was Iku-Turso—unfortunately not killed by Maden's shot—opening their cell gate and breathing in her face. And now, here they were on the bank of a little stream in a shallow cave that looked out onto the tundra of Ice-Dark.

A hiisi perched on a small outcropping of rock at the mouth of the cave, watching the group with its beady black eyes. Two more hiisi were sitting on the stone wall of the corral. Three black horses paced around, just a few meters beyond the wall.

Two black horses stood with her and Maden in the midst of the reindeer. "We have delivered you to your Kalevalan beasts, as King Hiisi-Hiisi commanded," Iku-Turso said. He tossed his mane and stomped a hoof, and Lyylia studied his movements, looking for any sign of injury from the bullet. "Prepare your magicks—Hiisi-Hiisi will be here soon, and if he does not find your magic or your beasts to be satisfactory, then he shall have no further use for you."

Iku-Turso looked at the other horse who had transported them. "Remain here and join the others guarding them."

The other Näkki hissed and bowed his head at Iku-Turso, then jumped over the wall.

Iku-Turso turned back to Lyylia. "You would do well to heed my words, little shamaness," he grated, his voice quieter than before. "Hiisi-Hiisi may not kill you, even if he is not satisfied with your magic. He is a weak king, curious and timid as a newly birthed youngling. But if he does not kill you, then Kipu-Tyttö will come for you."

Lyylia cast a quick glance over at Mađen, then looked back at Iku-Turso. She felt a chill that had nothing to do with the wind. She couldn't remember the exact details of the story, but she remembered that name from *The Kalevala*.

"Who's Kipu-Tyttö?" Mađen asked.

"Someone you should fear far more than our petty king," Iku-Turso grated. "You will beg for death long before she has finished taking all of your strength and magic." He tossed his mane again, spraying water droplets. "Perhaps it would be best for you to beg Hiisi-Hiisi to kill you."

With that, Iku-Turso tossed his mane again, then galloped into the stream and vanished.

Mađen put his hands on the backs of two of the reindeer, as the animals started at Iku-Turso's disappearance. "What was that all about?" he said, looking at Lyylia. "What kind of name is Kipu-Tyttö?"

"One that we should probably be afraid of," Lyylia said. If this Kipu-Tyttö was anything like her namesake, she was not a creature to be taken lightly.

"You don't seriously believe him, do you?"

Lyylia looked at him. "Not completely. Iku-Turso is arrogant to a fault, just like Hiisi-Hiisi, but we should consider his threat valid. Didn't you ever read *The Kalevala*?"

"Of course. Ages ago, in school. I don't remember much of it."

"I think Kipu-Tyttö had something to do with the nine

diseases and the underworld," Lyylia said.

"Well, until the Swan of the Dead comes to take me away, I intend on figuring out a way to escape," Maden returned. "At least your gamble paid off—we're out of the castle, and we found the reindeer."

Lyylia nodded as she surveyed the area. The tundra outside the corral's rock wall was a barren, rocky landscape fading into the distance. The vivid starlight afforded a good amount of ambient light. But there was no moon, and no sun or large central star. And no Dancing Lights.

However, the blue star that had been on the horizon when they viewed it from Hiisi-Hiisi's tower was now nearly forty-five degrees up in the sky, and much larger and brighter. Lyylia still had no idea how far away the border with Pohjola might be, but this much progress was encouraging.

Their hiisi and Näkki guards kept their distance, and the reindeer had calmed again, milling slowly around the cave and corral, nibbling at the small scrubby plants that grew on the dusty ground. Moss grew on the cave walls, and a heap of dried moss and branches was piled up in one corner near the little stream. At least Hiisi-Hiisi seemed to be taking good care of the reindeer—relatively speaking.

Maden moved amongst the animals, murmuring quietly in Sami. Lyylia took a position at the mouth of the cave, where she could be somewhat sheltered from the wind but still see their surroundings. She hadn't expected the reindeer to smell quite so strong, but she appreciated their body heat as two of them stood beside her to nibble at the little bush at her feet. Hopefully she and Maden could dry off without developing hypothermia. It wasn't nearly as cold here as in Pohjola, and she saw no snow—but it was far colder than their steamy jail cell. She unwound her soggy scarf from around her neck and wrung it out.

She squinted at the four black horses pacing in the distance beyond the wall. The two nearest ones she could probably shoot and hit, and Mađen could probably take out the three furry little hiisi with a well-aimed rock or even his fists. The other two Näkki were out of range. If she could take out the two nearest Näkki, the other two would no doubt move closer to investigate, and then she'd have a better chance of shooting them...assuming she had time to squeeze off more than one shot before one of the creatures screamed. Her earplugs had washed away during one of their trips through the water.

Several of the reindeer began snorting and tossing their heads nervously. Lyylia looked back at the stream to see if another Näkki had emerged, then looked over at Mađen. He was murmuring to the animals, and met her gaze with a concerned frown.

A faint vibration, so subtle that it might have been her imagination, trickled up from her boot soles. She stepped out of the cave into the outside part of the corral.

In the distance across the tundra, in the opposite direction from Pohjantähti, the far horizon was tinged red with the glow of the volcanoes of the Spine of Äi. Much closer, something that looked like smoke was billowing towards them through the air. Across the ground below roiled a blackness, and as the wind shifted, Lyylia heard a sound like the distant rumbling of an engine.

The sound was horse hooves, she abruptly realized—an army of Näkki, hundreds of them, galloping across the hard earth. The sea of Näkki blackened the landscape into the distance, and there was no doubt that they were headed towards the blue star on the opposite horizon.

Lyylia took a step back, wishing she was still inside the

cave so that she could lean against something.

"Kalevalans!" shouted one of their Näkki guards from the other side of the wall. "Come forward. The lord of Ice-Dark approaches!"

"Looks like it's show time," murmured Maden, smoothing his wet black hair back from his face. "Is this really going to work? What if he doesn't give us the flashlight?"

"What choice do we have? We have to try something. Iku-Turso is right about one thing: Hiisi-Hiisi is curious about us." Lyylia looked at Maden. "You've gotten us this far. Do you have the batteries?"

Maden unzipped his parka and patted an inner pocket. "Right here in the waterproof pocket."

The cloud above the army of Näkki was more than just the dust raised by their hooves, Lyylia realized. It shifted, settled on the ground, and the cloud abruptly cleared to reveal a giant ice-white horse with wings like solid smoke. He came towards them with huge purposeful strides while the Näkki army thundered on past behind him.

"Kalevalans," boomed Hiisi-Hiisi, his voice carrying easily over the wind and the rumbling of the distant army. "The time has come to prove your worth."

Maden squared his shoulders as Hiisi-Hiisi approached. "Give me my light talisman—the one that needs the magic of the reindeer to work—and I'll show you."

Hiisi-Hiisi came closer, and stopped at the edge of the stone wall. He could have stepped over it with little effort, but instead he spread his shadowy wings and held out Maden's flashlight in his talons. Maden slowly approached and took the flashlight.

"With my reindeer, I can now give it power," Maden said. He turned his back on Hiisi-Hiisi and walked amongst the fitful animals. With the flashlight in one hand, he made a show of rubbing it on the backs of the reindeer, while he reached inside his coat with his left hand. His back still towards Hiisi-Hiisi, Maden then squatted down between two reindeer so that even the Näkki couldn't see him, and stuffed the batteries into the flashlight.

"Maden!" Hiisi-Hiisi shouted. "My patience grows thin."

Maden stood up and faced him. He flicked on the flashlight, and the beam of light shot into the air. The dust raised by the galloping Näkki caught the light. Then he switched it to the laser pointer on the other end of the flashlight. He pointed it at the hiisi perched on the rock outcropping at the cave entrance. A tiny red glow appeared on the hiisi's foot; it gave a hiss and jerked its foot away, only to have the glow transfer to its abdomen. Then Maden flicked his wrist and the light shot straight into the hiisi's eyes. It shrieked and clawed at its eyes as it tumbled down off the rock. Maden then angled the laser pointer at the nearest Näkki—it gave a gasping hiss and darted back several paces as the laser beam hit it in the face.

Hiisi-Hiisi gave a low hiss, and reached out with the talons of one of his wingtips and took the flashlight from Maden. "Not very powerful magic, but intriguing. But interesting as it is, it seems hardly something that could help me defeat Kuu and her army, which is what you promised."

"Technically, I didn't promise to help you defeat Kuu," Maden said. Lyylia was impressed at the confident, haughty tone in his voice. "I just promised to show you my magic."

Hiisi-Hiisi tossed his glittering white mane and blew smoke from his nostrils. "Arrogant mortal! If this is the extent of your powers, then I have no further use for you. Give me the gun talisman."

"Uh…" Maden hesitated and glanced back at Lyylia.

"Give me the gun talisman or your beasts die." Suddenly one of the reindeer let out a strangled bleat as it was yanked into the air by an invisible force; it dangled in the air, legs thrashing, as if being hung by a noose.

"I gave the gun to Lyylia for safekeeping," Maden stammered. "I...I didn't trust the Näkki not to try to take it from me." He looked back at Lyylia with a desperate expression and gestured toward the struggling reindeer.

She couldn't just hand over her firearm to this monster—but if she didn't, he'd kill all of the reindeer, and probably her and Maden, as well. Slowly she reached both hands up under her coat and slid the gun out of the holster. Carefully she detached the magazine before she pulled the gun out to show Hiisi-Hiisi. There was still a bullet in the chamber, but there was no way to safely or secretly remove it.

Hiisi-Hiisi stepped over the wall and came towards her. The reindeer scattered, fleeing as far as they could into the shallow cave. Hiisi-Hiisi's giant shadowy wing swept down and the talons grabbed the gun out of her palm. Lyylia held her breath to keep from trembling.

Hiisi-Hiisi raised his wing to examine the gun, then lowered his head toward Lyylia. "Where is the rest of it?"

Her heart pounded. How could he know that she'd pulled out the magazine? "The rest of it?" she repeated, hoping she sounded convincingly ignorant. "I don't know what you mean."

"This part is hollow." Hiisi-Hiisi angled the gun in his talons to show her the empty grip where the magazine would go. "And yet, after Maden used this talisman to wound one of my Näkki, I smelled smoke from this end." He angled the barrel at her, and she tried not to flinch. "This talisman is incomplete."

"No, it's complete," she stammered, but even as she said

the words, hearing her voice quivering, she felt herself lifting her left hand out from under her coat.

Hiisi-Hiisi snatched the magazine out of her hand, his smokey black talons scraping against her palm. She stared at the narrow stripe of blood forming on her hand, unable to move.

"You two will live, for now," Hiisi-Hiisi grated, and stepped back over the wall. The reindeer that had been hanging in the air dropped to the ground, limp. Maðen hurried over to it.

Lyylia lifted her head, still feeling frozen to the spot. In the distance, the Näkki army had passed, the rumbling of hooves and the clouds of dust fading.

Spreading his shadowy black wings, Hiisi-Hiisi reared up and let out a piercing scream. All four of the Näkki guards answered him. Lyylia collapsed; it felt as if every organ in her body were on fire, and blackness spotted through her vision.

Slowly the pain faded and her vision cleared, and she sat up stiffly. Hiisi-Hiisi was gone.

Maðen was hunched over the collapsed reindeer. "She's dead," he grated. "Hiisi-Hiisi strangled her."

Lyylia crawled over to him, still feeling shaky and lightheaded. "I'm sorry, Maðen." She reached out and touched the animal's shaggy, dusty fur.

Maðen growled in Sami under his breath.

Lyylia sat back on her heels and examined the palm of her left hand where Hiisi-Hiisi's talon had cut her. At least it wasn't a deep gash; the blood was already slowing and clotting.

"You all right?" Maðen asked.

"He mind controlled me, didn't he? I didn't want to give him the gun, and I sure as hell didn't want to give him the magazine full of bullets. But I did anyway."

Maðen's dark eyes narrowed as he frowned. "Hiisi-Hiisi would have killed you. Killed us both. I wish I'd stabbed him."

"Then he definitely would have killed us," Lyylia said.

Finally feeling steady enough to stand, Lyylia rose and went over to the little stream at the back of the cave. She rinsed her wounded hand and took several gulps of the cold water, hoping there were no hidden toxins. Apparently they were far enough away from the volcanoes that the water was no longer warm.

She made her way back over to Maden. The remaining reindeer had calmed and had gone back to grazing on the limited shrubbery.

"We need to work on an escape plan," she said quietly to him. "This is the best opportunity we've had so far."

"I know," Maden murmured back. "But I'm not leaving without my reindeer. The living ones, that is."

Lyylia gave a small curt nod. Overcoming their guards and traveling with sixteen—now fifteen—reindeer in tow would make their escape that much more difficult, but she couldn't blame Maden for wanting to save them. And after all, her original assignment had been to find the missing reindeer and the culprit responsible. Well, she'd now done that, but getting them home was another matter. Especially now that they were missing their most powerful weapon.

"Let's start brainstorming then," she said. "And we're going to need to figure out something to do for food."

He looked down at the dead animal at their feet. "I've eaten raw reindeer before."

Lyylia tried not to make a face of disgust, though she knew Maden had a point. They'd had a meal of raw fish shortly before being transported here, but that wouldn't sustain them long. The longer they were here, the slimmer their chances got for food, escape, or anything else.

"If Kalevalans are flesh-eaters, you now have fresh food,"

grated a voice. A black horse had put its head over the rock wall; the other three Näkki guards still paced several dozen meters away.

"Go to hell," Mađen growled at it.

"I hope you have more magic than the light you gave to Hiisi-Hiisi," rasped the Näkki. "My eyes can see again—it creates only temporary blindness."

"I wasn't foolish enough to give my most powerful talisman to Hiisi-Hiisi," Mađen said.

The Näkki gave a high-pitched cackle that was probably supposed to be a laugh. "No, I am sure you did not." The horse regarded them with its glittering ice-white eyes. "And what of the other talisman Hiisi-Hiisi took from the female?"

"Mind your own business."

"Guarding you is my business," the Näkki returned.

"Well, go guard over there and leave us alone, or I'll put a knife in your face," Mađen snarled. Bending down, he pulled his knife from his boot, and took a step towards the Näkki.

Lyylia grabbed his arm. "Mađen..."

"Iku-Turso was right, the female is the one with the wisdom."

"So you're close to Iku-Turso, are you?" Mađen yanked his arm away from Lyylia and advanced towards the wall. "One more reason I should kill you."

"I did not say I was close to him," hissed the Näkki, putting its ears back. "The female divined his name, and she knows when to stay your hand. Hiisi-Hiisi was deceived into thinking that you were the more powerful shaman, was he not?"

Mađen stopped less than a meter away from the Näkki's head, his knife out in front of him. "We are both powerful shamans."

"Then what is my name?"

Maden glanced back at Lyylia. "Um, your name…"

Lyylia approached the wall. This Näkki, she realized, was the first one she'd seen that wasn't dripping wet. It must have been out here for a very long time, guarding the reindeer. "Your name..." she said slowly, peering over the wall at it. Then she saw. "Your name is very different from Iku-Turso's…because you're a female."

Maden gave her a startled look. The Näkki uttered a quiet hiss, and then lowered her head over the wall, as if bowing. "You speak the truth. If you will put away your weapon and withhold your magicks, I will swear that I will not harm you or your beasts."

Slowly Maden returned his knife to the top of his boot. "You're not supposed to be harming us anyway—you're supposed to be guarding us so that Hiisi-Hiisi can come back for us later."

"And I obey Hiisi-Hiisi out of necessity, for now. As many Näkki do. A true Näkki serves no master."

"Iku-Turso said that, as well," Lyylia said.

The horse hissed and put her ears back again. "Iku-Turso is the most corrupt of them all. He loudly voices that Näkki serve no one, but he himself is a servant of Kipu-Tyttö."

Lyylia exchanged looks with Maden. "Who's Kipu-Tyttö?" she asked.

"She is the Näkki who truly is the master of all who follow her. Hiisi-Hiisi and his companion, Syöjätär, are the rulers of Ice-Dark and the protected ones of Äi, but they are a mild foe compared to Kipu-Tyttö. If you meet her, you shall wish for the mercies of Hiisi-Hiisi.

"I do not serve Kipu-Tyttö, nor do I serve Hiisi-Hiisi," the Näkki continued. "And I care nothing for the fate of the people of Pohjola or of Kalevala, either. Therefore, if you live and take your beasts back to Pohjola, I care not and will not stop you."

Lyylia glanced at Mađen. Was this Näkki really offering them a chance to escape, just like that?

"Why should we believe you?" Mađen asked.

"If you wish to see me proven right, then simply remain here until Kipu-Tyttö finds you. She will likely come for you while Hiisi-Hiisi is engaged in his battle. And then I shall suffer alongside you, as Kipu-Tyttö does not kindly tolerate Näkki who are not loyal to her." The horse tossed her mane. "And that is a fate I refuse to accept."

"It's possible we might be able to help each other," Lyylia said carefully. There was no reason to think that this Näkki was different from Iku-Turso or any of the others. But Lyylia knew to trust her gut, and she felt oddly compelled to try to work with this creature. "But we still can't be sure that you're actually telling us the truth. What if you're just trying to trick us into using our magic against you so you can kill us?"

The Näkki regarded them in silence for a moment, then lowered her head again as far as the wall would allow and closed her eyes. "To prove what I tell you is true, I offer you my name, mighty shamans. I am called Vellamo."

Ávgos tightened the straps of the ice cleats around his boots one more time. Kied-Kie-Jubmel had roused everyone from their camping preparations about thirty minutes ago and had organized them into battle-ready positions. Ávgos stood with Shaun, Boots, and about two hundred other Menninkäinen arranged in ranks across the lake. Several rows of spearmen and swordsmen stood on the ice and on the little islands dotting the lake. More ranks of Menninkäinen stood behind them on the shore, and behind them archers lined the top of the ridge. A few men sat on horseback, and reindeer were dotted amongst the men. A few dozen meters in front of them, Kuu sat on her horse in the middle of the lake.

Presumably scouts farther across the lake had noticed some movement from Ice-Dark, though for the past twenty minutes, Ávgos hadn't seen or heard anything. He could hear the nervous murmurs and the subtle jostling of weapons from the Menninkäinen all around. Thin wisps of clouds had started crawling across the sky, making a hazy halo around Pohjantähti overhead. He hoped it wouldn't become fully overcast or snow.

Child of Light, sitting on the ice several paces behind Kuu, suddenly sprang to her feet, ears alert and her attention focused out towards the other side of the lake. All of the reindeer shifted their stances and pricked up their ears.

Out in the far distance across the lake, too far away to see clearly, something was moving. Like fog or smoke, drifting slowly across the lake from the other side. A smaller shape seemed to detach itself and move towards them.

"Stay your weapons!" came Kied-Kie-Jubmel's voice. "Hold until I give the signal!"

The shapeless blob of fog drifted towards Kuu, and then a voice boomed out. Harsh and grinding, low yet shrill—like a Näkki voice, the sound pierced through wind and distance. The voice didn't send his muscles into a lock or his head into a whirl of dizziness, but Ávgos felt a chill prick down his spine.

"Queen Kuu, you have requested an audience with the ruler of Ice-Dark," the voice grated and rolled through the air. "So speak."

"King Hiisi-Hiisi!" Kuu called. "You have poisoned my land with Näkki—I demand that you remove them immediately. And you have captured two Kalevalans who are under my protection—they must be returned."

"My Näkki have served me well," boomed the voice. "Pohjola is theirs, as promised, if they can keep it—I will not intervene against them. If you wish them gone, moon queen, then drive them out yourself."

The foggy shape came closer, and solidified as it landed on the ice. It was a giant horse, but white, not black like a Näkki; lifting from its back were black translucent wings. Even at this distance, Ávgos could see that its eyes glowed red. He remembered the painting of the white horse from the Halls of Time, but it was still alarming to see the monstrous creature for real.

As the creature moved its shadowy wings, a black bird rose from its back and flew in circles above it. The giant horse stopped some distance away from Kuu.

"I know what you want, Hiisi-Hiisi," Kuu said.

"Do you now?"

"You want Pohjola's Dancing Lights. And so I propose an exchange. Son of the Mountains knows well the ways of the Lights." One of the reindeer standing in the front row of the army stepped forward. "Freely he offers himself to you, in exchange for the two Kalevalans."

"I do not accept your offer," sneered the white horse. "Your Beast would not speak truth to me, this I know. And I cannot give you the Kalevalans. The male Kalevalan has no wish to return to you, nor to his homeland. And the female is dead."

Shaun lurched forward and put his hand on his sword hilt. Ávgos reached out and touched his arm. "We have no reason to believe anything he says," he whispered. "I'm sure they're both fine." He hoped and prayed they were fine.

"You are lying," Kuu said.

"And you are a fool, if you truly expected me to accept a bribe of one lowly animal in exchange for a shaman from another world. The Kalevalan named Maden has joined me of his own free will, and has me given a powerful talisman to use on his behalf." The shadowy wings shifted.

"Oh God," whispered Shaun.

"What is it?" asked Boots. "I can't see that far."

"He's got Lyylia's gun."

Boots started to ask another question, but Hiisi-Hiisi was speaking again.

"He gave me this talisman and showed me its secrets. The female Kalevalan was not so cooperative, and so Maden demonstrated to me the power of this talisman and killed her with it."

"No!" Shaun rasped in a strangled whisper.

"He's lying, Shaun," Ávgos hissed, keeping his hand on the other man's arm. His cousin would never do such a thing. He stared at the handgun, a tiny, dark speck in the inky black talons of the giant wings.

Ávgos couldn't see the expression on Kuu's face since her back was to them, but her firm tone never wavered. "I have no reason to trust any of your words," she said. "But that still does not change the fact that you have brought death and fear to my land, and you have captured and tortured countless Kalevalan Gentle Beasts."

"This I do not deny," Hiisi-Hiisi returned. "And so it would seem that we now have nothing more to say to one another."

"So be it."

The monstrous horse turned and began walking back towards the fog bank at the far side of the lake.

"He's leaving!" Boots whispered.

"I doubt it's as simple as that," murmured Ávgos. His hands felt sweaty inside his mittens.

"Put in your earplugs, men!" Kied-Kie-Jubmel shouted. "And ready your weapons, but do not strike until I give the command!"

At that moment, Hiisi-Hiisi turned around again to face Kuu and the army. He reared up and let out a wail—as mind-numbing as the piercing shriek of the Näkki, but deep enough to make the ice under their boots tremble with the sound. Ávgos clapped his hands over his ears, nearly dropping his spear, even though he'd already put in his earplugs.

The fog began to move again—or rather, something moved within it, and a roaring sound filled the air. It was hundreds of hiisi, all snarling and hissing and racing pell-mell across the ice.

"Hold your weapons!" shouted Kied-Kie-Jubmel.

Kuu raised her arms, her drum in her hands. She beat several rapid tones and sang a tune; if there were words, Ávgos couldn't hear at this distance. A faint sheen of blue light surrounded her hands, and all around, a blue glow began beneath the ice. A thin wall of blue mist rose up from the ice just as the swarms of hiisi were approaching. With snarls and shrieks, the creatures passed through the glowing mist and lost their footing and their strength. Piles of hiisi, either dead or stunned beyond usefulness, slid to a halt a few meters in front of her.

Boots lifted his spear.

"Wait for the signal," Ávgos murmured, as much as a reminder for himself as for Boots.

At that moment, the dark fog across the lake cleared to reveal another line of hiisi; and behind them, in a stark contrast to the white of the hiisi and the ice all around, was an army of Näkki.

Hiisi-Hiisi reared up, and a fireball shot from his mouth. Ávgos instinctively ducked, even though Hiisi-Hiisi was dozens of meters away. Kuu's horse shied away, but she stayed in the saddle, yanking her sword out of the scabbard. She deftly deflected the oncoming fireball; it smacked into her sword and then evaporated, like snuffing out a candle. Exclamations of shock came from the men gathered behind him.

With hisses and shrieks, the Ice-Dark army advanced. A deafening rumble filled the air as Näkki hooves came pounding across the ice. Kied-Kie-Jubmel's voice rang out: "Archers! Loose your arrows!"

"Oh God…I can't do this," said Shaun.

"You can. You've got this," Ávgos said with far more confidence than he felt. His stomach quivered. "We can do this. Here they come."

Sounds erupted all around—the hissing of bow strings and arrows, and screams as hiisi and Näkki fell to the ice by the dozens. But more kept coming. Heart pounding, Ávgos lifted his spear.

"All men, attack at will!" Kied-Kie-Jubmel's command was faint but clear.

Everything dissolved into a blur of noise and chaos. A Näkki came at him. A dog and two Menninkäinen were already attacking it, but the creature lashed out with its hooves and Ávgos hit the ice, feeling pain in his side. He rolled away as Menninkäinen with swords and spears took over, but then he quickly had to roll again and thrust with his spear as another Näkki reared above him. Its flailing hooves met the antlers of a reindeer, and the two creatures went down.

Still on his stomach, Ávgos stabbed the spear at the rump of the Näkki. It shrieked and thrashed, jerking the spear out of his grip, but that gave the reindeer the edge it needed to disengage itself and get back up. With a loud bellow it brought its broad hooves down on the Näkki's head, and the black horse lay still.

Ávgos didn't have a chance to get up, though, before more creatures were coming at him. Yanking his spear out of the dead Näkki and rolling over onto his back, he frantically jabbed his spear at every blur of white fur and black horse or wolf legs that came near.

Then there was a sudden lull, and a hand reached down to him. "Ávgos!" said Boots' voice. "Are you injured?"

"No, I think I'm all right." His side still hurt where the Näkki's hoof had struck him, and he realized his heart was hammering wildly, but he didn't feel otherwise injured.

He let Boots help him up, then he pulled his spear out of a wolf-Näkki that lay beside him; the wound gushed clear water, running down the creature's thick black fur to the blue ice of the lake.

The battle had come to a pause; all across the lake lay hiisi and Näkki bodies, but there were far too many Menninkäinen bodies among them. Ávgos frantically looked around for Shaun, then spotted him standing, still holding his sword, on one of the little islands nearby.

Back on the shore, more Näkki and hiisi lay scattered in the snow, and reindeer were busy reforming the defensive line in front of the ridge. Kuu was still on horseback out on the ice, her eyes a blazing purple; her sword glowed a faint blue, and dripped with water and red-black blood.

From across the lake in the direction of Ice-Dark, a new sound came towards them on the wind. A rumbling, but this time different; the low grinding noise sounded almost like a train. Then there was an echoing boom.

A ball of metal slammed into the lake a few meters away from Kuu, and exploded. The shockwave sent her horse stumbling backwards and she slid out of the saddle and hit the ice. Ávgos ducked as chunks of ice and metal went hurtling in every direction.

Shouts of shock and alarm went through the Pohjola army. *Ice-Dark has cannons?* Ávgos thought with horror. How were they supposed to fight against that?

"I bring you the guns of Ice-Dark, little moon queen of Pohjola!" roared Hiisi-Hiisi's voice. "Forged in the fires of the Mouth of Äi and imbued with her power, and created and named by the warrior shaman of Kalevala! Your magic that can turn back the living creatures of Ice-Dark cannot prevail against metal and fire that falls from the sky!"

More booms sounded, and cannonballs came screaming through the air, shattering the surface of the lake and sending Menninkäinen and reindeer scattering.

"Back to the shore!" Kuu shouted over the explosions. "Fall back to the ridge!"

Everyone ran, stumbling over bodies as the ice shook with each explosion. Kied-Kie-Jubmel pulled a line together at the shore of the lake.

"My Queen, I count at least twelve platforms of metal across the lake," said a reindeer. "And they are on wheels, advancing towards us."

Kuu had remounted her horse and had joined them on the shore. "Hold the line here at the shore. No weapons or creatures of Ice-Dark must be permitted to enter Pohjola. Kied-Kie-Jubmel, select twelve of the best archers and have them join me out on the ice. We must stop these weapons of metal and fire. And put anyone still fully fit and uninjured back out on those nearest islands." She pointed with her sword at the nearest skerries.

The Ice-Dark army was regrouping in the shadowy distance across the lake. The grinding rumble of the advancing canons sounded through the air, though they had paused in their firing.

"He said that the shaman of Kalevala had created those things," Boots said, his voice tight.

"That's not true," said Ávgos. "It can't be true, because Mađen would never do that. He would never help Hiisi-Hiisi, even if he was under a magic spell."

"And there's no way those cannons could have been built in like four or five days," Shaun added. "Which means that Hiisi-Hiisi—or someone over there—invented them." He looked at Ávgos and lowered his voice. "Ice-Dark has gunpowder and projectile weapons. And Pohjola is still in the iron age. What else do they have that Pohjola is totally unprepared for?"

Ávgos met Shaun's gaze with a worried frown and just shook his head. He was trying not to think about that.

"God, I hope Lyylia is still alive," Shaun then murmured, lifting his sword. "She's got to be alive…"

Ávgos took a deep breath. He hoped Lyylia and Mađen were both still alive, but he wondered how likely it was at this point that Eider would find them and they would be able to get back to Pohjola.

He looked at the spear in his hands. The silver tip was still shiny and still sharp, and covered with water from Näkki wounds, which had now turned to ice. Of all the ways he'd thought he might meet his end, he had never expected anything remotely like this. And the worst part was that Sirkka would never know.

Mađen looked at Lyylia, and then at the black horse with its head hung over the stone wall of their corral. The black horse who had just willingly given them its name, and was potentially going to let them escape. He had no idea what to say next, and hoped that Lyylia's police experience would give her some sort of negotiating tactics.

"Let's say we believe you, Vellamo," Lyylia finally spoke. "If we work together, then maybe all of us—you included— can escape the wrath of both Hiisi-Hiisi and Kipu-Tyttö. But first we have to get past the other guards."

"I can lure them closer," Vellamo said. "That one there— Sydämen-Syöjä—is old and weak, and has a leg that often goes lame when he runs." She gestured with her nose at the horse on their far right, out on the plain. "If he can be felled, he will not rise again."

"Okay, so that's one," Mađen said. He felt confident that he could handle an old, weak Näkki, even if it screamed.

"Small knives are the only weapons we have left," Lyylia said.

"You have your Kalevalan beasts," Vellamo returned. "Can you not use their magic? You need not fear using your powers in front of me—I have no desire to tell either Hiisi-Hiisi or Kipu-Tyttö of the extent of your magic."

Mađen glanced at Lyylia. She pursed her lips.

"We'll need a moment to think of a good plan," Lyylia then said. "You'd better get back out there and look like you're guarding us—otherwise the others might wonder why you've been talking with us for so long."

"A wise observation," Vellamo said. She retreated several steps back from the wall and tossed her head. Mađen noticed that the other three Näkki turned their heads to look at Vellamo, but none of them approached or seemed alarmed. The one she'd called Sydämen-Syöjä wasn't even pacing slowly like the others; he stood still, with one ankle cocked in a resting position. This really was their best chance.

"Any ideas?" Lyylia murmured as Vellamo wandered away. "Could we start a stampede with the reindeer?"

"We could," Mađen allowed, "but I'm not sure how effective it would be, except maybe to cause a bit of chaos. Fifteen reindeer isn't much of a stampede. Getting them to panic around Näkki wouldn't be too hard, but they're more likely to run away from the Näkki than try to fight them."

"And we've got those three hiisi to contend with, too," Lyylia said. "They're less dangerous than the Näkki, but they're still nasty fighters. Damn, I wish I still had my gun."

Mađen wished she did, too, but he could hardly blame her for giving it up. If he'd had the gun on him, he wouldn't have given it to Hiisi-Hiisi, and now they'd both probably be dead.

"Lyylia! Mađen!" came a soft voice suddenly from the other side of the wall.

Mađen started and looked around. Vellamo had retreated several meters away and was now slowly pacing back and forth like a good guard.

Lyylia glanced around the area. "Who's there?" she asked in a whisper.

"It's Eider!" came the voice. "I'm right here beside you, on the other side of this wall. Do not look for me—I'm cloaked in a spell of invisibility."

"You're invisible?" Mađen said, looking around anyway. "How is that possible?"

"Queen Kuu put a spell on us," came the reply from the other side of the wall. It sounded like Eider's voice, all right. "As long as we wear the talismans she gave us, we cannot be seen or smelled by any living creature."

"But you can be heard and touched," Lyylia said. She'd laid her hand on the top of the wall, and her eyes widened slightly and Maden saw her hand twitch. "Who's with you?"

"Two Gentle Beasts," Eider's voice said. "They are keeping their distance, out past the Näkki guards. They believed I could move more quietly to approach you. We found these Kalevalan Gentle Beasts yesterday, and we were trying to decide whether to wait here or travel onwards towards the fiery mountains when you arrived with the Näkki."

"How far away are we from Pohjola?" Lyylia asked.

"Not far at all. Barely a day's travel on foot, and a shorter time than that going at the speed of a Gentle Beast's gallop. The light of the stars is deceptive here—Pohjantähti looks no brighter than the star of the huntsman's dog right now, but it is truly very close. The light from Pohjola just doesn't reach across into Ice-Dark."

Maden felt an unfamiliar surge of hope. With three invisible—and presumably well-armed—allies, they just might be able to do this.

"What weapons do you have?" he asked Eider.

"I have my bow and arrows, as well as a sword and two knives."

"Give me the sword, and I can definitely take out that weak old Näkki with it," Maden said confidently. He'd never handled a sword in his life, but it was a better weapon than hurling his boot knife or throwing rocks.

"Queen Kuu said that the weapons will remain unseen, even if they leave my body, as long as I wear the invisibility talisman. The moment I take it off, the spell is broken."

"Let's not break the spell yet, Eider," Lyylia said. "And let's not start handing out invisible weapons just yet, either. I think I have a plan..."

Maðen remained leaning nonchalantly against the wall, staring around at his grazing reindeer, while Lyylia talked. She also stood relaxed, moving her head around as she surveyed the area, but rarely looking directly at him. A quick glance over his shoulder out to the tundra showed Maðen that none of the guards appeared to be suspicious of their behavior. Vellamo was still the closest Näkki to them, but she was pacing slowly like the others.

The first part of the plan was for Eider to approach Vellamo and talk to her. Maðen thought that was unnecessarily risky, but Lyylia reasoned that it was safer than either of them trying to get her attention, or simply waiting for hours for her to decide to come back over.

The next step was to cause a ruckus and kill the three hiisi. Eider was confident that he could take out at least two of them with arrows before they even realized anything was wrong. He left the sword and a knife on top of the wall for Lyylia and Maðen before he went to approach Vellamo.

The next part was dependent on Vellamo cooperating—or at the very least, not betraying them by raising an alarm or turning against them. Maðen hated that they were relying on a Näkki for anything.

Maðen rested his elbows on the top of the stone wall and idly moved his hands around until he felt the metal handle of a dagger. The sword hilt, leather wrapped around metal, it felt like, lay right beside it. He carefully lifted them down off the wall, trying not to look like he was lifting something. Hidden from view behind the wall, he extended the dagger, hilt first, towards Lyylia. She felt around and slowly took it from him without making eye contact.

At this point, after shape-shifting talking horses and everything they'd encountered in Pohjola, Maðen found he wasn't the least bit startled by the idea of a magic spell of invisibility. What he was still grappling with, though, was realizing how much work and risk the people of Pohjola had put into rescuing them. Queen Kuu had cast an astonishing magic spell, and Eider had risked his life in an unknown and dangerous land. As had two Pohjola reindeer, who apparently were as intelligent as Kied-Kie-Jubmel and, despite having been stuck in a magical limbo in the sky for five hundred years, had decided to risk their lives to rescue people they didn't even know. Maden vowed to thank them when this was all over, if they all survived, but he was sure a simple "thank you" would be woefully inadequate.

He carefully watched Vellamo out of the corner of his eye. She gave a sudden start, probably as Eider got her attention, but thankfully she didn't attack or scream or otherwise react dramatically enough to raise an alarm. Maden hefted the sword in his right hand, getting a feel for the weight and length of it, since he couldn't see it. A few minutes later, the hiisi perched on the outcropping of rock above the cave entrance gave a strangled squeal and toppled from its perch. The second hiisi sitting on the wall at the far end toppled over right after it.

Maden shoved away from the wall and swung at the third hiisi, the one lounging on the end of the wall closest to them. He had the satisfaction of hearing it squawk as his arm hit resistance. The creature thrashed away from him, nearly falling off the wall, inky blood gushing over its white fur. Maden slashed again, drawing more blood, and the creature fell over the wall.

"Get ready!" he heard Lyylia shout.

Spinning around, he saw all four Näkki charging towards them. Vellamo was the closest—he hoped it was Vellamo, since that horse was coming from the position he'd last seen her. Vellamo leapt over the wall with ease—the wall was high enough to give both reindeer and regular horses pause, unless they were trained jumpers. Or desperate.

Mađen moved his invisible sword to his left hand and yanked out his boot knife. He ran at Vellamo with a shout, waving the knife dramatically above his head so that the other Näkki could see it. He really hoped Eider had convinced Vellamo to play along with this part.

The big black horse sank down and rolled over in the dirt. "Stab me and I will bite your arm off," she hissed up at Mađen.

"It's just for show, so the others think you're out of commission," Lyylia said. "Here they—" The rest of her sentence was drowned out by the screams of at least two Näkki.

Mađen dropped both his knife and the sword as he crumpled to his knees beside Vellamo. He squeezed his eyes shut and hung his head down, willing himself not to vomit or pass out. Dimly he heard hissing and snarling and crashing amid another mind-numbing scream.

Something struck his hip, knocking him flat into the dirt. He rolled away, and finally dragged his eyes open. A wide hole had been punched in the stone wall, the rocks scattered on both sides of the opening. That's probably what had hit him, he realized, seeing a rock the size of his head lying near him.

A hand grabbed his shoulder. "You okay?" he heard Lyylia's voice in his ear.

"Yeah." He scrambled up and looked around. The battle was already almost over. One Näkki lay motionless out on the tundra, still several meters away from the wall. Another lay just inside the broken section of wall, water gushing from a bite wound in its neck. A black wolf stood over it.

"Vellamo?" he asked carefully.

"Yes," rasped the wolf. The voice sounded the same as

when she was in horse form.

Maðen looked around for the last Näkki. He spotted a black horse out on the tundra, kicking and flailing as if it were fighting something. The invisible reindeer, presumably. It let out a scream, which was blessedly cut short as it collapsed to the ground. It didn't try to get up.

The fifteen reindeer had all fled from the scene as best they could and were huddled in the back of the shallow cave, just past the stream. They were clearly scared, snorting and stamping, but none of them looked injured.

Turning back to look through the broken wall, Maðen started as there was suddenly a Menninkäinen there, clad in fur with a bow and quiver on his back, just a few meters away and jogging towards them.

"Good shooting, Eider," Lyylia said with a smile.

Eider grinned. "Dream be praised that you are alive and well!" He climbed over the pile of rocks in the broken section of the wall.

Vellamo put her ears back, but made no threatening movements. "Impressive indeed are the spells of Pohjola's queen," she said flatly, staring at Eider.

Eider squared his shoulders and met her gaze, but didn't say anything.

Vellamo hissed quietly, then looked up at Maðen and Lyylia. "I leave you now, shamans. I have fulfilled what I pledged to do, and I intend to be far from this place when Kipu-Tyttö comes or Hiisi-Hiisi returns. You are free to return to Pohjola, at your own risk."

"Thank you, Vellamo," Lyylia said.

The dog gave a quick bow with her nose to her paws, and then ran towards the stream. The reindeer skittered away from her approach. She splashed into the water and dipped her nose below the surface, and in a blink she vanished from sight. Mađen let out a breath.

"Is everyone all right?" Lyylia asked.

Mađen's right hip ached, but he could walk just fine, so he nodded.

"I am uninjured," said Eider.

"As the Näkki said, the sooner we are away from this place, the better," came a deep voice nearby. Mađen's hand automatically went for his boot knife that was no longer there.

Eider reached out, fumbling his hands around erratically in the air for a moment, and then suddenly a reindeer appeared beside him. Eider held up a long, thin rope with a small rock tied to it. The starlight glinted off something shiny embedded in the rock.

"Greetings, Kalevalans," said the reindeer, bowing its head. "I am Silence of the Sky."

"And I am Forest Wanderer," came another voice. Eider pulled the invisible necklace off and another reindeer appeared. So apparently all the Pohjola reindeer could talk, not just Kied-Kie-Jubmel.

Both reindeer had saddlebags draped over their backs, presumably carrying food and other supplies. Eider had his quiver on his back, but no pack of any sort.

"These silver protection stones kept the spell of invisibility intact," Eider said, holding up three slender ropes with lumps of rocks tied to them.

"Thank you for coming to our rescue," Lyylia said. "All of you. How did you manage to find us?"

"I caught the scent of your Gentle Beasts some time ago," said Forest Wanderer. "Though we dared not approach them because of the Näkki guards. Eider had suggested that we continue on towards the fire mountains in the distance, but then we saw you arrive through the water."

"We were in the fire mountains," Lyylia said. "Hiisi-Hiisi's castle is there. But now, we should move. Vellamo's right—eventually someone's going to come back here."

"I will speak with your animals, to make sure that they are fit and willing to travel," said Silence of the Sky.

"I never thought I'd need a reindeer translator," Maden murmured, as Silence of the Sky went over to the other animals.

"It was odd enough to see Kied-Kie-Jubmel talk," Lyylia added. "I didn't know that they all could talk."

"Your Gentle Beasts can talk, as well," put in Eider, pulling his now-visible arrows out of the dead Näkki and hiisi and restocking his quiver. "Just not in a tongue that you can understand."

Maden wasn't sure what to say to that. He scuffed around in the dirt till he found his boot knife. He spotted the hilt of Eider's sword under the fallen Näkki and pulled it out.

Silence of the Sky reported that all the reindeer were eager and willing to make an escape, despite the potential dangers up ahead. "Maden, I will bear you as a rider—I am the largest and strongest. Lyylia, you will ride Forest Wanderer. And Eider, you will ride Vuordámuš."

"Um, none of these reindeer have been ridden before," Maden said, wondering what he meant by *vuordámuš*. His reindeer didn't have names. "Most of them have never even been harnessed to pull a sled."

"Vuordámuš understands what he must do," Silence of the Sky assured him, nodding at the largest of the males. Eider jumped up on the animal's back. To Maden's surprise, the reindeer just stood there patiently, as if it had been in a tourist petting zoo its whole life. He helped Lyylia to mount Forest Wanderer.

"I've never even ridden a horse before," she said. "How am I supposed to stay on?"

"I will not let you fall, my lady," said the reindeer.

"Just grip with your knees and your lower legs," Mađen said. "And grab the thick fur on his back, or put your arms around the lower part of his neck. Don't grab his antlers."

Lyylia nodded nervously, fingering Forest Wanderer's fur.

Mađen mounted Silence of the Sky, feeling almost as awkward as Lyylia looked. He carefully arranged his legs around the saddlebags draped down the reindeer's sides. Finnish reindeer were too small to be effectively ridden by anyone but children, so it had been more than a few years since he'd sat on the back of one. Some were trained to pull for work or sport, but all of his animals were tundra-raised reindeer that were bred for their meat and their fur. He looked over at Vuordámuš, hoping that he wouldn't suddenly panic and dump Eider off.

Silence of the Sky navigated through the broken section of wall, and soon everyone was out of the corral. Then he gave a loud bellow; several other reindeer gave responsive cries, and the entire herd broke into a run.

Mađen squeezed his legs, as he'd told Lyylia to do, and hunched as low as he could over the reindeer's back to avoid its antlers, gripping the long coarse fur of the animal's shoulder hump. The terrain was rough, the ride rougher, and the cold wind became a dusty gale blowing in their faces. All fifteen reindeer kept pace with Silence of the Sky and Forest Wanderer, and soon the broken corral and dead Näkki had disappeared into the distance behind them.

Teija sat in the blustery cold wind, huddled into her coat and hood, with a blanket around her shoulders for extra warmth. The blanket was actually for Shaun's computer equipment, to cover up the laptop in case it started snowing. Thin clouds were starting to fade out the stars and Dancing Lights, but so far no snow.

With nothing to do except worry, she'd spent the last two days napping and wandering the castle corridors, and the nights outside on this small turret of Kuu's castle, where Shaun had set up his aurora scanning equipment. She didn't remember much about what Shaun had briefly told her, but after two nights of staring at the numbers and graphs and all the English words in the programs, she'd figured out some of it. Apparently the Dancing Lights made sounds that were inaudible to the human ear, and one of those sounds meant that a reindeer was returning from its magical slumber in the Lights and materializing on the earth again. Shaun had programmed a yellow blip to appear every time the microphones recorded that sound.

As strange as it was to learn that the aurora made sounds and that computers could record it—even sounds made by magical reindeer in the sky—it was oddly comforting to sit here clicking the mouse and watching numbers and graphs on a screen. It was like a little bit of home.

Since Shaun and the others had left for the lake two days ago, one hundred and nineteen blips had appeared. These blips were appearing in different locations all over Pohjola. Teija clicked on map of Pohjola that Shaun had transferred to his computer and watched the overlay of the yellow blips. Three reindeer had just appeared at the far south of Pohjola. Teija wondered how many kilometers away the Southern Fens were, and if any Menninkäinen or reindeer from the south would make it up to the lake in time to join the battle.

The battle. She wished she knew what was happening. The young shaman's son named Gray was still in the castle, to use the moon mirror if needed, but apparently he'd heard no updates from the army at the lake. And no updates about Lyylia and Maðen, either.

Another yellow blip flashed on the screen. Checking the overlay map, she saw that this blip appeared almost directly over the castle. Teija pulled Shaun's binoculars out of the scanner's carrying pack and peered over the wall of the tower. She saw movement, but then it flicked out of view.

She looked down without the binoculars, to get a broader view. The rocky face of the mountain tumbled down to the snow-covered tundra; in the far distance was the gray blur of trees. Several little black dots were moving along the white of the tundra. She focused in with the binoculars again.

It was a horse, black mane and tail streaming back in the wind as it galloped across the snow. Frantically Teija scanned the landscape with the binoculars, praying to spot reindeer; but all she saw were more horses. Five black dots, at least, spread out across the kilometers; but they were all headed in the same direction. Towards the castle.

Teija stuffed the binoculars back into the backpack and hurriedly tossed the blanket over the laptop in case it started snowing. Yanking open the door into the castle, she dashed down the spiral steps and into the corridor.

"Näkki!" she shouted, her voice echoing off the stone walls as she ran. "There are Näkki coming! Can anyone hear me? Help, there are Näkki coming!"

No one answered her. Kuu had said that she was leaving two Gentle Beasts and half the complement of guards and workers at the castle. Teija had no idea how many half the normal amount was, but she'd been well fed and usually saw a handful of Menninkäinen throughout the day. Right now, though, no one seemed to be nearby. All the corridors looked the same—carved walls inlaid with silver, blue-white outdoor light streaming through windows, and torches guttering on wall posts in the windowless hallways.

She hurried through endless corridors, up and down stairs, peering into rooms that had doors standing open. Hearing what sounded like reindeer hooves echoing, she called out again and tried to follow the sound, but found no one. She spotted an open door that looked like it led to a spiral staircase—perhaps she should go up to another turret and see how close the Näkki were by now. She started up the stairs.

At the top, she staggered to a halt in the sudden brilliance that assaulted her. Starlight, aurora, and the blue-white pseudo-sun were reflected and magnified by a polished floor and pillars of ice and silver. Under the brilliant vault of the sky, the wall-less space seemed to expand in the light. Her head swam with vertigo as she blinked in the brightness. This must be the Moon Tower.

As her eyes adjusted, she saw tall pillars scattered throughout the room, along with wooden chests, and an assortment of ice constructs. At the far end of the room were five doors leading into the rock wall of the mountain. One door stood open.

A familiar sound echoed off the clear walls and ceiling—the abrasive hiss of a Näkki. A black wolf appeared in the open doorway. Teija ducked behind the nearest column, but it wasn't exactly a good hiding spot. How had the Näkki gotten out of its prison? And why wasn't there a guard posted?

The Näkki hissed again and advanced directly towards her. Heart pounding, Teija fumbled in the front pocket of her coat for her earplugs, and jammed them into her ears.

"Tell me, weakling, where is your queen?" the Näkki rasped, its voice muffled only slightly by Teija's earplugs. She didn't answer.

Teija noticed that it had a thin silver halter around its head and muzzle, and wondered if that was limiting its screaming power. It was still more than dangerous, though. She glanced back at the entrance to the stairs, and wondered if she dared make a dash for it. The Näkki was still advancing with slow deliberate steps, and could definitely outrun her.

A small wooden chest sat beside her at the base of the ice column. Pulling her gaze away from the Näkki, she tugged on the lid. The chest was not locked, and inside were three small rolls of dark blue fabric. With quick glances back at the slowly approaching wolf, she dug frantically through the cloth, hoping for a weapon of some sort.

All she found in the chest besides the fabric itself were two small leather pouches. A handful of small clear crystals fell out of one pouch onto the blue cloth. The other pouch held a mouth harp. She grabbed it up and put it against her teeth, and struck the little metal tongue.

The twang of the mouth harp sounded straight and clear through her earplugs, and the echo seemed to hang in the air. The Näkki froze and put its ears back. She thumbed the mouth harp several more times, the echoing twang deepening into a steady thrumming sound that filled the entire chamber. She stood up, still thumbing the mouth harp, and the Näkki took a step back.

Emboldened, Teija stepped forwards, and the Näkki retreated another step, ears back and tail between its legs. On impulse, she paused long enough to scoop up the handful of crystals from the chest. Then she hurled the handful at the

Näkki. The little pebble-sized crystals scattered, and Teija couldn't tell if any of them even came close to hitting the Näkki, but the creature skittered back several more paces. Then it gave a loud grating hiss, and giving her a wide berth, it fled for the stairs.

Teija stood in the empty Moon Tower, the mouth harp against her lips, holding her breath as the sounds faded away. Had she really just driven off a Näkki with some tiny crystals and a mouth harp that she didn't know how to play?

But that meant that there was now a Näkki loose in the castle. Spotting a large, jeweled dagger protruding from a table made of ice in the center of the room, she hurried over it. Tugging on the dagger didn't budge it. Spotting another chest nearby, she opened it to find a long overtone flute, two silver bowls, and several wooden drum strikers, but no weapons.

She tried the doors at the far end of the Moon Tower; all were locked except the one that stood open. A narrow tunnel led into complete darkness; she assumed that was the dungeon, and didn't venture into the tunnel. As she hurried back across the room to the stairs, her boots crunched on the crystals she'd thrown. She stopped and picked up several of the tiny rough-cut gems. They glittered in the light, and the palm of her hand tingled. For some reason she was suddenly reminded of the locked door she'd found behind the bear pelt at the end of the Halls of Time.

Even though she needed to leave the Moon Tower to warn someone about the Näkki, she felt compelled to retrieve all of the crystals. Teija crawled around on the smooth stone floor, finding it surprisingly easy to spot the crystals. Hoping she had them all, she returned them to their leather pouch, along with the others that were still loose in the trunk. She closed the trunk, pulled out her earplugs, and with the mouth harp still in her pocket, she hurried for the stairs.

"Help!" she hollered again as she ran through the empty corridors. "Help, there's a Näkki in the castle!"

Rounding a corner, she slammed into a reindeer. She stumbled back against the wall with a yelp, feeling a flash of gratitude that she'd hit the side of the animal instead of its wide antlers. The reindeer jumped back as well, giving a snort of surprise.

"Kalevalan," it said, in a voice that was almost a growl. "Why are you still here?"

She recognized the voice—Night-Fire Desolation. Why had Kuu left *him* here to guard the castle?

"I…Queen Kuu told me to stay here," she stammered.

"The Queen has gone to battle," he said, taking a step towards her.

"Yes." Teija shrank against the wall at her back. "Please, Night-Fire Desolation, sir—there's a Näkki loose in the castle. We need to find it and—"

"Simpleton!" shouted the reindeer, tossing his antlers. Teija flinched. "To keep the Näkki here would have been death to us all."

Still trembling, Teija gaped at Night-Fire Desolation. "You released the Näkki? But—"

"Foolish little Kalevalan witch!" Night-Fire snorted and tossed his head. "The Näkki has joined his kin outside the castle walls. The other Näkki had come to collect him. They will now no doubt head for the Dark Water Lake, where the Queen and her army fight a losing battle. But at least the poison of Ice-Dark is now gone from this castle." The reindeer cocked his head at Teija, his ears back and his brown eyes wild. "The poison of Kalevala remains, but I have done all I can to protect this place."

Teija held her breath and tried to keep from crying. One small thrust of Night-Fire's head and he could ram her with his antlers. Night-Fire gave a loud snort, then reared and spun on his hind hooves, and galloped away down the corridor.

As Teija sagged against the wall, Night-Fire rounded the corner, and there was a strange flare of yellow-green light. Goosebumps pricked down her arms, and her scalp suddenly felt tingly. Teija hurried down the hall to the corner, but there no was sign of the reindeer—not even the sound of hooves on the stone floor. He'd vanished.

Teija stood in the empty corridor, heart pounding, wondering what to do. She had no idea where she was now, so she should probably just keep roaming until she finally found someone. And what about Night-Fire Desolation? Had that flash really been aurora energy, inside the castle, and had he transported himself back to the Dancing Lights?

That seemed like a ridiculous idea, but it was the only thing that made sense. The yellow blip she'd just seen on the computer had been near the castle—what if it was Night-Fire appearing within the castle walls? That meant that he could appear and disappear at will.

And he'd just released the Näkki prisoner and abandoned everyone.

Wiping at her eyes, Teija set off down the hall. She passed by a window; green and gold Dancing Lights rippled calmly across the sky, still bright through the increasing clouds. No Näkki—or reindeer—were visible on the white tundra far below.

Rounding another corner, she spotted a Menninkäinen at the far end of the corridor.

"Help!" she called, running towards him.

He hefted his spear and started towards her. "What is it, my lady?"

"I need to find Gray!" she panted. "Näkki—Night-Fire Desolation—we have to tell the Queen!" Teija knew she wasn't making much sense, and her throat felt tight as she struggled not to burst into tears. "I think there are more Näkki headed for the lake," she said as she and the man reached each other. "And Night-Fire Desolation just left. He vanished."

"I will take you to Gray at once, my lady," said the little man, gently taking her arm. "Are you hurt?"

Teija shook her head and gratefully followed the man through the long castle corridors. She hoped Gray would be able to get word to Queen Kuu. And she hoped that somehow, somehow, she'd get to see Lyylia again.

Ávgos stood beside Shaun and Boots again, back out on one of the little low islands in the lake. They were only a few meters from the shore, where the bulk of the army remained.

For right now, the Ice-Dark army was regrouping, just as they were. Kuu's current tactic was to stop the cannons. A line of archers stood some distance out on the ice, in front of Ávgos' group.

"If those cannons are mechanically powered, or built at all like tanks, archers won't do a bit of good," Shaun muttered.

Ávgos glanced at him. "I wish we could see them better. They're still too far away. I wish I had my herding binoculars."

"My binoculars are back at Kuu's castle," Shaun said. "Not that seeing the cannons would do any good, really. We can't fight gunpowder and mechanized warfare with swords and spears."

"The Queen will stop them," Boots said confidently.

Ávgos looked down at him, feeling simultaneously encouraged and saddened by the Menninkäinen's cheerfully naïve outlook. Shaun was right—iron age weapons in the hands of a few hundred farmers was no match for magical monsters and industrial age weaponry.

Then again, the three of them were still standing, and relatively uninjured. Ávgos' side still ached from that early blow from a Näkki, but he was pretty sure nothing was broken. He knew he had a cut on his cheek, but the blood had dried quickly in the cold.

Kuu stood in the distance out on the ice, no longer on her horse, but with her dog beside her. Ávgos could just make out that she'd plunged her sword into the ice. It stood upright, glinting in the light, like the dagger she'd driven into the ice table in the Moon Tower. She had her frame drum in her hands and Ávgos assumed she was singing, but she was too far away for him to hear anything except the distant grinding rumble of the cannons. He wondered why Hiisi-Hiisi hadn't given an order to resume firing yet. The Pohjola army needed the respite, but charity was probably not the reason for the delay.

"Is the ice glowing?" Shaun said, pointing out across the lake. "There, where Kuu's sword is in the ice."

"It does kind of look like that," Ávgos said, squinting. The Dancing Lights had just begun, but the light under the ice was not a reflection of the sky.

A distant boom sounded, and a second later a cannonball exploded not far from Kuu's position. It was followed almost immediately by another shot, and then another.

"First line archers, fire!" shouted the reindeer who stood with the archers out on the lake. Son of the Mountains, Ávgos thought his name was. Kied-Kie-Jubmel was still on the shore.

Ávgos stuffed his earplugs back in and tightened his grip on his spear. Even standing on the earth of the skerry, he could feel the vibrations of the explosions as the cannonballs pounded the ice. He could now clearly see four cannons approaching, with the shadowy shapes of others behind them.

Suddenly a loud crack sounded over the booms of the cannons, and Ávgos squinted out at the lake. The blue light had spread, and the nearest cannon was tipped nearly on its side, two of the platform's wheels sunk into the ice. There was another crack, and the cannon toppled over and began to sink through the broken chunks of ice around it.

Kuu was thawing the lake.

Shouts and commotion came from the shore behind them, and Ávgos looked over his shoulder to see a man on horseback pushing his way through the assembled army. "My lord Kied-Kie-Jumel!" he shouted.

Shaun and Boots turned around, as did several others who were stationed on the nearest skerries. The man pulled up his horse as the big reindeer approached.

"My lord! Näkki—coming from the south! My party was traveling from the Southern Fens to join the battle when we were attacked. I escaped—I don't know if anyone still lives. The Näkki are headed this way!"

Ávgos looked at Shaun; the other man's face was pale. "We'll be surrounded," Shaun murmured.

Kied-Kie-Jubmel was barking out orders. "Runs in the North, take twenty men and as many Gentle Beasts as you can and protect our southern flank. Someone get this man a fresh horse and ensure he is properly armed. Everyone else—keep to your positions and stand strong!"

Ávgos turned back around to face the slowly approaching cannons. The blue glow beneath the ice was increasing, and the air smelled like gunpowder.

"All men, prepare for battle!" Kied-Kie-Jubmel's voice bellowed from behind them. A moment later, Näkki screams pierced through the air, not drowned out by the cannon fire. Ávgos winced and felt a wave of dizziness, despite his earplugs. Beside him, Boots crumpled to his knees; Ávgos grabbed his shoulder and helped him back up. Boots nodded at him, and stuffed his earplugs in.

Son of the Mountains bellowed something at his archers, but then the air was thick with Näkki screams and an oncoming tide of black horses. Ávgos barely had time to flinch in horror as the line of archers in front of them were all trampled under the wave of galloping Näkki, and then he was surrounded by the chaos of battle again. He couldn't think about Sirkka now, couldn't think about Näkki coming up on their rear flank, and he couldn't spare a glance towards the center of the lake to see if the thaw was spreading or more cannons had sunk. All he could do was fight.

After hours of riding, Maðen was grateful when Silence of the Sky and Forest Wanderer halted the group. They stopped beside a narrow stream that ran through a low depression between hills, not quite low enough to be called a valley, but offering them a bit of shelter from the wind. Small scrubby plants grew along the water's edge, and the rocks were covered in moss.

Maðen worried about Näkki suddenly popping out of the stream, but the reindeer needed to rest, and everyone needed food and water. Eider shared the food that he'd brought with him. Hard bread, mutton jerky, and dried fruit had never tasted so good. The two Pohjola reindeer took turns eating and patrolling the area; right now, Forest Wanderer walked a slow circuit a dozen or so meters away, his ears alert and his nose to the wind. So far they'd been fortunate and had encountered no other living things, not even birds.

Looking over at Lyylia, Maden saw that she'd hardly touched her food, and was staring into the distance with a dazed expression. Her lips were blue and she was visibly shivering. Setting his jerky and lump of bread on a rock, Maden leaned over and touched her shoulder. "You okay, Lyylia?"

She started, then looked at him and nodded, but her expression was glassy and dull. She was still wet, Maden realized. They hadn't had a chance to dry off properly after their trip through the water to the reindeer's corral hours ago. Maden's clothes were mostly synthetic fibers designed to wick moisture and dry quickly—and he had a lot more body mass than Lyylia, too. But she was wearing Pohjola clothes made of wool and fur, which were great at keeping one warm only as long as the garments stayed dry.

"Take off your coat," he instructed her. "And your boots and socks. Eider, do you have any extra clothing with you?"

"I have an extra pair of socks," Eider said. "What—" He then looked at the shivering, unresponsive Lyylia, and his eyes widened with understanding.

Scrambling up, Eider went over to where the reindeer had dumped their packs. "Here are the socks," he said, tossing them to Maden. "And I have my sleeping blankets. A tent was too large to carry, but the Queen sent me with a small blanket to lie on and a larger one for warmth." He came back with two tightly rolled blankets.

Lyylia had pulled off her coat, but was now shaking more dramatically and having trouble with her boots. Maðen and Eider helped, getting her boots and socks off, and the new dry socks on. Maðen also pulled off her damp tunic, leaving her in her undershirt, and wrapped her up in the larger blanket. He put the smaller blanket around her legs and feet, then pulled off his now-dry coat and draped it over her shoulders, pulling up the hood to shield her head from the wind. He shook and wrung her clothes as best as he could, then laid them out on rocks. They couldn't linger here long enough for everything to fully dry, but letting Lyylia succumb to hypothermia wasn't an option, either.

When he finished with the clothes and turned back around, he saw that Eider had started a fire and had a small metal cup filled with water perched at the edge of the flame. "I have some dried long-leaf and a bit of healing moss, so I'm making a hot drink," he said.

Still shivering, Lyylia shook her head. "No, they'll see the smoke."

"It's only a small fire," Maðen said, squatting down beside her. He took hold of her hands, which were stiff and cold but didn't show signs of frostbite. Then he tucked her hands inside the blanket, and held a hunk of bread to her lips. She hesitated, then took a bite.

They stayed by the stream for probably at least an hour. Eider made Lyylia drink two cupfuls of hot long-leaf and moss, and Maðen fed her so she could keep her hands inside the blanket. Eventually Lyylia stopped shivering and some of the color came back into her face, so they packed up to leave. Maðen insisted that she wear his coat, which was completely dry at this point. Maðen wrapped the smaller of the two blankets around his shoulders to help protect him from the chilly wind as they rode, and he rolled up her still-damp coat and tied it to the reindeer's packs. They dared not leave anything behind that could be used to track them.

The bright blue star in the distance grew bigger as they traveled, and rose higher in the sky, though none of the other stars were rising or setting. Like in Pohjola, the stars of Ice-Dark wheeled around a central axis.

The land gradually became hillier, though no less rocky and desolate. The reindeer's galloping eventually slowed to a trot, and finally a walk as the slopes got steeper and the loose rocks became more prevalent. Maden and the other two dismounted to give the reindeer a respite.

As they struggled to the top of an unusually high slope, they were met with an encouraging view. Right in front of them, high in the sky, Pohjantähti blazed a warm radiant blue, and illuminated the land below it. Oddly, the light didn't seem to illuminate the landscape of Ice-Dark, even though Pohjantähti was bright enough to make them squint. A ribbon of silvery-white stretched across the land below them—the river that served as the border between Ice-Dark and Pohjola. And on the other side of the river, just at the horizon but definitely visible, a soft landscape of white snow.

"Pohjola!" Eider cried happily, lifting his arms.

"We can't just march across the river, easy as that, though," said Maden. "Look."

Black and white shapes dotted the Ice-Dark bank of the river. Näkki and hiisi, as far as they could see in both directions.

"Listen," Lyylia said. "What's that sound?"

An irregular rumbling drifted faintly from their left. It sounded like distant gunfire.

"It's the cannons," Maden gritted. "They're bombing Pohjola."

"What is this you speak of?" Silence of the Sky asked.

Lyylia briefly described gunpowder and explosives, and the cannons that Hiisi-Hiisi had showed them. "We've got to stop those cannons," she said.

"And how exactly do you propose we do that?" Mađen asked, staring at her.

She just pursed her lips and shook her head.

"Where did you cross the river?" Mađen asked Eider and the reindeer.

"More than a day's journey to the west," said Silence of the Sky, nodding away towards their right. "And that was before the battle began, and there were only small troops of hiisi along the riverbanks, and very few Näkki. Invisible as we were, it was an easy matter to slip past them. Now that the battle has been engaged and Näkki by the hundreds have come, I fear that even a journey of several days may not take us to an unguarded crossing."

"We'll have to figure out a way to fight them, then," Lyylia said.

"We got lucky and killed three of them," Mađen said. "How can we fight a whole army?"

Suddenly several of the reindeer snorted and stamped in alarm, skidding on the loose rocks. Glancing around, Mađen saw a black wolf standing a few meters behind them on the slope.

Eider swung his bow off his shoulder, and Mađen bent to pull out his boot knife.

"If you wish to approach the border unseen, I can show you the way," the Näkki rasped.

Mađen lowered his knife. "Vellamo?"

"What are you doing here?" Lyylia said. "Have you been following us?"

"No. I came to see the battle, and to hide myself among

the numbers of Näkki. I could not return to the waters where I normally dwell—Kipu-Tyttö has dispersed her spies. And she knows that you have escaped—you will be found by her Näkki if you remain out in the open much longer."

"Why are you offering to help us?" Lyylia asked. "You said you didn't care whether we lived or died once we escaped."

"I offer to help you not out of concern for any of you, but for my hatred of Kipu-Tyttö. She will find you, before Hiisi-Hiisi has finished his work here. She will steal your magic and the very energy of your lives, and then she will launch her fight against Hiisi-Hiisi. Kipu-Tyttö and Hiisi-Hiisi have fought before—this is not the first time she has sought to usurp his rule. But this time I fear she may succeed. A war between Hiisi-Hiisi and Kipu-Tyttö and the Näkki loyal to each will destroy us all."

Maden and Lyylia exchanged worried looks at Vellamo's grim prediction.

"All right," Lyylia said finally. "So how do you propose to help us get across the border?"

"I did not say I could get you safely to Pohjola," Vellamo grated, coming up the hill towards them. "But I can get you to the edge of the battle, and you will not be seen until you choose to show yourselves. There are tunnels under these hills. The tunnels are emptied of Näkki right now, as they are all above the ground, fighting for Hiisi-Hiisi."

"Lead the way, then," said Lyylia.

The Näkki trotted down the other side of the slope, and then led them for a short distance to the base of another network of slopes. Scratching at the loose rocks, she revealed the opening of a tunnel.

Maden was about to protest that the reindeer would be both unwilling and unable to fit through such an opening, but

Silence of the Sky was already moving among them, grunting and whickering. Forest Wanderer ducked his head and followed Vellamo into the tunnel, Vuordámuš right behind him.

Complete blackness surrounded them. Mađen had to lower his head and hunch his shoulders, but the tunnel was tall enough for Lyylia, Eider, and the reindeer. He walked with one hand on Vuordámuš' rump in front of him and his other hand on the neck of the reindeer behind him. They followed the sound of Vellamo's claws scuffling the rocky soil. Periodically Mađen saw her white eyes as she turned her head, glowing like two tiny frosted light bulbs in the darkness. He heard water trickling nearby.

Then there were other sounds—a faint distant roaring like wind, and an intermittent rumbling. A dim light glowed up ahead, and Vellamo slowed.

"Here I must leave you. This is as close to the border lake as you can be and still remain hidden underground; but I would caution you not to remain here long, whatever you choose to do. Kipu-Tyttö is hunting for you. She will not think at first to look for you at the front lines of the battle. But once the battle has ended, Näkki will return to these tunnels and you will be found."

"Thank you, Vellamo," said Lyylia. "We couldn't have done this without you."

"Thanks, Vellamo," Mađen put in. "Good luck to you in staying hidden from Kipu-Tyttö."

"Thank you, shamans of Kalevala. Good fortune to you, as well." Vellamo's glowing white eyes blinked in the darkness, and she trotted away down the tunnel back the way they had come.

Mađen, Lyylia, and Eider carefully approached the tunnel exit and one by one peered out. They were fairly high up on the side of a rocky hill, but the exit hole was well hidden by outcroppings, so they had to crawl outside to see where they were.

The roaring and the rumbling, Maden realized, were the sounds of battle. The lake was right in front of them. Ranks of Näkki were scattered everywhere along the shore. The lake lay in a valley of sorts. The valley between the hills led up to the lake, almost like a road—that pass was probably the way that the army had come, and the hiisi who had been dragging the cannons.

The frozen lake was swarming with Näkki and hiisi, and Maden counted nearly a dozen hulking black cannons. The guns were mounted on giant wheeled platforms, and were rolling slowly across the ice towards Pohjola, firing as they went. Dozens of little white hiisi swarmed across each of the cannons, refilling them with ammunition and lighting the fuses.

"How can we ever get past that?" moaned Eider.

"If we can find a break in their ranks, we could make a run for it," Lyylia said. "There's no way we'll be able to fight our way through."

"Look," said Maden. "It must be night. The Lights have started."

Above the lake, filling the sky in the distance, the Dancing Lights swirled with every color imaginable. Pohjantähti's blue-white brilliance shone through the display. Thin clouds did nothing to block the light, instead scattering the colors into a dazzling rainbow of light. It was breathtakingly beautiful. And none of it was in the sky directly above them, even though they were only a few hundred meters from the border.

"Hiisi-Hiisi was right," Lyylia murmured. "The Lights are only in Pohjola. It's like there's an invisible wall in the sky that keeps the aurora from crossing the lake. How is that possible?"

"I don't know, but something's happening down there,"

said Mađen. "See, that cannon has stopped rolling. And those two stopped firing. And that line of Näkki on the shore are going out onto the lake."

Silence of the Sky joined them out on the hillside. "All of your Gentle Beasts are safe," he said to Mađen. "They have left the tunnel, but they are hidden behind this part of the ridge. They await your signal."

Mađen nodded at him.

A blue sheen was spreading across the lake. At first Mađen thought it was just the reflected light of Pohjantähti, but it was growing brighter. "Do you see that?"

"The magic of Dream," said Silence of the Sky.

"Look," said Eider, pointing.

One of the cannons in the center of the lake tipped over as the ice all around it broke into loose chunks.

"Somehow, I think Kuu thawing the lake to stop the cannons," Lyylia said. "Come on—I think this the best chance we're going to get."

As they scurried back around the edge of the hill to get the reindeer, Mađen thought of Ávgos and Sirkka and Piijá.

The snow was packed slick from tramping feet and bleeding Näkki, and some small part of Shaun's mind marveled at his own ability to keep his footing while slashing with his sword. The ice cleats on his boots worked better on the ice of the lake than on uneven packed snow. He had to let only one thought dominate his mind: Kuu's orders to defend the shore at all costs.

Defend the shore. Bring back Lyylia. Shaun repeated those

thoughts like a mantra as he swung at every blur of white or black fur. *Defend the shore. Bring back Lyylia.* He couldn't think about the pain in his knee when he'd fallen earlier, or wonder whether the moisture he felt running down his neck was sweat or blood, or how his right arm ached to the point of deadweight now. He felt Ávgos beside him, but he'd lost track of Boots some time ago. They'd been driven back from their position out on the skerry by the unceasing wave of Näkki and hiisi. And despite Kuu's thawing of the ice, the cannon fire was getting closer, too. *Defend the shore. Bring back Lyylia.*

"Melting the ice—a clever trick, little moon queen." Hiisi-Hiisi's voice boomed louder than the cannons.

Shaun spun to look out across the lake. The giant white horse was striding purposefully towards Kuu across the thinning ice. All around, the Näkki and hiisi seemed to slow as their master spoke.

"You may have slowed my fire-mouths," said Hiisi-Hiisi. "But you forget—water is the domain of the Näkki."

Dead center of the lake was where broken chunks of ice bobbed loose in the water, and where one cannon had already sunk and another lay on its side, wedged between ice floes. Opaque shadows like giant batwings lifted from Hiisi-Hiisi's back as he rose into the air and flew over the thawed section of the lake.

Kuu hooked her frame drum over the knife on her belt, and yanked her sword out of the ice as Hiisi-Hiisi landed a few yards away from her. The blade glowed with a blue sheen.

Even at this distance, Shaun could see the long curved talons on the ends of Hiisi-Hiisi's wings. In one set of claws he held the handgun.

Shaun slashed at the nearest Näkki, and ran out onto the lake. He faintly heard Ávgos calling after him. He had to get to Kuu. Lyylia hadn't explained how her gun worked, only that it was a dangerous weapon, so Kuu didn't know what it could do. Her leather breastplate wasn't going to stop a bullet. Shaun slashed and hacked with his sword, plowing through Näkki and hiisi and shoving past Menninkäinen and reindeer.

Hiisi-Hiisi had stopped just a few paces away from Kuu. She held up her sword, the glowing blade pointed at the giant horse head looming above her. Hiisi-Hiisi swept his wings down, the gun angled directly at her.

"Kuu!" Shaun shouted, his voice lost amid the yelling and snarling and rattle of weapons. He slashed at a black wolf that lay writhing and hissing on the ice, stumbled over a dead hiisi, and shouldered past two Menninkäinen, nearly stumbling again as he tried to break into a run. "Kuu!"

"A noble effort, moon queen," Hiisi-Hiisi's voice rumbled and rolled through the air. "But the lake must stay frozen. My fire-mouths will reach your shores." He fired the gun.

The crack of the gunshot cut through all the other noise. Kuu fell backwards and hit the ice, her sword clattering from her hand. With a snarl, Child of Light leapt at Hiisi-Hiisi, and he fired another shot at her.

There was a pause as the gunshots echoed across the lake. Kuu sprawled on the ice, her dog collapsed on top of her; her drum rolled away until it hit the fallen sword and stopped.

"No!" Shaun cried. With a surge of adrenaline, he finally broke through the crush of battle and ran.

"Defend the shore!" he heard Kied-Kie-Jubmel's voice shouting to the army behind him. "Hold the line—none must reach the ridge!"

Hiisi-Hiisi had turned his back on the scene and was striding back towards his oncoming cannons. With a collective shout, a group of Menninkäinen took off after him, but before their spears and swords even came close, he turned around and spat a fireball.

Shaun tried to block out the image of the flames engulfing the group of Menninkäinen, but it was all happening in front of him as he ran across the ice. Boots had better not have been in that group. Shaun stumbled over one of the little skerries, dodged around the bodies of several Menninkäinen and hiisi, and finally hit his knees and slid to a halt beside Kuu.

Several reindeer had gathered around her, and one had pulled the dog off of her. Child of Light's white fur was red with blood.

"Kuu!" Shaun stuffed his sword into its scabbard as he bent over her. Her eyes were closed and her face pale. The bullet had pierced her chest right in the center of her breastplate. A powder burn dusted the tan leather and blood was seeping out.

Shaun looked up at the reindeer. "Can she die?"

"Dream will heal her," one of them said. "But we must move her to safety."

Shaun gathered his feet under him and carefully picked Kuu up. Either she was lighter than she looked, or he was still on an adrenaline high, but she felt almost frail as he cradled her body against him. One of the reindeer laid down so that the others could slide the dog onto its back. Other reindeer picked up the sword and the drum in their mouths, and they all set off towards the shore.

"Defend the shore!" Kied-Kie-Jubmel was galloping along the ice near the shore and trying to keep the stunned army together. "Archers, maintain your positions! Men—form a protective flank and make way for the Queen!"

A large group of Menninkäinen and reindeer moved in to surround them and clear a path for them to retreat. Shaun managed not to stumble as he carried Kuu back to the shore, then through the snow and over the ridge to the camp. He went into the nearest tent and laid her down.

Ávgos burst in right behind them. "Let me look at her."

"Dream will not permit Hiisi-Hiisi's magic to bring permanent harm to the Queen," said one of the reindeer calmly.

"This isn't Hiisi-Hiisi's magic," Ávgos replied, squatting down next to Shaun. The two of them worked together to carefully remove Kuu's sword scabbard and breastplate. Blood gushed more freely now, the red stain spreading across her white tunic. "Hiisi-Hiisi stole that gun from the Kalevalans he captured. This is Kalevala magic that wounded her."

Ávgos looked at Shaun. "Every herder learns some basic first aid for when they're out on the land—that includes accidental gunshot wounds." He looked up at the reindeer gathered around. "I need something to slow the bleeding— bandages, blankets, clothing, anything. And a knife, and clean water."

Two of the reindeer began nosing around in the packs of supplies in the corner of the tent, and another one went back outside. One reindeer tossed several articles of clothing towards them, and another found a knife.

"Press the clothes against the dog's wound," Ávgos said to Shaun, picking up the knife.

Shaun balled up a tunic and pressed against Child of Light's side. He couldn't tell if she was still breathing. Ávgos cut away Kuu's tunic, slicing it open down the center; the thin undertunic was drenched with blood. Kuu had not responded at all, her breathing now raspy and shallow. The bracelet on her wrist was glowing blue.

Two Menninkäinen rushed into the tent. "We were told to tend to the wounded," said one. "We have—"

Both Menninkäinen froze as they saw Kuu. Ávgos had cut

off the undertunic, and the wad of clothing he had pressed between Kuu's breasts was already turning red. The sharp smell of blood was filling the tent, and Shaun felt lightheaded.

"The Queen needs you," said one of the reindeer gently. "You are shamans skilled in healing?"

Both men nodded, and then knelt down beside Ávgos. Shaun moved back and handed his work off to one of the Menninkäinen. One of them had a satchel slung over his shoulder, and he slid it off and began pulling out bundles of herbs and small carved stones. A reindeer came into the tent with three water skins hanging from its antlers. It would have looked almost comical if the situation wasn't so serious.

"I have water," said the reindeer, lowering its head and depositing the skins beside Ávgos.

Shaun backed towards the tent entrance. There was nothing more he could do here—Ávgos and the shamans knew more about treating wounds than he did. There wasn't much he could do outside, either, though—he wasn't a soldier, and his whole body felt numb from fighting. But he couldn't just sit here and watch Kuu die.

Could she die? She'd said she was immortal, but could even her magic overcome a bullet in the heart? Anger swelled up.

"I'm going back out to fight," he said. "Ávgos, you've got this?"

The other man glanced over his shoulder at him and gave a tight nod.

Back outside, the noise of battle echoed from the other side of the ridge. Shaun saw a small contingent of Menninkäinen on horseback galloping away through the forest. Briefly he wondered why they were fleeing the battle, until he remembered about the Näkki that had infiltrated Pohjola that were coming up from the south. Anger surged through him again, and he pulled his sword out as he clambered up the snowy ridge.

He paused briefly at the top of the ridge to catch his breath. The melee of battle spread out before him, on the snowy shore and all across the lake. Menninkäinen and reindeer still fought valiantly, but for every Ice-Dark monster that fell into the snow, three more were on the lake behind it. Shaun could see the cannons clearly now—iron behemoths on wheeled metal platforms, advancing slowly and steadily like tanks. The blue light beneath the ice had faded and the thawed patch in the center of the lake was frozen again.

He glanced up at the sky. Tonight's aurora was an unusually impressive display of both warm and cool colors, swirling brightly through the thin clouds. He wished he could stop this hideous battle so he could just watch the Lights. Drawing a deep breath, he slid down the snow of the ridge, and charged towards the fray.

And then skidded to a stop as a brilliant green streak flashed in front of him. Like a long celestial wave, green aurora light swept down in front of him, making the air crackle and his entire body tingle. Earth-walking Lights.

The sword vibrated in his hand with the energy. All around him, the battle paused as ribbons of colored light danced across the landscape. The air hummed audibly, and the analytical part of Shaun's mind told him that with this much electromagnetic energy so close, they should all be dead.

A yell like a cheer rose, and Shaun looked over to see a tendril of golden light curling back up into the sky, leaving behind three reindeer where there had been none. A dark-colored reindeer with wide-sweeping antlers reared up and tossed his head.

"My lord Kied-Kie-Jubmel!" he shouted. It was Night-Fire Desolation. "We have come to drive this poison from our land! For Pohjola and Queen Kuu!"

Every place where the Dancing Lights touched, reindeer appeared in their wake. The reindeer lit into the Ice-Dark army, and every moment dozens more joined them as the Dancing Lights continued to swirl and sweep the snow like a living thing. The Gentle Beasts of Pohjola were returning, and they were ready for war.

Lyylia peered down the hill. The low pass between the hills was like a black sea. From her vantage point, it looked like the entire pass was filled with Näkki as they continued to pour out across the lake.

"Look!" exclaimed Eider. "The Lights are dancing on the earth!"

Tendrils of colored light swept down from the sky, weaving and curling along the Pohjola side of the lake. Ground level aurora, Shaun had called it, when they had witnessed the phenomenon shortly after arriving in Pohjola. But this display was even more intense: every color of the spectrum, and the webs of light kept rising and falling and rising again like a choreographed dance. It was breathtaking.

Abruptly, Lyylia realized that the battle had changed. The sea of Näkki on the Ice-Dark shore had stopped advancing out across the lake. The faint din of shouts and fighting that had been floating periodically up on the wind was now suddenly louder. And most of the cannons had stopped firing.

"Come on," said Lyylia, standing up. "This might be our chance."

She climbed onto Forest Wanderer's back, and Maden and Eider mounted their reindeer. Forest Wanderer and Silence of the Sky led the way down the hill, and the rest of the herd followed. A cascade of loose rocks preceded them down the hill, but they were still too far away for any of Ice-Dark's army to notice.

"Are they retreating?" Maden said.

The Ice-Dark army was definitely scattering. The thick ranks along the shore were thinning and spreading back up through the pass. Lyylia couldn't tell what was happening out on the lake. The earth-walking Lights seemed to have stopped.

"If we do not go now, we will be overrun by the retreating Näkki," Silence of the Sky said. "If you have weapons, prepare them. We will run through the field of battle."

Eider handed his sword to Maden, then pulled his bow off his back. Lyylia pulled out the knife that Eider had given her, and clutched at Forest Wanderer's fur with her left hand. She wasn't sure how effective she could be at fighting Näkki with a small dagger from the back of a running reindeer. She wished she had her gun.

As the reindeer broke into a gallop, Lyylia kept her focus on the white bank across the lake. The lower they descended down the slope towards the shore, the farther away it seemed. Over the pounding of hooves and the distant shrieks of Näkki, she heard a strange trumpeting roar that came rolling down from above like thunder.

She looked up and saw a white horse, surrounded by a cloud of fire, streaking by overhead. He roared again as he wheeled around like some monstrous bird of prey.

"Hiisi-Hiisi!" she shouted, though she doubted if Forest Wanderer could hear her. "Faster!"

The reindeer's gallop quickened, and it was all Lyylia could do to hold on as he careened through a crowd of Näkki and hiisi, swinging his head wildly to clear a path. Lyylia slashed at the rump of a black horse, but just hit air.

Hiisi-Hiisi's roar thundered down from above, and a ball of flame shot down and blasted the ice mere meters away. Lyylia felt the flash of heat as Forest Wanderer galloped past. Näkki screams came at her from all directions, and she felt the dagger slip from her hand as dizziness washed over her. Clutching the reindeer's fur with both hands, she lay down on his back to keep from falling off.

Suddenly there were two reindeer running beside Forest Wanderer, and more moved in to surround their group. A crowd of Gentle Beasts ran with them across the ice, and Lyylia lifted her head to see the Pohjola shore in detail. Näkki and hiisi streaked past them, going the opposite direction, with Menninkäinen and reindeer and dogs in pursuit. The Ice-Dark army was in retreat.

Forest Wanderer slowed as his hooves left the ice and hit the snow on Pohjola's shore. The group kept going, still surrounded by their guardian Gentle Beasts, through the remains of the battle until they came to the base of a low ridge.

Lyylia released her grip and slid off the reindeer, letting herself tumble into the snow. She never thought she'd be this happy to see snow, or a strange magical land that wasn't her home.

Eider landed in the snow beside her, then righted himself and reached down to help her up.

"My God, I can't believe we made it," Maden said, dismounting from Silence of the Sky.

Lyylia looked around. The chaos of battle was happening far out on the lake, with the Näkki and hiisi fleeing and a herd of reindeer in pursuit. A cloud of flame and smoke still circled in the sky, but was growing smaller as Hiisi-Hiisi flew back to his land.

One cannon lay half submerged in the ice, but the others were rolling back across the lake. The Ice-Dark shore was shrouded in darkness. The black starry sky and the rocky hills where they had just come from were lost in shadow, as if they had passed through an invisible curtain that spanned the lake. On this side of the lake, though, far too many Menninkäinen lay motionless in the snow and scattered across the ice, some reindeer and dogs among them.

"Lyylia!"

She turned her head at the shout, and saw Shaun running towards her. He dropped his sword in the snow and grabbed her in a ferocious hug, lifting her off the ground. She clutched him and put her face in his shoulder, surprised at the tumble of emotions going through her. She'd worked so hard not to think about him, or Teija, or anyone—only focusing on getting herself and Maðen out of Ice-Dark. But now...a sudden swell of relief and happiness went through her and tears pricked her eyes. She wanted to ask him if Teija was all right, or tell him that she'd missed him, but no words would come.

Shaun's hold lessened enough for her to finally pull back and look at him. His hair was matted and his face flushed, and there was a streak of blood across his temple. She probably didn't look any better.

"You are hurt?" she finally managed to ask.

"I'm fine," he said with a grin. "I'm better than fine. I knew you had to be alive." He pulled her closer again.

"So...we won?" Lyylia asked when Shaun released her again.

"I guess so," he said, looking around. "It was the reindeer. Hundreds of them, coming down from the Dancing Lights. They just kept appearing and tore into the Ice-Dark army. The

Näkki didn't know what to do. It was amazing."

"We saw the earth-walking Lights across the lake," Lyylia told him. She then quickly translated for Mađen what Shaun had just said.

"My lord," Silence of the Sky said, lowering his head at a large reindeer approaching them. "We have fulfilled our mission."

Kied-Kie-Jubmel came up to them. "Mađen and Lyylia, we rejoice that you have returned. Silence of the Sky, Forest Wanderer, Eider, this deed you have done is worthy of more honor than I know how to put into words. This is a great day for the songs—the battle is won, and the Kalevalans have returned."

Eider bowed low, and the two reindeer lowered their heads.

"The time for celebration will come soon. But for now, we must heal our wounded and make sure that Pohjola is cleansed of all creatures of Ice-Dark. If you will excuse me, Kalevalans." Kied-Kie-Jubmel walked back towards the lake, calling out orders. "Make sure the area is secure! Leave no hiisi or Näkki alive. Spread out and search—we cannot permit a single creature of Ice-Dark to remain! Tend to the wounded!"

Lyylia looked around. "Where is Ávgos?"

"He's probably still with Kuu. She's—" Shaun cut himself off.

Lyylia raised her eyebrows at Shaun's worried expression. "What happened?"

He didn't answer right away. "Hiisi-Hiisi took your gun," he said finally.

"I know." But how did Shaun know that?

"And he…" Shaun hesitated. "He shot Kuu."

"*What?*"

"Lyylia, what's going on?" Mađen asked with a frown.

She translated what Shaun had just said.

Maden swore in Sami. "It's my fault," he then said in Finnish. "I shouldn't have told him that I gave you the gun."

"He would have killed us," she said. "It's not your fault, Maden." No, it was her fault. It was her weapon. And Hiisi-Hiisi had figured out how to use the gun, but Kuu had never even had the chance to learn, because Lyylia had never explained it to her.

"Come on," Shaun then said. "Let's get you—both of you—back to the tents. Are either of you hurt?"

Lyylia looked over at Maden. He was moving amongst his herd of reindeer, and talking with Silence of the Sky. "No, we're not hurt."

"I haven't seen Boots in a while," Shaun said quietly. "I hope…" He didn't finish the sentence, and then his arm tightened around her. "Come on, Lyylia. Let's get you to a tent where you can rest and get something to eat."

Lyylia wanted to stay and help. Eider had joined the other Menninkäinen who were tending to the fallen. She knew what it was like to have a comrade-in-arms go down. These Menninkäinen didn't even have the benefit of psychological training like she'd had. But she let Shaun lead her up over the snowy ridge and towards an encampment at the edge of the trees.

Many of the tents were already full. Menninkäinen scurried from tent to tent, asking about bandages and healing moss. Still more wounded were coming towards the camp, carried by their fellows or draped on the backs of reindeer. Many of the reindeer were limping or sporting bloody gashes. Lyylia ached to see these peaceful, happy people brought down by the crush of war. They had won this battle, but at what cost?

Lyylia wanted to ask Shaun more about what had happened

to Kuu, but he set her down on a fur beside a campfire, and thrust a water skin at her.

"Drink this. I'll see if I can find you some food. Are you sure you're not injured?"

She gratefully took several swallows of water, and shook her head. "I'm not hurt. But you—your head."

"I'll be okay."

She tugged on his arm. "Sit. Let me see."

He sighed and sat down on the fur next to her. She dabbed some water on the back of her coat sleeve and wiped it across his temple. "A cut, not so deep," she said. "You need a bandage so you can press and stop the bleeding."

"I'll be fine. Save the bandages for the ones who really need them."

Lyylia took another swallow of water, then handed him the water skin. He started to shake his head, but then took it from her and drank.

"I watched her get shot," Shaun said after a moment. "It was happening right in front of me, but I couldn't get to her in time."

Lyylia had seen people shot. And more than once, she'd been the one pulling the trigger. It never got easier. She slipped her arm through his and leaned her head on his shoulder.

"I know she's immortal," Shaun continued. "But Hiisi-Hiisi shot her at point-blank range, right in the middle of her chest."

"*Perkele,*" Lyylia muttered, and squeezed his arm. She felt cold—a cold deeper than the chill of the air and her still slightly damp underclothes. If she sat here much longer, exhaustion and despair would take over.

She released his arm and stood up, her muscles already aching and stiff. "Come," she said. "Let's help the others."

Shaun looked up at her. She saw the haunted expression in

his eyes, but then he shook it off and scrambled up. "You're right. We can't just sit here while everyone else tends to the wounded." He grabbed her hand, and together they headed back towards the ridge.

Lyylia had no idea how long she wandered across the snow and the frozen lake, checking bodies for breathing or a pulse, and calling to Shaun or Maden when she found someone still alive. Cold and exhaustion pulled at her more heavily, and she found herself stumbling, and struggling to stand back up each time she knelt down. Shaun came over and put his arm around her again.

"You need a break. Let the others keep working for a while. You sure you're not hurt?"

Lyylia shook her head as they walked back towards the ridge. Just then there was a shout from the top of the ridge, and she looked up to see Ávgos hurrying towards them. Maden jogged towards him, and the two men embraced.

"Lyylia! I'm so glad to see both of you!" Ávgos said in Finnish when they got closer. "We were so worried; we had no idea if... So Eider and the reindeer found you?"

"They did," Lyylia said. "Maden and I can tell you all about it, but first—what about Queen Kuu? Shaun told us what happened."

Shaun was looking back and forth between them, probably wanting a translation, but Ávgos continued in Finnish for Maden's benefit.

"I don't know," he said solemnly. "The bullet was in deep, and I didn't have any forceps or tweezers or anything. I'd slowed the bleeding a bit and the two healers and I were going to try to stitch the wound closed, when she started...glowing. Her bracelet had been glowing blue, but then the light spread and surrounded her whole body. The reindeer said it was Dream healing her. We backed off, but then the light got so bright we had to leave the tent." He looked back over his shoulder, though the tents were hidden behind the ridge. Then he looked back at Shaun and repeated himself in English.

"I know you did everything you could, Ávgos," Shaun said. "I'm going to take Lyylia back to the tents to rest and eat—she looks like she's about to collapse."

Lyylia wanted to protest, but at this point she felt like she was about to collapse. She'd lost track of how long it had been since she'd slept or eaten anything.

"Are you injured?" Ávgos asked her in Finnish, and then looked at his cousin. "What about you, Maðen?"

"We're not injured," Maðen said. "But Lyylia had a close call with hypothermia a few hours ago. We were wet, and even though there's no snow in Ice-Dark, it was still chilly."

"What's he saying?" Shaun asked.

"I'm fine," Lyylia groused in English, as Ávgos translated what Maðen had said.

"Hypothermia?" Shaun exclaimed in alarm. "Why didn't you say something? I wondered why you were wearing Maðen's coat. Come on—you're going to get warmed up and have some food."

Lyylia was determined to keep pace with him as he hustled her up and over the snowy ridge; she didn't want him carrying her. Shaun sat her down at the nearest campfire; a cooking pot hung over the fire.

"That's barley stew with healing moss in it," said a Menninkäinen who was just going into the tent, rolls of blankets under his arm.

"Perfect," Shaun said, spooning some into a wooden mug and handing it to Lyylia.

She gratefully sipped at the warm thick stew. "You should

eat, too, Shaun," she said.

"I will in a minute."

A clamor and commotion arose away to their right, and Shaun stood up to look.

"What is it?" Lyylia asked, setting down her mug and struggling up.

"I don't know. There's a whole crowd of reindeer, and—"

"All hail the Queen!" bellowed a voice. It sounded like Kied-Kie-Jubmel. "Praise be to Dream! All hail Queen Kuu!"

Shaun took Lyylia's arm, and they hurried over to the gathering crowd.

Kuu stood at the center of the crowd. Her blonde hair was disheveled and escaping its braid, and she wore a loose brown tunic and no coat. But she was smiling, and very much alive.

The crowd of adoring Menninkäinen and bowing reindeer parted for Lyylia and Shaun as they approached, and for Ávgos and Mađen as they arrived from a different direction.

"Lyylia, Mađen—praise be to Dream that you are returned to us!" Kuu came forward and embraced Mađen and then Lyylia.

"Your Highness," Lyylia said. "Thank you for sending Eider and the others to find us. We all made it back safely, along with fifteen reindeer from Kalevala."

Kuu smiled and her silver eyes sparkled. "A tale indeed you all will have to tell." Then she turned to Shaun and embraced him. "They told me what you did, that you went out onto the ice to rescue me."

"I'm just glad to see you recovered, Your Majesty," he said, returning her hug.

Kuu smiled, then turned to Ávgos and embraced him. "And I have you to thank, as well, for working to heal me."

"I wish I could have done more, Your Highness."

"Though Dream has restored me, I appreciate your desire to help and your healing hands. I cannot be killed by any weapon or magic, and Hiisi-Hiisi knows this. He sought to confound my army by removing my leadership, but I see that even that tactic failed him. Ice-Dark was no match for our determination, the strength of Menninkäinen and Gentle Beasts, or the resourcefulness of Kalevalans."

Kuu looked up at the Dancing Lights overhead, then smiled again as she spread her arms and addressed the crowd. "The battle has been won, but there is still much work to be done. Together, we will make Pohjola whole once again."

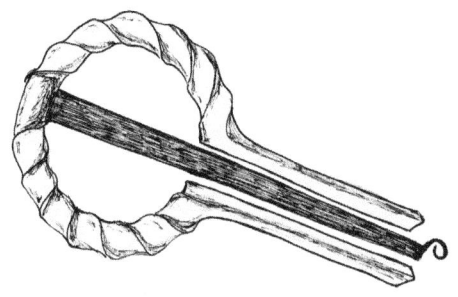

CHAPTER 9: SUOMI

For the past three days, Teija had found herself suddenly very busy. Gray had received word from the Queen that the battle was over, Ice-Dark had retreated, and Lyylia and Maden had been rescued. Teija had spent most of that first night out on the cold high turret, crying tears of relief and watching the graphs on Shaun's aurora computer.

Then the first of the wounded arrived at the castle. Most of the wounded were returning to their home villages, Gray said, but those who lived south of the Dancing Ground Island and had a journey of many days were sent to Kuu's castle since it was closer and had more resources.

Teija had no nursing experience, but she eagerly helped as well as she could by changing bandages, cleaning wounds, and feeding. Gray took charge by organizing most of the female castle workers into shifts, and turning several large open rooms into hospital wards of sorts, with blankets and bedding in rows on the floor. It was ghastly to see so many injured, traumatized Menninkäinen, and they all were pathetically grateful whenever Teija changed a bandage or brought a bowl of porridge.

On the third day, Queen Kuu arrived on horseback, followed a few hours later by a caravan bringing more

Menninkäinen, along with Lyylia, Shaun, Maðen, and Ávgos. And Eider. Teija shed more tears as she greeted them all, and was relieved to find that none of them were severely injured. She was told that Boots had been wounded and had gone back to his village to recuperate.

And now they were all eating dinner, clean and safe and together again. As they ate, Lyylia, Maðen, and Eider told their stories of everything that had happened in Ice-Dark. The two reindeer who had gone with Eider were also in the room, along with Kied-Kie-Jubmel.

The three reindeer had been given large bowls of moss, herbs, and other greenery, and were standing at the table to eat. Teija found that she wasn't the least bit bothered by reindeer eating off the table—at this point, it seemed almost normal, and oddly comforting. The report of what had happened to Lyylia and Maðen in Ice-Dark, however, was anything but. Equally horrifying was hearing that Hiisi-Hiisi had shot Kuu with Lyylia's gun. Kuu's magical immortality had saved her, but sadly her dog Child of Light had not survived.

"Eider, Silence of the Sky, and Forest Wanderer, you have the thanks of all of Pohjola for your brave deeds," Kuu said when the others had finished their tale. "And because you brought Maðen and Lyylia safely back to us, we also now know more than we have ever known about Ice-Dark." Kuu paused, and looked at Kied-Kie-Jubmel, who was standing beside her at the head of the table. "What concerns me the most out of everything you have told us is Kipu-Tyttö."

Teija blinked in surprise at that. She'd been alarmed by the stories of cannons and volcanoes and the descriptions of Hiisi-Hiisi himself; one random Näkki who supposedly hated Hiisi-Hiisi seemed unimportant.

"Vellamo told us that Kipu-Tyttö has challenged Hiisi-

Hiisi before," Lyylia said. "And she seemed convinced that a war was coming between the two factions of Näkki who were loyal to each. Iku-Turso warned us about Kipu-Tyttö, as well, but there's no guarantee that either one was telling the truth."

"I believe they both spoke the truth," Kuu said solemnly, exchanging another look with Kied-Kie-Jubmel. "We have met Kipu-Tyttö before."

Everyone stared at her.

"We had a great battle with Ice-Dark, over five hundred seasons ago," Kied-Kie-Jubmel said. "You have heard the tale?" Everyone nodded.

"Hiisi-Hiisi had requested that we meet on the ice of the Dark Water Lake, to learn more about one another," the reindeer continued. "And then when his army attacked us, he accused Pohjola of instigating the battle. But I saw what happened. A line of Gentle Beasts stood face to face with a line of Näkki, but none moved while Kuu and Hiisi-Hiisi spoke. But then suddenly a small patch of ice gave way beneath the front hooves of a Gentle Beast at the end of the line; he fell forwards, and his antlers struck the Näkki in front of him. The Näkki gave a great cry, calling treachery, and Ice-Dark attacked.

"As the battle progressed, the ice was broken in many places, and Näkki thawed much of the lake, to put the Pohjola army at a disadvantage. Hiisi-Hiisi had no fire-mouths then, so he did not need the ice to remain solid. However, the ice was thick and firm across the lake before the battle began, except for that one small space beneath the hooves of one Gentle Beast. That Näkki had thawed that place intentionally, to give the Ice-Dark army a reason to attack us."

Kuu picked up the story when Kied-Kie-Jubmel paused. "That Näkki was Kipu-Tyttö. She was a commander in Hiisi-Hiisi's army, directing much of the battle. And she loudly proclaimed her name throughout the battle, taunting us with threats of her own might and the might of Ice-Dark. After the battle was over and we were tending to our wounded and dead, I thought no more of her. Hiisi-Hiisi had made himself my enemy, and to me Kipu-Tyttö was nothing more than one of his vicious servants. But it would seem that she is more than that."

"A potential civil war in Ice-Dark," Kied-Kie-Jubmel rumbled thoughtfully. "This could be safety for us, if Hiisi-Hiisi's eyes are turned towards his own land. Or, it could be deeper danger for us—war, like poison in a river, can spread quickly and reach wide."

"So Näkki live at least five hundred years?" Lyylia asked.

"I confess I do not know," Kuu said. "But it would seem so. Or, at least, Kipu-Tyttö does."

There was an uncomfortable silence. Teija shivered in spite of herself, and she felt Eider touch her hand under the table.

"I will meditate with Dream about what you have told me," Kuu said after a moment. "But in the meantime, we have much work to do. I will be leaving tomorrow, after I have finished tending to the wounded here in the castle. I must visit as many villages as I can, to help heal the wounded and preside over burials of the dead." She paused, and seemed to draw a breath. Teija could only imagine how painful it must be to have to attend so many funerals.

"Kied-Kie-Jubmel will also be away from the castle," Kuu resumed. "He will be organizing Gentle Beasts all across Pohjola to make sure that our waterways are clear of Näkki. The small contingent of Näkki that came up on our southern flank during the battle has been dealt with, but we need to be sure that not a single creature of Ice-Dark remains in our land. You are all welcome to remain here—you will be well cared for, and Gray will remain here should you need to contact me with the moon mirror."

Across the table, Teija noticed Ávgos shifting in his seat. "Your Highness?" he said. "I know you have duties elsewhere, and the lake is frozen, but...we still need to get home."

Home. Teija realized with some surprise that she hadn't thought about home in a while. She still missed her mother and her friend Johanna, of course. But for a couple of weeks now, the focus had been evading Näkki and worrying about rescuing Lyylia and Maden. She hadn't spared any mental energy to think about her life or loved ones back in Finland.

Kuu looked at Ávgos and her expression softened. "I had not forgotten. Once we can be assured that all of Pohjola—as well as the lake—is clean and safe, we shall begin in earnest to search for the gateway. Hiisi-Hiisi found it, so we can, as well."

"I have some ideas about that," Shaun spoke up. "I might be able to adjust my aurora computer—my Light-listener—to help search for the portal. But I, uh, might need to borrow some tools and other supplies, if you have them, Your Highness."

"Of course," said Kuu. "Come to the Moon Tower, Shaun, when we have finished here, and tell me what you might need. I will give you what I can before I leave in the morning."

He smiled. "Thank you."

"Now, it grows late and we are all weary, so I will bid all of you a good night." Kuu pushed her chair back and stood up, and everyone got up from the benches.

Kuu lingered a moment to speak quietly to Kied-Kie-Jubmel, and Teija followed the others towards the door. In the pocket of her breeches, she felt the shape of the mouth harp shifting around against her leg. She'd kept the mouth harp with her night and day since she'd driven that Näkki from the Moon Tower, but now that Kuu was back, she should probably return it to her.

Kied-Kie-Jubmel walked past her as she paused and turned back around. Kuu was still standing at the head of the table, finishing off the drink in her goblet.

"Um, Your Highness?" Teija began. "I need to return this to you." She pulled the mouth harp out of her pocket, and then told Kuu about facing off with the escaped Näkki prisoner in the Moon Tower. "I found it in a wooden chest. I know I shouldn't have been going through your stuff, but I was looking for a weapon."

Kuu smiled. "That was very brave, Teija, and very wise. Silver can be as effective against Näkki as swords and arrows, and it would seem music may be, as well. And both are much more suited to your skill."

A strange little flutter of pride went through her, and she smiled. "There was also a little bag of crystals in the chest, and I threw those at the Näkki, too. I put them all back in the chest. At least, I tried—I hope I got them all."

"The crystals were another wise choice to use against the Näkki," Kuu said. "Although I would not recommend it as the most ideal one if other options are available. Those are moon mirror crystals, and they possess a rare magic."

"I'll have to remember that."

Kuu smiled again. "In your world, Teija, are you a 'detective' like your sister, or a 'scientist' like Shaun?"

"Neither one. I'm a software engineer."

Kuu raised her eyebrows.

"It would take too long to explain, Your Highness. It's kind of a boring job, really." Proof-reading lines of code looking for errors and typos would seem even more boring after all of this.

"Well, in this world, you show much aptitude for music

and magic."

She never would have thought of that. Too bad those weren't viable career options on Earth—especially the magic one. Teija smiled again, but a memory suddenly sprang to her mind, of the strange door she'd found at the end of the Halls of Time. Why had she remembered that at this particular moment?

"Was there something else you wished to talk to me about?" Kuu asked kindly. It was almost as if Kuu could read her mind.

"Um," Teija said, feeling suddenly awkward. Why did she feel like this was important to tell Kuu? She forced herself to look Kuu in the face, and tried not to feel completely unnerved by her bright silver eyes. "I'm not sure why I remembered this just now, but a few days ago, before everyone left for the battle at the lake, I was in the Halls of Time looking at the paintings, and...I found a door."

For the first time, Kuu's face turned grave. "A door?"

"Behind the bear skin, at the end of the hall."

"Did you open the door?"

"No. I...well, the latch wouldn't move, and then I thought I should probably just leave it alone."

Kuu nodded. "Another wise choice."

"I'm sorry, Your Highness." Teija swallowed and forced herself not to look at the floor.

Kuu did not look angry, but her pensive expression was somehow just as disturbing. "That door is not a secret," she said finally. "If I wished that door hidden from all eyes, I would have disguised it with more than a bear pelt. But do not try to open it."

Teija shook her head vigorously. "I won't." She wanted to ask where the door led, why it was such a secret-but-not-secret. But clearly it was something that bothered Kuu.

Kuu's serious face softened. "You wish to know what is

behind the door."

Teija shook her head again. "It's none of my business, Your Highness."

Kuu gave a mild smile. "That is true. There is much I could tell you, but now is not the time for such tales." Her face grew serious again. "What is behind that door is the beginning."

"The beginning? Of what?"

Kuu smiled again, in a cryptic sort of way, and her eyes sparkled brighter. "Good night, Teija, and sleep well tonight. You have earned it." She smiled, more kindly this time, and lifted the mouth harp. "May you dream of music and every pleasant thing." She touched Teija gently on the arm, and walked with her to the door.

Lyylia and Shaun were waiting in the hallway outside. Kuu said goodnight to Lyylia, and invited Shaun to go with her to the Moon Tower.

"What were you talking with Kuu about?" Lyylia asked as they headed down the hall. A castle guard stood at the intersection of corridors, waiting to escort them back to the sleeping chambers. That was good, because even after several days with nothing to do but wander the halls, Teija still hadn't learned her way around.

"I was returning a mouth harp to her," Teija said, feeling oddly reluctant to talk about the strange conversation regarding the door behind the bear pelt. "I'll tell you all about it tomorrow. I'm tired of thinking about danger and battles and Näkki right now."

"I know what you mean. I'd rather think about a hot bath and warm bed for the first time in ages."

Teija hugged her sister's arm. "I'm so glad you're safe."

Lyylia smiled at her. "Me, too."

Arm in arm, they walked the rest of the way to the sleeping

chambers in happy, contented silence.

Shaun stared at the graph spiking across his laptop screen. After almost two weeks of scanning—and nearly three weeks of tinkering with his computer, microphones and receivers, and software programs—he had found the portal.

The only sure-fire way to test it was to try going through it. But all of his tests and scans showed positive. He could go down in history as the first scientist to not only locate and track a stable wormhole, but to travel through it. Assuming, of course, that the scientific community back home believed him. And assuming they all got back to Finland in one piece in the first place.

His computer equipment sat on a sled in the middle of the Dark Water Lake. A few feet away was another sled, with a moon mirror and several stones that Shaun had rigged up with the help of the Gentle Beasts. Kuu had put Night-Fire Desolation in charge of the gateway search, which Shaun had initially been concerned about. Night-Fire Desolation had helped win the battle with Ice-Dark by bringing the rest of the reindeer down from the Lights, but Shaun wasn't sure how reliable he'd be in searching for a magical wormhole. Kuu's reasoning was that Night-Fire knew what the portal felt like because he'd traveled through it to Earth and back again—except that had happened five hundred years ago, and Night-Fire hated all things related to Earth and humans. But thankfully Night-Fire had mostly stayed out of Shaun's way and ignored him.

Now Shaun looked up from his computer screen and over at the other sled nearby. A reindeer named Snow on the River had been helping him the most, as they methodically dragged the sleds around the ice of the lake, scanning.

Snow on the River was staring down at his sled, and raised his head to look at Shaun. "The moon mirror has begun to hum," the reindeer reported. "At the exact same pitch as the other times we believe we caught the gateway."

After glancing at his computer screen one more time, Shaun scrambled up from the fur he was sitting on and went over to the other sled. The moon mirror, positioned in the center of the sled surrounded by several wire-wrapped stones, was emitting a very faint humming sound. Tiny ripples vibrated across the surface of the water in the mirror. One of the many bizarre but fascinating properties of the moon mirror was that it took water about four times as long to freeze when in the silver dish than it would anywhere else.

Shaun grinned. "We did it, Snow on the River. We found it! And I've got the frequency logged on my computer now, so even if we lose the gateway again, we should be able to find it pretty quickly."

"*You* found it, Light-Whisperer," the reindeer answered. "We could not have done this without you."

Light-Whisperer. Night-Fire Desolation had called him that the first day they came out to the lake, but with his pinned-back ears and sarcastic tone of voice, Shaun assumed he'd meant it as an insult. However, the term was quickly adopted by all the other reindeer and Menninkäinen at the camp with them, and now it seemed to be Shaun's title. He liked it, though. Since he hadn't stayed in school long enough to get a Ph.D. and become a doctor, "Light-Whisperer" was the next best thing.

"I will inform Night-Fire Desolation," Snow on the River

then said. "The Queen should be notified at once."

The reindeer left Shaun with the sleds and headed back across the ice towards the shore. A small camp had been set up on the shore, with two other reindeer and three Menninkäinen to help them. After two fresh snowfalls, all traces of the battle with Ice-Dark had been obliterated from the area.

After about twenty minutes, there was a flash of green light on the shore. Squinting, Shaun could make out Kuu and Kied-Kie-Jubmel standing where the light had just flashed. A vanishing stone, a magical teleportation talisman—the same thing that the Näkki had used to kidnap Lyylia and Mađen. It felt like forever ago.

Kuu headed out onto the lake, followed by all of the reindeer and Menninkäinen. "You have found the gateway?" she asked as she approached.

"We believe so, Your Highness." Shaun glanced down at his computer screen—the graph lines were steady. "It's about seven meters below us—that's about the distance from me to that skerry over there." He pointed.

"Impressive indeed are the skills of Kalevalan shamans," said Kied-Kie-Jubmel, inclining his head at Shaun. "We searched for many seasons—and Kuu for longer than that—and you have found it in mere days."

"Well, we've learned that the gateway moves," Shaun said humbly. "We thought we had it a couple of times, but then it disappeared. So far, at least, we haven't been able to determine if there's a pattern to the locations or the interval of time between moves."

"I told you that the gateway moves," put in Night-Fire Desolation. "When I was trapped in Kalevala and found it again by chance, it was in a different place from where I had come through before."

Shaun nodded at him, then looked back at Kuu. "Now that we know the frequency of the gateway, if it moves again, we should be able to find it again pretty easily."

"Please, tell us how you have done this," Kuu said. She looked down at the laptop and receivers sitting on the sled. "I wish to know every detail."

"The talismans of Ice-Dark were the key, Your Highness," Snow on the River said.

Night-Fire Desolation snorted, but Shaun ignored him. "He's right, Your Highness." He walked over to the other sled and picked up one of the stones. "It was a combination of magic and science that enabled us to find it. This is one of the lodestones that the hiisi were wearing around their necks when they first captured us and brought us through the gateway. The stone is magnetic, but after I studied it a bit more, I realized it's also laced with copper ore." He brought it over and showed Kuu where he'd chipped away a tiny piece of the stone to reveal a patch of rough green color. "Copper is a great conductor of electricity.

"Electricity is a type of energy, or force," he hurried to add, before Kuu could ask what it meant. He'd thought a lot over the past couple of weeks of how he could explain his scientific process, and the general concepts of physics and electromagnetism, in a way that Kuu might understand. "The gateway emits energy that we can't see. Some electromagnetic energy we can see, like visible light, but the gateway emits a very specific frequency that we can't see."

Shaun hefted the Ice-Dark lodestone in his hand. "I believe that the hiisi could track the gateway with these stones because when the stones get close to the gateway underwater, they receive an electrical charge—that is, the stones warm up and begin to vibrate. We tested it a couple of days ago, the first time we thought we caught the gateway's signature; the men chopped a hole in the ice, and I lowered one of these stones into the water. My computer picked up a mild electrical charge on the stone when we brought it back up."

"The Ice-Dark stones also have a magic spell upon them," Night-Fire Desolation put in. "The scent of magic still lingers. You yourself said as much, Highness, when we were in the Moon Tower preparing for this expedition."

Kuu nodded. "Yes, I could tell the stones had a mild enchantment upon them. Perhaps to make them more sensitive to this energy from the gateway?" She looked at Shaun.

"It's possible," he said. At this point, he was beginning to wonder if magic—which in this world was obviously very real—was really just a form of quantum physics that humans had yet to figure out. "At any rate, I'd suspected that electromagnetism had something to do with it, which is why I asked you for all these metal ores and wires." He gestured down at the sled; besides the lodestones, the rest of the rocks were chunks of silver and iron ores, with copper wires wrapped around them.

Shaun knelt down to put the lodestone back. "Since we weren't going to swim around in freezing water waiting for a rock to vibrate, that's why I asked for a moon mirror to go with these stones. The moon mirror is acting like a receiver and translator—it displays the electromagnetic frequency that the rocks are responding to. My computer does the same thing—it receives information from those black wires and boxes, and displays it in a way that I can understand. And see—the moon mirror is vibrating."

Kuu knelt down on the other side of the sled and peered at the silver dish. Kied-Kie-Jubmel moved closer, as well, and hovered his nose a few inches from the moon mirror.

"It is humming," he said. "Nothing like the sound it

makes when contacting another mirror. I have never heard such a sound."

Kuu held her hand above the dish. "I feel the vibration," she said. "The 'energy,' as you called it." She looked at Shaun with shining eyes. "I wish to know more about this 'electricity,' and 'science.'"

Shaun grinned. "I'd be happy to teach you everything I know, Your Highness. But maybe right now isn't the best time."

Kuu nodded at him as she stood back up. "Now is the time for you to return to my castle, to rest after your work, and to tell your fellow Kalevalans of your discovery. And to make a decision."

Shaun knew what she meant. Now that they'd officially found the portal, they had to decide whether to brave the ice and risk going back now, or stay in Pohjola for another five or six months until the spring thaw.

"I'll bring my computer with me," he said. "So that I can show them everything. Now that we know how to find the gateway, we should be able to locate it any time we want."

"Very good," Kuu said. "When you are ready, Shaun, meet us back on the shore. Kied-Kie-Jubmel and I brought another vanishing stone with us, so we can return directly to the castle."

Shaun nodded at her. As she and the others turned to head back across the lake, he knelt down and began disconnecting the receivers from the laptop. He'd actually done it—he'd found the wormhole with nothing more than wires, rocks, a computer designed to read the aurora, and a magic silver dish. A surprising tumble of emotions went through him as he closed the laptop.

He felt elated that he'd achieved a highly improbable scientific breakthrough, stunned that he'd done so with such a primitive assortment of tools—and now apprehension wormed its way into his chest. What if he'd miscalculated? What if they couldn't get home after all?

What if they *could* get home?

He missed Earth, of course, but he didn't feel quite ready to leave just yet. Making sure all of the wires and receivers were secure on the sled, he set off towards the shore, dragging it behind him. He left the sled with the stones and moon mirror where it was; if the portal moved by the time they returned, that would be the clue. And if another storm came through, Snow on the River could move the sled or cover it up.

He glanced up at the wide expanse of sky, clear and bright and full of stars. It was early evening—the Dancing Lights would be beginning soon. He missed the sun, and the changing constellations of Earth's sky—but this sky had become familiar, too. At least he'd taken a lot of pictures.

Back on the shore, Kuu was waiting. Shaun went into his tent to pack up his computer and gather the rest of his belongings. He was accustomed to camping, and he'd enjoyed this time out in the wilderness, just running scans and experiments and logging data. But a warm bed and a hot bath would be nice, and he'd desperately missed Lyylia.

Ducking out of the tent, Shaun swung his backpack over his shoulder and went over to Kuu. She smiled at him.

"You are ready to tell the others the news?" she asked.

"I'm ready." He returned her smile. "Let's go."

Ávgos lowered his head against the wind as he and Maden rode on horseback along the winding snowy trail up the mountain. For the past three weeks they'd been staying in a small village not far from the base of the mountain where Kuu had her castle. That village was where most of the castle workers lived, they'd learned. Some of the castle workers had their own wing of living quarters and stayed there full time, but most of the workers who had families lived in their own homes at the base of the mountains.

That village also managed Kuu's horses during the summer months. There were several large fenced pastures, so it was the ideal place to contain all of their reindeer. Over the past three weeks, Menninkäinen and Gentle Beasts had brought Finnish reindeer to the castle, as they'd found them scattered all across Pohjola. Many had been taken up into the Dancing Lights while the reindeer spell had still been active, and a few were even still in their Menninkäinen changeling forms.

It had been several days without any more arrivals of reindeer, and Ávgos figured that they had all of the surviving animals at this point. Ninety-eight reindeer, out of the one hundred thirty that had originally been captured by the hiisi. That wasn't bad, all things considered. They'd be going home with more than two-thirds of the missing herd.

Home. They were really going home. Last night a Menninkäinen had come down from the castle to tell them that the Queen had just returned from the lake with Shaun, and that he'd found the gateway. So this morning after a quick breakfast and checking on the reindeer, he and Maðen followed their guide back up to the castle.

Ávgos hadn't ridden a horse in years, but he was grateful that he didn't have to walk for the long steep journey up the mountain path. When they arrived in the large stone courtyard, two stable workers took their horses, and the castle guard named Stone was waiting to escort them into the castle.

Lyylia, Shaun, and Teija were seated around a wooden table when Stone showed them into the room. Kuu sat at the head of the table, with Kied-Kie-Jubmel standing at her side. A fluffy white puppy came bouncing towards them as Ávgos and Maden seated themselves on the bench.

Ávgos smiled as he bent to rub the puppy on the head. Since Child of Light had died during the battle with Ice-Dark, Kuu had gotten herself a new dog.

"Bright Ice, come," Kuu said. The puppy perked up its ears, and went bouncing back to Kuu. "Stay on your blanket," she instructed it, pointing at a blanket on the floor behind her chair. The puppy obediently went to the blanket and set about making a nest for itself.

"Ávgos, Maden, welcome," she then said, looking at them and smiling. "I trust you and your reindeer have been faring well in the workers' village?"

"Very well, thank you, Your Highness," Ávgos said. "We've been very comfortable and well fed, and our reindeer are happy in your pastures."

"Good." She smiled again. "As my messenger told you, there is good news. Shaun has found the gateway to Kalevala."

Belatedly, Ávgos realized that Shaun had his laptop sitting open on the table in front of him.

"I knew you'd be able to rig up your computer and other gadgets to find it," Ávgos said to him, quirking a smile.

"With lots of time and trial and error," Shaun replied with a grin of his own. "And it was actually a moon mirror and the lodestones from Ice-Dark that did most of the work and gave me a template to work with." He then began to explain about searching for electromagnetic frequencies underwater, and turned his laptop around so they could all see the graphs on the screen.

The graphs didn't make much sense to Ávgos. He murmured a Finnish translation to Mađen, but once Shaun started using scientific words besides "electricity," "energy," and "magnets," Ávgos got a bit lost trying to translate the technobabble. He knew his cousin wasn't much for science and math anyway, so he figured that it didn't matter if his translations weren't exactly accurate.

"So we don't know where in Lake Inari we're going to come up?" Mađen asked, and Ávgos repeated the question in English.

Shaun shook his head. No translation needed for that one. So they might wind up seventy kilometers away from Inari village, at the eastern end of the lake near Norway or Russia.

"How big is the gateway?" Ávgos asked.

"I don't know," Shaun said. "Obviously it's big enough for humans and reindeer to pass through, but I don't know if we all have to go through single file or what." He looked at his laptop screen, and then shrugged. "I can pinpoint the exact location and depth of the gateway, but the electromagnetic resonance from the gateway doesn't really give me an indication of size."

"What if the gateway moves while we are traveling through it?" Lyylia asked.

That was a disturbing thought.

Shaun shrugged again, an apologetic expression on his face. "I'm afraid I have no idea."

There was silence for a moment.

"Whenever you decide to leave, I will do all I can to assist you and make your journey easier," Kuu said.

"We appreciate that, Highness," Lyylia said in Finnish. "Ávgos, I think it should be up to you and Mađen to make the decision, since they're your reindeer." She then repeated herself in English for Shaun.

Ávgos was ready to head for the lake this instant, but they needed to be practical about this. "The reindeer will be fine," he said at last. "They can swim, they can handle cold temperatures, and they're all strong and healthy now. Maden and I can manage the whole herd, especially if you three are able to help. The only question is the ice."

"I can clear the ice for you," said Kuu. "But only in Pohjola. I can send ice axes with you, to break through in Kalevala. I can also give you talismans to help you to breathe while under water."

"Thank you," Ávgos said to her. "In that case, I vote for going back now. The longer we wait, the thicker the ice will get."

"I agree," Maden added.

Lyylia translated what Ávgos had just said, and then said in English: "I say we go now."

Teija nodded in agreement, and then Shaun nodded, as well.

"Tomorrow, then," Lyylia said in Finnish, looking at Ávgos. "Would you and your reindeer be ready to leave for the lake tomorrow, or do you need more time?"

Ávgos felt a shudder of excitement. "We'll be ready tomorrow morning."

"Tomorrow it is," Kuu said. "Kied-Kie-Jubmel and I shall accompany you to the lake to see you home."

"Thank you, Your Highness," Ávgos said. He looked around the table at these people who had been complete strangers two months ago, and now he considered friends. It would be sad to part ways with them, and to say goodbye to Kuu and the Menninkäinen he'd gotten to know. But it was high time to see his wife and the rest of his family again, and to tell them of everything that had happened in Pohjola.

It was time to go home.

Lyylia stood in the Moon Tower surrounded by light. Even with the moon only a sliver of a crescent in the sky, and no Dancing Lights because it was still mid-afternoon, the glass walls and ceiling and all the reflective surfaces made the space stunningly bright.

Shaun had asked Kuu if he could see the Moon Tower one last time, and Lyylia had decided to go with them. She hadn't seen the Moon Tower since they'd first arrived at the castle and Kuu had transformed that Menninkäinen changeling back into a reindeer. So many even more incredible things had happened since then. As eager as Lyylia was to get back home, she found herself suddenly wishing that they could stay in the castle just one more day. She'd already been in the castle for over two weeks now since the battle, but now that Shaun was back from the lake...

Pushing those thoughts away, she turned her attention back to Kuu. The Queen was standing by the little table of ice in the center of the room. A jeweled dagger protruded from the center of the table; Lyylia didn't remember seeing it there the last time she'd been in the Moon Tower. Kuu ran her fingers along the jewel-studded gold hilt, and grasped it as if she were going to pull it out of the ice. But then she released it, and let her hands fall by her sides.

Shaun was taking pictures with his phone. Kuu went over to him.

"How does it replicate such a perfect image?" she asked, looking at the phone.

"Well, light passes through the lens," Shaun said, showing her the back side of the phone. "A silicon pixel grid then stores each photon as an electrical signal, and the image is then displayed on the screen here. Basically, it's just tiny points of light arranged and displayed in such a way that our eyes can recognize the image."

"Fascinating," Kuu said. "Yesterday at the lake you said that you would tell me about 'electricity.' I would like to know more about the 'science' of Kalevala before you leave."

"I'd love to, Highness," Shaun said with a grin. "Well, I went to school for six years to learn what little I know, and I'm hardly an expert on anything—not even the aurora. But I'll try to give you a crash course in basic physics. Do you have something I can write and draw with?"

Kuu headed for one of the five doors on the rock wall of the mountainside, and emerged a moment later with a large sheet of parchment and a stick of charcoal. Shaun took it from her, and since there wasn't a table in the Moon Tower—besides the small ice table—he sat down on the floor. Curious, Lyylia went over to join them—not that she expected to understand much of what he said.

Shaun drew a horizontal line across the page. "Okay, so this is the electromagnetic spectrum. At this end we have radio waves, which are very slow and have a long wavelength. At this other end are gamma rays, with a short, fast wavelength. This small bit in the middle here is visible light." He drew a few lines.

As he talked, Kuu asked numerous questions. Even with Shaun's simplified answers, Lyylia quickly became lost; she didn't have much of a head for science and mathematics, and she didn't know what many of the English words meant. But as she sat beside Shaun and watched the two of them talking away like old friends, she smiled to herself. Kuu's eager expression was full of child-like wonderment, and Shaun's delight in talking about science was strangely alluring. She wanted to always remember this moment.

After a while Shaun had filled both sides of the parchment with drawings and equations. "We'd probably better stop there," he said. "Before I get into quantum electrodynamics and special relativity."

Kuu held up the parchment, her silver eyes sparkling. "This is wonderful. Thank you, Shaun, for teaching me so much."

"You're welcome. I hope my scribbles make some sense to you. I guess your magical ability to understand languages doesn't extend to reading, does it?"

She looked at him. "Reading? What is that?"

He pointed at the parchment. "Words, written down. You don't have a written language?"

"We speak our language," Kuu replied.

"What do those symbols mean?" Lyylia spoke up. She pointed at a set of tubular chimes beside one of the tall ice pillars. The chimes were metal, and hung from a wooden frame. The wood was carved with the angular runic markings she'd seen other places. "Those symbols are on gravestones, and on your drum."

"That is music," Kuu said. "Music for spells." She stood up and went over to the tubular chimes. "The first symbol shows the type of spell, such as a spell of healing, or blessing at a birth, or a spell of change. The rest of the symbols indicate what instruments to play or the types of sounds."

Shaun pulled out his phone again and took another picture. "That's amazing—I had no idea. We have written music, too, but it's nothing like that. So you don't write down the words that you say, or the sounds of your language?"

Kuu shook her head.

Lyylia briefly wondered if Ice-Dark had developed a written language, since they seemed to have other advancements that Pohjola did not. Thinking about Ice-Dark reminded her of the mountain of paperwork she'd have to go through when they got back to Finland, to report her missing firearm. And that reminded her that she had something she had been wanting to tell Kuu.

Shaun was wandering around taking pictures again, and Kuu was staring at the drawing of an atom on the parchment sheet. Lyylia stepped closer to her.

"Kuu, I want to apologize to you," she began.

Kuu looked at her. "Whatever for?"

Lyylia drew a breath. "You saw my gun once, but I never explained it to you, or showed you how it worked. So when Hiisi-Hiisi took it from me and..." She pursed her lips. "I just keep thinking that if I'd actually showed you what it could do, how dangerous it was, you might have been able to protect yourself against it."

Kuu laid the parchment down on the top of a chest sitting near the tubular chimes. "You have nothing to apologize for, Lyylia," she said. "You are not responsible in any way for Hiisi-Hiisi's choice to steal from you, or his desire to do harm. Though I can be wounded and feel pain, I cannot be permanently harmed or killed by any weapon or magic— even from another world. The magic of Dream protects and sustains me."

Lyylia nodded. "I know. But...well, I'm sorry, anyway. And I'm very glad that Dream fully healed you."

"As am I." Kuu smiled gently. "I shall miss you, Lyylia. It has been an honor knowing you—knowing all of you. I have learned so much from all of you. And all of Pohjola is in your debt for showing me the truth of what happened to the Gentle Beasts. Kalevala must be a truly wonderous place to have such people in it."

Lyylia blinked back a sudden sting of tears. "I'll miss you, too, Kuu."

Kuu smiled again. "But now is not yet the time for goodbyes. It is nearing time for the evening meal, and tomorrow morning we shall set out for the journey to the lake."

Shaun had come back over, and Kuu looked up at him and smiled. "Come. Let us eat together, and enjoy these last hours before you return to your home."

She turned and headed for the stairs. As they followed her, on impulse Lyylia reached out and grabbed Shaun's hand. He looked at her and smiled, the bright light reflecting in his hazel eyes, highlighting the amber and green flecks of color. Lyylia smiled back, and hand in hand they left the Moon Tower.

"So tomorrow it's goodbye," Shaun said as they walked back towards their chambers after dinner. "Goodbye to the Menninkäinen and Kuu and the reindeer, and this castle and the magic aurora..."

Lyylia didn't say anything, but she looked somber. The goal had always been to return to Finland. But now that the moment had finally come, after everything they'd been through in Pohjola, Shaun didn't want to leave. He wondered if Lyylia was having similar thoughts, but he wasn't sure how to ask her.

And one more goodbye they'd have to face—saying goodbye to each other. He wasn't sure what to expect when they arrived home—after being gone for two months, they might all be listed as dead at this point. But even once life returned to normal, Lyylia's work would take her back to Kokkola, and Shaun's work would take him to some other Arctic country...

They'd come to the corridor of sleeping chambers, and as everyone else headed down the hall, Shaun found himself hesitating. There was no way he'd be able to get to sleep right now. Lyylia had paused beside him.

"I'm not really tired yet," he said. "I think I just want to walk for a little while." He looked at her. "You want to join me?"

She gave a small smile and nodded eagerly. He grinned. They set off down the corridor in the other direction.

For a while they just wandered in silence. Shaun let his gaze linger on the intricate carved patterns on the walls, the curling shapes of snakes and full and crescent moons, inlaid with thin bands of silver. He never wanted to forget.

He hadn't learned his way around the castle, aside from memorizing the route between the corridor of bed chambers and the dining chamber. Most of the corridors they wandered down looked the same. Then they came to one with windows—not the Halls of Time, just a hall with two large windows overlooking a lower courtyard of the castle.

They stopped to look out on the vista: the snowy terrace with ice statuary scattered around, a lower turret of the castle visible just beyond the courtyard wall, and the white tundra far below. The sky was bright with shifting greens and yellows of the Dancing Lights.

Lyylia rested her hands on the wide stone windowsill. Shaun did the same, feeling the cool stone, then slid his hand over to take hers. She looked up into his face. In one smooth motion, he pulled her into an embrace and kissed her.

She wrapped her arms around his shoulders as she returned

the kiss. He clutched at her tightly, desperately, and he could feel her heart beating against his chest. Eventually they parted, slowly, and Shaun didn't loosen his hold around her.

"Lyylia," he said quietly. "I don't want to say goodbye to you. But..." He shook his head.

"I know." Her fingers trailed across the back of his neck and through his hair. "I don't know what's to happen, either."

His throat tightened as he looked down into her face. He'd spent his whole adult life traveling, never getting attached to a person or a place—and he'd loved every minute of it. He could call any circumpolar country home, and sometimes he'd called coworkers and team partners friends. But never had he been so reluctant to leave a place or a person.

Lyylia put her head down on his shoulder, one arm still wrapped around him, her other hand resting on his chest. He gently rubbed his cheek against the top of her head.

"I want to still talk to you," she said quietly after a moment. "On the phone or the computer."

"Of course I'll stay in touch with you," he said, smoothing a hand across her back. "I'll call you every day, no matter where in the world I am. Or email you, or video chat, or mail you a letter, or use a moon mirror."

She laughed softly against his shoulder.

"I could never just leave you, or stop talking to you, or say goodbye to you forever. Lyylia, I love you."

She lifted her head to look at him. "Don't say that. That just makes it harder."

"I know." His chest felt tight at the thought of never seeing her again, never holding her again. "But it's true. I think I've been in love with you since you came to my hotel room in Inari to question me about missing reindeer."

She smiled and shook her head. "*Olet hauska,*

Shaun," she said.

"What's that mean?" His heart skipped a beat, hoping it was good.

"You're funny." She smiled again.

"Well, I try." He gave her his best grin. "I was serious about being in love with you, though."

"I know." She rubbed her hand in a slow circle on his chest, then turned her head up to kiss him.

He loved the way she kissed him, slow and gentle and deep. He loved the way she said his name, pronouncing it like *Sone*, since the Finnish language didn't have the s*h* sound. He loved the way her curls seemed to wrap around his fingers of their own accord as he tangled his fingers in her hair.

There was no way he could just leave her for months on end, when his science team went back to Norway, and then to Canada or Siberia or wherever they were headed next. Maybe he could find a job with a Finnish science organization, so he could at least come back to her between projects.

He felt slightly breathless when they finally parted. He didn't think he had the air or the brainpower to talk to her about that idea just yet—and he should probably wait and see if his current employer had declared him dead and dropped him from the organization. So he tucked that thought away in the back of his mind and focused on fondling Lyylia's hair and admiring her beautiful face.

She wasn't smiling; she looked almost sad as he trailed his thumb across her cheek. "*Minä rakastan sinua*," she said quietly, her voice almost a whisper.

His heart skipped a beat again. "And what's that mean?"

"Something I shouldn't say, because it makes goodbye hard." She still wasn't smiling, but she reached up and touched his face. "I love you."

His heart suddenly pounding, he grinned and tightened his arms around her. "You didn't fall in love with me when you questioned me about missing reindeer in Inari, though, did you?"

That finally got a smile out of her. "No. Not then. You annoyed me."

He laughed. "Hey, I tried to cooperate. I didn't want to get my Finnish work visa revoked because I honked off the most beautiful police officer in the country."

This time she laughed. "You cooperate, you did. But all suspects annoy me until I solve a case."

"Suspects?" He raised his eyebrows at her. "I thought I was just a witness. You seriously suspected me of stealing a hundred and thirty reindeer?"

Now she was laughing *at* him, he could tell. "Suspect, witness..." She shrugged, as if the important distinction between those two words didn't matter.

"Good thing we got kidnapped and brought to Pohjola, then," he said with a grin. "Or I might have wound up in a Finnish jail on charges of reindeer thievery."

She laughed, her blue eyes sparkling.

"But you love me anyway?" he then asked, just to make sure he'd understood her properly. "Even though I annoyed you?"

"You annoy me now," she said, still smiling. "But I love you."

He pulled her close against him, feeling suddenly giddy. He wanted to kiss her, and hold her at arm's length and just look at her, and wrestle with her in the snow, and kiss her, and lie beside her out under the stars and the aurora...

She kissed him, just briefly, and then put her head down on his shoulder again. Keeping his arms tightly enfolded around her, he kissed her forehead, then looked out the window at the white landscape and the glowing sky.

If they loved each other, then they could figure out how to be together, no matter what happened. They'd just survived a war with Ice-Dark—they could survive anything.

"I can see the Dark Water Lake in the distance," Eider said as he leaned out the side of the sledge. "We're nearly there."

Teija had been riding in a sledge with Eider for the past four days, as they traveled from the castle to the lake. The traveling was slow enough that sometimes they'd gotten out to ski alongside the horses, just to stretch their legs. The caravan of four sledges and five people on horseback was herding Ávgos' reindeer so they could take them home.

They were finally going home. As excited as she was about that, she knew she'd miss Pohjola and everyone she'd met here. Especially Eider.

Eider had gone back to his village to see his parents and sister, and to visit Boots. But he'd returned to the castle the day before Shaun had returned with his news of finding the gateway.

"I'm glad you came back to the castle in time to ride with me to the lake," Teija said. "Even if it has been a long slow trip. I'm sure your parents would rather you had stayed at home."

Eider smiled at her. "I will return home again soon enough. But you have been away from your home for far longer."

"I miss Helsinki—that's the name of my village. But I've come to really like Pohjola, too. I'm going to miss it." She looked over at him. "I'm going to miss you."

Eider stared at her a moment, a strange look in his light

brown eyes. Then he dug in the pocket of his breeches and pulled out a small knife.

"I want you to have this," he said. "I wish I had something nicer to give you, but this is all I have." He held it out.

The little knife was shorter than Teija's hand, with a bone handle and wrapped up in a soft leather sheath. She carefully took it from him.

"I use it to carve arrows. I'm sure you won't have a use for it in Kalevala, but I want you to have it, to remember me by."

Teija blinked back tears. "I could never forget you, Eider. And I can't take this—how will you make your arrows?"

"I can get another knife," he said with a smile. "Take it, please."

She ran her finger along the smooth bone handle. She wished she could give him something, but everything she had with her was Pohjola-made. Except for her necklace.

She reached inside the collar of her coat and tunic and unclasped the thin gold chain with the heart charm. "My father gave this to me the year before he died. The shape of the charm is a heart—we use it to symbolize things or people we care about." She placed the necklace in his hand.

"I can replace my knife," he said. "But you cannot replace a gift from your father."

"I have other things from him that I can remember him by. Just keep it, Eider. Please?"

Eider closed his hand around the necklace and nodded.

The sledges were slowing. Teija leaned over and hugged Eider; he returned the embrace, and Teija tried not to cry.

When the sledges stopped, they climbed out. A small collection of tents sat near the shore, and the blue-white lake stretched into the shadowy distance. Teija shuddered slightly, remembering the horror stories she'd heard from Lyylia and

Maden about Ice-Dark. It was scary to think that all that separated Pohjola from Ice-Dark was a lake and a river. She hoped that the underwater portal wasn't all the way across the lake near Ice-Dark.

A familiar Menninkäinen came out of one of the tents. Eider gave a wave. "Boots!"

They all went over to greet Boots. Even though he'd been injured in the battle, he'd traveled back to the lake, along with his wife Silver and son Track, to say goodbye to them. He was walking with a sturdy stick to support himself, but he seemed in good spirits.

"I couldn't let Eider be the only one to bid you farewell," Boots remarked. "We have known you since we first rescued you from the hiisi and pulled you from the lake."

"And we're very grateful you did," said Shaun, grinning and clapping him on the shoulder.

Teija stayed with Lyylia and chatted with Silver and Boots, while Eider and Shaun joined the two Sami men in consolidating the reindeer herd and making sure the animals weren't preparing to move on again. Soon they rejoined the others near the tents. Kuu came out of one of the tents. Her white puppy, Bright Ice, bounced through the snow behind her.

"Your traveling clothes and packs are prepared for you," Kuu said, nodding at the tents behind her. "But first, there is something I must say to all of you."

The five of them gathered in front of her in solemn silence.

"Although no words of gratitude can fully express how much all of Pohjola is in your debt, I must say thank-you to each one of you for everything you have done. There will be new paintings in the Halls of Time—pictures to tell the story of the return of the ancient forest lords, the victory over Ice-Dark, and the Light-Whisperers from Kalevala who were responsible for these great deeds of valor. You have helped to save a land that wasn't yours to save, and proven yourselves to be courageous and honorable people. It has been an honor and a pleasure knowing you all."

As one, they all bowed before her. Teija couldn't help sniffling, and out of the corner of her eye she noticed Shaun wiping at his eyes.

"And now," Kuu continued, her tone lighter. "I have some parting gifts for all of you."

Kuu had a leather satchel slung over her shoulder, and she reached into it and pulled out a long silver dagger in a shiny metal sheath.

She held it out to Mađen. "You are a protector, Mađen. May this knife protect you and others whenever you need it."

He bowed and mumbled, "Thank you, Your Majesty."

"A healing stone for you, Ávgos. You have the hands and heart of a healer, as I now well know." Kuu smiled as she handed him a small black stone.

Teija had seen a number of healing stones when she'd been helping Gray with the wounded at the castle after the battle. Small flat black stones, that fit easily in the palm, and carved with the snake-and-moon design on one side and a rune on the other. She wasn't sure what they were supposed to do, but Gray had thought it important that every patient have one next to them.

Ávgos bowed and thanked Kuu.

Next she pulled out a moon mirror. "For you, Shaun. I doubt that this will reach across the worlds, but I hope that somehow it can aid you as you listen to the Dancing Lights in Kalevala."

Shaun grinned as he took the silver dish. "Thank you, Your Highness."

"And for you, Teija, a mouth harp." Kuu smiled as she handed her a soft white leather pouch. "I think perhaps that music and magic are stronger in your spirit than you might think."

"Thank you," Teija whispered as she slid the mouth harp out of the pouch. Tiny runic markings were carved around the frame, and the little silver instrument glinted in the light. Its smooth weight felt both warm and cool in her hand.

"And for you, Lyylia, I have something special and unique. This is the only one of its kind." Kuu handed her a thin wooden stick, easily thirty centimeters long, with a round glass decoration at one end.

Since she was standing beside Lyylia, Teija could see that both the stick and glass bauble were carved with the angular symbols of magic spells. A drop spindle, she finally realized. She'd seen them in museums and depicted in artwork. Lyylia wasn't a seamstress or a folk artist—it seemed an odd gift.

As Lyylia took the spindle, Kuu laid a hand over Lyylia's, and looked into her eyes.

"Only one who has known the moon in full can discern its hidden meaning. Keep this well, Lyylia. Protect it always—it holds the key to a powerful magic."

Lyylia nodded. "I will, I promise. Thank you, Highness."

Kuu reached into the satchel again. "And I have silver protection stones for all of you." She handed each of them a small rough pebble. Silvery veins threaded through the gray rock. Teija squeezed the little rock in her hand, and thought about the opal protection stone that Shaman Pike had given Mađen and then he'd given to her. She had so many things now to remember Pohjola by—she wished she had something else she could give to Kuu or Boots.

At least she'd been able to give Eider something. As Kuu

instructed them to head for the tents to change their clothes, Teija looked over at Eider. His hood was pushed back, and the light breeze ruffled his sandy hair. He smiled at her, and patted his pocket; she knew he was indicating her necklace, and she returned his smile.

Putting the mouth harp and protection stone into her own pocket, she headed for the nearest tent. She was ready to go.

Maðen looked out across the frozen lake. A Pohjola reindeer—Snow on the River, Kuu said his name was—stood on the ice several dozen meters away, marking the exact location of the gateway. Apparently it was in the same spot as it had been when Shaun had discovered it several days ago. Maðen tried not to think about what might happen if the gateway suddenly moved to a new location while they were in the middle of traveling through it. Would the rest of the group just emerge in a different place, or would they be killed, like getting trapped by a heavy door closing? Maðen hated the uncertainty, but there was nothing to do except just try it. After all, they'd all made it through to Pohjola in one piece.

He absently adjusted the oilskin pack strapped to his back. They had all been given outfits of lined oilskin clothing—certainly not the same as a drysuit or even a wetsuit—but hopefully enough to protect them from the frigid water long enough to get to the surface. Assuming it didn't take them too long to break through the ice.

They each had an oilskin backpack containing a change of clothes, blanket, a firestarter, and food, since they had no idea how far away from Inari village they might emerge. Each backpack had a small ice axe strapped to it.

Maden glanced over at Shaun, who was busy strapping his oilskin pack to his computer backpack, which he was wearing. It looked awkward, and potentially heavy; Maden hoped Shaun was a strong swimmer. Lyylia was helping him and discussing with him in English, but she didn't seem concerned, so Maden assumed Shaun would manage.

"Before you enter the water," Kuu said to them, "place your breathing stone beneath your tongue, and keep it there. Keep your mouth closed while below the water, and you will not drown."

Maden lifted the thin rope looped around his neck and examined the pendant. Each oilskin outfit had come with a necklace. The small flat brown stone had several runes carved on one side, and the other side had a stylized etching of a fish.

"What about the reindeer?" Maden asked.

"Kied-Kie-Jubmel will give them the strength to hold their breath for as long as needed," said Kuu. "And he is reminding them to always stay with you and follow your lead."

Maden looked over at the herd. Kied-Kie-Jubmel was moving slowly among them, touching each animal with his nose. He towered over them all, his massive antlers like trees in comparison to even the largest bucks. Every single reindeer was standing still and watching him.

Maden glanced at Ávgos, and saw bewilderment and awe in his face. Suddenly their animals no longer seemed like normal Earth reindeer. With ears alert, the entire herd, nearly one hundred strong, watched Kied-Kie-Jubmel, and parted to let him through as he moved among them. It was as if he were truly the lord of all reindeer, not just the Gentle Beasts of Pohjola. Suddenly Maden had absolutely no doubts that five people, swimming under water, would be able to keep the herd together and not lose a single one.

Kuu approached the edge of the lake and knelt down in the snow. Kied-Kie-Jubmel emerged from the herd of reindeer and stood beside her. She laid both hands, bare with no mittens, on the ice, and Kied-Kie-Jumbel lowered his head and breathed. Slowly a narrow swath of ice dissolved into open water, creating a channel all the way to where Snow on the River stood.

Ávgos walked into the water first. The herd immediately began to move, and by twos and threes followed him into the narrow channel of water. Lyylia and Teija walked in with the animals, and Shaun waited with Maðen to bring up the rear. As he watched his cousin and the reindeer nearing the end of the channel, he heard Kuu and Kied-Kie-Jubmel behind him begin to sing.

Lights in the north
The battle is won
Peace comes to the north
Our victory song

Ice in the north
Shadows have gone
Cry to the north
Our victory song

The sound of Kuu's strong clear voice sent a sudden strange ache of homesickness through him, and Maðen had to force himself not to turn back around. The last of the herd entered the lake, and he put the breathing stone in his mouth, glanced at Shaun, and headed into the water. As the icy water climbed up his legs, he looked out across the lake, the ice shining silvery-blue in Pohjantähti's light. *Light comes to the north,* the voices of Kuu and Kied-Kie-Jubmel came to him before the water closed over his head. *Our victory song.*

The frigid water sent his heart pounding and his limbs into momentary frozen shock, despite the primitive wetsuit. The fish stone talisman was under his tongue, but he still automatically held his breath. After a few moments he got his body to work again and he started swimming, and abruptly realized that his lungs weren't aching and he didn't feel like he even needed to take a breath. Trying not to think about the fact that he didn't need to breathe, he swam downwards after the reindeer, who were all swimming in tight formation and still following Ávgos.

Snow on the River had dropped a weighted line down to mark the exact spot of the gateway. Even though Maden had been conscious when he'd first come through, following the hiisi that had abducted Teija, he had no idea what the gateway looked like. He didn't remember seeing anything "gateway" or "magical" looking in the water. He didn't see anything now, except what looked like an odd patch of faint light in the watery dimness this far below the surface. Ordinarily he would have just thought it was light filtering through from above, except the stone tied to the end of the rope was hanging immediately above it.

And the reindeer in front of him were disappearing. No dramatic flashes of light or anything else "magical looking." He just suddenly realized that the animals he could faintly see in the murky distance were no longer there. Heart pounding, he blinked against the cold water stinging his eyes, and swam towards the faint smudge of light, following what was left of the herd.

Then the light disappeared behind him, and suddenly the herd and everyone else were there again, all swimming upwards towards the grayish-blue haze of ice above them. Maden looked around to see if there were any stragglers, but the reindeer all seemed to be still keeping their tight formation together.

He spotted Teija treading water nearby, trying to pull her axe off the strap on her backpack. Maden swam over and helped her, then pulled his own axe out. Above them, Ávgos, Lyylia, and Shaun were already pounding on the ice with the sharp spiked ends of their axes.

They were near an island, which was good. Shaun stood on the slope of earth, pressing his shoulder against the ice as he swung the axe. With water plants swirling around his legs, Maden planted his feet on the island and heaved his spike upwards.

Eventually they broke through the ice, and kept chopping to get the hole big enough for several reindeer to pass through at a time, and to make sure that it wouldn't start freezing over before they were all out. Shaun crawled up the slope of the island, pushing chunks of floating ice out of his way, and broke the surface. A moment later, he plunged his arm back into the water and gave a thumbs up signal.

Ávgos swam for the hole. The reindeer followed him, their hooves churning the water and the broken ice as they scrambled up the slope of land. Maden's entire body was starting to ache, but he stayed in the water until the two women and all of the animals were out. Then he climbed up onto the island, grabbing at rocks and water plants as he went.

The cold air struck him more sharply than the cold water had when he'd first gone in. Maden spit out his breathing stone pendant and took a breath of the sharp cold air. The little island was big enough for a hundred reindeer; the animals milled around, all stamping and blowing and shaking water from their fur. The water lapped behind him, the chunks of broken ice bobbing and cracking against each other. All around was the smooth frozen lake, the ice interrupted frequently with little skerries and larger islands, all covered with snow. And above, through a thin layer of white-gray clouds, a bright yellow sun hung low in the sky.

Shaun gave an exclamation in English. Lyylia and Teija hugged each other, and Ávgos grinned and let out a long breath.

Home. They were really home. Mađen looked around; everything looked so familiar and yet so strange.

"Let's change, before we freeze," Lyylia said.

Lyylia and Teija went a little ways inland and around a rise in the land. Mađen had secured his gift from Kuu around his waist—the knife was smooth, but the silver sheath was engraved with the snake-and-moon designs that covered the corridor walls in the castle. He drew the knife and used it to slice open his backpack. The oilskin and tight stitching had worked—everything inside was dry. Shivering, he peeled off his soggy outfit and put on the warm woolen underclothes and fur boots and coat.

Ávgos was peering up at the sky when they all gathered back together. "I think Inari village is roughly that way," he said, pointing off to their right across the lake. "It wasn't even midday yet when we left Pohjola, so I'm guessing it's the same time here, too." He squinted at the huge yellow sun. "We should have at least two or three hours of daylight left."

Shaun said something, and he and Ávgos and Lyylia all conversed briefly in English. Shaun had his cell phone in his hand.

Ávgos looked back at Mađen. "Shaun says his phone isn't picking up enough of a signal for the GPS to work," he said. "So he thinks we're at least a good ten kilometers away from Inari."

Mađen looked at the sky. "If that's the case, we should be able to get close enough to town to know exactly where we are before it gets completely dark."

Ávgos nodded in agreement.

Everyone gathered up their packs, and together they spread out across the island to surround the reindeer. Ávgos set off walking, and the herd obediently fell in behind him.

"Let's remember what we talked about before we left," Lyylia said as they walked. "About what we should say when we get back to Inari."

When they'd camped during the evenings on their trek from Kuu's castle to the Dark Water Lake, they'd discussed options about what they should or should not say upon their initial arrival back in Inari. No one knew what sort of search might still be going on for them—if any—but their arrival would certainly be noticed.

After much discussion, they eventually all agreed that when they were questioned by reporters or authorities—which they probably would be—the truth was really the only viable option. It was likely they'd all be branded as liars or insane, but there was no sort of plausible cover story that could be made up to explain everything. They had also agreed, at Lyylia's suggestion, to minimize as well as they could any mention of Ice-Dark, Hiisi-Hiisi, or the Näkki.

They walked for well over an hour. The reindeer were all still calm and following Ávgos in a surprisingly organized manner. Mađen was starting to feel hungry, but since they didn't have a lot of daylight left, it wasn't prudent to stop just now even for a short break. He snugged the hood of his fur coat tighter around his wet hair.

Shaun said something in English that sounded like a question.

Ávgos answered, and then said in Finnish: "Do you hear that? It sounds like engines."

Maðen pushed his hood back to hear more clearly. A distant whine was growing gradually louder. "Snowmobiles," he said. "Several machines, and they're headed our way."

The noise of the engines quickly came closer, and soon three sets of headlights flashed in the gathering dusk across the lake. The reindeer pricked up their ears and went alert, but none of them panicked.

The three snowmobiles spread out as they approached, blocking the group's progress. Ávgos held up his hand to stop everyone, and the reindeer obediently stopped walking when he did.

The snowmobiles halted a few dozen meters away. The machines all bore the blue-and-white, lion-headed sword emblem of the police. A man in a blue uniform climbed off the nearest snowmobile. He had a police rifle slung across his chest, which he held onto securely but did not point at them. Maðen moved his hand to the hilt of the dagger on his hip.

"Stop where you are!" called the man with the rifle. "This is the police! You are all under arrest!"

Lyylia sat on a hard bench in the lobby of Sajos, the Sami Parliament building at the outskirts of Inari. Officers from the National Bureau of Investigation had taken over several of the meeting rooms as their temporary offices during the past two months, as they'd been investigating the disappearance of five people and a herd of reindeer.

Three days ago, police drones flying over the lake had detected them emerging from the ice, and ever since, Lyylia had felt like prisoner. Once the five of them had convinced the Bureau officers that they were, in fact, the missing people in question and not Russian terrorists trying to sneak into Finland via Lake Inari, they'd all been separated. Several doctors had been flown in from Rovamiemi by helicopter, since Inari didn't have a hospital. Lyylia had been given a clean bill of health, but she hadn't heard any details about the others.

She stared at a picture hanging on the wall across the lobby—an oil painting of a reindeer standing on the snowy tundra, with swirls of the aurora above it. As beautifully realistic as the painting was, she wished she could see the murals in the Halls of Time again, with the stylized reindeer and the bright primitive colors.

Shaun had taken pictures of all the murals, but she hadn't seen him since the police had escorted them and the reindeer herd off the lake and back to town. Jassu had told her that the two Sami men were back at home, and Teija and Shaun were fine, as well, but nothing more. Because Lyylia was a government employee, more rigorous security measures applied to her. That made sense, but it still felt a bit demeaning to be escorted everywhere, and prevented from seeing or talking to her sister or anyone else. At least the Bureau officers and the Border Guard were keeping reporters away.

She looked up at the sound of a door opening. Jassu stepped out of one of the meeting rooms. Lyylia stood up from the bench.

"They're ready for you," he said, nodding at the door behind him.

Lyylia picked up the police jacket from the bench and shrugged into it as she headed for the room. She was wearing all her own clothes again, at least, courtesy of her luggage that she'd brought to Inari two months ago. Her coat, however, had been left behind in Pohjola when she'd been given Menninkäinen-made clothing, so she now had a donated, too-large blue police coat. Her wallet, her blue-and-purple scarf, and the gold studs she kept in her ears were the only items that had survived and stayed with her, even in Ice-Dark.

Straightening the oversized jacket as best she could, Lyylia went into the small meeting room and stood in front of Agent Vaara. Vaara and two other men from the Bureau of Investigation sat at the table. The huge stack of papers that was Lyylia's report was spread out in front of them.

"Detective Niiranen," Vaara began. "Your record on both the Helsinki and Kokkola police forces has been exemplary. Therefore, based on your past record, and corroborating evidence from the other prior missing persons in this case, we have decided to accept your report in full. You are reinstated to the Kokkola force, effective immediately, and can return to duty at the discretion of your immediate superior."

Lyylia let out a silent breath. "Thank you, sir."

Vaara pulled a folder out from beneath the pages of her report. "This is a confidentiality agreement, prohibiting you from speaking about your experience with anyone not directly involved or anyone who does not already know the details of your report. In the interests of national security, this portal must not become public knowledge."

"Yes, sir," Lyylia said again, accepting the folder of papers. She assumed that the others had had to sign a similar document. That was fine—who would believe them anyway, if they went around talking about Pohjola?

"Once you've signed, you are free to go," Vaara said, handing her a pen.

Lyylia sat down at the table and went through the document as quickly as she could without looking like she was irresponsibly rushing through it. After signing, she handed the paperwork back to Vaara, thanked him, and left the room. Jassu was on her heels.

"I don't need an escort anymore, Jassu," Lyylia said, striding through the lobby towards the exit.

"I know. I'm sorry all that took so long, Lyylia, but like Vaara said, because of national security—"

"I know, and I'm not mad," Lyylia said. "Not anymore, and I'm not mad at you." She pushed open the door and left Sajos, grateful to feel the cold air on her face. "This was an unprecedented incident, so they had to take extra security measures. I know it wasn't personal. But now maybe you can tell me what's happening with Teija and Shaun and the two Sami men."

"They all signed the confidentiality documents yesterday morning. Your sister is still in town—she said she was going to stay here until you were cleared. The American will have to deal with his own set of red tape from that Norwegian science organization he works for. I think their group is leaving for Norway today or tomorrow."

Lyylia's heart skipped a beat as she walked through the snowy parking lot. She wanted to be able to see Shaun one more time.

"Um, the snowmobile is parked over there..." Jassu pointed across the lot, then hurried to catch up to her.

"Feel free to use it," she said. "I'd rather walk." She wasn't sure how many kilometers it might be to get back her to hotel in town, but she didn't care. After weeks and weeks of walking and basically living outdoors, she felt stifled being inside. A snowmobile wasn't as bad as a car, but she wanted to feel the snow beneath her boots.

"So…" Jassu said, keeping pace with her. "Now that you've signed all the security documents and gotten the all-clear, is there anything you want to…you know…tell me off the record?"

Lyylia stopped walking and stared at him. "Everything is in my report. I told the truth. You don't believe me, do you?"

Jassu was silent for a few beats too long. "Your report has been accepted by higher authorities," he said at last. "That's good enough for me."

"But you don't believe me." His doubt stung her. Granted, it was an unbelievable story, but he should know that she wasn't given to absurd stories or outrageous lies.

Jassu rubbed his forehead. "You've been through a lot recently. I'll call the Chief and give him the good news, but you should probably take some time before coming back on duty. I'm sure he'll give you a few weeks to—"

"I don't need time off," Lyylia said. She wondered if Chief Sjöberg would believe her, even after reading her report. "I think I'd like to take a couple of days to go to Helsinki and see my mother, but I'm ready to get back to work as soon as possible."

Jassu nodded. "It'll be good to have you back, Lyylia. You're a good cop, and the best partner I've had in a while. Whatever the hell you've been through in the past two months, I hope… well, I'm just glad to have you back. And that's the truth."

"Thanks, Jassu." She managed a smile. "Thank you for staying here and never giving up on me."

"That's what partners are for." He returned her smile. "Enjoy your walk, and go find your friends. I'm going to go back and get my snowmobile."

Lyylia smiled at him, and headed down the road. The sun was rolling along the horizon, at its peak for the day and already setting. The brief yellow sunlight and the wintertime darkness hurt her eyes in a way she hadn't expected. In her mind, she still saw everything sharply illuminated in shades of blue and silver.

As she neared the edge of town, she paused as a small group of about a dozen reindeer crossed the road, a teenage boy and a dog following the herd. It felt strange that the reindeer didn't look at her, didn't pause and speak to her in low, gentle voices. She tightened her scarf and zipped her coat collar up against a cold gust of wind.

"Detective Niiranen!" a voice called from down the road. Two Sami women were walking towards her, leading a reindeer.

Lyylia recognized Ávgos' wife from when she'd met her two months ago. "Sirkka!" she greeted the woman who was leading the reindeer. "And you're Ávgos' sister, right?"

"That's right. Elbmá Somby." The other woman smiled and shifted the package she was carrying so she could extend her hand.

The reindeer was pulling one of the round-bottomed wooden sleds that the Sami used; Ávgos' little daughter Piijá was riding in it, along with several shopping bags. The little girl looked up at Lyylia and gave her a shy smile.

"How are Ávgos and Mađen?" Lyylia asked.

"They're out with the herd right now," Sirkka said. "It's such a relief to have them home. Thank you for everything you did to keep them safe and bring them home."

Lyylia smiled at her. "Just doing my job." Which was technically correct, but Ávgos and Mađen deserved just as much credit for the group's survival as anyone. And they never would have found all the reindeer or made it back home without Shaun. And the Menninkäinen, and especially Kuu.

"I can still hardly believe it," Elbmá's voice broke into her thoughts. "It all sounds so fantastical, like something out of an old folk song. Oh, we're not supposed to talk about it, are we?" She looked worried.

Lyylia gave her a reassuring smile. "The confidentiality agreement applies to anyone who wasn't directly involved. So don't spread it around town, but you can talk to each other about it. And to me."

Both women smiled and looked relieved.

"I'd like to see Ávgos and Mađen before I leave," Lyylia said. "Would that be all right?"

"Of course," Sirkka said with a grin. "I know they'd love to see you. Please come by any time, Detective."

"Thank you. And you can call me Lyylia."

She smiled again. "Lyylia. Thank you, for everything."

Sirkka and Elbmá continued down the road, and Lyylia started walking again, heading for what passed for downtown Inari. She didn't know which hotel Teija might be staying in, so she went into the first one she came to.

She spotted her sister immediately: the only person sitting in the small café area of the lobby, staring forlornly into a cup of coffee.

"Teija!"

Her sister looked up and burst into a smile. "Lyylia!" Teija scrambled up and threw her arms around Lyylia. "What happened? The police wouldn't let me talk to you or even see you. Are you okay?"

"Everything's fine. Just extra security, because I'm a government worker." Lyylia didn't want to talk about her grueling and repetitive interviews over the past three days. "But I'm all clear now."

She fixed herself a cup of coffee, black with just one packet of sugar, and savored the bitter warmth. The people of Pohjola didn't know what they were missing by not having coffee.

Sitting down at the table with Teija, she saw a mouth harp lying next to Teija's cup—Kuu's parting gift to her. Lyylia's gift had been thoroughly examined by forensic officers before being pronounced a harmless and ordinary drop spindle and returned to her. Lyylia had been puzzling over the odd gift and Kuu's parting words, but even if she never understood, it didn't matter; she'd promised she'd protect the spindle, and she would do so.

"I called Mom yesterday," Teija said. "Once I signed all those papers and they said I could make phone calls and talk to people. They said it was okay to tell her the truth. I'm not sure if she believes it or not, but she was so happy that we were both okay."

Lyylia smiled. "I'll call her this afternoon."

"I called Johanna, too. She said they cleared out my desk at work a couple of weeks ago." Teija shrugged and took a sip of her coffee. "I can find another job." She looked at Lyylia. "You should go to the bus depot, though. We can talk more later today. I saw Shaun and his coworkers leaving the hotel with their luggage about an hour ago. I think the next bus leaves for Rovaniemi this afternoon."

Lyylia's heart lurched. She gave Teija's hand a brief squeeze, and leaving her coffee unfinished on the table, she got up and hurried out of the hotel. She could see the bus depot from the hotel entrance, and as she got closer, she recognized the Norwegian man who was the leader of the science group. She didn't see the other three men. A bus sat, engine rumbling, and a worker was loading luggage in the underside hold.

"I'm looking for Shaun," she said to the Norwegian man

in English, figuring that he didn't speak Finnish.

He eyed her blue police coat. "He's been cleared to leave Inari," he said. "Agent Vaara authorized it yesterday."

"I know." She didn't bother to explain that she wasn't on duty and had, in fact, just been through the same thing Shaun had been through. "I just want to talk to him."

"He and the others went to get coffee." He pointed at a café down the street. "You can tell them that the bus is leaving in about ten minutes."

Lyylia nodded at him and headed for the café. She'd almost reached it when Shaun and the other two men came out.

"Lyylia!" Shaun's face lit up when he saw her. He thrust his coffee cup at the man next to him, who managed to grab it before it fell, as Shaun rushed forward and enveloped Lyylia in a tight embrace.

She could hear the other two men talking and snickering, but she didn't care. She wrapped her arms around Shaun and buried her face in his neck. For a moment they just held each other in silence.

"So they finally let you go?" Shaun said, pulling back to look her in the face.

"Yes. I just signed the papers, and I can now go back to work. Are you going back to work?"

Shaun made a face. "I don't think so. The foundation wants to claim the rights to my laptop and all my equipment that I had with me in Pohjola, as well as all the data I collected. I think I can claim my rights to keep it, but I have to go back to Norway to deal with the head directors. I might even have to go to court."

"I'm sorry," Lyylia said with sympathy.

"And I'm leaving basically right now." He glanced over her shoulder at the bus depot behind her. "Yeah, that's Pål flagging me down." He released one arm from around her and dug in his coat pocket. "Here, this is my phone number and email, so we can stay in touch." He handed her a folded piece of paper. "I wish we had more time..."

"I know." Lyylia stuffed the paper into her coat pocket. "I'll call you when I have a new phone." There were so many things she wanted to tell him, but it would have to wait.

She kissed him, not caring that they were standing on a public street, and in full view of his—probably soon to be former—coworkers. He obviously didn't care, either, as he grabbed the back of her head and kissed her deeply.

Then he released her, and jogged down the street to the bus depot. Lyylia stayed where she was and watched until everyone had finished boarding and the bus pulled away.

It wasn't goodbye forever, she reminded herself. And in the meantime, she had a job to get back to. And she should call her mother. Snugging up her scarf, she headed back to the hotel.

Ávgos closed the gate behind the last reindeer as the animals trotted into the corral. Maden was still in the corral, moving amongst the reindeer, checking the animals and talking to them.

It was so gratifying to have Maden back with the family, and back working with the reindeer. His time with that gang in Rovaniemi was truly behind him now, Ávgos knew. His cousin had even stopped smoking.

Maden made his way through the herd to the corral gate. He tossed a shed antler at Ávgos, then climbed over the gate.

"Is it just me," Mađen remarked. "Or are they calmer, almost more organized than reindeer ever are?"

"I know what you mean," said Ávgos. "It's not like they've suddenly become intelligent like Pohjola reindeer, but…" Ávgos let the sentence hang. Of course the memory of their experience in Pohjola was still as fresh as ever in his mind, and in Mađen's too, he knew—but surely the reindeer weren't still remembering the other world weeks after returning home. And half of the herd had stayed here.

As they headed back towards the snowmobile, a reindeer went wandering past them.

"Now how did that one get missed in the round-up?" Ávgos said, handing the antler to Mađen and sliding his lasso off his shoulder. "I thought we had them all."

The reindeer stopped and turned its head to look at them.

"Hey, I think…I think that's Vuordámuš," said Mađen. "The reindeer that Eider rode when we were escaping Ice-Dark."

Ávgos looked at him and paused in unwinding his lasso.

Mađen waved his arms at the reindeer. "Come on, Vuordámuš. Into the corral."

The reindeer obediently went up to the gate, and waited while Mađen opened it.

Ávgos could only shake his head as Mađen latched the gate again. Just because Eider had claimed the reindeer had a name, why would it still be responding to the name now? And what an interesting name, too—it meant *hope*.

They climbed on the snowmobile and sped through the snowy darkness back home. Piijá greeted them with a squeal and a hug as they shed their coats in the mud room and came into the kitchen.

"Elbmá and Osku just arrived for dinner," Sirkka said

from the stove. "How is the herd?"

"Doing fine," Ávgos said. "We finished the sorting and they're all corralled." He kissed Sirkka, and gently laid a hand on her pregnant belly. She was due in mid-January—just a few more weeks now. He would be home for the birth of his second child. All the time that he'd been in Pohjola, he'd wished for a way to send Sirkka a message to tell her that he was all right. And now, back home, he wished again that he could send a message, to thank Kuu for everything she did and to tell her they all were safely back home.

Piijá came into the kitchen carrying a small gray rock— the protection stone that Kuu had given Ávgos. He'd put the protection stone and the healing stone in a place of honor on the end table next to the sofa.

"Daddy, silver," said Piijá, holding up the little stone. The thin veins of silver in the gray ore glinted in the warm overhead light in the kitchen.

Ávgos squatted down and took the stone from her. "That's right, Piijá, silver. Just like Grandma's necklace that she wears at Christmastime."

Piijá grinned. Ávgos' mother always wore a necklace with a large silver medallion of the traditional Sami sun disk during the winter days of twenty-four-hour darkness. Ávgos took his daughter's hand and they went back out into the living room. His sister Elbmá and her husband Osku were chatting with Maden and Ávgos' mother Máddji. Piijá ran over to them.

Ávgos smiled as he turned the protection stone over in his fingers. He glanced out the window across the room, and saw the green flare of the northern lights in the sky. They were less vibrant than in Pohjola—and of course didn't show up with the same predictable regularity—but this way was comfortingly familiar. He crossed the room, setting the protection stone back on the end table.

He took one last look out the window at the northern lights, and closed the curtain.

Shaun stood on the snowy sidewalk. It was late afternoon and the sun had already set, and heavy clouds were rolling in over the city of Tromsø, Norway, threatening more snow. All of his worldly possessions were in his backpack and two suitcases beside him. He had no job and no place to live, and his phone battery was dead.

But Shaun didn't care about any of it—he'd never felt so free.

He had been invited to leave the employ of the aurora organization, and because his apartment was paid for by them, he was now homeless. But after nearly three weeks of interviews, emails, and finagling of contractual and legal loopholes, he had full possession of his computer and scanning equipment, phone, and all the data from Pohjola. The only stipulation was that he not share any of his modifications with anyone—the cell phone parts and silver wires he'd used to repair the computer, or the reprogramming he'd done to make the scanners sensitive to magic reindeer and wormholes. Since he was bound by the Finnish government to similar secrecy, he didn't mind one bit. And he'd accomplished all of this without having to go to court, and before all the directors turned on their out-of-office email replies for the Christmas holiday.

So now he just had to use the remaining kroner in his bank account to get back to Finland.

He hauled his luggage down the sidewalk to a café, and set himself up in a corner out of the way and plugged his phone into the wall. After he'd ordered some food, the phone had enough charge to make a call.

"*Hallo,* Niiranen," the clipped voice answered halfway through the first ring.

"Lyylia, it's me."

"Shaun!" Her tone immediately softened. "You are okay? I was going to call you soon. I haven't heard from you today or yesterday."

"I know, I'm so sorry. Things got kind of busy." He realized guiltily that he'd forgotten to send her a good-night text last night. "I had to clear out my apartment in Tromsø. They wanted me out by today." He then explained all the updates and the final ruling about his equipment.

"That's so good you can keep everything," Lyylia said. Shaun could hear the smile in her voice. "So now what will you do?"

"I want to stay in Finland. I'll have to re-apply for a work visa, since my previous work visa was through an organization that I no longer work for. I know you have organizations that study the aurora, and lots of universities with physic departments. I haven't really investigated all the options yet—it's been kind of hectic, and I wanted to make sure that I knew what I had first. I'll get a job sweeping floors if I have to—but I want to come to Finland."

"I'm glad," Lyylia said. Shaun could hear her smile again. "You can stay with me."

They'd discussed his potential living arrangements before, but they hadn't decided anything, since he hadn't been sure if or when he might lose his place in Tromsø. As giddy as he felt about living with Lyylia, whether just as roommates or something more, he didn't want to be a burden or impose on her space and her lifestyle. "I have enough money to pay you rent for a while," he said. "And I'll get a job just as soon as I can get a work visa."

"It's okay," she said. "Where are you staying now?"

"Nowhere. I'm in a café right now. If I can't get a flight to Finland later today, I'll have to get a hotel room here."

"Please come, Shaun."

He smiled. "Don't worry, I will."

He searched for flights while he ate. The best he could find was a red-eye flight into Tampere, Finland, which was as close to Kokkola as he could get on such short notice. He called Lyylia again, and she promised to meet him at the airport, even though it would be two in the morning.

Despite the late night and his general exhaustion from the stress of the past couple of weeks, Shaun was wired and didn't even doze on the flight. This was the start of a whole new life for him. True, he had a two-month gap on his resume that he couldn't talk about, aurora-scanning equipment that he couldn't show to anyone, no income, and a family back in the U.S. who thought he was a crazy geek and had given up on him years ago.

But none of that mattered. He'd had an amazing adventure, and had pictures and a moon mirror to remember it by. And he had Lyylia.

The Tampere airport was quiet and empty. As he went through the one open customs lane, a changing LED sign greeted him alternately in Finnish, Swedish, and English:

Tervetuloa Suomeen!

Välkommen till Finland!

Welcome to Finland!

Suomi. Finland. His new home.

Lyylia stood just on the other side of the turnstile, hands in the pockets of her gray coat, her curly blond hair spilling over her shoulders and the purple and blue scarf around her neck. Her face lit up with a smile, and Shaun literally ran to meet her.

He scooped her into a tight embrace. "Oh, Lyylia, I've missed you so much."

She mumbled something in Finnish in his ear, but before he could ask for a translation, she kissed him. He kissed her back and held her, not ever wanting to let go.

"The train is two hours back to Kokkola," she said as they went to retrieve his luggage from the baggage belt.

"That's fine," he said. "I mean, as long as you don't mind. You really didn't have to come all the way here to meet me in the middle of the night. I could have found my way to Kokkola by myself."

"I know," she said, taking the smaller of the two suitcases to pull behind her. "But I missed you."

His heart swelled, and he had to stop himself from dropping his luggage and pulling her into a passionate kiss again.

As they headed out into the cold for the walk to the train station, Shaun pulled on his gloves, and noticed Lyylia putting on fur mittens.

"Pohjola mittens?" he asked her.

She smiled. "They're warm."

Pulling his large suitcase behind him, he reached out and took her free hand, squeezing his synthetic gloves against the fur of her mitten. Overhead, bright colors penetrated through the glow of city lights as the aurora borealis danced in the sky.

APPENDIX

Appendix 1: The Kalevala

The Kalevala is a 19th-century epic poem, compiled by Elias Lönrot. He collected the tales from Finnish and Karelian mythology and the oral folklore of old rural storytellers. *The Kalevala* is considered the national epic of Finland and one of the most significant works of Finnish literature. The story begins with the of the creation of the world, and follows various heroes and other characters as they live in a fairytale-like world of gods, witches, monsters, and magical talismans. Finnish cultural icons such as the mythological Sampo, and legendary characters whose names are still used in artistic and commercial venues, all have their basis or origin in the stories from *The Kalevala*.

Appendix 2: Finnish Language

The Finnish language is unique in Scandinavia, because it is not related to other Nordic languages such as Swedish or Norwegian. The languages most closely related to Finnish are Estonian, Hungarian, and the various Sami dialects.

Every letter in a Finnish word is pronounced, and the stress or emphasis is always on the first syllable of a word. Double letters (such as in *Kuu*) are simply pronounced longer than a single letter—the sound does not change.

A – *ah*

E – *eh*

I – *ee*

O – *oh*

U – *oo*

Y – *oo* (with a more intense lip puckering than the *u*. Example: Lyylia – *LOO-lee-ah*)

EI – *ay* (long *a* as in "gate." Example: Teija – *TAY-yah*)

Ä – *a* (short *a* as in "cat")

Ö – basically pronounced as a sound about halfway between *U* and *Y*

J - *y*

All consonants are pronounced similar to English, though usually the R is rolled.

Appendix 3: Sami Culture and Language

The Sami people (also sometimes called Saami, Same, or Lapps) are the indigenous people of northern Europe. There are several different Sami people groups or tribes, speaking several different dialects, who live in the northern parts of Norway, Sweden, Finland, and Russia. They are traditionally nomadic, but most now live in established villages or towns. Reindeer are a key part of Sami culture, though not every Sami family owns or herds reindeer for a living. The terms "Lapp" and "Lapland" are often considered to be derogatory by today's Sami.

Sápmi is the geographic region across the four countries where the Sami have traditionally lived, and the four countries give the Sami people varying degrees of autonomy in local and cultural affairs.

There are upwards of eight or nine dialects of Sami that are spoken across different regions of Norway, Sweden, Finland, and Russia. Most of the Sami words and phrases used in this story come from Northern Sami and Inari Sami, the most widely spoken dialects in northern Finland.

For the most part, similar to Finnish, every letter in a Sami word is pronounced. Usually the first syllable of a word is stressed, and double letters are pronounced longer than the single letter. Often the *t* at the end of a word is softened or not pronounced at all.

A – *ah*

E – *eh*

I – *ee*

O – *oh*

U – *oo*

J – *y*

Á – indicates more emphasis on this letter, even if it is not the first syllable

Č (č) – *ch*

Š (š) – *sh*

Đ (đ) – a softer *d* sound; almost a cross between *d* and *th*

Ŋ (ŋ) – a softer *n* sound (similar to *ng* in "ring")

Ž (ž) – a softer *z* sound; almost a cross between *z* and an English *j*

Y is generally not used

Appendix 4: Music

Most of the musical instruments featured in this book are based on real Finnish folk instruments.

Silver-string: Based on the Finnish kantele. This dulcimer-like instrument is made of wood; it is usually held in the lap, and played by either plucking the strings or hitting the strings with a light hammer. The most ancient kanteles had five strings; modern kanteles can have as many as thirty-eight strings.

Horsehair-string: Based on the Finnish jouhikko, also known as a "bowed kantele." The jouhikko typically has only two or three strings, and one string serves as a drone sound during playing, as it is touched only by the bow and never by the player's fingers.

Mouth harp: The mouth harp is also known by the name "jaw harp" or "Jew's harp." (It is called *munniharppu* in Finnish, which translates to "mouth harp"). The mouth harp is one of the most ancient instruments in the world, and is commonly used in folk music throughout Scandinavia, as well as Siberia, Mongolia, and other parts of Eurasia. Many different styles of mouth harp exist in different cultures, but all function on the same basic principle of a tongue of metal producing the sound, and the human mouth acting as the resonating chamber.

Drums: Another ancient instrument in every culture of the world. In ancient Sami culture, as in many others, the drum was associated with magic. The *noaidi* or shamans of the Sami were believed to be able to cast spells using frame drums that had designs and symbols painted on the skin.

Bells and chimes: Like the drum, simple percussion instruments like a single-tone chime are common and ancient in every culture. In this story, the use of chimes (and other instruments) made of ice is based on a modern musical practice rather than a historical or mythological precedent.

Long-flute: More commonly known as an overtone flute in Scandinavian and eastern European folk music. It usually does not have any holes besides the two open ends. It is played by blowing into one end and moving the fingers across the other open end. While an overtone flute can be any size, it is typically longer (and wider) than a flute or a whistle that is played with finger holes or keys.

Fells-cry: Based on the style of singing known as *kulning*, a high-pitched song full of half- and quarter-tones, giving the sound an eerie, melancholy tone. *Kulning* is traditionally used as either a cattle-call, or a way of communicating over long distances. The high-pitched tones resonate off mountains and hills and can carry vast distances. *Kulning* is more common in Sweden and Norway than Finland, however, as it is most effective in a mountainous region and Finland has flatter topography. In recent times, *kulning* has found its way into modern Scandinavian folk music.

Author's Note

I have the greatest respect for the Finnish and Sami people and their cultures, and I appreciate the Finns whom I've learned from and befriended. Any inaccuracies with lifestyle, language, geography, or other cultural misrepresentations are purely unintentional.

I also have a great love and respect for *The Kalevala*. This book is not intended as any sort of analysis or retelling, but only as a work of fantasy fiction inspired by the epic.

My hope is that I have provided not only an entertaining story, but perhaps an inspiration to read more about the folktales of the Finnish people. The great old stories live on and can be enjoyed, learned from, and reimagined with each new generation.

About the author:

Grace E. Robinson is a lover of stories, both real and imaginary. Born and raised in Virginia, she currently lives in Idaho with a cat and a lot of books.

Visit her website at StorytellerGirlGrace.com, and connect with her on social media.